I0788583

THE
SHIELD
AND
THE
THORN

Also by C. J. Brightley

A Long-Forgotten Song:
Things Unseen
The Dragon's Tongue
The Beginning of Wisdom

Erdemen Honor:
The King's Sword
A Cold Wind
Honor's Heir

Fairy King:
A Fairy King
A Fairy Promise

The Wraith:
The Wraith and the Rose

Other Works:
The Lord of Dreams
Twelve Days of (Faerie) Christmas
Heroes and Other Stories

THE SHIELD AND THE THORN

C. J. BRIGHTLEY

Paperback ISBN 978-1-954768-03-1
Hardback ISBN 978-1-954768-04-8
Ebook ISBN 9781005168605

Published in the United States of America by Spring Song Press, LLC.

www.cjbrightley.com
www.springsongpress.com

Cover design by Kerry Jesberger of Aero Gallerie.

For my wonderful children, Natalie and Timothy, who brighten the
world with their love and laughter.

ACKNOWLEDGMENTS

Many thanks to my wonderful friends Sarah, Suebee, Constance, and Janice, who offered encouragement, helpful feedback, and friendship throughout the writing and editing process. You are all delightful, and I am glad to have you as friends.

CHAPTER ONE
An Unsettling Guest

Lord Fenton Selby raised his hands placatingly. "I would much prefer not to be punctured, my lady. What exactly do you want from me?"

"I want Juniper Morel!" She glared at him fiercely.

Lord Selby took another cautious step backward and found to his dismay that he had been backed into a large rose bush and could not easily retreat farther. The sword point jabbed the hollow at the base of his throat as he swallowed.

"I do not know what you mean by that," he said carefully. "Is it a plant?"

Her brilliant blue eyes flashed. "Where is Juniper Morel?"

"I cannot say, since I do not know what you mean." Lord Selby did, in fact, know exactly where young Juniper Morel was, but he was not about to betray the fairy to this woman.

She was nearly as tall as he was, though she was willowy and slender in comparison to his broad-shouldered strength. The faintest edge of glamour caught his eye, but he could not tell what she was doing with it. It might have been as minor as darkening her hair color one shade to better set off her blue eyes. If she were one of the Fair Folk, she might have changed her appearance completely. Fair glamours were too skillful for a human to tell even what they did, much less see through them.

However, it was clear that she must be a fairy, for she held the sword with too much familiarity to be a human woman. Women of Valestria did not train with swords; if one had, for her own reasons, it was unlikely that she was also this skilled at glamour, and tall and willowy like a fairy besides.

Juniper had much to fear from fairies, though he was one himself. He had faithfully served Lord Selby's friend Theodore Overton, IV, as Theo had carried out his courageous rescues of Arichtan children and even more audacious strategem to end the kidnappings permanently. When Juniper had been discovered some three months earlier, he had fled into the veil between the Fair Lands and the human world, and eventually had found refuge with Theo and his parents, Sir Theodore, III, Baronet, and Lady Overton.

Lord Selby had just returned from the Overton estate some three miles away, having ascertained that Theo, after having somehow pulled a bloody triumph from what appeared to be disaster, was now blissfully drunk on Lord Cedar Mosswing's healing magic and deliriously pleased with the world in general and his wife in particular. Fenton had also aided Theo, though not as much as he had wanted to. The veil had taken an especially strong disliking to him for unknown reasons, and Theo had adamantly refused to take him on a fourth rescue mission after the veil had tried to choke him to death. Again.

The fairy woman glowered at him. Her glower was as beautiful as the point of her sword was sharp, and Fenton took a deep, slow breath.

"While I cannot aid you in your search, I will gladly offer you hospitality this evening, if you would so honor me," he said carefully.

She tilted her head and studied him. "Why would you do that?" she said at last, withdrawing the point of the sword half an inch.

"I'm a gentleman," Fenton said kindly. "And you appear to be far from home."

"Why do you say that?" Her blue eyes glittered dangerously.

Perhaps voicing that thought had been a mistake. With Theo so recently on his mind, Fenton decided to take a page from his friend's strategy by diving right on in to the mistake and brazening it out rather than attempting to backtrack. "Your glamour is exceptionally good," Fenton said. "I guessed you might be one of the Fair Folk. I do apologize if I have offended you."

She straightened and stared at him, withdrawing the sword point further. "How can you tell I'm wearing a glamour?" She sounded so confused that Fenton felt a little more confident.

"I can just see the edges a little," he said, sounding vaguely apologetic. "The rest was conjecture. A Valestrian lady wouldn't know how to hold a sword as well as you do, for one thing."

She frowned at him and dropped the sword to her side. "I still want Juniper Morel," she said fiercely, as if angry at herself. Then, under her breath, she added, "He must be so frightened."

"Is it a he, then?" Fenton asked carefully.

"My cousin," she sighed. "Why would you offer hospitality to someone who threatened you with a sword? I do know how to use it."

Fenton smiled and lowered his hands slowly. "I think if you wanted to stick me with it, you'd likely have done so already. Anyway, I have a large house and a dozen empty guest rooms. You can eat dinner in the second dining room and stay the night and never even see me, if you desire."

She tilted her head. "Why?"

"Why what?"

"Why do you have a large house with a dozen empty guest rooms? Did you steal it from someone?"

Fenton blinked and stared at her. "No. I inherited it. My father passed away three years ago. My mother lives with me, but other than her, the servants, and me, the house is empty."

The woman glanced around. "What is your name?" she said. "Where is this?"

"Lord Fenton Selby, The Marquess of Ambervale. This is my back door. We're not far from Ardmond, the capital."

"So I am in Valestria?"

Fenton nodded.

"What is Ambervale?"

"The property I hold. It's about forty miles east of here. I have a house there too, but I'm here for the season." Fenton's lips curled with amusement at this. The season had become interesting with the appearance of Miss Lily Hathaway, with whom he had shared one delightful dance before she had fallen madly in love with Theo. The wedding had been only four and a half weeks earlier. While Fenton was sincerely delighted for his friend's wedded bliss, especially now that the little misunderstanding between the newlyweds had been resolved, he could not entirely help lamenting his own unsuccessful season.

Not that he had no prospects at all. There were, of course, families of lesser means or status who would be delighted to attach their name to his, and there had been no shortage of young ladies being paraded before him at the various social engagements of the Ardmond season. But he had held out for someone irresistible, like Theo had found in Lily, someone delightful in heart as well as appearance.

"The season?" The lady stared at him. "It is the end of summer, or the beginning of autumn, depending on how you count the seasons and their changes. Is it different in Valestria?"

"The social season," Fenton clarified. "The season of endless parties at which young ladies and gentlemen are expected to pair off in happy couples. The first of the weddings for this season was four weeks ago, and others will follow soon." There was no bitterness in his voice, only a gentle, restrained melancholy that no one who did not know him well would hear at all.

"Are you marrying someone then?"

The directness of the question startled him, and he said, "No."

The woman looked him up and down. "You're already married?"

"No."

"If the offer is still open, I believe I will accept it," she said.

Surprised, he blinked and then said, "It is. May I ask what prompted that decision?"

The corners of her mouth lifted in a soft, amused smile. "Someone who answers such questions so patiently after being threatened is probably mostly trustworthy, and it would be convenient both to have more questions answered over dinner, and have a place to sleep tonight before I continue the search."

Fenton nodded. "You are welcome. If I might open my door, please?"

She hesitated, then stepped back and sheathed the sword at last. "You may."

He opened the door and stepped aside to let her enter first. She did so, moving to the side immediately so she could keep her eyes on him as he entered in turn.

He offered his arm, and she glanced at it, then at him curiously. "What is that for?" she said cautiously.

"It is courteous to offer a lady one's arm when acting as host." He found himself amused by the whole situation, including his own reaction to it. He had always had an even temper, and, like all Valestrian nobility, had had courtesy ingrained in him since birth. The absurdity of being threatened at swordpoint by a Fair lady at his own back door, after being told he could not accompany Theo on any more rescues because of the danger, tested the limits of his serious demeanor, tempting him to laugh at the world as Theo did.

Having been blessed in looks, name, title, and wealth, he did seem to have been particularly unlucky of late.

"Is it?" She eyed him cautiously, then placed her hand on his arm as if it might turn into a snake and bite her at any moment.

He escorted her through the first floor to one of the many guest suites. Her blue skirt rustled softly as she walked, and her hand was so light upon his arm he barely felt the touch at all.

Fenton opened the door and gestured for her to enter first.

"There is a water closet through that door where you may refresh yourself before dinner, if you would like."

She stepped in and slipped away from him cautiously, then strode to the window.

"The window looks upon the eastern garden, and the morning light is lovely. Do you need anything before dinner?"

She turned to look at him with a steady, evaluating gaze. "No, thank you," she said quietly.

"Please excuse me a moment. I will let Richard know that I have a guest."

Lord Selby bowed slightly as he stepped out of the room. He left the door open as he strode away.

What a strange evening!

Richard, his manservant, was waiting in the foyer with a curious look on his face.

"She's staying for the night. Please ask Millie to prepare a meal for her at dinner."

"Who is she?" Richard asked with interest.

"I have no earthly idea," said Fenton. "One of the Fair Folk, although you probably should keep that to yourself."

"One of Lord Willowvale's?"

"I doubt it. His assistants all seem better versed in Valestrian court manners. But it is wise to be cautious." With this, he immediately went to his study and dashed off a quick note.

Theo, a Fair lady has come to my estate seeking J. I've offered hospitality for the night and do not know how long she will stay. Please keep J. safely out of sight until I have ascertained her motives.

Fen

He sent it with one of the young stable boys, along with an admonition to accept tea and refreshments at the Overton household if such were offered.

Fenton then went to wash his face and refresh himself before dinner.

When dinner was ready only a short time later, he went back to his guest's door and knocked.

She opened it. "Yes?" she said cautiously.

"Dinner is ready."

"Thank you." She accepted his arm with a smile, and he could not help smiling in return, equally bemused by the situation.

He held out her chair for her, but she stared at him. "I'd rather not have you behind me," she said apologetically. "I've heard humans can lie, and if you can lie, I assume you can be equally deceptive in other ways."

"We can, indeed." Fenton nodded. "As a beautiful young lady traveling alone, such caution is certainly warranted. But you will find no such danger in my home." He meant it, too, whether she believed it or not. Nevertheless, he stepped away, for it was certainly more courteous to make a lady comfortable than to insist upon performing actions for one's own pride. He waited by his chair for her to sit first, which she did with a perplexed look.

"What may I call you, my lady?" asked Fenton as Richard placed spinach and strawberry salads in front of them.

She looked at him steadily without answering for a moment, her clear blue eyes thoughtful. Finally she said, "Crocus Firethorn. Juniper is the only son of my cousin, who died several years ago. He has no one to look after him."

"He's a fairy, then?" Fenton inquired mildly. It was widely understood that fairies could not lie, and Crocus' concern seemed genuine. But the Fair Court was also known for exceptionally intricate games of deception among the nobility, and most humans did not know enough to hold their own against a fairy in a game of twisting words. It would not do to betray Juniper now, when Theo had already wrested victory from defeat.

"Yes. You're sure you don't know anything of his whereabouts?" the young lady asked again, daintily dabbing her rose-pink lips with her napkin.

Fenton shook his head regretfully. "I am afraid I can be of no help. Why do you seek him?"

"I heard he was in danger." The lady's eyes held his.

Fenton looked up at Richard, signaling that they were ready for the next course, a cold cucumber soup.

"Since I have already guessed you are a fairy, may I ask to see your true face?" Fenton asked. He felt it rather bold, but then the situation was already strange.

She studied him again, then let the glamour drop, at least as far as he could discern. Her features were not much changed, but her true hair color was a bright, ice blue, and it fell in jubilant waves past her shoulders. Her eyebrows were a blue a shade or two darker, and the irises of her eyes were the same color as her hair. Her skin was a creamy alabaster, not quite as pale as Lord Willowvale but lighter and cooler even than Theo's fair coloring, and without freckles. The lovely rosebud pink of her lips was unchanged.

Her gaze rested upon him steadily, and she said, nearly under her breath, "I cannot read you. Are you displeased or merely shocked at what a fairy looks like?"

Fenton blinked and said, quite honestly, "How could I be displeased, my lady, when presented with such beauty?"

"Am I not too strange for your human tastes?" Her question had a mocking tone.

He met her eyes. "If you want compliments, you may have them. But I did not think that was your purpose here."

She broke into a delighted smile. "Such a gentleman! A genuine compliment is indeed worth much more than flattery upon demand." She tilted her head to the side and looked at him again. "I have heard many disparaging things about humans. I doubt all of them are true. What is the worst thing you have heard about the Fair Folk?"

Fenton waited while Richard took away the soup bowls and replaced them with steaming plates of roast chicken in a savory sauce.

"Well, when Lord Willowvale was sent to discover the identity of the Wraith, there was of course much speculation about what the Fair Folk needed with human children." Fenton watched her reaction surreptitiously as he appeared to focus on his meal. "One theory was that the Fair Folk were eating the poor waifs."

Crocus choked, swallowed, and stared at him. "What a horrible thing to say!" she breathed. "And I thought you were a gentleman."

He blinked at her. "You just asked…"

"Did you believe it of us?" She stared at him with wide eyes.

"Of course not. If you wanted to eat humans, underfed little street urchins would hardly be your first choice. Although I suppose not all of them were starving orphans." His sharp eyes caught her outraged gasp, and he softened. "If I had believed that of you, I would not have invited you into my house."

She blinked dampness from her eyes and raised her chin. "What a horrible thing to think of us," she said.

"I am sorry to have upset you," Fenton said sincerely. Now he was almost entirely sure that she could be trusted with Juniper's safety, but he did not want to lead her to the young fairy with no warning. Juniper had never indicated that anyone in the Fair Lands would miss him while he was gone.

At this moment, Richard entered with their dessert of raspberry compote and cream. He also held out a sealed note.

Fenton said, "Pardon me," and read it immediately.

Understood. I have relayed the message on Theo's behalf, as he is sleeping.
Theodore Overton, III, Baronet

Fenton slipped the note into his pocket.

"All is well?" inquired Crocus with a delicate uplift of her brows.

"Yes." Fenton smiled.

After dinner he offered her tea and a book from his library, if she wished. She hesitated, then said, "I suppose all your books are in Valestrian?"

"Indeed."

"Then I must confess I cannot read them. I speak Valestrian but was not educated in it well enough to enjoy a book." Crocus's cheeks grew ever so slightly pink, and she raised her chin.

Fenton smiled. "I can't read any of the Fair languages, so it would be hypocritical of me to think less of you for that. Is there anything else that would make your stay more comfortable before I bid you goodnight?"

"No. Thank you."

They walked in silence to her door, and he bowed courteously.

"Goodnight, my lady."

"Goodnight," she said softly.

He strode away, willing himself not to look over his shoulder at her as she stepped into the room and closed the door behind herself. The lock gave a soft click.

What a strange evening.

CHAPTER TWO
Breakfast with a Fairy

A note arrived at first light from the Overton estate.
All well here. Do you need reinforcements?
Theo

Fenton smiled to himself. Theo's brotherly affection had taken on a slightly solicitous air in the years since Fenton's father Lord Alistair Selby had passed away. His mother, always a quiet lady, had grown more reserved and solitary since her husband's death. Fenton ate either lunch or dinner with her every day, kept her well supplied with books, embroidery supplies, and sheet music, and was otherwise unsure what to do with her. She both accepted and issued few invitations for tea with other ladies, but when she did visit or have visitors, she was charming and sweet. Her closest friend, if she could be said to have one, was Lady Helena Overton, Theo's mother.

Fenton had always been rather reserved, and in this he had taken after his mother. Though they said little to each other, there was a long undercurrent of tenderness in their relationship. He wrote a quick reply to Theo, saying:

Not yet. However, if you are up to it, I should like to hold you to your promise of luncheon in my garden on Thursday. Mrs. Overton is, of course, invited to attend as well. Please convey my regards to her, your parents, C., J., etc.
Fen

After dispatching this with one of the young stable boys, Fenton went to his mother's wing and told her of their overnight guest.

"You say she's a fairy?" Lady Selby said in surprise.

"Undoubtedly." Fenton had not told his mother of his own involvement in the activities of the Wraith, nor that the mysterious hero was Theo, whom she had known since they were both boys.

So he was surprised when she said thoughtfully, "I should like to meet her before you have Theo and his bride over. Young men are easily deceived by a lovely face."

"Mother?" he said gently.

She looked at him with her steady, dark eyes, so much like his own, and said, "Surely you don't think me that unobservant. Several times I sat with Helena when Theo got lost in the veil; I've prayed for that dear boy for months. Who else has both the ability to traverse the veil and the ridiculous audacity to play the part of a Fair nobleman?"

He blinked helplessly at her. "You knew?"

She smiled. "I did wonder when you would tell me."

"I didn't want you to worry." He looked down at the rug with a rueful smile. "I wasn't as much help as I wanted to be, anyway. The veil seems to have a particular dislike for me, and Theo refused to take me back in after it tried to kill me three times in a row."

She stood and, in an unusual display of emotion, wrapped her arms around him. "I wish you had told me that," she said quietly. "I prayed for you anyway, of course, but I wish I had known how disappointed you were. Did you speak to Sir Theodore about it?"

He huffed a gentle laugh over her head, his arms around her much smaller form. "I did. He was encouraging and sympathetic, as I'm sure you can imagine. As difficult as it was for me to stay behind, it must have been even more difficult for him."

She nodded and stepped back. "Now, may I meet this guest at breakfast?"

Fenton knocked at Crocus's door.

He was not entirely surprised when she opened it cautiously. She was already dressed and had one hand on the hilt of her sword, as if unsure of whether she might need it. She looked convincingly human, except for the fact that she wore a sword over her simple blue dress. The faint edge of glamour was barely visible at all, and if Fenton had not known to look for it, he might have missed it altogether.

"My mother and I are having breakfast in the little dining room, if you wish to join us." Fenton bowed politely.

Crocus blinked. "Breakfast."

"If you would prefer to eat alone, I can ask Richard to bring you a tray."

She hesitated, then said, "Thank you. I will join you, if I may."

He offered her his arm. Her cheeks flushed rather becomingly, and she said, "I can walk perfectly well, you know."

"I don't doubt it. I meant merely to be respectful." He maintained his carefully schooled expression of serenity, though he was amused by her reaction to his gallantry. It was rather formal for breakfast, but he had never had an overnight female guest, other than his now-deceased aunt and her daughters some years ago. He had assumed that formality would help maintain the correct distance between him and his Fair guest. Informality could be misconstrued, whereas overzealous adherence to etiquette could not be questioned.

Crocus stared at him cautiously, then said, "I have the feeling you're mocking me, and I don't like it. Is that your intent, sir?"

"It is not." He met her eyes and said sincerely, "I am not accustomed to having female guests in my house, and I intended to make you feel safe by offering you every courtesy."

He realized, with an uncomfortable sort of twinge, that her eyes were a very similar shade of blue to that of Lord Ash Willowvale, the horrid Special Envoy of the Fair Court who had been dispatched to Ardmond, the Valestrian capital, some months before to identify the

Wraith, whom the Fair Court called the Rose. The Wraith had become a national hero, and everyone in Valestria had supported the man's efforts. Only a very intimate group of friends, all Valestrian noblemen, mostly young, had known that this hero was Fenton's oldest and dearest friend, Theo.

From what he had heard the previous afternoon, Lord Willowvale had last been seen in the Fair Lands the day before, when Theo and the Fair monarch His Majesty Silverthorn had come to their unexpected agreement. Fenton's mind shied away from imagining too vividly the scene that Cedar and Oliver Hathaway, Mrs. Lily Overton's brother, had described.

Crocus put her hand on his arm cautiously, and he felt a twinge of delight that she had decided to accept his courtesy. Then he gave himself a mental shake; it would be monstrously inconvenient to develop feelings for a fairy, especially if she turned out to be an adversary.

He escorted her to the breakfast room, asking if she had slept well and whether the room was to her liking, and receiving polite assurances that everything had been perfectly pleasant.

When they entered the room, Fenton's mother stood to greet their guest.

"Mother, this is our guest, Miss Crocus Firethorn. Miss Firethorn, this is my mother, the Honorable Lady Valeria Selby, Marchioness of Ambervale."

Crocus smiled and gave a slight bow in the Fair fashion rather than a curtsey. She regarded the lady with a steady sort of wary attention.

Lady Valeria blinked, but did not comment on the strangeness of this greeting. "You are welcome here, of course, Miss Firethorn."

They sat at the table, and Crocus watched as Richard put plates in front of them bearing eggs, sausage, sweet green melon, late strawberries, raspberries, and fluffy pastries with a swirl of soft sweet cream filling. He filled their teacups with hot black tea.

"Thank you, Richard," said Fenton. Proper high society manners had previously dictated that servants were not to be acknowledged as they carried out their duties, but neither the Overtons nor Selbys had ever abided by this rule. Their unfailing courtesy to those of lesser station had contributed to their popularity among the staff of many noble houses. Sir Theodore's adherence to always thanking his staff had, many years before, set off something of a trend in acknowledging the servants, though this practice had hardly gained universal acceptance.

Crocus watched Richard as he retreated. While acknowledging servants was no longer universally frowned upon, a simple expression of thanks was considered more than enough.

Fenton watched her watch his servant, wondering why she seemed to be so fascinated. "May I ask your plans for the day?" he asked.

"I will seek my cousin," she said. "I believe him to be somewhere nearby, and I intend to find him."

Lady Selby asked, "Why do you believe him to be nearby?"

Crocus looked at her, then glanced at Fenton, apparently unsure how much to say. She studied the food on her plate for a moment and took a sip of tea. Finally, she said, "I heard that when Lord Willowvale was seeking the Rose, he concentrated his search on the Valestrian noblemen in and around Ardmond."

Lady Selby smiled kindly. "And you believe your cousin to be with the Rose?" she prompted.

"I don't know." Crocus's voice was tight. "I should hope the man wouldn't abandon a child after taking advantage of the child's position in the palace for his own purposes, but I am not sure what to think."

Fenton frowned and glanced at his mother. "I do not believe the Rose to be so selfish as to abandon any child, certainly not one who aided him at great risk to himself. Have you heard that the Rose's efforts in the Fair Lands were concluded recently?"

Crocus blinked. "No." She straightened. "I had not. How did you hear that?"

"I am not at liberty to say." Fenton swallowed and looked down at his breakfast, suddenly less hungry than before. "I heard there was a dramatic confrontation in the Fair Court between the Rose and your king."

The Fair maiden's eyes widened, and she stood, leaving her breakfast mostly uneaten. "I will go immediately. If the Rose is dead, then…" She sucked in a breath, and her white teeth worried her lower lip. "I must find him," she said, referring to Juniper.

"The Rose is not dead!" Fenton said hurriedly. "I heard that he and your king came to an agreement."

Crocus stared at him. "Did he best the king, then? How is that possible?"

Fenton said carefully, "Well, I certainly wasn't there to see how it was done, but I heard that there was an agreement. In any case, I don't think Juniper's situation is urgent enough to prevent you finishing your breakfast."

She sat and resumed eating with quick, purposeful efficiency. "I will inquire in the Fair Lands. What you've said is difficult to believe. Maybe someone there can tell me more."

"Isn't the veil dangerous?" said Fenton, with an edge of concern in his voice.

The fairy shrugged one elegant shoulder. "Juniper is my responsibility." She finished her tea and stood again. "Thank you for your hospitality."

Fenton stood with her. "If you do not find your cousin, please do come back." Why should he feel this sense of loss at the thought of her leaving? It was ridiculous and unjustified, and he squashed it mercilessly. "I would be honored to host you again, if you should find yourself in the human world again."

Her lovely blue eyes softened in a most enchanting way, and his heart gave an uncomfortable little skip within his breast. "Thank you, my lord." She bowed in the Fair fashion to him, and then to his mother. "You have been exceedingly kind, and I am most grateful."

Then she turned and strode from the room, her steps long and graceful.

Fenton stood for a moment, looking after her, but she did not look back. It would have been polite to escort her to the door, but she had departed so hurriedly that she obviously did not expect or desire this courtesy.

He sat down again.

His mother said quietly, "She will probably be back."

"I know." This knowledge only made the guilt heavier, for it galled him to think of her risking the veil again in hopes of finding Juniper, who was already safe.

Everything in him wanted to trust her, but he did not have the right to make that decision on Juniper's behalf.

That afternoon he went on a solitary ride around the estate and up into the hills, from whence he could see the trees beginning to show their autumn shades. When he crossed between his estate and the Overton estate, he considered going to visit Theo. Then he refrained, for Theo and Lily ought to be delighting in each other's company, not in his. Besides, the question was hardly urgent, for Miss Firethorn had not returned yet.

The wind, unexpectedly chilly, ruffled his hair as he turned toward home.

A note awaited him, asking him to meet Theo and Lily at the palace the following morning, when Theo would give his report to His Majesty Lance Alberdale.

CHAPTER THREE
A Report to the King

T he next morning, Fenton stepped out into the beautiful golden fall sunshine and was startled to see Miss Crocus Firethorn standing upon the patio. She looked as though she had been debating whether to knock on the door or not.

"Good morning," he said.

She twisted her hands uncertainly. "I… Well, I haven't found Juniper and… well, I was wondering if I might stay here for another night."

"Of course." His voice was warm and kind. "Come in, please." He led her inside and said reluctantly, "I must apologize, Miss Firethorn, but I have a prior engagement this morning. My presence is required at the palace for a few hours. Please make yourself comfortable here. Would you like some breakfast?"

She hesitated, then nodded once. She was a little pale, and Fenton wished fervently that he did not have to leave. But he had promised Theo he would be there, and one did not want to be late when meeting the king.

Fenton's manservant Richard was standing close by, having just bidden Fenton farewell, and so Fenton said to him, "Richard, please ensure that Miss Firethorn is cared for. Breakfast in the white room, I think, and tea. Would you like a fire in your suite, Miss Firethorn?"

She nodded again. "I am rather tired," she admitted, as if embarrassed.

Fenton bowed deeply. "Please ask for whatever you need, Miss Firethorn. You can eat and rest and be refreshed here."

"Thank you," she said, and her lovely blue eyes shone with gratitude.

He bowed again and then set off for the palace.

After learning of Theo's triumph, the palace had requested a full report as soon as Theo was able to give it. His Majesty Lance Alberdale offered to visit Theo, if he did not feel up to traveling the ten miles to the palace, but Theo had demurred, stating in his note that he felt marvelous and would be delighted to deliver a full report in two days' time. In truth, he had not felt particularly energetic when he sent his reply, but two days later, the words were true.

"May I come with you?" Lily asked that morning.

"Of course, my love." He seemed startled by the thought. "I didn't think you would want to, or I would have asked you."

"I want to be with you." She met his eyes. "I love you, Theo, and I don't want to be separated any more than necessary."

Theo nearly danced to the stables when he went to ask the grooms to ready the horses and phaeton. The elegant phaeton was made of polished dark wood and drawn by two matched bays, and Lily already knew he drove it well.

The bright autumn sunlight gleamed on his auburn hair and lit his hazel eyes, and Lily leaned against him, unwilling to be even a few unnecessary inches apart.

A carriage passed them going the opposite direction, and then they were alone on the road again.

Lily admired Theo's skillful hands on the reins and the fine line of his jaw.

"What are you looking at?" he murmured with a sidelong look at her.

"At you. I feel quite fortunate, if you must know." She smiled primly and slipped her hand in the crook of his arm, feeling the lean, strong muscles of his arm and side. "Not only am I blessed with a husband who is generous, kind, and heroic, he is handsome to look at, too."

She was delighted to see his cheeks flush deeply.

"My love!" His eyes sparkled with surprise and delight. "I did not think you so forward."

"I'm not usually," she added even more primly. "I only dare say such things because we are alone, and because I think it is long past time that you understand that I adore you just as much as you do me."

He shifted the reins to one hand and twisted to kiss her with passion that made her heart beat faster. "Did you know, Mrs. Overton, that I adore you even more than I did this morning? I did not think such was even possible, so delighted was I with you, and yet I find myself completely overcome."

Theo looked back at the horses but caught her hand in his and kissed it with great enjoyment.

"You are ridiculous," Lily laughed as he pulled her closer.

"Ridiculously in love."

Fenton met them just inside the palace gate, having arrived just a moment before they did on a magnificent chestnut mare. "Good morning," he greeted them.

"Good morning, Lord Selby!" Theo used Fenton's title, since there were palace guards nearby. To Lily, the formality merely reminded her what close friends they were, for she had more often heard them use each others' first names, as if they were family.

Fenton dismounted with easy grace and handed the reins to the waiting groom. Theo jumped out of the phaeton and helped Lily down, then handed the reins to another groom. They walked into the palace together.

"How is your mother?" Theo asked.

"Quite well. I think she would enjoy seeing your mother again soon." Fenton would have brought up the topic of his Fair guest, but there were servants bustling about in this section of the palace.

Instead, he asked quietly, "I really do not know what I can add to this discussion, Theo. I was not with you in the Fair Lands when you confronted Silverthorn."

Theo glanced at his friend, his eyes bright and warm. "You helped courageously on several missions, and you were invaluable in planning." There was no mistaking the sincerity in Theo's voice, but Fenton suppressed a sigh. He had not been able to help his friend in the Fair Lands much at all, much less in the terrifying confrontation with the Fair monarch. Theo had been essentially alone, pitting his courage and his cleverness against the Fair crown, unwilling to risk Oliver, Lily, or even Cedar enough to let them speak, for words could be perilous in the Fair Lands.

When they reached the king's private study in which His Majesty Alberdale had requested Theo to meet with him, Fenton bowed and stepped aside, as if to let Theo go in alone. But Theo urged him to accompany him and Lily into the room, and Fenton graciously assented. The king had been enjoying some excellent tea while he looked over some papers, which he neatly stacked to the side when Theo, Lily, and Fenton arrived. He stood to greet them.

Edouard, the leader of the royal guard, stepped inside the room and closed the door behind himself.

"Sit, please." The king smiled them as he gestured at the chairs across from his own. Lily's eyes widened, and she glanced at Theo before complying. His Majesty Alberdale was not particularly pretentious, for a king, but he was nevertheless a king.

Theo bowed deeply and then sat across from the king, one long leg elegantly crossed over the other. Lily sat to his left side, and Fenton at his other side.

With admirable clarity and conciseness, Theo told the king how he had used the binding magic which the league, and the king himself, had given him, how Lord Willowvale had suspected Oliver Hathaway of being the Rose and attempted to use Lady Araminta Poole as bait, how Oliver had courageously gone into the veil after Lady Araminta, and how Theo had extricated them from their respective predicaments. He explained how his young Fair ally Juniper Morel had taken refuge with the Overtons and how Juniper's binding magic had been so critical in Theo's confrontation with the Fair king, Silverthorn. With a modest flush, he told of his bargain with the king, how the king had stabbed him, and how his blood, glittering with healing magic and binding magic, had soaked into the ground and made the very soil of the Fair Lands yield to him.

Through it all, he commended the courage of his allies, especially Fenton, Cedar, and Juniper, with sincerity and warmth.

"How do you feel now?"

"Perfectly fine. Lord Mosswing's magic is incredible."

"And Silverthorn promised not to take or harm humans again?" the king said in wonder.

Theo sparkled with delight and triumph. "Indeed." Then his smile dimmed a little. "He cannot harm humans either directly or indirectly, but I confess I was not thinking clearly enough to ensure that he extended that order to all of his subjects. I shall attempt to remedy that when I return to the Fair Lands."

The king blinked. "You're going back," he said flatly. "Why?"

"I promised Silverthorn I would tell him why I am a friend of the Fair Lands when I could think more clearly."

The king's eyes widened slightly, but he said only, "Hm. I've half a mind to expel Willowvale completely, but I suppose it would be unwise not to have a Fair presence in Valestria."

"Indeed."

His Majesty Alberdale looked Theo over again. "I am glad to see you're whole. Please convey my deep gratitude to Lord Mosswing."

Understanding this as the gracious dismissal it was, Theo stood and bowed deeply to the king. "Thank you, Your Majesty."

"Thank you, Theo," the king said affectionately. "You are a truly remarkable young man, and I am glad to call you a friend. Valestria, Aricht, and the Fair Lands all owe you a great debt."

Theo flushed and bowed again. "Thank you, Your Majesty," he said. "I was wondering if it would be all right if Mrs. Overton and Lord Selby and I went to visit the children before we depart for home."

"Please do. I think Mr. and Mrs. Porter would like to see you well, too. They were informed of your triumph, of course, but not having seen you, they have likely been imagining the worst."

Theo gave a smile of radiant delight. "Then I shall be glad to show them that all is well. Lord Selby, I wonder if you might be willing to glamour me, please?"

"Why should you be glamoured?" his friend replied with a frown.

The king looked at him severely. "Indeed? Is there any remaining threat from the Fair Court?"

"I shouldn't think so," Theo replied. "It is only that… well, isn't it awkward if the children know who pulled them from the Fair Lands?" His cheeks flushed. "I shouldn't want them to be reminded of that difficult time if they were ever to see me again."

His Majesty Alberdale said quietly, "Dear boy, I should very much like to use my royal authority to command you to let them see your face, but I won't, because I don't wish to be an utter tyrant. I will say only that I believe from the bottom of my heart that you deserve to receive their gratitude wearing your own face for once."

Theo looked down and murmured, "I didn't do it for accolades, Your Majesty."

The king said, "I am aware of that, and thus I have refrained from proclaiming your heroism across the entire nation. Nevertheless, don't you think that if you had been so courageously rescued from such dreadful circumstances, you would like to thank the hero face to face?"

Theo's blush deepened, and he muttered, "Your Majesty, I do think that is an unfair question."

"Only because you're too modest." The king clapped him on the shoulder and began to walk him toward the door. "Theo, you will be doing them a kindness by letting them see that their rescuer is human after all. They will admire and love you all the more for it, and it will be good for them to see how very great a human heart can be."

The young man nearly groaned. "You've made your point. It's a moral imperative. Thank you, Your Majesty."

The king chuckled and said, "Thank you, Theo. You understand me perfectly. I do hope you enjoy your time."

A few minutes later, Theo, Lily, and Fenton strolled across the wide courtyard and along the flagstone path to the spacious manor house where the children and their guardians were currently housed. Lily looked around in awe.

"Do you come here often, Theo?" she asked.

"It depends. Sometimes I'm here nearly every day, sometimes only once a month." He blinked, then added, "It occurred to me that I once told you my Arichtan and Rulothian were quite bad. I was not entirely truthful in that, and I must beg your forgiveness for my dishonesty. My family spent a little time in both Aricht and Ruloth when I was young, while my father was developing business connections. So I'm next to fluent in both Arichtan and Rulothian, and His Majesty has asked me to interpret a few times when his court interpreters were ill or otherwise unavailable."

Fenton made a sound low in his throat, and Lily looked at him questioningly. He said, "Your husband is a bit more than a backup interpreter. The king leans on him to help manage a number of challenging political relationships."

Theo shook his head wryly. "He doesn't need much help. I think he has me just for another set of ears."

At this point they reached the low, white-painted gate of the fence that separated the little garden of the manor house from the larger garden and courtyard. Fenton opened it and stood aside as Theo and Lily stepped in, then followed them up the path to the door, which was not quite wide enough for three to walk abreast.

The light, cheerful sound of laughter came from outside, and Theo turned from the door to lead them around the side of the house to the back, where they found a crowd of children playing lively games of jumping rope, stick and hoop, and a particularly animated version of Follow the Leader. Essie held one end of the rope with her back to the newcomers, and John was sitting on the steps deeply engrossed in a book.

Theo, always ready to smile, beamed in delight, though he said nothing at first.

Fenton said quietly, "I know you don't want the attention, but isn't it good to see how they're healing?"

"It is," Theo replied. "You're right, as usual. This was the one little bit of delight that was lacking in my triumph." He sighed, and Lily glanced up to see that his bright hazel eyes were nearly glowing with satisfaction.

One of the younger girls saw them and promptly lost her place in the jumping rope rhyme she was singing. "Mr. John! Mrs. Essie!" she cried. "There are gentlemen here, and a lady!"

Essie and John both looked up with sudden shock. "Mr. Overton! Lord Selby!" Their eyes widened even more when they saw Lily. "Children, line up right away, quick as you can!"

Theo winced and hurried forward. "No, no, please, Essie. Let them play!"

The children lined up as quickly as any schoolmaster might wish and stared at Theo with lively interest, though with caution as well.

Theo reached John and Essie, his cheeks hot and flushed. "I didn't mean to stop their merriment," he said quietly. "Please, let them play. His Majesty made me come, and I'm glad I did. It's good to see them playing."

Lily followed in his wake, feeling everyone's eyes on her. Several of the little girls smiled at her, unaware of anything but the sweet times they had shared when Lily and Oliver had previously visited the children's home, but Essie and John eyed her coolly.

Theo smiled down at Lily, then back at the caretakers. "You've met my wife, Mrs. Lilybeth Overton, but not since the wedding. Lily, these are some of my oldest friends, Essie and John Porter. They worked for my parents for a while when I was young, and I trust them implicitly."

Essie's cheeks pinked, and she said cautiously, "May I assume that the little misunderstanding has been resolved?"

"Entirely." Theo turned to Lily and bent to kiss her hand with infinite tenderness, though Lily knew it was not entirely for her sake that he did so. When he straightened, he said, "I would very much like it if you could rejoice with me, Essie."

Essie nodded, though her eyes lingered on Lily for a moment longer. Then she turned to the children and began, "Children, this is—"

"No, don't, please!" Theo said hurriedly. "It's unnecessary."

Essie smiled impishly at him and continued, unruffled, "Lord Fenton Selby, the Marquess of Ambervale, Mr. Theodore Overton the Fourth, and Mrs. Lilybeth Overton."

Fenton bowed slightly to the children without saying a word, though humor danced in his dark eyes.

Theo narrowed his eyes at Essie, then swept an exaggerated bow toward the children. "It is an honor to meet you all," he said with a genuine smile lighting his face.

One of the little girls blinked. "I know you," she said in sudden recognition.

Theo frowned at her. "I don't believe we've been introduced before."

Her face broke into a delighted smile. "You're the Wraith. I know your voice."

Theo blinked, momentarily nonplussed. He didn't want to lie to the poor child; she'd already suffered so much, and telling her that she could not trust her own ears seemed too unfair to contemplate.

"Are you sure?" he said uncertainly.

An older boy in the front said, "I am. You carried my little brother through the veil for four hours before we got out. I think I'd know your voice after that."

The entire group of children was suddenly exclaiming in wonder at once, and Theo flushed as pink as Lily had ever seen him.

Lily, to her surprise, felt his hand trembling in hers, and leaned closer. "Let them love you," she whispered to him.

He took a deep breath and nodded. He knelt before the youngest girl in the front row. "You're Gertie, aren't you?" he said with a smile.

She nodded shyly. "Thank you for stealing me," she said in her tiny, soft voice. She was only six years old and small for her age, for she had not been fed well even before the Fair Folk had taken her.

"It was my honor and my delight." His voice was as warm and sincere as his heart.

Gertie asked, "Would you play stick and hoop with me, sir?" with her blue eyes wide and filled with innocent hope.

Theo could not have refused, nor did he want to.

He spent the next hour playing stick and hoop, jumping rope, and Follow the Leader with the children, who whooped and laughed in delight at their hero's antics. Between games, or sometimes in the middle of them, the children came up to him one by one and thanked him. Most were shy, but some were enthusiastic and demonstrative, throwing their arms about his neck with joyful abandon. One girl brushed tears from her eyes as she thanked him, and Theo surreptitiously wiped dampness from his own eyes.

When they played Follow the Leader, Theo called out, "Lord Selby, it would be shabby of you not to join us!"

Fenton, with a shy smile, joined the end of the line.

At last, grinning, Theo stood beside Lily and Fenton again at the edge of the yard as the children began a game of croquet. He sighed in contentment. "What a satisfying morning! Thank you for sharing it with me."

Lily slipped her hand through his arm and leaned close, though she said nothing. The entire garden was bright and joyful with the sound of the children laughing. A cool breeze barely snuck over the wall, tickling the sweat-dampened curls at Theo's temples.

Fenton said, "I cannot think of a better way to end your work in the Fair Lands than to see the smiling faces of the children you saved. Not to mention that His Majesty was right."

Theo blew out a breath and gave a wry smile. "Shall I admit it to him, or let him simply bask in knowing it?" He cast his gaze over the happy chaos. "I think I'd like to sneak away. Your family is visiting this afternoon, aren't they?" He glanced at Lily, who nodded.

They walked back through the garden in a companionable silence, then Theo led them through the courtyard. Fenton's horse and the Overton phaeton would be waiting for them near the front of the palace, and the shortest way there took them through the palace itself. Theo led them through spacious halls lined with paintings and past several smaller studies and sitting rooms.

Fenton said, "Thank you for your note about my houseguest. I think—"

Exquisite agony bloomed in Theo's chest.

The world collapsed inward. There was nothing but a terrible, relentless, gnawing grief, an abyss of screaming pain that divided muscle from bone and heart from heart.

He fell to his knees and retched, only distantly aware of Fenton whispering, "No no no, Theo, don't die like this," with desperate, sick fear in his voice. He couldn't hear Lily's softer voice at all over the ragged thunder of his own heart as it skipped and danced an uneven rhythm through the pain.

Threads of fire wove through his heart. They burned down his arms and through his belly, outlining each nerve, blood vessel, and muscle fiber in a fine lacework of searing anguish.

A single thread pulled, and pulled, and *pulled*, as if it would rip his heart out through his chest.

Then there was a terrible *snap*, as if the offending thread of fire had been about to break and snapped back into place.

The pain disappeared as quickly as it had come.

Theo found himself sprawled on the floor, his head in Lily's lap and Fenton looking down at him.

Tears slid down Lily's face, and he stared up at her, unable for a moment to comprehend anything other than the great, blessed relief of the absence of pain.

"Are you still with us?" whispered Fenton.

Theo tried to say something witty and reassuring, but when he opened his mouth, he could only manage a low groan. He blinked, dazed, and pressed a hand to his heart.

"What happened?" whispered Lily.

Theo closed his eyes and concentrated on breathing, which seemed to require a great deal of focus at the moment. The blood roared in his ears, and the whole world seemed to be swaying with the force of it.

"Are you well, Lord Selby?" Lily asked quietly. "You're nearly as pale as he is."

There was a silence, in which Theo intended to open his eyes but didn't quite manage it, and then Fenton said, "When my father died, he clutched at his heart the way Theo did just now."

Theo groped blindly for Fenton's hand and grasped it, putting all the reassurance he could not yet voice into the strength of his grip. Warm fingers felt his pulse at his wrist and throat, and someone murmured something that sounded reassuring, though Theo didn't hear the words.

His heartbeat thundered in his ears, but the rhythm was steady and strong, as if he had been running hard. With a grunt of effort, and a few deep breaths to quell a rising nausea, he managed to turn over to his side, and then shoved himself up to hands and knees.

Fenton's strong hands steadied him a moment there, as he stared at the floor.

"Are you sure you're ready to sit up?" his friend asked under his breath.

Lily's delicate hands touched his shoulders, as if she wanted to help him but wasn't sure what to do.

"I'm all right." His voice sounded weak and strange in his ears.

He staggered to his feet and leaned on Fenton a moment. The hallway wavered before him before it steadied.

"You're paler than Juniper," said Fenton. "Sit down."

The king and the royal physician, Bertrand Southwick, were already there; Theo wondered how long he had been on the floor and when the men had arrived. Fenton and Mr. Southwick helped Theo solicitously to the nearest sitting room, where he collapsed onto a velvet settee.

"I'm all right," he said again, feeling that it was not entirely a lie, but not yet entirely true, either.

"You don't look it," said Southwick. "What happened?"

Theo felt a great lassitude coming over him, as if he had not slept in weeks, and it was all he could do to sit reasonably upright. Beside him, Lily put her arm through his, as if for reassurance, but he felt with surprise that she was also supporting him in the most subtle way possible.

They were talking again, and he could not muster the attention to clearly decipher the words. He laid his head on Lily's shoulder and let his mind wander.

The king was speaking urgently with the physician, who, after an apology for his presumption, began unbuttoning Theo's jacket.

When the physician pushed him against the back of the settee, he murmured only, "I'm fine," knowing that no one believed him, and not entirely sure whether he believed himself.

CHAPTER FOUR
Repercussions

Lily watched worriedly as the physician unbuttoned Theo's jacket, vest, and shirt. What a strange way to see her new husband's disrobed body! For those difficult weeks after the wedding, they had maintained nearly as much formality as before the wedding, and then, after their delighted reconciliation, he had been drunk on Lord Cedar Mosswing's healing magic for two nights. Only last night had been a little closer to what one might expect of a newly married couple.

His sweet smile and the elegant lines of his face were familiar and beloved. The taut lines of the muscle and sinew of his long, well-knit torso, and the smooth, pale skin of his chest and stomach dusted liberally with freckles, she had only seen by lantern light. The terrible wound he had received only three days before in the Fair Lands was nearly gone; the only sign of it was a bright red line scarcely an inch long just to the right of and a little above his navel, and a matching scar on his back.

The physician probed and poked and listened and asked questions, and Theo endured it all with an unsettlingly quiet sort of fatigue.

He actually fell asleep on Lily's shoulder, and Mr. Southwick was unable to wake him until he opened a little jar of smelling salts, which made Theo groan in protest.

"I can't find anything wrong with him," the physician said after his examination. "You say it was pain, not pressure?"

Theo blinked blearily at him, nodded, and then, with shaking hands, began rebuttoning his shirt. "Can I smell that again, please?"

The physician offered him the jar of smelling salts, and Theo sniffed it.

The sharp smell helped focus his muzzy mind, and he said, with a hint of his usual brightness, "Is Lord Willowvale still in Ardmond, Your Majesty?"

"I believe so. Why?" The king sat across from the settee where Theo had slouched against Lily. Fenton hovered protectively above Theo and Lily, one hand clenched on the arm of the settee as if to pretend he were not shaking.

Theo took several deep breaths, feeling the fatigue recede to his trembling fingers and his legs, which felt oddly hollow and weak. He was almost thinking clearly; he was nearly sure of it, though his thoughts were certainly slower than usual. He focused on the puzzle of his last shirt button and, after some difficulty, managed to get it in the hole. He began on the little silk-covered buttons of his vest, which seemed significantly more fiddly and difficult than they had that morning.

"I believe I should pay him a visit," he said at last, when his scrambled thoughts finally consented to behave logically.

"Do you think he's responsible for this?" The king's voice held a dangerous edge.

Theo considered the question. "Yes, but I doubt he intended the result he got."

"I'll send a contingent of soldiers and have him brought in."

"Wait," said Theo.

The king studied his friend's face, then nodded. He looked toward the physician. "Anything else, Mr. Southwick?"

The physician shook his head. "He's entirely healthy, as far as I can see. I cannot deny that something happened, but I do not see any lingering illness or damage. If the heart itself were damaged, I could not tell, but his pulse seems strong and regular at the moment. Circulation is good."

Fenton caught his breath and turned away. He strode to the window and looked out, his shoulders stiff and his back erect.

Theo found that his hands steadied as he focused on his buttons, and by the time he finished the last button of his jacket, he felt almost functional. He looked across to meet the king's eyes.

"Your Majesty, I don't think your soldiers are necessary. I would like to visit Lord Willowvale myself."

"Why?" His Majesty Alberdale said with open skepticism.

"I think he needs help."

Fenton turned from the window and stared at him. "What do you mean?"

Theo shoved himself to his feet and managed to stay upright with only a slight wobble, which Lily's grip upon his arm helped steady. He looked down at her with a grateful smile, then turned back to address the king and Fenton.

"I believe, Your Majesty, that there is nothing wrong with my heart at all. I believe Lord Willowvale tried to rip the binding magic from me, but it is twined far too deeply for any attempt of that sort to work." He felt suddenly breathless with the effort of staying upright and talking at the same time. Darkness seemed to be creeping in from the edges of his vision, and he leaned more heavily on Lily.

Fenton stepped closer and wrapped a strong arm around his shoulders. "Can it wait?"

"He's probably in worse shape than I am." Theo's vision cleared with a few deep breaths. "I'm all right. Just… tired."

The king looked at the physician, who shrugged.

"I have no objection, I suppose, provided you take a contingent of soldiers," said His Majesty Alberdale. He stepped to the corridor and spoke to the guard for a few moments.

While they waited for the escort to be arranged and a royal carriage made ready, for so the king insisted, Theo sat back down on the settee and laid his head against Lily's shoulder again.

"How do you really feel?" she murmured.

"There's no pain at all," he replied reassuringly. "I'm only tired and a little dizzy, but that is fading." Without opening his eyes, he brought her hand to his lips and kissed it. "I adore you so," he breathed.

Within a few minutes, the soldiers and carriage were ready. Fenton insisted upon accompanying them, and Theo made no objection. Fenton asked, "Mrs. Overton, would you like to be alone, or might I ride with you and Theo in the carriage?"

"You are welcome to ride with us, Lord Selby," Lily said with a smile.

He gave her a slight, grateful bow and replied, "Thank you, Mrs. Overton."

The soldiers strode along beside the carriage, which went at a slow, steady walk. At this relaxed pace, it took over half an hour to reach the house Lord Willowvale had rented during his time in the Valestrian capital of Ardmond. Theo regained a little color and smiled reassuringly at both his wife and friend.

"Let me out first, if you please," said Fenton nearly under his breath.

"I'm not going to fall out of the carriage, Fen," said Theo with a gleam of laughter in his eyes. "I'm quite revived, actually."

Nevertheless, he clutched at the edge of the carriage door as he exited rather than leaping out with his customary vigor. Then he stood straight and tall, and offered his hand to his beloved wife as she stepped out behind him.

The garden was well maintained, but at this time of autumn none of the flowers were blooming. Instead, the trees had just begun to show their warm autumn colors. Red, orange, and yellow vied for prominence, and the wide patio in front looked inviting, if mostly unused.

"Mr. Overton, His Majesty said that we were not to leave your side, and that we were to run the fairy through as many times as we like if he offers you any hint of violence." The guard bowed sharply to him.

Theo grinned. "Thank you, Edouard. I doubt that will be necessary."

"I should like the opportunity," the guard said grimly.

"Let me go first, if you please." Theo slipped Lily's hand into the crook of his arm and proceeded up the path as if he were on a social visit.

He knocked at the door, and they waited almost a whole minute before it was opened. A fairy with pale green skin and reddish-brown hair pulled back in an elaborate braid said, "What do you want?"

"I would like to see Lord Willowvale," said Theo.

The fairy's eyes flicked from Theo's face to Fenton's, then to the soldiers behind them. "My lord has not finished breakfast," he said finally.

Theo blinked. "Really? It's nearly ten o'clock."

The fairy shrugged. "It is not my place to dictate my lord's schedule."

"Have you seen him recently?"

"My lord eats alone."

Theo frowned. "When did he begin breakfast?"

"At the usual time, eight o'clock." The fairy looked at him with a vague sort of resentment in his eyes.

"I should like to see him," said Theo.

"My lord eats alone," the fairy repeated.

"He must be finished by now." Theo stepped forward, pushing the door open with one hand.

The fairy did not offer any more objection, though he studied Lily, Fenton, and the soldiers with interest as they followed Theo down the hall.

Two other fairies were sitting at a table in a nearby room, and they jumped up at the sight of Theo and drew their swords.

"My lord has not given leave for you to enter his house," said one.

"I'm here on my king's business." Theo stepped in front of Lily and raised his hands placatingly. "I bear no weapon, and I will not harm Lord Willowvale."

The senior of the two studied him, then said, looking vaguely affronted, "All right. He's been at breakfast for nearly two hours. Enter if you like." He indicated a door to his left with the tip of his sword. "The soldiers stay out here."

Edouard began to protest, but Theo said, "Peace, Edouard. Let me open the door before you tell me I'm a fool, please."

Theo opened the door.

The late morning sun spilled golden across a table which held a plate bearing a few remaining crumbs of a scone, a cold teapot, and a butter dish. Lord Willowvale lay crumpled on the floor beside it. He appeared to have fallen from his chair. One arm was flung out at an awkward angle, as if he'd tried and perhaps failed to catch himself, and the other was under his body. His face was mashed into the hardwood floor.

"You poor, disagreeable wretch," muttered Theo under his breath.

One of the two fairies snorted derisively, and neither made any move to help him. "He's breathing," one of them said. "Leave him."

Theo shot him a cold look. "I will not." He stepped carefully into the room, watching for any sort of reaction from Lord Willowvale. "Lily, if you would stay safely out of his reach, I would be much obliged," he said quietly.

Lily stayed several feet back, and Theo knelt at Lord Willowvale's head, with Fenton just beside him. "What are you doing, Theo?" Fenton asked under his breath.

Theo felt Lord Willowvale's pulse at his throat and found it weak and thready. "Come on, you prickly fairy," he muttered. "Wake up." He took off his jacket and folded it, then slid it under the fairy's head when he rolled Lord Willowvale onto his side.

The movement provoked a convulsion of coughing. Lord Willowvale gasped and spit pale blue blood onto Theo's jacket. He groaned and half turned toward the floor, as if intending to push himself up.

"I suggest waiting a few more minutes before trying to stand up," said Theo.

Lord Willowvale made a choked sound of dismay and shoved himself up to hands and knees. He drew a dagger from some hidden sheath, and, with a groan, clawed his way up to a kneeling position. "Keep away," he gasped.

Edouard's sword was at Lord Willowvale's throat before Theo could raise his hands.

The fairy bared his teeth and, with a hiss of desperate fury, tried to rise, then fell back to his knees.

"Edouard, please back away," said Theo.

"His Majesty gave me leave to——"

"I know. *Please*, Edouard. Lord Selby, you as well, please."

The soldier snarled his dismay but stepped back two steps. "If you hurt him, I'll take great pleasure in poking cold steel through your innards," he said to Lord Willowvale.

Theo raised his open hands toward the fairy. "I'm not armed, Lord Willowvale."

The fairy's pale blue eyes blazed with fierce anger and pride, but he said nothing. He tried to rise again, then, apparently overcome by dizziness, nearly fell on his face.

Theo caught him.

"You're a fool," the fairy gasped. He wrapped one arm around Theo's neck and the other pressed the point of the dagger to Theo's side.

"I'm unarmed, my lord, and I have promised your servants I will not harm you," said Theo quietly.

Lord Willowvale's chest heaved as he tried to catch his breath, and Theo felt in him the same desperate, yawning abyss of fatigue that had nearly swallowed him whole.

The Fair lord shoved Theo away and fell back onto his heels. "Curse you and your idiotic chivalry," he muttered. He swayed on his knees. "How did you get here?"

"You did something with the binding magic, didn't you?"

The fairy didn't answer, but the bleak, terrible look in his eyes gave the answer.

Theo said, "Mrs. Overton, Lord Selby, Edouard, would you please leave us alone for a few minutes?"

Fenton said, "Lord Willowvale, if you harm my friend, you'll wish Edouard had gotten to you first. Have a care."

The fairy nodded once, his gaze not leaving Theo's face.

With that, the others left reluctantly, and Fenton pulled the door nearly closed behind them.

"My lord, I wager you didn't intend for that to go as it did," said Theo.

The fairy leaned against the leg of the breakfast table and coughed. He doubled over and vomited a little more pale blue blood onto the floor.

"What were you trying to do?" Theo asked gently.

Lord Willowvale groaned something unintelligible and nearly fell on his face. Theo caught at his shoulders and helped him shift to sit against the wall.

"Get your hands off me," the fairy coughed.

"You'd rather lie in your own blood?" Theo pulled his jacket closer and offered a clean sleeve to Lord Willowvale, who used it to wipe the blood from his lips.

Theo sat back and rested his arms on his raised knees. Lord Willowvale glared back balefully, though blearily.

"I think," Theo said quietly, "that you wanted to rip the binding magic out of me."

"It isn't right!" Lord Willowvale's voice cracked. "Why should a human, weak and stupid as you are, hold the Fair Lands together?" His chest heaved. "It is shame on us all!" He gasped for breath, his head thrown back against the damask wallpaper.

Theo stood, then took several slow breaths to steady his own dizziness. He stepped to the door and said to Fenton, "If you wouldn't mind having someone bring us water and perhaps a little fruit, it might help." He returned to his place near Lord Willowvale.

A few minutes later, one of the fairy servants brought a tray bearing a plate of starfruit, a pitcher of water, and two glasses.

Theo waited until the servant left the room again before pouring water for Lord Willowvale and himself.

"I think I've demonstrated my love for the Fair Lands, my lord," Theo said quietly. "If you fear that I'll not value your beloved country enough, please rest assured that I do."

Lord Willowvale curled his lip in scorn but said nothing immediately. He raised his eyebrows in surprise when Theo offered him one of the glasses.

"It affected you?" the fairy said at last.

"Indeed." Theo smiled ruefully. "Although I gather the effect was worse on your end of the effort."

Lord Willowvale made a soft *pfft* of irritation but could not deny this. "It is not right," he murmured again.

"It is difficult to let someone else protect you, when you're so accustomed to being the protector, I imagine."

Lord Willowvale looked at Theo sharply.

Theo sighed and rubbed both hands over his face. "It was a valiant attempt," he said quietly. "You nearly killed us both, I think, but I don't know if it would have worked before we died."

The fairy sighed and stared bleakly at the cup of water. "I barely had a grasp of one of the strands," he said. "I could neither shift nor break it, and it was only one of thousands."

This honesty, along with the raw grief that roughened Lord Willowvale's voice, startled Theo, but he knew better than to show his surprise.

"Did your king ask you to take the binding magic?" he asked quietly.

Lord Willowvale glanced at him, then stared back at the water. "He holds to your agreement."

Theo considered this in silence. The fairy leaned his head against the wall behind him and closed his eyes. After several minutes, his labored breathing grew a little easier.

Lord Willowvale muttered, "I won't stop you if you inform my king of my failure. There's little hope of a better second attempt."

"Why would I do that?"

"Why would you not?" The fairy's cold blue eyes stared at him, bleak and hard. "He'd likely kill me for it."

Theo smiled with as much warmth as he could manage. "You seem to believe I hate you, Lord Willowvale. I don't. I despise how you and your king thought to save your land, but I cannot deny that anyone in your situation would be tempted by methods that seemed likely to succeed, regardless of the cost. Now that the danger is past, I should hope you might realize the error of your ways."

Lord Willowvale gave a soft, dismissive grunt. "You're an idiot, Overton," he said.

Theo chuckled, low and amused. He thought of several clever retorts, most of which noted that he was the only one who had bothered to see if Willowvale was still alive, but he said only, "Perhaps. I don't plan on notifying your king, in any case."

The fairy raised a skeptical eyebrow at him, pale as moonlight.

Theo added, "Eat some fruit. It ought to help a bit."

Lord Willowvale could barely lift the slice of starfruit to his lips, and he closed his eyes as he chewed.

When he finished the fruit, he murmured, "Even an idiot can be useful sometimes."

Theo laughed under his breath. "And even a prideful fairy lord can unbend enough to take a gift when it is offered, I should hope."

"I owe you nothing," Lord Willowvale said, with a hint of his usual icy contempt.

"Of course not," Theo agreed. "Compassion is not an exchange. It is always a gift."

Lord Willowvale groaned. "You're intolerable."

Theo grinned at him. "Shall I leave you here on a floor to recuperate a bit more in privacy, or shall I help you up?"

"Leave me."

Theo stood, with a little effort, and offered his hand. The fairy scowled at him.

"Leave me," he repeated icily.

"As you wish, my lord." Theo sketched a polite bow.

CHAPTER FIVE
A Quiet Afternoon

Theo told Lord Willowvale's servants that he was resting and that he might appreciate luncheon a little earlier than usual today.

They climbed into the carriage and rode back to the palace. Theo was unusually quiet, and Lily said, "How are you feeling, my love?"

"Fine." He smiled reassuringly at her.

At the palace, he met briefly with the king and relayed to him that Lord Willowvale had been similarly affected and was now recovering.

"It was not act of war, if that is what concerns you," he concluded.

"I shall take your word for it, at least for now." The king looked him over critically. "Theo, dear boy, you've done quite enough. Go home, enjoy your lovely wife, and rest a while."

Theo smiled radiantly. "Thank you, Your Majesty." He bowed. Fatigue was rising like a great wave, but the crash was yet distant. With Lily's hand on his arm, he kept his steps steady through the long corridors to the palace door.

When they exited the palace, the Overton phaeton in which he and Lily had arrived was waiting, along with Fenton's tall chestnut mare.

Fenton stepped closer to say to Theo, "Shall I drive you home? You're nearly as pale as Lord Willowvale, and it's only three days since…."

Theo took a deep breath, and for a moment he considered arguing. Then he saw Lily's sweet, concerned face, and he imagined what would happen if the darkness at the edges of his vision overcame him while he was driving.

"All right," he said, surprising both Fenton and Lily. "I am rather fatigued."

Fenton nodded. He looped his own horse's reins around the back rail of the phaeton and helped Lily up, then watched with concern as Theo clambered aboard.

The vehicle was only built for two, but it was clear Theo was in no condition to drive. Fenton climbed easily up beside him, and Theo murmured, "Fen, I might fall asleep on your shoulder. Forgive me."

Fenton said, "I'll catch you if need be. You've done magnificently." He clucked to the horses, and they started off.

Theo managed to stay mostly upright for the trip, as Lily kept her arm wrapped tightly around him and steadied him against the few bumps of the road.

When they pulled up in front of the house, Theo roused enough to walk inside with one arm slung around Fenton's shoulders. After some discussion, it was decided that he would take a nap on the sofa in his sitting room with his head in Lily's lap.

Fenton relayed the morning's events to Sir Theodore and Lady Overton, who thanked him for his steadfast care of his friend.

"There's also the matter of the fairy at my house," he said. "I wanted to talk to Theo about her, but there wasn't time this morning."

"She's still there?" Lady Overton asked.

"We ate breakfast together yesterday, with my mother. She left to seek news of the Rose in the Fair Lands, and she returned this just as I departed this morning. Is Juniper still staying with you?"

"Yes. I did relay the fact of her presence to him, but I did not know her name at the time. Would you like to speak with him?"

"Yes, please." Fenton smiled his appreciation at Sir Theodore.

Several minutes later, Anselm brought the young fairy to the sitting room where the elder Overtons and Fenton waited. "Shall I bring tea?" Anselm asked.

"Yes, please," said Lady Overton. "How do you feel today, Juniper?"

"I'm quite recovered, Lady Overton. Thank you for asking." The young fairy smiled shyly and added, "I was watching Mrs. Sophie make scones."

Several days before, Juniper had collapsed after giving Theo an incredible amount of binding energy twice in two days. His sacrifice had been a critical part of Theo's daring plan to save the children held captive in the Fair Lands, as well as the Fair Lands themselves.

The young fairy still looked a little pale, for Lord Cedar's healing magic had worked differently on him than it had on Theo. But his hand did not shake when he lifted the delicate china teacup, and his smile was as full of bright gratitude as ever. He had found not only refuge, but compassion and friendship here in the human world.

Fenton said, "Do you know a fairy named Crocus Firethorn?"

Juniper blinked. "Yes. She is a distant cousin. Is she the fairy you asked Sir Theodore about?"

"She met me at my door several days ago with a sword, wanting you. She said she was concerned for your safety." Fenton smiled at Juniper's wide eyes. "Don't worry, I didn't tell her that I knew who you were, much less where you are. Do you trust her?"

Juniper swallowed. "Thank you." He sounded slightly dazed. He looked down at the teacup and frowned a little. "I should like to think I can trust her." His voice was low and sad. "But His Majesty Silverthorn has hold over many of my kind, and I cannot imagine she would value my life over advancement in the court."

Fenton said, "I am inclined to believe she means you no harm. But you know the Fair Court better than I do."

The young fairy looked up at him. "What has she said?"

"She has given no particular indication of hostility toward you, or me, for that matter. She said you had no one to look after you. She asked the worst thing I had heard about the Fair Folk, and I allowed that one theory about why the Fair Folk were stealing children was that they ate the poor waifs." At Juniper's horrified look, Fenton said, "Her expression was much like yours, and I doubt a fairy could pretend such horror."

Juniper said thoughtfully, "I doubt it too. We are, as a species, much more transparent than you humans. I find it frightening to think of how easily your kind lie to each other, and perhaps to me." He blinked, and added earnestly, looking between the Overtons and Fenton, "I do trust you and Theo. Your courage and compassion speak for themselves. But we do not have the habit or skill of lying convincingly. If she says she is concerned for me, and has shown other signs of compassion, perhaps I should trust her."

Fenton studied the young fairy. "I would not risk you unnecessarily, Juniper. What shall we do to gain a little more confidence in her motives?"

Sir Theodore said, "Are you still planning to have Theo and Lily over for lunch tomorrow?"

Fenton said, "If he feels up to it." At Juniper's concerned look, the young nobleman relayed the events of that morning again.

Juniper said, "I have never heard of binding magic being removed from anything, or anyone, by a third party. Lord Willowvale must have been desperate to attempt it." He frowned. "I shouldn't wonder that Theo is tired, but I think he will be recovered by morning."

"He believed the binding magic still intact, and Lord Willowvale said as much, too."

The fairy nodded. "If he is recovered, and he and Mrs. Overton do visit you tomorrow, might you dine outdoors? I could sneak into the garden and observe your interactions with her from a hiding place."

"Of course." Fenton nodded. "I will await your decision, then, on whether she can be trusted."

"What did your mother think of her?" Lady Overton asked.

"My mother," said Fenton, slightly aggrieved, "has known for months that Theo was the Wraith and that I was in league with him.

She didn't see fit to mention it to me, but she knew. To the point, she didn't see any particular reason to distrust my Fair guest, but she did urge caution."

Lady Overton smiled and looked at him compassionately. "You underestimated her, didn't you?"

"Apparently. I will endeavor to have our luncheon outdoors tomorrow. But I do hope you will help Theo be rational if he's not up to it yet." He looked down at his teacup and murmured, "Actually, I would prefer to have the luncheon next week. Perhaps Tuesday. It was… I don't want to see him like that again."

"Thank you for being there," Sir Theodore said quietly.

"I don't even know why I was," Fenton said. "He asked me yesterday to meet him at the palace and to be there during his conversation with His Majesty. I had little of worth to contribute, since I wasn't in the Fair Lands when he… when it happened. I honestly think his whole purpose in having me there was to say kind things about me to the king."

Lady Overton smiled and reached across to pat his hand. "He means every word."

"I know."

Fenton ate lunch with Sir Theodore, Lady Overton, and Juniper. They were nearly finished when Theo and Lily entered the room. Theo smiled, pale and sweet, and said, "My dear Fenton, I am delighted that you are still here. I wanted to talk with you about your guest."

"Sit down, please, Theo," Lady Overton said.

"I'm all right, Mother." He smiled reassuringly at his mother as he held out Lily's chair, then sat beside her. "There's no pain. I'm only fatigued."

"All the same, Theo," Fenton said firmly, "I would much rather see you looking like yourself. Have some lunch." He looked up to see that Anselm had already appeared briefly in the door, noted Theo and Lily's presence, and hurried away to bring them lunch.

Fenton repeated what he had told Sir Theodore and Lady Overton again, along with Juniper's suggestion of an outdoor luncheon. Theo listened intently, his fingers laced through Lily's. With his other hand, he absently rubbed his chest over his heart.

"Yes, we'll eat outside." Theo agreed, then looked at the young fairy. "You have friends here, Juniper. Don't worry."

"Thank you, sir."

"Just Theo is fine." He smiled tiredly, and Juniper flushed and looked down. The young fairy held Theo in the highest respect for many reasons, and this was the continuation of a gentle, ongoing argument.

Lily leaned closer to murmur into Theo's ear. He nodded and took a bite.

Fenton studied him. "You don't look much better than you did this morning, Theo. Are you sure you feel all right?"

Theo blinked several times, then said quietly, "I don't think I've ever felt so tired in my life, but I don't think there's anything to be worried about." He took a sip of his tea and closed his eyes for a moment. "If anything, the binding feels stronger."

At his mother's alarmed look, he smiled again. "I think I'll be back to my usual troublesome self after about three days of sleep."

Juniper said, "But why should Lord Willowvale's attempt to rip the binding magic out of you make you tired? I understand the pain, but I would not have expected the fatigue." He frowned. "Is there a way to send for Lord Mosswing and get his opinion?"

Theo replied, "I really don't think that's necessary."

"I would feel better if you did," Lily said.

He lifted her hand, with their fingers still interlaced, and kissed it tenderly. "As you wish, my love."

Anselm stepped away to send a message via bird through the veil.

"Where is your guest now, Fenton?" Theo murmured thoughtfully.

"Probably resting, but I'm not sure. She was tired when she returned, but when she's recovered, she probably intends to search the surrounding area."

Lily said quietly, "My love, I would be very much pleased if you could eat a little more."

At this moment, Anselm stepped back into the room and said in a low voice, "Sir Jacob, Lady Hathaway, and Mr. Hathaway are here.

What shall I tell them?" He glanced from Theo to Lily and then to Sir Theodore, his brows lowered in concern.

Lily began to rise, but Theo said, "Please show them in, Anselm."

A few moments later, Lily's parents entered the little dining room, followed closely by Oliver.

Theo rose to greet them, blinking back a sudden wave of fatigue that threatened to crush him. He bowed and smiled, focusing on the warmth and affection he felt toward his lovely wife's family.

Oliver said, "Theo! What happened?"

To Theo's surprise, remaining upright seemed entirely too complicated of an endeavor. He sat down with little of his usual grace and polish, and breathed, "If you would be so kind, Lord Selby…" He closed his eyes.

Lord Selby introduced Juniper to the elder Hathaways and explained the morning's events again, though he left out a little of the conversation between Theo and Lord Willowvale. Oliver had already explained to Sir Jacob and Lady Hathaway the events of the previous few days and Theo's heroism as the Wraith. They had come to congratulate him on his triumph and express their appreciation for his kindness to Oliver, as well as their delight that he and Lily had resolved their little misunderstanding.

"That's concerning," Sir Jacob said gravely, when Fenton had finished relating the events of that morning. "You say you're only tired now?"

Everyone looked at Theo, and he roused enough to say, "Yes, I'm all right." He smiled as reassuringly as he could, which was not entirely convincing to the others. Even his lips were pale, and his coppery eyelashes looked even brighter than usual against his wan skin.

"We ought to let you rest," said Lady Hathaway gently. "We came only to tell you how proud we are of you, and how delighted we are to be able to call you our son by marriage. Do rest, please." She and her husband rose, along with Oliver.

Theo stood to give them an unsteady bow. "Thank you, Lady Hathaway. I'm honored to be part of your family." His words felt thick and difficult because his mind was so foggy and the fatigue so overwhelming. "And I adore your daughter with my whole heart," he added.

Sir Theodore stood. "Anselm, would you please help Theo to his suite? I'll walk with the Hathaways to the door."

Theo would have protested, but at Lily's pleading look, he consented without argument. The rug waved and rippled before him, and darkness fluttered at the edges of his vision. He leaned hard on Anselm on his way up the stairs, and he had no silly quips or reassurances to offer because his mind was entirely occupied with the effort of each next step.

Sir Theodore and Lady Overton accompanied the Hathaways only a short distance down the hallway before Sir Theodore said, "I would actually be delighted if you would stay for dinner this evening. We had hoped to spend more time with your family after the wedding rather than less. It's only that I don't believe Theo would have gone to bed if he didn't think you were leaving."

Sir Jacob glanced at his wife.

Lady Overton added, "Please do stay a little longer, at least."

"If you insist," said Lady Hathaway with a smile.

Fenton bowed. "I will leave you, then. I pray you have a wonderful afternoon with no more excitement."

Sir Theodore frowned at him. "Don't be ridiculous. You're family, too! Stay as long as you like."

The young lord would have demurred, but Lady Hathaway said kindly, "Please don't leave on our account. We would be delighted to know you better."

Fenton smiled. "As you wish."

Sir Theodore led them out the front door and around to the stables. "I believe it has been a while since you've been able to see Dandelion, Mr. Hathaway. Would you like to see him now?"

Oliver said, "Please call me Oliver, sir, and you as well, Lord Selby."

"You may call me Fenton."

Oliver followed Sir Theodore into the stable and down the stalls, greeting each magnificent horse. Sir Jacob and Lord Selby followed, while the ladies walked together toward a little gazebo tucked beneath some flowering myrtles.

Dandelion nickered and tossed his head before letting Oliver rub his long, elegant nose.

"What a lovely horse you are," Oliver murmured. "You really are beautiful, and with such good manners, too." The younger man looked at Sir Theodore. "Did you know Theo was going to give me Dandelion?"

Sir Theodore gave a low chuckle. "No, but I wasn't surprised when I heard it later. Would you and Lord Selby like to take him out this afternoon?"

Oliver glanced at Fenton, who nodded obligingly. "I don't believe I'm needed at home yet," Fenton said.

"Why don't you take Milo out? Theo hasn't ridden in several days, so he needs the exercise." Sir Theodore indicated the tall gray gelding in a box stall across the aisle, who snorted in response.

"Yes, sir," said Fenton. "Thank you."

The two of them saddled the horses and set out on a leisurely ride around the Overton estate. Fenton led the way up a hill to the northeast and then across the ridge to the west, from which they could see much of the surrounding land. The golden afternoon sunlight warmed their shoulders, and the wind swept across the high hills with merry little gusts that tugged at the horses' manes and tails and made the young men's cheeks flush. From atop the ridge, Fenton pointed out the limits of the Overton estate, the distant hills of the Radclyffe estate, and his own land.

"That's your pond, isn't it?" Oliver asked, pointing toward the little pond at the rear of Lord Selby's garden. Though it was still quite a distance away, the beauty of the estate was clear from their elevated position. "It's a lovely place to work."

Fenton reined to a halt and stared. "I wonder who that is." The figure was difficult to make out at this distance, but he was reasonably sure he had never met the man before, much less invited him to poke around the rear of his garden while he was not at home.

Oliver looked at him. "That's not your gardener?"

"No." Fenton turned Milo toward the garden and urged the horse into an easy trot.

The intruder looked up at them briefly but continued walking around the edge of the garden looking into bushes and beneath the weeping willows, as if searching for something.

Something about the man struck Fenton as strange, but he was not at first able to discern what it was. The man's clothes were unremarkable: grey-green trousers of some rough fabric and a lighter shirt with the sleeves rolled up to his elbows.

"Good afternoon," Fenton called when they were within earshot. "May I help you?"

The man looked up at them again, and then, apparently having decided to ignore them, continued his search beneath the willows.

As they drew closer, Fenton said quietly, "Mr. Hathaway, do you have the gift of glamour?"

"No. Why?" Oliver glanced at him. "Is he using a glamour?"

Fenton replied, "I can't tell, but my gift is not particularly strong." It would be convenient if Juniper were nearby, but that would hardly be safe if this were one of His Majesty Silverthorn's underlings hunting the young fairy.

"Good afternoon," Fenton said again, and this time the man did not pretend he had not heard.

The man looked up at them only a few dozen feet away, then ducked beneath the drooping limbs of the willow and disappeared.

Fenton dismounted and jogged toward the tree, calling, "Excuse me! What are you doing in my garden?"

The man had vanished, as far as he could tell. Fenton looked around beneath the tree branches, then emerged on the other side and looked around before checking under the nearby willows and in the bushes.

Oliver held the reins of the two horses while he looked over the garden.

Fenton strode through the garden with increasing annoyance and concern, though his voice remained polite as he called out several more greetings. Only the sound of birdsong and rustling leaves answered him.

At last he returned to where Oliver had remained.

"I take it you didn't find him," Oliver said.

"No." Fenton mounted his horse again with effortless grace and led Oliver through the garden in a meandering route. "I'm not well pleased to know there's a man skulking through my garden who won't answer a polite inquiry. I might have had him in for dinner if he'd simply met courtesy with courtesy." This he said in a clear voice, half hoping the intruder would make himself known.

"Indeed."

These efforts did not produce any results or any evidence of where the man might have gone. Fenton eventually stopped at his front door and spoke briefly with Richard to alert him to the intruder.

"Is our guest here?" Fenton asked him a low voice.

"No, my lord. She rested for a little while, asked for an early lunch, and departed immediately afterward."

Fenton nodded, looking over the grounds again. A hint of movement some way distant caught his eye, but when he focused on it, there was nothing but the reflection of the clouds upon the surface of the pond and the cattails dancing in the breeze.

"If you see her, let her know about the intruder, please, and let me know how she reacts to the news. I'll be back this evening."

"Yes, my lord." Richard nodded.

Fenton and Oliver trotted around the Selby estate for another hour, both enjoying the weather and looking for any other sign of the mysterious lurker.

Neither Fenton nor Oliver found anything amiss, nor any evidence that there had ever been an intruder. Finally they meandered back toward the Overton estate.

When they made their way back inside, they were surprised to see Theo and Lily in the green parlor. Lily was playing the piano quite skillfully, and Juniper was watching with fascination from an almost excessively proper distance. Theo sat with his eyes half closed in a comfortable chair nearby, one hand resting on his stomach where he had been stabbed.

Fenton and Oliver entered, and Lily looked up at them and smiled, taking their quiet entrance as an invitation to continue playing. Fenton sat in the chair nearest Theo and studied his friend surreptitiously.

When Lily finished, Theo said, "Thank you, my love. That was delightful." He smiled sweetly at her, his hazel eyes warm. Then he turned to Fenton and Oliver. "Have you returned, or have you been here the whole time?"

"Oliver and I went on a ride. I took Milo out for you; he needed the exercise," said Fenton.

"Thank you," Theo said sincerely.

They ate dinner with Sir Theodore, Lady Overton, Sir Jacob, and Lady Hathaway, Juniper, and Cedar, for he arrived a few minutes before they began. Anselm hurried the Fair lord through the hall to the parlor, where everyone was listening to Lily play a more challenging song than she had attempted earlier. She stopped playing to stand and curtsey to him.

"Cedar!" Theo said with delight. "Welcome back! Is everything well with you?"

"Indeed." Cedar strode directly to Theo and put a hand on his shoulder to slide a little magic tentatively into his friend. "The Fair Lands are entirely in an uproar over what you have done."

Theo blinked at the gentle swell of golden magic that slid through his veins, and said, a little shakily, "That's enough. Thank you."

Cedar bowed to the others a little belatedly. "What happened?"

So Theo and Fenton repeated the story yet again as they sat down to dinner. Theo felt fizzy and bright, not quite drunk on magic but considerably more alert than he had fifteen minutes earlier.

Cedar stared at him over their salads. "You don't think Willowvale will try again?"

Theo shook his head. "No, he was entirely out of sorts. I don't think we need to worry about a second attempt." He smiled reassureingly, and his eyes sparkled with both his customary good humor and the golden magic that made his skin tingle and his heart skip lightly over the yawning chasm of fatigue that still lurked at the edge of his awareness. "Please tell us about the Fair Court, my lord."

The Fair lord sat back in his chair with an air of satisfaction. "You have uprooted and overturned everything the Fair Court thought and believed it understood about itself and about humans. His Majesty

Silverthorn has paced the throne room for hours each day, and his magic seethes beneath the palace and throughout the garden like a nest of snakes.

"Lord Larch has been to see him several times, and I would that I could have listened to their conversations, for I fear they contem-plate some deception. However, His Majesty has not issued any orders against you, and indeed seems more confused and troubled than angry."

Juniper shifted in his seat. Cedar looked at him inquiringly, and the younger fairy ventured, "Has there been any mention of clemency?"

Cedar's turquoise eyes softened. "No. I would like to believe His Majesty would understand that Theo's bargain included your safety as well as mine, but I wouldn't risk returning yet, if I were you. I will investigate further, though; you have every right to keep your position in the palace."

Lady Overton said, "We are delighted to have you here, Juniper. You are welcome to stay as long as you like, you know."

"Thank you." Juniper ducked his head.

Theo looked compassionately toward the young fairy, then turned toward Fenton. "Fenton has an interesting situation at his estate. I'd like to get your opinion on it."

Cedar listened with interest as Fenton explained his Fair guest's quest to find Juniper, and the plan to determine her trustworthiness with the luncheon the following week. Fenton's eyes had an unusual sparkle of excitement when he spoke of Miss Firethorn, and he described her as "quite lovely, in fact, though of course that does not mean she can be trusted." Yet his cheeks had a faint flush, and his lips kept turning up in a soft, secret smile.

Theo hoped desperately that Fenton's Fair guest was worthy of his attention.

Cedar said at last, "I don't know her, nor of her, but I hope it turns out well. Do let me know if I can be of assistance."

CHAPTER SIX
An Autumn Squall

The following morning was cold and gray, entirely unsuitable for a luncheon in the garden. Fenton ate breakfast with his mother and his Fair guest in the white room, which was not only bright and calm, lit by what little eastern sunlight made its way through the leaden sky, but also given a spot of cheerful color by the brilliant red spikes of gladiolus in a cut crystal vase in the middle of the table.

The Fair maiden was quiet, and it seemed that was her nature, but she responded courteously to Fenton's gentle inquiries about her comfort the previous night.

"I will return this evening, if I may presume upon your hospitality again," she said reluctantly.

"You are welcome here," Fenton said, his heart twisting guiltily within him. "But I believe the weather is growing colder. Perhaps you might rest today and resume the search tomorrow?"

She stared at him. "A delay might cost my cousin his life. I cannot know what danger he is in, whether he is lost out in the cold or held captive by some human who holds the entire war against a young fairy or perhaps wounded by some horrible animal of your world against whom he has no defense. I cannot rest until I know he is safe."

Fenton flushed, ashamed and sorely tempted to reassure her. "Forgive me, Miss Firethorn. But did you not say he was believed to have fled to our world for safety? Perhaps he has found it."

Her eyes flashed. "How am I to be sure of that? No, I will search your world until I have found him."

The young man inclined his head. "Of course." He swallowed. "Will you at least accept a cloak while you search? I will ride with you, if you like." If he could not assuage her fears, perhaps he could offer his company while she searched.

She hesitated, then said, "Thank you. I would appreciate use of a cloak. But there is no reason to believe your presence would reassure him. The offer is kind, my lord, but I will search alone."

Lady Selby said, "As you wish. Please do come back for dinner, Miss Firethorn."

Crocus stood. "Thank you."

At Fenton's request, Richard brought one of Fenton's own cloaks of dark blue wool, heavy and warm. Fenton held it out, and, beneath the guilt, he felt a little frisson of pleasure when her fingers brushed his as she took it from him. She did not, however, accept a horse, for she said she had no experience with the creatures in her own world, much less those of the human world.

She strode off into the chill, foggy day with long steps and her head high.

Fenton, unable to sit at home in the warmth and comfort of the library while she was out in the cold and damp, busied himself by brushing down his favorite mare, and then saddling her for a ride. The creature tossed her head, wanting to run, but in such thick fog, it was hardly safe even on the road, much less on the hills. Fenton kept her to a quick walk and meandered over the estate for hours, halfheartedly searching for the intruder.

Crocus returned late that night, well after Fenton and his mother had finished dinner, but she accepted Fenton's offer of refreshment. With a cup of steaming tea, he sat with her while she ate. She offered little information about her efforts, other than to thank him for the use of his cloak.

When she had finished with a weary sigh of satisfaction, he escorted her to her suite.

"Thank you for your hospitality," she said quietly. "You are very kind."

Guilt twisted within him, but he said only, "I pray you rest well tonight, Miss Firethorn. Will you rest tomorrow?"

"No, my lord. If I might keep the cloak tonight, I will depart before breakfast."

Fenton hesitated, then said, "I was hoping to introduce you to a friend of mine. Perhaps the following day you might have luncheon here with us? I believe the weather may clear and we can eat in the sun outdoors."

She looked away, her hands trembling at her sides, and chewed her lower lip. "As you wish, Lord Selby," she said at last. "If I have not found him by then, I will oblige you."

"Thank you, Miss Firethorn."

Yet the morning of the planned luncheon, the Selby household awoke to a crack of lightning so shatteringly loud that Fenton wondered for a moment whether the house itself had been hit. Heart thundering, he dressed quickly and hurried out into the hall.

In moments he found Richard, who was coming to see him with wide eyes.

"It hit the oak in the front, my lord. Not the house." Richard followed him to the front door.

Fenton opened it and looked out into the pouring rain, thankful for the wide portico that kept it off their heads. Even through the downpour, the scent of wet, scorched wood reached his nostrils. He let out a soft, relieved breath.

"What was that?" Crocus's shaking voice came from behind them.

Fenton turned to see her wrapped in the borrowed cloak, her eyes wide in her white face.

"Lightning struck the oak there." He pointed and then stepped out beneath the portico into the cold, misty air. The roar of the rain filled his ears.

She stepped closer, then, carefully, stepped barefoot onto the tiled patio to stand near him, shivering. "Does it often storm like this?"

"I would not say often, but it is not rare in the autumn. The icy winds come down from the heights and collide with the warmer air here in the south." He smiled a little. "I've always loved the storms, but I must admit that lightning was a little too close for comfort."

She shuddered beside him. "How long will it last?"

"A day or two, perhaps three." He looked down at her.

Her bare toes curled away from the chilly tile, and she shivered again.

"It is a little early to begin the day, but I doubt I will sleep again this morning. Perhaps we might have an early breakfast in the green room? Would you care to join me?"

She looked out at the downpour, so heavy she could no longer see the oak which the lightning had hit. She swallowed and said, "I suppose there is little use in going out in that. I couldn't see him even if he were near."

They spent that day indoors, for the rain did not let up until nearly midnight. Fenton did his best to amuse her; he read to her from a book of poetry which his mother had recently enjoyed, and offered her the use of his piano, but she said she did not play.

Lady Selby raised one eyebrow in faint surprise at this, but made no comment, and Crocus's alabaster cheeks flushed. "I did not have opportunity to learn," she said, with a strange tone halfway between apology and defiance.

So the day was quiet and tense. None of Fenton's efforts or gracious hospitality could soothe Crocus's gnawing worry, and she grew more pale and troubled by the hour.

Her distress, carefully contained, as if she had been long accustomed to keeping fear and emotion to herself, only increased Fenton's aching guilt.

In the afternoon, Lady Selby played piano for quite some time with admirable skill, hoping to distract the Fair maiden from her worry. Crocus managed a pale smile and a compliment, which tore at Fenton's heart.

After dinner, Crocus pled fatigue and said she would retire early. "I would like to go out early tomorrow, if I can," she said.

By this time the rain had settled in to a steady downpour, and if there had been light, perhaps she might have ventured out already.

"As you wish," Fenton said. "Please stay for lunch, though. It would grieve me to think of you out alone."

Crocus's pale blue eyebrows drew downward. "I cannot stay, my lord, for I cannot rest until I have found my cousin." At his gentle, steady look, she said softly, "But if it is so important to you, I shall endeavor to return for a brief lunch."

"Thank you, Miss Firethorn." Warm gratitude filled his voice, and the fairy's pale cheeks flushed pink.

She looked down and clenched her hands. "You are most kind, Lord Selby," she murmured.

The following morning dawned glittering and bright, for the ground was soggy and every leaf was edged in water drops. It was cold, but not quite cold enough for frost, and Fenton found to his chagrin that his Fair guest had departed before the sun rose.

Nevertheless, he sent a message to the Overton estate reminding Theo of his intention to host the young Overtons for lunch in the garden. Then he went to check the rear patio, which he found already nearly dry in the brilliant sun, despite the chill in the air. He breathed a sigh of anticipation, for the hours before lunch seemed long indeed.

CHAPTER SEVEN
Luncheon in the Garden

The morning of the rescheduled luncheon with Fenton and his Fair guest, Theo rose with the sun, refreshed and delighted in the bright promise of a new day. He dressed casually, though with his usual exquisite style.

"You seem cheerful," said Lily with a smile.

Her husband beamed. "Should I not be? I woke up next to the most beautiful woman in Valestria!" He kissed her, laughing low under his breath at her blushing delight.

"I am the fortunate one!" She laughed. "I married you knowing you to be kind and generous, but I did not realize you were also a dashing hero!"

He swept her off her feet. "You give me too much credit, my love, but I fear I do not want to shatter your sweet illusions about me. I am hardly dashing, except when I'm in a hurry."

Lily laughed into his chest, for he had pressed her close, his fingers tangled in her hair. "And modest too," she added.

"Occasionally, but only by accident." He grinned at her. "As much as I enjoy hearing your compliments, I should like to enlist your aid at our luncheon with Fenton and his guest." His hazel eyes sparkled at her, bright with love and wit. "We shall, of course, engage in all the usual polite conversation. However, if it seems prudent, I shall, in the course of the conversation, reveal that I am the Wraith. By her reaction, we will learn something of her opinion of what has happened, and perhaps that will help inform Juniper a little more about whether she can be trusted. We shall also question her about the intruder around Fenton's estate; I would not be entirely surprised if it were her, trying to seem inconspicuous, but if it is not, we must be extra wary."

"If it isn't her, who might it be?" Lily stretched to kiss him as he set her on her feet again, and he returned the kiss a dozen times over.

"If it isn't her or one of Lord Willowvale's minions, I suspect it might be Lord Larch or one of his servants. Larch was Willowvale's counterpart in the Fair Lands, charged with rooting out any hint of sympathy for the Rose among the Fair Folk."

"What is he like?" Lily looked up at Theo's face in concern.

"I've never met him, only overheard half a conversation once. I imagine he's a true believer in the superiority of the Fair Folk, much like Willowvale. He and Willowvale were remarkably casual with Silverthorn in the conversation I overheard, so I imagine all three have known and trusted each other for years." Theo smiled disarmingly. "Don't worry, my love. Fenton and I will figure something out."

With a bounce in his step, Theo strode to the stable to let the grooms know he wanted the carriage ready before lunch. The wind was fresh and cool, promising glorious autumnal colors soon in the leaves of the trees around the estate. He would take Lily on a drive to the top of the hill and picnic from the best vantage point to see the trees dressed in their autumn hues. The burgundy, crimson, scarlet, orange, and yellow would delight her, and he would delight in her, for her smile would be brighter and more beautiful to him than any view of his beloved Valestria.

He greeted the horses by name and rubbed each of their noses, promising to take them out for a good run soon. He took Shadow out for a quick ride around the estate, taking the time to ascend the low hill from which he could see the rear of Lord Selby's garden in the distance. No intruder was visible, and from this distance Theo could discern nothing about the feel of the magic. Even if he had been in the garden, he doubted he would have noticed anything unless the intruder had done some spectacular magical feat there; his sense of the magic in the land, and what had been done in a particular location, was not strong, even for a human.

No matter. He would be there soon, and more information would be gained from conversation than from his meager magic.

He trotted back and left Shadow in the capable hands of the groom, then jogged back to the manor.

"Are you ready?" Theo caught his breath at Lily's beauty.

She smiled shyly at him, and his heart seemed to skip and dance within his breast.

He caught her in his arms and kissed her with great enjoyment, then murmured into her ear, "When you smile at me, it feels like the sun's warmth on my face, Lily." He withdrew just a little so he could meet her eyes. They were a soft gray-blue, so different than his own sparkling hazel, and alluring for that difference. He rested his forehead against hers for a moment. "I am entirely, unreservedly, brilliantly delighted with you. But it occurs to me, belatedly, that my dear friend Fenton cannot yet enjoy the affection of a beloved wife. It would be kind not to flaunt our happiness more than necessary while we visit him."

"Of course," Lily said gently. "I am just as delighted with you, Theo, but I would not want to cause him any distress."

"I imagine you will more skillfully rein in your shows of affecttion than I will." At her affronted look, he chuckled and said, "I mean no insult, my love. I meant only that such overt displays come more naturally to me, or so it appears, and I would like for you to know, now, that if I seem even a jot less affectionate than usual, it is only that I do not wish to grieve him by reminding him of what he does not yet enjoy."

He frowned then. "Also, it grieves me to my very soul that he has not yet found a woman worthy of him. Do you know, Lily, that he is the very bravest and best man I think I have ever met? With the possible exception of my father, who boasts years on him, and excepting of course your father and brother, whom I would not disparage. He deserves every human joy."

Lily's gentle smile had deepened while Theo spoke, for of all the many traits she loved in Theo, perhaps the most endearing was his love for his friends.

"Well, I shall endeavor to assist in this matter, if I have the opportunity."

At this moment Juniper stepped into the hallway with a shy smile.

"Juniper! I hope you've had a pleasant morning," said Theo with warmth. "Are you ready?"

"Yes, sir."

Theo led them out to meet Anselm at the waiting carriage and they set off toward the Selby estate. In the carriage, Theo said, "Juniper, if you have any trouble at all, do not hesitate to call for help. Lord Selby, Anselm, and I are all armed and ready to defend you."

He pulled a sheathed dagger from an inside pocket of his jacket, much to Lily's surprise, and offered it to the young fairy. "Take this for yourself. I doubt you will need it, but I should hate for you to be without a blade in case the intruder Lord Selby sighted was not his guest but another more dangerous person, perhaps still lurking about."

Juniper swallowed and took the dagger gingerly.

"Do you know how to use it?" Theo asked.

"Not well." The fairy looked up at him. "I know not to touch the blade, if that's what you're asking."

Theo smiled kindly. "Hold the hilt like so. The pointy end goes away from you—"

Juniper huffed a quiet laugh.

"—and use it only at need. Call for us, and we'll come running."

"Thank you, sir."

When they reached the Selby estate, Theo hopped out of the carriage with his customary cheerfulness and helped Lily descend the steps with love sparkling in his eyes. Having already bidden Juniper a brief farewell, he did not acknowledge him before closing the carriage door. Anselm drove the carriage around the house so that Juniper could slip out undetected, or so they hoped, by anyone in the garden.

Theo, as comfortable at Fenton's estate as at his own, offered Lily his arm and escorted her around to the garden, where Fenton had said they would dine.

A table, chairs, and china were already set out on the flagstone patio, along with croquet wickets in the nearby grass. An elegant vase in the middle of the table held long branches of goldenrod, gardenias, fiery red gladioluses, red and yellow daisies, and deep purple dahlias.

"Theo. Mrs. Overton." Fenton strode toward them with a warm smile. "Good morning. My guest will join us shortly." He lowered his voice. "I asked her last night, and she said she would be here. She was gone this morning but returned a little while ago. I think she's nervous."

At this moment, the door opened and Crocus stepped out. Fenton could not tell if her dress was a new one, obtained from the Fair Lands or in the human world, or the one he had seen before, glamoured to appear different. There was the edge of faint glamour about her, but that told him nothing, because her hair was a pleasant, medium brown and her eyes were a slightly less icy blue. There was no sign of her sword, though Fenton imagined she was armed.

Theo bowed with exquisite courtesy, and Lily curtsied to her. She returned the curtsey with a faint, nervous smile.

Fenton introduced them properly. "This is my friend, Theodore Overton the Fourth, and his wife Mrs. Lilybeth Overton. Theo, this is Miss Crocus Firethorn, my guest."

The Fair lady glanced at him, wide-eyed, as if she had not expected him to reveal her name.

Theo beamed. "What a pleasure to meet you at last!" he exclaimed. "I was surprised and delighted to hear that Lord Selby had such a lovely guest. Have you been able to accomplish your mission here in the human world?"

Crocus's eyes widened a bit more, and she glanced at Fenton. "I…" She hesitated. "No." She swallowed, then added coolly, "I had not expected Lord Selby to have betrayed my confidence in him by sharing it."

Fenton blinked, then replied, "I apologize most sincerely, Miss Firethorn. I had not anticipated that you would expect me to lie to my dearest friend on your behalf."

Crocus flinched, then said, "I'm sorry, my lord. I had not expected you to lie. I only hoped you would avoid the question."

Theo said kindly, "I would be much obliged if you wouldn't blame him too much, Miss Firethorn, for I can be quite insistent when I'm interested in a topic, and what could be more fascinating than a mysterious, lovely visitor staying with my dear Fenton? If you must blame anyone, it ought to be me, I'm sure."

The Fair woman blinked and glanced between them.

When she did not say anything, Fenton said, "I do hope we can still enjoy the meal, Miss Firethorn."

They strolled to the table, where Fenton held Crocus's chair for her. Lily had the distinct impression that the Fair woman was even less accustomed to aristocratic customs than she herself was, and felt a rush of sympathy for the fairy, though she did not yet trust her. It must be frightening indeed to be alone in the human world, especially if she truly were attempting to find and rescue Juniper.

For several moments they spoke only of the beauty of the garden and the freshness of the air. Theo mentioned hosting an autumnal ball, and solicited Fenton's and Lily's opinions on whether it ought to be a masquerade ball or not. Lily eyed the flower arrangement in the middle of the table with interest, then looked up at Fenton. A faint flush came to his cheeks, and he looked down at the table.

When the first course was laid, Fenton said, "Miss Firethorn, I do not believe I mentioned it earlier, but I saw an intruder in my garden yesterday afternoon. Do you know anything about it?"

The fairy blinked. "In what way?"

"Well, I was hoping that perhaps it was some misunderstanding, and perhaps it was you yourself, or perhaps you have a friend who ought to be offered hospitality?" Fenton was almost sure this was not the case, but it seemed a worthwhile question, if only to see her reaction.

"I was not near your garden yesterday afternoon," she said. "Are you sure it was a fairy?"

"Reasonably sure. He disappeared when I called to him, and I believe I searched well enough that if he had not been wearing a Fair glamour, I would have spotted him. He appeared male, and a friend who also saw him thought him at first to be my gardener, but he was not. Can you guess who it might be?"

Crocus glanced between Fenton and Theo, then briefly at Lily before focusing on Fenton again. "Perhaps." She looked down at her food, avoiding everyone's eyes.

Theo said brightly, "I heard that the Fair Court has been in an uproar since the Rose, whom you call the Rose, met His Majesty Silverthorn. Do you think it might be related to something the king is doing?"

The Fair woman blinked and stared at him. "How would you hear that?" she asked. "Are you in contact with many Fair Folk?"

Theo gave her a sparkling smile. "You might say a little birdie told me," he said confidingly. "The uproar in the Fair Court makes me wonder what this intruder's purpose is, and whether it aligns with yours or not." His keen eyes rested on her face, thoughtful and evaluating.

She swallowed and said carefully, "I doubt his purpose aligns with mine."

"Why do you say that?" Theo asked.

"I seek to protect my cousin, if I can." The fairy raised her chin. "He was accused of conspiring with the Rose and fled, or so it is believed. I doubt the intruder wishes him well."

Fenton said gently, "If we knew a little more, we might be able to assist you in the search for your cousin."

Crocus sighed, then said reluctantly, "Lord Willowvale, Special Envoy of the Fair Court to Valestria, has several members of his staff here in Valestria. There is also his counterpart in the Fair Lands, Lord Larch, and he has been pursuing a number of leads to identify and capture the Rose's Fair allies. He might have sent someone here, if he had reason to believe Juniper is here."

Theo looked surprised. "I wonder what would make one of them think to look out here in the countryside for a fugitive fairy. I dare say they will be disappointed." He took a bite and chewed meditatively.

Fenton said, "You've had no luck yet, I take it?"

"No." Crocus shook her head. Her lips trembled, and she looked down. "Your world is strange to me, and I can't help thinking of him being alone and frightened somewhere."

Theo said kindly. "If he is here at all, I'm sure he has managed to find somewhere safe. You Fair Folk are said to be quite clever. I can't imagine he is entirely helpless."

Lily almost added some reassurance, but thought better of it. Theo seemed to be choosing his words with care, though he seemed so light and cheerful, and her well-intended words of reassurance had already once caused grief. So instead Lily smiled and said, "Would it encourage you to tell us a little about him?"

The Fair woman smiled a little. "I don't know him well. I haven't seen him in years. I remember him as a bright-eyed child, gifted in glamour and binding magic, and very shy. I heard he got a position in the palace after his father died years ago."

"He's younger than you are?" Lily prompted, although she knew the answer.

"He must be thirteen by now, maybe fourteen." Crocus blinked. "He was not more than six when I saw him last."

Theo glanced at her. "Are Lord Willowvale and Lord Larch the only ones who might be targeting him, or might there be others?"

She blinked at him. "I do not know."

Theo said thoughtfully, "I wonder whether the Fair Court has a few members who are growing bolder in pursuing their own individual interests. Who might stand to gain from some nefarious action in the human world?" He tapped his fingers on the table. "If we do not know who the intruder is, we cannot be sure whether he is targeting your cousin or the Rose. Perhaps your cousin is not in as much danger as you believe."

Fenton said, "I'm not sure anyone stands to gain from targeting the Wraith, or the Rose, or whatever he's called. Shall we assume then that it is someone working for either Lord Larch or Lord Willowvale?" He addressed this last to Crocus.

Crocus glanced between them. "I wonder at your knowledge of the Fair Court, sir," she said at last. "It seems unwise to me to share my own thoughts too freely, since I do not know your purpose or interests."

"Nor do we know yours, but I should hate to think we are at an impasse," said Theo. He turned to smile at Lily, then turned back to the fairy. "I wonder what *you* think of the Rose, Miss Firethorn, and whether you believe your cousin might have some connection to him."

Crocus hesitated. "I believe he fled because His Majesty had planned to detain him for some perceived connection to the Rose, but I do not know if the king's belief in that connection was correct or mistaken."

Theo's eyes gleamed with humor and curiosity. "I notice you do not give your opinion of the Rose," he said.

"I was not there when His Majesty Silverthorn parlayed with the Rose," Crocus said quietly. "All I know is that the indigo forests have solidified, and the mountains seem to have their peaks again, and everyone says that is the Rose's doing. If that is so, I, along with all Fair Folk, owe him a great debt. But it is difficult to believe the rumors I have heard, and I imagine there is some sort of misunderstanding."

Theo sat back and glanced at Fenton, his eyes sparkling with delight. "Rumors can grow with the telling," he said with a low laugh.

The Fair lady said, as if she wanted to be understood, "I do not seek to aid Juniper because I believe him to be heroic, but because he is my responsibility. I was not able to offer him any help until a few weeks ago. I searched for him in the Fair Lands for a week before I heard he was rumored to have fled. Now I feel more than a little guilty that he apparently believed himself entirely without allies in the Fair Lands and fled to the human world."

"Why were you unable to offer him help earlier?" Lily asked gently.

Crocus' eyes hardened, and she looked back at her plate, avoiding everyone's eyes. "My situation gave me little agency." She stabbed a piece of roasted potato with precision and slightly more force than necessary. "It took me several years to understand how trapped I was, and then several more to do anything about it. I made use of the time by learning to wield a sword and studying what little I could of the human world, for I thought your kind fascinatingly exotic." She met everyone's eyes in turn and gave a prim little smile with her pink rosebud lips. "So I reclaimed my freedom."

Her smile faded, and she said more quietly, "When I heard that my cousin was missing, it seemed to me that I had waited too long to break the bonds that had trapped me, and I have been filled with guilt and fear for him ever since. I ought to have been braver sooner, and not required a human legend to show me what love looks like."

Fenton glanced at Theo, wondering whether he would choose to reveal himself yet. The young nobleman's tender heart wanted to reassure his lovely guest of Juniper's well-being and of his own compassion in the face of her apparently troubling memories.

Theo smiled, his eyes warm and kind, and said, "It sounds as though your own situation was quite challenging enough. I'm sure that if Juniper knew of it, he would not hold the delay against you." Then he said, "If you will excuse me for a moment, I have just remembered that I ought to ask my footman something." He stood and bowed. "I shall return right away."

He strode away with a cheerful spring in his step.

Fenton said, "I wish I could reassure you about your cousin's safety. Unfortunately, all I can offer is my assurance that, should it be in my power, I would aid a young fairy fleeing from unjust accusations, especially one allied with the Wraith."

Lily felt her heart warming even more toward the young nobleman, whose dark eyes were so kind and gentle. She added to Crocus, "I don't mean to pry, Miss Firethorn, but it sounds as though your last few years have been difficult. If ever you would like to confide in another woman, I will hold anything you say in complete confidence."

Around the corner of the house, Theo jogged to Anselm, who stood just beside the carriage. The fact that Anselm did not come to meet him, but maintained his position at the carriage, told Theo that Juniper had likely taken refuge in the vehicle again.

"Is all well?" Theo asked in a low voice when he reached the faithful servant.

"He heard much of the conversation, but then saw someone lurking the bushes some distance away. He said it was a fairy, perhaps one of Lord Willowvale's lackeys, and fled, as you suggested. He does not think he was spotted, but he thought it safer to hide here than continue to listen."

Theo nodded. "I don't like to leave you here alone. I'll make some excuse and we'll depart momentarily. Did he say whether he learned anything about Lord Selby's guest?"

"No, sir."

Theo opened the carriage door a crack, then slipped inside.

Juniper flinched when the door opened, then said, "I'm sorry. I didn't mean to cut your luncheon short." His pale cheeks flushed.

"Think nothing of it," Theo said gently. "Did you recognize the intruder?"

"No, sir." He frowned, troubled. "His glamour was exceptionally strong, and I could not see through it."

"Did you learn enough about your cousin to trust her, or be sure she cannot be trusted?"

"I think I ought to trust her," Juniper said earnestly. "She seems sincere, and she was very clear with her words. I cannot think how she could be malevolent after what she has said."

Theo nodded. "I agree, but I would not take action without your consent. Shall I invite them for lunch soon, then?"

"Yes, sir." Juniper smiled, his eyes shining with hope. "Thank you."

Theo slipped back out the door, closing it carefully behind him so as not to reveal Juniper's presence in case the mysterious intruder was watching. He murmured to Anselm, "Be careful, my friend."

Anselm gave a quick, businesslike nod.

Theo strode back around the house, whistling a jaunty little tune. He smiled brightly at Lily, Fenton, and Crocus as he sat back down and leaned forward eagerly. "Forgive me, but I wanted to confirm that we're free for lunch in two days. Anselm has a better memory for my schedule than I do." He gave a self-deprecating little laugh. "Would you honor us with lunch at our estate?"

Fenton, with a gleam of understanding in his eyes, said warmly, "I would be delighted to. Would you accompany me to the Overton estate, Miss Firethorn?"

Crocus looked between them with an air of caution, but even a Fair woman, accustomed to the astonishing and varied beauty of the Fair Folk, was not entirely immune to the charm of Theo's sparkling smile or Fenton's quiet kindness. She swallowed, and said, "If I am still here, and have not yet found my cousin, then I should be pleased to, my lord."

Fenton's answering smile had not only warmth, but a deep, subtle pleasure that he was not ready to acknowledge to himself, much less to the others.

"I should prefer to keep you all afternoon," he said sincerely to Theo and Lily, "but I believe you had plans later, didn't you?" He knew nothing of the sort, but he had been friends with Theo long enough that he understood Theo's absence had been to check on Juniper's safety. Theo didn't look concerned, but that didn't tell him much. So he offered his friend an easy way to extricate himself and Lily, if Juniper needed to be taken to safety.

Theo said reluctantly, "Indeed, but I shall look forward to seeing you again soon." He stood and bowed with utmost courtesy to both Fenton and Crocus, then took Lily's hand and smiled at her. "I am sorry to tear you away, my love, but I hope you and Miss Firethorn will have the opportunity to spend a little more time together very soon."

Lily curtsied politely to both Fenton and Crocus. "It was lovely to meet you, Miss Firethorn, and equally lovely to see you again, Lord Selby."

Fenton bowed, and Crocus followed Lily's lead and curtsied, though she looked a little confused about it all.

"It was lovely to meet you," she said, with a glance at Fenton.

CHAPTER EIGHT
A Meeting with the Fair King

At breakfast the next morning, Theo said to his parents, "Fenton and his Fair guest are coming tomorrow for lunch. I would have had them come today, except it occurred to me that I told His Majesty Silverthorn that I would return and tell him why I am a friend of the Fair Lands. I think it is time."

Lady Overton blanched and said quietly, "Must you go so soon?"

"I'm fully recovered, Mother," Theo said with a brilliant smile. "I believe it would be discourteous to wait longer when I did promise to return when I could think more clearly."

She pressed her lips together and looked down.

Theo added, "Besides, he has every reason to want me alive now, and he will keep his word."

Lily said quietly, "I would like to go with you."

Theo blinked. "Why?" he said blankly. "Was your first visit to the Fair Lands not entirely horrifying?"

"It was. But I think I have the right to stand at my husband's side." Lily met his eyes. "Besides, if you love the Fair Lands, I would like to understand why, so that I may grow to love them too."

For a moment, Theo seemed to have been rendered speechless by shock. Finally he said, "You are right, as usual, dear Lily. Nevertheless, there is danger there that I would prefer not to let anywhere near you."

Lily's eyes lit with restrained passion. "I could say the same; I do not want it anywhere near *you*, either."

Sir Theodore and Lady Overton had said nothing during this exchange, though they looked pleased with Lily's unexpected spirit.

Theo gazed at her thoughtfully. Then he smiled with his usual warmth, and said, "Your courage is exemplary, my love. I will be honored to show you the Fair Lands."

"When will you leave?" Sir Theodore said.

"I don't see any reason to delay. I would like to depart this morning, after we finish eating." He glanced at Lily and said, "Since we are to call upon His Majesty Silverthorn, we ought to be dressed appropriately. We'll change clothes first."

Theo had selected one of his most exquisite suits of pale green silk that set off his auburn hair. The jacket was cut in the most modern fashion, and the lace at his throat seemed to accentuate the sharp, elegant lines of his face. Lily felt a surge of pride when she looked at him; he was quite extraordinarily attractive, and she felt fortunate indeed to have somehow married such a delightful man.

"I don't know what to wear," Lily said, standing helplessly in front of her wardrobe. Secretly she still felt a little overwhelmed by Theo's effortless elegance, and his clothes were the least part of that sophistication.

Theo gave a dismissive *pfft* and said, "Well, His Majesty ought to be honored by your presence and your beauty." He pulled out a dress. "This one coordinates well with my jacket. Do you like it?" At her nod, he tossed it upon the bed, which she had not slept in since their reconciliation some days before. "Anyway, attempting to outdo the Fair Court in beauty and extravagance is a quick route to madness. I would much prefer you wear something that makes you feel comfortable and at ease, at least as much as possible in the Fair Lands."

He stepped closer and put his hands upon her shoulders, his touch gentle and reassuring. His warm gaze held hers. "Don't worry, my love. I am delighted that you want to know the land I love so deeply." He took one of her hands and pressed her palm to his chest, where his heart beat strong and steady. "Love for you makes my heart thunder within me. I swear on my life to keep you safe there."

Lily swallowed, pushing away thoughts of his bloodied face and terrible injuries from her memory. "I want *you* to be safe, Theo."

He smiled sweetly. "I will not do anything unnecessarily foolish," he said, with a gleam in his eye. "It is the same promise I've made my mother a hundred times, and I've always kept it."

"Always? Even… then?"

Theo wrapped his arms around her and kissed her. Between kisses he murmured, "That was necessarily foolish."

The two young Overtons stepped out into a crisp fall day. The air was cool, but the sun was warm upon their heads and shoulders, and the breeze was mild.

"How do you get to the Fair Lands?" Lily asked.

"I might ask you the same," Theo said, with a teasing light in his eyes. "I open a door to the veil and walk through it." He offered her his arm, and she took it with a smile.

He wore an elegant rapier on his left hip.

"Are you expecting there to be trouble?" she asked.

"If I were, I would not allow you to accompany me, my love." He added more softly, "I do regret that you had to see what happened in the Fair Lands last week."

Lily shuddered and pressed closer to him for a moment. "I should have told you how silly you were being when you told me you didn't want the blood to soil my dress."

Theo blinked. "Oh. I suppose it did sound rather doltish, but it made sense to me at the time." He smiled down at her. "I wasn't concerned about your dress, you know. It was just that you were so pale and spotless and beautiful. I didn't want to…"

She closed her eyes and wrapped her arms tightly around his lean waist. "You were being ridiculous," she said into his chest.

"I am sorry, my love," he whispered. He could feel her trembling as she held him, and he tightened his arms around her. "I am completely recovered, though, so please don't let it trouble you." He bent to kiss her, at first with tender reassurance, and then with barely restrained passion, partly because it delighted him, and partly to prove to her that there was no need to worry.

"How am I supposed to think clearly when you kiss me like that?" she gasped at last.

He laughed, low and delighted, and kissed her again.

Then, with a flourish, Theo opened a door to the veil. "Did you have any trouble when you passed through with Lord Mosswing?"

"No, but he was wary."

"I am sure he was." They stepped into the veil, and Theo let the door close the behind them, leaving them in darkness. Theo's grip on her hand was strong but gentle, and he shifted beside her. "If anything troubles you, tell me immediately. Don't wait until you're injured or cannot speak."

She nodded, then said, "All right."

They set off at an easy pace, and Theo murmured lighthearted comments to her at intervals just to hear her laugh.

Theo opened the door and peered out before stepping out with a smile for his wife. "This is His Majesty's garden. Just over there is Lord

Willowvale's estate. Most of the children were kept in or around the palace. Lady Araminta and your brother were kept in Lord Willowvale's estate."

He offered her his arm and led her confidently across the lawn toward the enormous, gold-chased double doors of the palace entrance. The wide marble steps had gleaming veins of gold and violet, and Lily sucked in an astonished breath.

"It's so beautiful," she whispered. She turned her head to look at the moss-covered patio half hidden behind a lush fall of fuchsia blooms to the left, then back to the right to the white walls of Willowvale's elegant manor looming behind banks of bushes blooming in a thousand shades of gold.

Autumn in the Fair Lands was colder than it was in the human world, and, as in Valestria, it had come suddenly. Autumn in the Fair Lands was as lovely as any other season, though, and Theo was not immune to its beauty, either.

"Isn't it?" Theo agreed. As much as he loved the Fair Lands, he could not tear his gaze away from her wondering face, with her wide, admiring eyes and her sweet smile.

He knocked on the palace door. A moment later, a fairy with dark blue skin and pale pink hair opened it and stared at them. Her hair was caught up in an elaborate fall of braids, and white feathers were woven throughout the arrangement.

She blinked at them in open confusion and a faint air of superiority. "Yes?"

"I'm Theo Overton, and this is my wife. I've come to see His Majesty Silverthorn, if he will see me. I promised to return and speak with him."

The fairy blinked her violet eyes. "Overton." Then she bowed low, extending one hand to them gracefully. "Follow me."

Her hair swung with the rhythm of her long steps as she led them through the spacious hallways of the Fair palace. Lily's eyes were wide, and she kept craning her neck as they walked. One corridor was floored in white tiles with an opalescent sheen. Another hall was carpeted in a lovely blue moss with mounds of star-shaped white flowers.

The fairy stopped before an open door curtained by long strands of vines covered in deep green leaves.

"Wait here," she instructed, then stepped through the vines. Her next words came through the vine curtain slightly muffled, as if there were a faint magical barrier which they could not see. "Your Majesty, two humans have requested an audience. Theo Overton and his wife."

The magical barrier theory was validated by Theo's complete inability to hear Silverthorn's response.

The fairy stepped back through the door and motioned them to follow.

Theo bowed, and Lily curtseyed deeply as they entered the throne room, and the fairy motioned them forward. She stayed just inside the door, so they were left to advance alone.

They walked hand in hand the full length of the room. The floor was white marble, which gleamed in the sunlight that streamed in through a vaulted glass ceiling that refracted the light so that it seemed they walked through a kaleidoscope of rainbows. Some sections of the walls were mirrored, others were windows that showed views of the garden, and yet others were covered in fine mosaics of brightly colored glass depicting flowers and mountains and other natural wonders of the Fair world.

The brilliance of the light and the dancing rainbows of hues upon the floor served only to highlight the otherworldly beauty of the Fair Folk who attended the king. The throne itself was made of gold inlaid with silver, and the glitter was so intense that for human eyes it was difficult to discern the design at all.

When they reached the foot of the dais, Theo bowed low before the Fair king again, and Lily followed his lead with a deep curtsey. The king's beauty was the most terrible of all, his violet eyes bright and hard. He wore a bright raspberry silk shirt and well-cut trousers of sky blue, with soft white boots upon his feet, and a white cloak of luxurious fur draped his shoulders. The cloak was clasped with an enormous ruby set in a nest of silver thorns. The spike-covered crown upon his head gleamed silver against his cobalt hair. The contrast of his pale, robin's egg blue skin and dark hair against the pink silk and white fur only served to highlight the alien beauty of his angular face.

By contrast, the Overtons' dress looked restrained and almost anemic, for all the Fair Folk attending the king were dressed in similarly bright colors, though few dared challenge the king's resplendence.

"Your Majesty, I promised that I would return to tell you why I am a friend of the Fair Lands. I am here to fulfill that promise."

His Majesty Oak Silverthorn surveyed Theo with a faint, bemused smile. "Proceed."

Theo smiled radiantly at him, all kindness and warmth. "The story is long, Your Majesty. Might I suggest a more comfortable setting? I should like to tell you the story as if we are friends, for so I should hope to be by the end."

The king's violet eyes narrowed. "I said proceed."

Theo sighed softly, as if grieved, and replied, "As you wish." He turned to Lily and clasped both her hands for a moment. "My love, I beg your patience. The story is long."

She smiled up at him trustingly, and the light of love in her eyes made his heart beat faster. "I am delighted to hear the story, too, Theo."

He nodded and turned back to the king, who had been watching this exchange with interest.

"Your Majesty, the story actually began when my father was ten years old. One of the Fair Folk stole him from the garden of a family friend and took him through the veil to that nobleman's estate in the outskirts of your Fair capital. The way my father told the story, this Fair nobleman used my father primarily as a status symbol; my father was expected to serve refreshments at parties, learn the Fair dances and customs, and generally be paraded about in front of the nobleman's acquaintances." Theo kept his eyes on the king, though he was intensely aware of his wife's tension and grief beside him.

"My father was captive for some five years under these conditions. He attempted to escape several times; humans in general, and Valestrians in particular, do not take well to being used as chattel, even relatively well-treated chattel. The Fair lord who held him punished him more brutally each time, using his healing magic to bring his prisoner back to health." Theo swallowed, resolutely ignoring Lily's horrified expression.

His Majesty Silverthorn stared at Theo with his face set in an expression of cold fascination.

"After five years, it had become clear to the youth that he would not be able to escape Lord Tanglesage unless he were also able to enter the veil, for the Fair lord's ability to track him far outstripped his human ability to flee through the Fair Lands without being caught. So he bided his time, testing his own small gift of binding magic against inanimate objects and small animals.

"Some time later, when my father was sixteen, my mother was caught and brought back to the Fair Lands by Lord Spiderfrost. Lord Spiderfrost was also interested in having a human captive, but not for the same reasons. He and His Majesty Alder Silverthorn, your father, had long suspected that the slight fading in the land that your father had noticed had something to do with human captives dancing. Lord Spiderfrost had taken it upon himself to venture through the veil and obtain a talented dancer for himself, to test the theory against the fading at the edges of his own estate.

"The fading was little known then, and the land was much stronger. Nevertheless, Lord Spiderfrost was concerned because the fading that had been noticed was near to his own lands. Lord Spiderfrost took her from a garden party held at a family friend's house because he was delighted by her beauty and her dancing, which he accounted quite skillful for a human.

"When he brought her back to the Fair Lands, she was at first held captive and forced to dance for hours as Lord Spiderfrost and His Majesty your father examined the fading. Lord Spiderfrost often danced with her himself, and though my mother was of course frightened by her situation and the Fair nobles around her, she said later that Lord Spiderfrost was both just and fair as a captor. She felt that he was grieved by an act that he felt his land required, and did not delight in cruelty. When her dancing seemed to make little difference, Lord Spiderfrost brought my father's captivity to the king's attention, and His Majesty required Lord Tanglesage to bring the youth to the palace for examination.

"My father and my mother, both young and frightened, were forced to dance with each other for hours each day and night for nearly two months. In that time, they formed a plan. My father had no gift for the veil, but my mother had discovered that she understood the magic of the veil, just a little, as Lord Spiderfrost had taken her captive. She did not, however, have the ability to open a door by herself.

"Your Majesty, I shall not tell you exactly how she freed them both, except to say that it took both courage and trust on the part of both captives. The success of this brave effort, and the resulting joyful return to the human world, formed the foundation of what became a beautiful love story that inspires me today.

"From my mother I inherited a gift for the veil, although mine is stronger than hers is. From them both, I inherited both great admiration for the beauty of your land and a healthy caution of your people." Theo met the king's gaze without flinching.

His Majesty Silverthorn raised a hand, and Theo inclined his head. "Did your parents never eat Fair food while they were captive?" the king asked.

Theo's eyes glinted with pride. "They did, Your Majesty. My parents are *very* clever."

The Fair king's eyes widened slightly, then he sat in silence for a moment. Then he said slowly, "I see no reason for you to show kindness toward the Fair Lands."

Theo smiled and said, "And if the story ended there, I would feel little but admiration for the beauty they described and dislike for your people." He sighed and glanced at Lily with warmth in his eyes, then he continued.

"When I was eight years old, I discovered my own gift for the veil by opening a door into it while my parents and I were visiting the seashore. I left the door open behind me and explored a little way into the veil before my father realized where I was and came in after me.

"They told me not to go into the veil again, but they did not tell me the whole story, for they did not want to frighten me and they thought there was little chance of me ever reaching the Fair Lands. Thus emboldened, I engaged in perhaps the only real disobedience of my young life; I ventured farther and farther into the veil and found the Fair Lands on my third attempt.

"By some mercy of God, I emerged from the veil in Lord Bitterberry Mosswing's garden only a few feet from where he was training his son Cedar in swordplay. Lord Mosswing immediately understood that I was human, and, being both honorable and kind, endeavored to help me return home. I begged him to let me learn about the fascinating place in which I had found myself, and so, with admirable patience, he gave me a tour of his garden and told me all about the plants therein.

"At last he insisted that I depart for the human world, but by this time Cedar—now Lord Mosswing—and I were fast friends. I returned several times to the garden, and I explored other locations within the Fair Lands as well, mostly alone, though sometimes Lord Bitterberry Mosswing and Cedar would accompany me. Lord Mosswing advised me to never be seen by other Fair Folk if I could help it, for many of your people were not so kindly disposed to humans; Lord Mosswing believed us equals in value and personhood, if not in magic or power.

"On my third visit to the Fair Lands, Lord Mosswing took Cedar and me to a particular precipice from which he enjoyed looking at the surrounding lands. He put a glamour on me, and we rode his horses some miles to our destination. Shortly after we arrived there, we were attacked by a peryton.

"In the attack, Lord Mosswing was gravely injured, and the peryton turned on Cedar and me. I was unarmed, but in the confusion, I was able to take Lord Mosswing's sword and kill the peryton while Cedar tested the limits of his healing magic on his father. Lord Mosswing had, unknown to me, and despite his kindness, distrusted me from the beginning, and he was surprised when I risked myself for him and his son rather than fleeing into the veil.

"After that, his kindness knew no bounds. He risked much to keep me safe, and I was deeply grieved when he died some years ago.

"The new Lord Mosswing, Cedar, has thus been a trusted friend for many years. He has known the kindness and forgiveness of my parents for what they suffered under his people, and he has shown them that not all Fair Folk are as cruel as Lord Tanglesage.

"I imagine that humans and Fair Folk are equally complicated, though perhaps in different ways.

"Your Majesty, you told me you do not love. But what is love but to put the needs and the well-being of others before yourself, not for the warm feeling that results but for the sheer joy of knowing that you have made someone's life better? To be sure, it is easier when there is a warm feeling that accompanies this act, but I do not think you ought to rely upon that feeling as a gauge of love.

"I chose to love the Fair Lands because Fair Folk like Lord Bitterberry Mosswing and Lord Cedar Mosswing exist. When I chose to see the beauty and nobility of their characters, I saw other things lovely and worthy of esteem in your people. I do not mean only the beautiful plants and animals that seem so exotic and wonderful to my human eyes, but you Fair Folk yourselves. You are just as varied as we humans are, and it would be cruel indeed to judge you all by the actions of one cruel Fair lord."

The king regarded Theo steadily. "I assume you are aware that Lord Tanglesage is yet alive?"

Theo swallowed. "I had heard so, Your Majesty."

"Do you wish to exact some vengeance upon him?" The king's voice was mild.

Theo licked his lips. "I do, yes, but I will not. God brought beauty out of my parents' captivity and suffering; I will not stain that grace with bitterness."

His Majesty Silverthorn stood at last and strode down the steps to stand only a short distance away. He was even taller than Theo. Perhaps another man might have been intimidated, but Theo's smile was patient and kind as he waited for the king to speak.

"What have you done with Lord Willowvale?" the king said at last.

Theo tilted his head. "Has he not returned to the Fair Lands?" he asked.

"No." His Majesty Silverthorn looked narrowly at Theo. "He has not returned from the human world, nor have any of his staff. If you did not kill him, what is keeping him there?"

Theo inclined his head courteously. "I cannot say, Your Majesty, but I'm sure he has a good reason. Lord Willowvale is entirely devoted to the Fair throne."

The king looked at Theo with sharp interest. "I do not hear anger in your voice when you speak of him. Is that because you humans lie so easily, or do you feel no anger?"

Theo smiled, feeling the warmth of Lily's hand in his. "Why should I be angry with Lord Willowvale now?"

"Do you wish for no vengeance upon him, either? What good came of the pain he inflicted upon you?" Silverthorn tilted his head, as if puzzled.

"I don't know yet," said Theo meditatively. Then, with a gentle smile, he said, "No, Your Majesty. Lord Willowvale is in no danger from me."

The Fair king's violet eyes glittered with some strange emotion, but he said only, "Fascinating."

Theo bowed deeply. "I do have one request, Your Majesty. When I was last here, you promised that you would not take or harm humans, directly or indirectly. Yet I have reason to believe there is someone sneaking around Valestria seeking to harm my human allies. Your vow ought to prevent this."

Silverthorn's eyes hardened. "I am not responsible for what my subjects do on their own initiative," he said in a low voice. "I wonder that you dare contend that I am."

Theo studied the king's face. "Perhaps you are not entirely responsible," he allowed. "But you could choose to honor the spirit of the agreement, as I choose to honor my friendship with the Fair Lands."

Silverthorn laughed, low and cold. "Our audience is finished, Overton."

The air had a crackling sense of danger in it, and Lily's hand trembled in Theo's. Perhaps, if he had been alone, he might have pushed the king a little and tried to negotiate some promise that Silverthorn would insist that his courtiers honor the agreement.

Instead, Theo merely bowed politely and said, "Good afternoon, Your Majesty. It has been a pleasure."

The king's gaze flickered, almost as if he were disappointed in the lack of argument. "A pleasure."

CHAPTER NINE
The Envoy of the Fair Court

When Theo and Lily emerged from the veil at the edge of the garden, Theo said, "I shall go see Lord Willowvale this afternoon, my love. Might we have lunch together in the garden before I go?".

She looked up at him with warm admiration. "I can think of nothing I would like better."

Theo twisted to kiss her on the lips, warm and soft and sweet, and she leaned in to wrap her arms around him. She reached up to twine her fingers through his copper curls, and he closed his eyes in bliss.

"Lily," he murmured between kisses. "It is probably obvious, but I feel I ought to emphasize how much I would rather spend the afternoon with you."

She giggled, and he swept her up in his arms and spun her around, smiling down at her. "It is truly a magnanimous sacrifice," she said softly. "Will you really help him?"

"If I can." He set her down on her feet again, and the light of love in his eyes warmed her heart.

"Theo, you are remarkably kind. What made you so?"

At her gentle, serious tone, his smile softened. "Haven't we all sinned, and don't we all need grace?"

"Yes, but we're not all kind enough to offer it the way you do."

"You did, to me."

Lily nearly gasped, for she did not feel that the sins for which Theo and Lord Willowvale were offered grace were remotely equivalent, but she did not have time to protest before he kissed her again. "Please don't let us talk of the grumpy fairy any more than necessary," he said softly. "I would rather hear your opinion on what sort of flowers you would like to add to the garden, and whether you would like to host a tea any time soon, and if you think you would enjoy a bonfire on the hill once it gets cold enough, and if there is anything I might do to make you laugh again, because your laugh sets my heart beating so fast I cannot think straight. Also," he lowered his voice until it was only a breath in her ear, barely audible over her own pulse, "I should very much like to spend a great deal of time in activities that are not appropriate for the garden."

"Oh," she said breathlessly, and he laughed, low and delighted and not at all repentant.

The autumn breeze was cool, but the sun was bright and warmed the flagstones, so the lunch on the patio felt delightfully refreshing.

When they finished, he kissed her again, for the warmth of her touch set his heart thundering.

"Are you sure you're not too tired?" she asked.

"Fit as ever," he replied. His radiant smile reassured her.

The crisp autumn breeze kept the sun from beating too hot upon Theo's shoulders as he trotted toward Ardmond. With his lovely wife's kisses upon his lips and the memory of her hands in his hair, he smiled to himself all the way to Lord Willowvale's rented manor house nearly on the other side of the capital.

The garden had the feel of unhappiness and an unpleasant, restless sort of Fair magic, and he stepped in with more caution than last time. He tied his horse to a post inside the gate and strode up the steps. He knocked briskly at the door.

The same fairy from two days before opened the door again and looked at Theo with surprise. "What do you want?"

"I would like to see Lord Willowvale, if I may." Theo beamed at the Fair servant.

"Just a moment." The fairy closed the door in Theo's face.

The young man laughed to himself and waited, trying to decipher the feeling of the magic in the garden. He had never been particularly good at sensing the latent magic in the land, so it was difficult to discern anything about the house at all. Still, it felt unsettled, somehow.

The door opened suddenly and the fairy said, "He doesn't want to see you, Overton."

The fairy began to close the door again, so Theo stuck his foot in the door and said, "I've just been to see His Majesty Silverthorn. I think your master might want to hear what he had to say."

The servant looked at him skeptically, then said, "I'll ask him."

With a smile, and with his foot still firmly preventing the door from closing. Theo replied, "I'll wait."

After another brief absence, the fairy returned. "He will see you."

The fairy led Theo through the halls to a sitting room and said, "Here he is, my lord."

Lord Willowvale lounged on a burgundy velvet settee, and he looked every inch a Fair lord. Not having expected a human guest, he had dressed casually in the current fashion of the Fair Lands, and it suited him particularly well. His boots were low and made of soft, black leather. His lower legs were set off in well-fitted silk hose, and above that he wore breeches of dark blue cloth that seemed at first like fine wool, but its folds caught the light from the window in shades of violet and gold, as if silk were woven through it. Around his narrow hips he wore a belt of gold studded with tiny purple gems, and his filmy white shirt was loose and open halfway down his chest, showing his lean muscle with careless elegance. A ring with a similar purple gem circled one forefinger.

He looked up at Theo with pale, hard eyes and motioned to the settee across from him, but he did not sit up. He lay upon the arm of the settee against a pillow, one arm behind his head; one bent leg was propped against the far end of the settee, and the other foot sat upon the floor.

"You told him, then?" Lord Willowvale said. "All right. When I can open a door, I'll be sure to let you know ahead of time so you can watch the execution."

Theo blinked. "What?"

Lord Willowvale shoved himself up to a sitting position, and the effort left him breathless and irritated. "His Majesty Silverthorn does not value my service to the crown enough to countenance my attempt to wrest the binding magic from you. Humans lie. Of course you told him, or he winkled it out of your simple human mind."

Theo laughed lightly. "Clever enough to evade you for months."

Lord Willowvale blew out a *pfft* of disdain and muttered bitterly, "I'm a fool, too. That's no great accomplishment."

The young man looked at him more closely, noting the shadows beneath the Fair lord's eyes. "I told you I wasn't going to tell him what you attempted."

"Humans lie," the fairy said again.

Theo said gently, "I lied to protect children, my lord. That's a far cry from breaking my word to you to exact some petty vengeance."

Lord Willowvale looked up. "You call it petty? I thought the vines looked rather painful, myself."

Theo laughed under his breath. "Ah, well, it was all in a good day's work, I think, and it ended as beautifully as I could have imagined. Anyway, that wasn't why I came."

"Why did you come?"

"This morning His Majesty Silverthorn said you had not returned to the Fair Lands. He assumed I had killed you, and when I assured him that I had not, he wondered what was keeping you here. Some of my research indicated that you Fair Folk are less able to recover from magical injuries in the human world than in your own, so I thought you might appreciate a little assistance returning to the Fair Lands."

Lord Willowvale blinked. "Appreciate a little assistance," he said flatly. "From you?"

"I would be honored and delighted to be of assistance in this matter," Theo said warmly.

The fairy sat back and swallowed. "You must be enjoying this immensely," he muttered. "To have me at your mercy in so many ways at once."

Theo said nothing, only held the Fair lord's icy gaze without flinching. A slight smile played about his lips, but it was not cruel, nor entirely mocking.

"What of your king?" Lord Willowvale asked at last. "Has he threatened me as well?"

Theo said quietly, "Not exactly. When I collapsed on the floor of the palace, no one knew at first what had caused it. But when I was coherent enough to guess what you had done, he was ready to bring you to the palace in iron chains, and I don't think I need describe what might have followed."

Lord Willowvale gazed at him without expression for several long moments. "Why didn't he?"

"I asked him not to."

The fairy blinked, then shifted again, his cold blue eyes intent on Theo's face. "You asked him not to." His voice shook a little.

Theo smiled, all warmth and sincerity, and said, "So you see, Lord Willowvale, I wish for no vengeance upon you."

The fairy sat back and stared at him, his mouth locked in an unhappy grimace. A muscle worked in his jaw for a moment, and then he said, as if it pained him, "If I accepted your assistance to open the door to the veil, which I should not, most of my staff would perish in it, for I am not strong enough at the moment to keep it from crushing them. My magic is barely sufficient at the best of times to fight my way through, but none of them have the gift at all." There was a question in this that Lord Willowvale was too proud to ask directly, but Theo understood.

"I would be delighted to escort you to your manor, my lord."

The fairy let out a soft, defeated breath and looked away. He swallowed.

In the thick silence that followed, they could hear the sound of a carriage passing by on the road and cheerful birdsong from several warblers in the tree just outside the window.

Lord Willowvale at last made a sharp gesture with his right hand, and the Fair servant stepped into the room a moment later.

"Pack the house. We're leaving."

The servant blinked. "Yes, my lord."

Lord Willowvale stared out the window a moment in thought, his thin lips turned downward. The shadows under his eyes seemed deeper, and the angle of his cheeks sharper than before. At last he said, "If you bring us safely to the Fair Lands, we will not repay you with treachery."

Theo smiled gently. "I trusted so already, my lord."

The fairy's lips curled, but he said nothing else for several minutes. Theo looked around the room, noting the sword lying on the floor within easy reach of Lord Willowvale's seat and the tea cup sitting nearly full of long-cold tea on the little table nearest the settee.

"Does anyone in your party have healing magic?" he asked quietly.

Lord Willowvale snorted softly, his eyes gleaming with bitter humor. "That gift is not common, but if any of my staff has it, they have not offered to use on my behalf."

Theo tilted his head. "You have not asked?"

The fairy shrugged one shoulder. "I am not inclined to ask for kindness, Overton." He looked away, his cold eyes focusing for a moment on the tree outside before drifting around the room, avoiding Theo's clear gaze.

"How many are in your party?"

"Six."

Theo leaned back in the settee, every line of his posture relaxed and comfortable. "Have any of them been skulking around the country near my estate or Lord Selby's estate?"

Lord Willowvale looked at him with an odd, still sort of caution. "Why?"

"Someone was sneaking around, and I wondered if he might be a fairy, and if so, if he were following your orders." Theo's voice was mild.

Lord Willowvale opened his mouth, as if he meant to say something, then he closed it again. He tapped his fingers meditatively against the arm of the settee, and finally he said, "No. It was not on my orders."

"Was it one of your staff?" Theo asked gently. "The intruder was seen in the afternoon, two days ago."

The fairy hesitated almost imperceptibly, then said, "No, I do not believe it could have been one of my staff." His eyes narrowed in thought. "Are you sure it was one of the Fair Folk?"

"We are not sure, but we believe it most likely. We believe he disappeared in a way impossible without the use of a glamour made by someone with Fair magic."

Lord Willowvale gave a faint, annoyed grimace, and said, "You've already gotten everything you want, and hold the Fair Lands captive besides. I doubt there is much any of us can do to threaten you."

At this moment, the servant knocked on the doorframe. "The house is packed, save this room, my lord."

"Pack it all." Lord Willowvale waved that he should enter.

The servant entered carrying a large trunk. He set it on the floor and opened it, then began putting items from the bookshelf into it. There was no packing material, and the trunk did not seem to overflow, though it always looked full.

"That's fascinating," Theo said in delight. "May I examine it?" He looked up at Lord Willowvale with a sparkling smile.

The fairy's lips twisted in irritation, but he said, "It's Fair magic. I don't think humans can do it."

Theo knelt by the trunk and examined it from all angles, moving obligingly to the side as the servant put in several books, a coverlet from the back of a chair, and a number of intricate wooden carvings. "I shouldn't think so, though it would be convenient."

"That is all, my lord." The servant straightened.

Theo looked around the room, which still contained a great deal of furniture, books, paintings, and smaller items such as the tea setting. "There's quite a lot left, I believe."

Lord Willowvale said, "The house was furnished. We only brought a little from the Fair lands." He picked up his sword and stood, and, though Theo would not have though it possible, grew even paler than before. He said, "Call the others. We're leaving."

The servant stepped into the hallway.

"Where will you open the door?" Lord Willowvale asked.

"I can open it here."

The servant returned with another four fairies behind him carrying two more trunks. Two of the Fair Folk were the ones who had let Theo in to see Lord Willowvale at his first visit, and these two wore swords; the other two, along with the one who had answered the door, were unarmed. All looked at Lord Willowvale with doubt.

With a twist and a pull of magic, Theo opened the door to the veil in the bookshelf.

Lord Willowvale's pale eyes widened and his lips trembled for a moment before he said in a low voice, "That is uncanny skill. Are you sure you're entirely human?"

"Without question." Theo gave him a sparkling smile. "I do not know how you traverse the veil, but I have found it to be quite a bit safer to travel without a light." He glanced between them. "We must walk in the dark, and so we must maintain contact with each other."

The three unarmed servants hoisted the trunks onto their backs, holding them with one hand on a handle above their shoulder and one hand on the lower edge at their backs. They looked toward Lord Willowvale, who nodded them toward the door into the veil.

Theo said, "If I might suggest—"

"What?" Lord Willowvale gritted his teeth.

"If you carry the trunks between you, we can more easily maintain contact between all of us. I believe it to be safer for those at the back," Theo said mildly. To the two armed servants, he said, "I suggest you two take the rear with swords drawn. Lord Willowvale, I'll take the lead, if you please, and I suggest you take hold of the tail of my jacket, and you take hold of Lord Willowvale's jacket."

The servant's eyes widened, but Lord Willowvale set his jaw, apparently resolving to accept such indignity in disgruntled silence. Thus organized, the whole group followed Theo into the veil.

The light of the human world disappeared when the door closed with a snap.

Theo led the way in silence, trailing his left hand along the wall beside him. There was a damp, squishy texture somewhat like moss, but it had a foreboding feel to it, and Theo hurried them onward.

After several minutes, he said quietly, "If something bothers you, let me know immediately, please." When there was no answer, he said, "Might I know your names? I am Theodore Overton the Fourth, but you may call me Theo."

There was a moment of silence, and then Lord Willowvale said, "You may answer him."

The names came in low voices from the back toward the front. The two armed servants at the back were Hemlock and Alyssum and the three unarmed servants were Poplar, Tansy, and Beech.

An unpleasant skittering sound came from behind them, and someone murmured something Theo did not hear.

Lord Willowvale stumbled and fell into Theo just as someone from the rear screamed.

Theo flicked light to his fingertips with a breath of magic.

Lord Willowvale had fallen to his hands and knees, and snarled something unintelligible as the brick writhed and closed over both his hands. It hissed as it touched the blade of his sword, and he jerked against the stone with a grunt of pain.

The floor did not let go. It crept up his wrist, and he let out a disgusted, furious sound from the back of his throat.

The plight of the fairies at the rear of the line was more urgent.

One had been almost entirely encased in stone, and he wheezed as the stone squeezed the breath from his lungs. The other one stabbed at a gray rat-like creature that lunged at his feet like a predator.

Theo darted around the servants who huddled against the trunks. Without a sword, he wanted the other fairy's rapier, but the fairy's wrist and hand were encased in stone and even if Theo could have reached him, he would not have been able to take it.

The fairy finally stabbed the creature through its neck, and Theo said, hurriedly, "Excellent. Give me the sword, please!"

Without hesitation, he lunged at the captive fairy. The one behind him cried out in outrage, apparently thinking Theo meant to stab his fellow, but Theo's aim had been true. The sword point slipped into the flowing stone at exactly the place where the stone from the left wall had not yet met the stone from the right, and both sides hissed when the metal touched it.

"Hold it!" he said tersely. The other fairy took the hilt again and drove it in farther, producing more hissing and popping from the angry veil. Theo pressed both hands to the stone nearest the captive fairy's face and shoved his magic into it, as bright and warm as his smile.

The veil reacted with what Theo later thought of as shock and awe, though at the time it seemed more like a painful, strained withdrawal. The rock receded from the fairy's face and loosened its hold upon his torso.

By this time, the fairy had been unable to inhale for quite long enough to be unconscious, and as the rock withdrew, he slumped forward.

Theo caught him, keeping one hand pressed to the rock as it sank back into the floor.

Then he darted back to Lord Willowvale, who was now encased nearly up to both elbows in quartz that sparkled brilliantly in the magic light that danced over Theo's head.

Theo pressed his hands to the floor and his magic with it, quick and ardent, full of life and love.

Lord Willowvale sagged sideways as the stone receded, and Theo wrapped one arm around his shoulders. The Fair lord's elbows buckled, and he would have fallen on his face if Theo hadn't caught him.

The light above them danced jubilantly, bouncing around as if delighted by both the danger and reprieve. Theo looked around. "Is everyone still with us?" he asked.

Hemlock, the fairy in the back who had been unconscious, had struggled to a sitting position with his head hanging down. He grunted, "I'm alive."

Lord Willowvale pulled away from Theo's supporting arm with a groan. "Get off me," he muttered.

Theo stood easily and offered a hand to the Fair lord, who stared up at him.

Lord Willowvale met his eyes for a moment, then sagged back against the wall. "You might as well leave me," he said in a low voice. "Take them and go."

Hemlock took several deep breaths and hauled himself to his feet.

"Lord Willowvale, please." Theo knelt in front of him, with warmth and compassion so clear in his eyes that the fairy was startled. "Let me help you," he said quietly.

"I don't want your help," Lord Willowvale snarled. Then he coughed, breathless and furious.

Theo smiled gently. "I am well aware of that, my lord. Yet can you not muster up the dignity to accept it gracefully?"

He reached forward, and Lord Willowvale flinched, as if he expected Theo to have some hidden weapon, but Theo knew the fairy would have been less angry if he had stabbed him. Theo slipped his arm behind the Fair lord's back and steadied him as he rose.

Lord Willowvale could barely stand upright, and Theo guessed he had expended the last shreds of his strength, both magical and physical, trying to free himself from the stone.

"Help Hemlock, please, Alyssum," directed Theo. "And be sure to stay together." He looked past the fairies to the dark tunnel behind them, then back at the servants. "Maintain contact, if you please." There was some rearranging of the trunks, and then they set off. Theo let the light go out.

Lord Willowvale could scarcely walk, and Theo kept them to a slow pace both for his sake and for that of the poor Fair guard in the back. The Fair lord leaned hard against Theo.

The fairy coughed, a short, hard bark that made him stumble.

"My lord, will you heal once you're in the Fair Lands?" Theo murmured under his breath.

"I don't know. I've never done this before," snapped Lord Willowvale. Then he coughed again, harder.

Theo led them on with his left arm wrapped around the fairy's ribs and his right holding the Fair lord's hand upon his right shoulder.

They walked for nearly an hour, and by the end, Lord Willowvale and Theo had managed to get into something approaching a rhythm with their steps, despite the fairy's resentment. They had no further major incidents, although there was a persistent growling sort of threat that seemed to be growing closer.

At last Theo felt the familiar pattern of the magic beneath the wall, which this time seemed to be covered in a dry lichen like that on the trees in the mountains. He opened the door with a twist and a tug of magic, then stood aside with Lord Willowvale still leaning upon him to let the servants out of the veil safely before stepping out himself.

The front door of Lord Willowvale's manor gleamed in the afternoon sunlight. The pale wood of the door was polished until it shone, and the silver inlay sparkled. Elegant topiaries flanked the door, and the broad marble patio was lined with white moonflowers and something much like white jasmine, though its leaves were a different shape.

"Your skill is quite remarkable," Lord Willowvale said, with both bitterness and honest admiration filling his voice.

"Thank you," said Theo.

Lord Willowvale leaned on Theo as they ascended the three steps to the front door, which opened easily at the fairy's touch.

When they entered, the spacious foyer was empty. Lord Willowvale gestured, and the fairies following him and Theo hurried off toward a door to their right.

"Where shall I take you?" Theo asked.

The fairy sighed. "Second floor, to the left." He coughed again and groaned almost inaudibly.

They made it up the stairs and down the corridor before Lord Willowvale turned toward a wooden door with golden accents.

"You've done more than enough," the Fair lord muttered. He opened the door and shoved himself away from Theo to lean against the doorframe. Through the open door, Theo could see a spacious, elegant sitting room that was likely part of Lord Willowvale's personal suite. Jasmine crept up the walls and around bookshelves to the left, while to the right a desk held several sheets of paper, a quill pen, and a pot of pink flowers that spilled out in exuberant disarray down to the floor. A patch of moss on the floor boasted tiny star-shaped blue flowers.

"Shall I send someone up to you?" Theo asked.

Lord Willowvale coughed again and closed his eyes. "For the love of all you hold dear, please just go, Overton," he breathed.

Theo hesitated, then said quietly, "As you wish, Lord Willowvale." He bowed, then opened a door to the veil and turned toward home.

CHAPTER TEN
A Furious Storm

The next morning after breakfast, Theo took Lily on a leisurely drive around the estate to admire the changing colors of the trees. The sky had been clear when they departed, but within an hour, the crisp, sunny day had turned dark and cloudy. The wind grew colder.

"I believe we ought to head home," said Theo, reluctantly. "I expect it will begin raining soon."

Lily snuggled closer to him and pressed her cheek against his shoulder. "Whatever you think best." She smiled up at him, enjoying the delight in his eyes. "I just want to be with you."

The wind gusted with a chill more like winter than autumn.

Theo shifted the reins to his right hand and wrapped his left arm around her with a sigh of satisfaction. "How can I be cold when my heart burns for you?"

She laughed softly. "You're silly, Theo. I think it's my love for you that's keeping us both warm."

Theo glanced down at her in delight, and, apparently unable to think of anything sufficiently clever or winsome, merely kissed her until they both felt much warmer.

Without any further warning, the sky above them let out a great *crack* of lightning, and the horses, even as well-trained as they were, startled into a gallop. With one hand Theo steadied Lily, holding the reins with the other, and once she was mostly upon the phaeton seat again, he worked to get the frightened animals under control.

"Are you all right?" Theo asked over the sound of the hoofbeats and the rush of the wind.

"Yes!" Lily cried.

With a suddenness that startled them both, frigid rain began to fall.

"Blast," Theo said, barely audible over a roll of thunder. "I'm sorry to get you cold and wet. I thought it would hold off a little longer." As he said this, the horses settled into a fast, but no longer panicked, gallop. Only a few minutes later, Theo brought them around the rear of the garden and to the nearest door, where he helped Lily down and left the horses in the care of the grooms.

Laughing, soaked to the bone, and shivering, they hurried upstairs to change into dry clothes and warm up before the fire.

"Do you think Lord Selby will still bring Miss Firethorn for lunch?" Lily asked. "Even in this weather?" Now dressed in a simple but elegant blue dress, she stood close by the fire Theo had lit, brushing her hair so that it would dry more quickly in the heat. Her skin prickled with residual chill, and the warmth of the fire felt heavenly.

Theo kissed her and stepped toward the window, looking up at the sky. "Probably. It might clear up a bit, and his estate is only three miles away. He's anxious to show her Juniper is safe."

Lily said, "Do you think she'll be angry with him?"

Theo's lips tightened. "It's quite likely. I'll take as much of the blame myself as I can, but I doubt he'll escape the brunt of it. Fairies don't really understand lying, even for the best of reasons. They can't do it themselves and see it as a grievous failing of the human species. It's probably one reason why most of them despise us."

A sudden sheet of rain battered against the window.

"While we wait for them, my love, shall I read to you?" Theo turned back to Lily with a sparkling smile.

"What will you read?" Her blue eyes were warm and expectant.

Theo looked meditatively toward the bedroom, where several books stood on the table beside his—their—bed. "I would very much enjoy reading you love poems, but it occurs to me that perhaps you would not mind too much if I selected something a bit more swash-buckling instead. What do you think?"

She smiled at him with such tender affection that he crossed to her and wrapped his arms around her again.

"Please do, Theo. I would much prefer to hear it in your voice rather than merely reading it, too." The fine, soft linen of his unbuttoned shirt let her feel the warmth of his chest against her cheek.

"How am I supposed to go find a book when you're right here, in my arms, looking so enchanting?" His voice roughened, just a little, and he murmured into her ear, "Do you know I find you significantly more exciting than any book I ever read?"

Her chuckle turned into a laugh, and she kissed the smooth skin just under his collarbone, which was what she could reach first. If there had not been a knock on the door then, they might have pursued the conversation, but the sound jolted them back to more serious matters.

Anselm's voice came through the door. "Lord Selby and his guest have arrived."

Theo cleared his throat and said, with admirable steadiness, "Thank you, Anselm. We'll be down in just a moment."

He put his forehead against hers and whispered, "I love you, Lily."

"I love you, too, Theo."

Theo pulled on a jacket, and they set off down the hall.

Anselm had been watching for the Selby carriage and had seen it while it was still some distance up the drive. Accordingly, he had alerted Theo and Lily to their guests' arrival as early as possible. Thus Theo and Lily reached the spacious entrance hall a moment before Fenton escorted Crocus up the steps.

The rain had subsided to a chilly drizzle, and the sky loomed gray and close over them, promising more, and heavier, rain later in the afternoon. Anselm took Fenton's greatcoat and a lovely warm cloak from Crocus, which Theo recognized as belonging to Fenton. All the same, it was a cloak, not a fitted jacket, and other than the length, there was nothing that marked it as unsuitable for any woman. Since Crocus was tall, it suited her well.

"I do thank you for coming in such weather," Theo said with a sparkling smile as he bowed to each of them in turn. "I have been looking forward to spending this afternoon with you."

He caught Anselm's eye and nodded, then escorted Lily and their guests to the smaller, more intimate dining room.

Crocus eyed their surrounding with what Lily took to be caution. The Fair woman seemed a little ill at ease, though not exactly frightened.

"Miss Firethorn," Lily said kindly, "I hope you and Lord Selby had a pleasant morning. Mr. Overton and I got caught out in the rain."

Crocus's pale blue eyes softened a little. Fairies did not show their fatigue easily, the way humans did, but there was something in her expression that seemed to Lily as if she were a little tired and worn. "I was up quite early looking for my cousin," the Fair woman said in a low voice. "I am very worried, for I have found no sign of him, and I have covered nearly every inch of your land for twenty miles in every direction." Her voice shook. "I have wondered whether he is even alive, and if so, if something terrible has happened to him. I wonder if I should look elsewhere."

Fenton said quietly, "Miss Firethorn, there is something I ought to tell you. When I said I did not know where Juniper was, I—"

At this moment, Anselm brought Juniper to the door of the room. Fenton's voice had been quiet, and with the sound of the rain beating against the windows again, neither Anselm nor Juniper realized that Crocus had frozen, her eyes locked on Fenton's face.

At the movement in the doorway, she glanced toward Juniper and her mouth opened in silent shock.

She stood. "Juniper," she said. "Do you remember me?" Her voice shook.

Juniper nodded. "Barely," he said. "I did not expect you to come look for me, and I am sorry to have caused you to worry." His voice suddenly sounded young, and Lily's tender heart ached for him. He sounded lost, and a little frightened of what might come next. He said, "Mr. Overton is… may I tell her?" At Theo's nod, he continued, "Mr. Overton is the Rose, and Lord Selby is his friend, and they protected me when I had no one in the Fair Lands. They've been very kind to me."

Crocus was trembling. She looked him up and down, then said, "You're not injured? You've been safe all this time?"

"Yes, Miss Firethorn." Juniper nodded, his eyes wide.

Crocus turned to Fenton. "You lied to me." There was blank incomprehension in her voice.

"Please forgive me," Fenton said, his voice full of sincerity. "It was his right to decide whether he trusted you; it was my right only to protect him."

"You lied to me." Her voice shook. She looked from Fenton to Theo and Lily, then back to Fenton.

"I am sorry, Miss Firethorn." Fenton stood, the movements careful, for she seemed suddenly brittle. He reached for one of her hands, intending to bow over it to show his humble apology.

She took a step backward, her eyes wide. "You all lied to me." She swallowed and looked back at the young fairy, and the air in the room grew colder. "I don't know how to protect you from them, Juniper."

"You don't have to." Juniper smiled reassuringly.

She took another step backward, and her ice blue eyes burned with anger. "Shall I leave you here, then?"

"Please stay." Juniper's voice was soft and pleading. He glanced at Theo, then looked back at his cousin.

Theo said, "Please forgive us, Miss Firethorn. I realize that lying is abhorrent to you, but we engaged in it only to protect Juniper, who was such a brave ally to the Rose in the Fair Lands."

Her lips tightened, and perhaps, if she had repeated the accusation again, Fenton might have tried to explain himself. Instead she said, "Faithless, deceitful humans! Stay with them, if you want. I have done with you all!"

She ran from the room.

Fenton, still standing, let out a soft, grieved sigh.

Theo stood and stepped closer to put a hand on his shoulder. "I'm sorry, Fenton."

Fenton looked down at the floor and closed his eyes for a moment. "It's not your fault, Theo."

He walked to the window and crossed his arms, looking out at the rain with a bleak sort of resignation.

Anselm had observed all of this with growing distress, and he stepped closer to say quietly, "Forgive me, Lord Selby. That was exceptionally bad timing on my part."

"It's not your fault either, Anselm," the young nobleman said.

Theo put one hand on Lily's shoulder for a moment, then stepped closer to stand by his friend in quiet solidarity.

The rain was falling so heavily that they could barely see the edges of the patio, much less the distant hedges at the edge of the garden. The hills beyond were entirely lost in the falling water.

A figure flitted across the patio and disappeared as it passed into the garden.

"Was that Miss Firethorn?" said Fenton, with an edge of concern in his quiet voice.

"I believe it was."

Juniper edged closer. "I'm sorry," he whispered. "I didn't mean to—"

"It's not your fault, Juniper," Fenton said.

He crossed his arms more firmly and pressed his lips together, staring out at the worsening storm. The wind threw the rain in sheets against the window, and then for a moment it lessened. They all looked for some sign of Crocus outside, but there was no sign of anyone.

Fenton took a steadying breath, then said, "Fair Folk don't have any particular resistance to cold, do you? It affects you the same way it affects humans?"

"I believe so, sir. I wouldn't want to be out in that if I could help it." Juniper added tentatively, "Though I suppose in general we're a little stronger and less likely to succumb to cold."

Fenton nodded, still staring out the window. "She won't want me to go after her." His voice was nearly inaudible.

Juniper shook his head.

A few moments later, Anselm silently put plates upon the table. The first course was tomato soup and toasted cheese crisps, which would have been perfect to welcome the autumn if they'd been eating together while listening to the rain battering the window. But instead of enjoying the contrast of the weather outside and the warmth of the Overton hospitality, they ate in troubled silence.

Anselm brought the main course, roast chicken with rosemary and other herbs. Fenton put his spoon down, having eaten only half of his small bowl of soup. "No, thank you, Anselm." He stood. "I can't do this. I'm sorry. I have to go after her. It's too cold for anyone to be wandering about."

Theo nodded and rose. "I'll go with you." He leaned down to kiss Lily's cheek, then said to Anselm, "Send a message to Lord Selby's estate to inform them she's missing, and to let us know if she arrives there. We'll do the same if she returns here."

"Yes, sir."

Juniper said, "I can search too."

Fenton swallowed, then said, "No, thank you, Juniper. We still don't know about the intruder on my estate, and I would hate for something to happen to you when we can't be there to help."

Theo nodded. "Let's go."

They hurried off, stopping only to arm themselves with Theo's swords and retrieve a heavy coat for Theo as well as Fenton's coat and cloak, which he rolled up and carried under his arm to put around Crocus, if and when they found her. As they saddled two of Theo's horses, they agreed on a search pattern, then set off into the icy rain.

The storm had come with a sudden wintery chill. The first fury of the storm abated not long after the two young men had separated to circle around the rolling hills north of Theo's estate. Fenton made his way north and east in long, curving sweeps that he hoped would let him find Crocus, if she were anywhere in the vicinity. Theo went west, criss-crossing the road that led past the Selby and Overton estates toward Ardmond. They avoided the highest peaks of the hills, for lightning still cracked too close for comfort.

The rain was so heavy that it would have been hard to see anyone without nearly stumbling over them. Theo followed the road for nearly a quarter of an hour, then turned back and checked a copse of trees to the west of the road, in case the Fair lady had taken shelter beneath them. Frigid water ran down his trousers into his boots and collected in the toes. He pulled his hat low over his eyes and peered through the downpour, hoping for any sign of Crocus.

"Miss Firethorn!" he called. "Miss Firethorn! You're welcome to be angry with us, but please come back and be angry by a warm fire."

To the east, Fenton was doing much the same. "Miss Firethorn! You have every right to be angry with me. I admit it. Miss Firethorn! Please allow me to beg your forgiveness under a roof. There's no need to be out here in the cold rain." He shoved his freezing fingers into Milo's mane, so the horse's heat could warm his skin a little.

After two hours he retraced his steps and returned to the Overton estate.

"She's not here. You just missed Mr. Overton. He's heading that way now." Anselm waved toward the south and west, then gave Fenton a cup of tea. "Drink this. You must be frozen."

Fenton's hands were so cold the warm teacup felt as though it were burning his skin, but he gulped the tea gratefully. "Thank you."

"Don't worry. She'll be all right, sir." Anselm's reassurance sounded rather thin, but Fenton appreciated the sentiment.

"Thank you," Fenton repeated, and, handing the teacup back, set out again.

He followed the same search pattern to the south and east, crossing back and forth over the stream and between the thickets of the edge of the wood. "Miss Firethorn! Please forgive me, and even if you don't, please don't stay out here in the cold. I'd never forgive myself if you were to become ill. Please, Miss Firethorn, at least come back until it stops raining!" His voice felt scratchy after hours of shouting. He turned back to make a wider circle, for he could see a little farther here under the trees, where the leaves softened the rain a little.

"Miss Firethorn, you don't have to talk to me at all, but please come in out of the cold and wet."

The dreary afternoon grew darker and darker. Fenton's stomach growled.

Perhaps she had returned to the Overton estate after all. Or perhaps she had returned to his estate; she had left her sword there, after all. If she intended to leave for the Fair Lands, perhaps she would have gone there.

Fenton turned toward his own estate. The torrential rain had finally softened to a steady drizzle, but he could see almost nothing, for it was now after sundown, and no hint of moonlight was able to fight through the thick clouds.

"Miss Firethorn! Where are you?" he tried again, a little more hoarsely than before.

"What do you want?" Crocus's voice came from somewhere to his left.

For a moment he was speechless. "I just want you safe and out of the cold, Miss Firethorn." He swung down from Milo and held the reins, looking into the darkness.

"What do you care, liar?" she snapped.

Fenton flinched as if she had struck him. "I am sorry," he said again. "Please. I just want you safe. There's someone, a fairy we believe, who has been lurking around my garden, and it's miserable out here anyway. Will you not allow me to offer you a roof over your head until it stops raining?" He said all this, unable to see her, hoping t hat though she were angry, she might at least hear the sincerity in his words.

She flicked a bit of light into being on the tips of her fingers and he blinked, momentarily blinded.

"Ah, you humans can't see well in the dark," she murmured. "No, you cannot offer me your hospitality, because I don't trust you. Have you forgotten how many times you lied to me?" Her voice cracked. "I trusted you! I let myself believe…" She snapped her mouth shut, and her blue eyes blazed. "I thought better of you!"

Fenton brushed water from his face, and if some of it were tears and not rainwater, he barely noticed. Crocus didn't.

"Forgive me, Miss Firethorn," he whispered. "I had to keep Juniper safe."

Crocus's mouth twisted in anger. "Of course you have a reason you lied. I never thought you didn't." She turned away and with a gasp of effort, opened a door to the veil.

"Miss Firethorn!" Fenton gasped. "Wait!"

"What?" She stopped and looked over her shoulder. The fairy light on her fingertips fell across her face. The passage in the veil behind her was a black hole in the darkness; only the strange stone wall beside her was visible with any clarity.

"The veil is dangerous. Please don't go." Fenton's voice shook.

"I know. But there is nothing for me here except lies, and nothing for me in the Fair Lands, except—" She shook her head. "Nothing. If I make it back, I'll… I don't know. I can't stay here, though."

She turned away.

Fenton dropped Milo's reins and stepped in after her as the door closed.

CHAPTER ELEVEN
The Shield

Crocus stared at him in shock. "What are you doing?" she snapped.

"Escorting you through the veil," Fenton said. His voice was, if not exactly steady, at least not as shaky as he felt. "It hates me, though, so we'd better move fast. I hope you know how to navigate in here, because I don't. I do, however, have a sword, and I'll protect you with my life."

The Fair lady stared at him, her lips twitching with fury. Finally she let out an angry huff and said, "I'd shove you out now, but I don't think I can open another door if I do. Can you open a door to the human world?"

"No."

"What will you do when we reach the Fair Lands?"

"I… well, the Rose has a few Fair allies. I'll figure out my own way back." Fenton pushed the fear of the Fair Lands and the veil to the back of his mind. He would see Crocus safely through the veil to the

Fair Lands, if she insisted upon leaving. "Will you not stay safely in the human world? Please?"

"There is nothing for me there except a reminder of what a fool I've been." She turned on her heel and began to walk away. "Come, if you're coming."

Fenton started after her.

For several minutes, Fenton merely followed Crocus in silence. His skin crawled; something followed them, something silent and terrifying, that would undoubtedly attempt to eat them in the very near future.

Crocus strode furiously through the veil, her jaw clenched. Her only concession to his presence was that she kept the fairy light on her fingertips, just bright enough that he could see the vague outline of the passage around them. Ahead, some sort of trailing vegetation hung at face level, and he edged around it, grateful for the small mercy that he hadn't walked into it face first with no warning.

Whatever followed them seemed to be getting closer. He wasn't sure how he could tell, and he tried to convince himself it was only his own terror, but after being attacked from the rear every other time he'd entered the veil, he felt that such a fear was justified.

"Miss Firethorn," he said at last. "Might I suggest putting out the light?"

"What? Why?" She turned to glare over her shoulder at him. "We're almost to the Fair Lands."

"Mr. Overton has discovered that, unpleasant as it may be, traveling in darkness is safer in the veil. The predators that live here seem to be drawn to the light."

She blanched. "Oh." The light disappeared from her fingertips, and they stood for a moment in the frigid gloom. Fenton had been able to ignore the icy chill of his clothes, but now, in the pitch black, he could not help a convulsive shiver. With a suddenness that startled him, Crocus grabbed his hand and hurried onward.

The tension in her fingers told him she was frightened, and he hoped she feared the veil, not him.

"It's getting closer," he murmured. "I cannot navigate in the veil at all. I am sorry."

"I can't either," she said. "Not with any accuracy. I can get us to the Fair Lands, that's all." Her voice was as cold as her hand.

But in her coldness, Fenton heard her fear and grief and disappointment, and his tender heart ached. "I am sorry, Miss Firethorn," he said softly. "I won't trouble you once you reach the Fair Lands."

"I should hope not."

A moment later, he said, "Let me switch hands. I believe I shall need my sword in a moment." He shifted her hand to his left and drew his rapier with his right.

Crocus opened a door in the veil and stepped out, pulling him after her, just as something dark and shadowy flicked at his ankles. Off balance, he stumbled out into the Fair forest and whirled, eyes searching the darkness of the veil.

He saw nothing, and took a shuddering breath as Crocus let the door close.

"Lord Selby," Crocus said in an odd voice.

He turned to see her staring up at a monster.

The creature had a face that would have been human, albeit too big, if it had not hissed, revealing rows of sharp, triangular teeth. Its body was the size of a large draught horse, but shaped more like that of a great golden cat, and its paws were larger than Fenton's face. A strangely segmented tail curled behind it, as golden as the horrible creature's fur. Its strange face was ringed by a tawny mane.

It hissed again, and moved toward Crocus. She edged backward.

"What is that?" Fenton whispered.

Crocus sucked in a terrified breath. "Manticore."

"Dangerous?"

Its eyes were locked on them, and there was no mistaking the bloodthirsty glint there. The creature meant to devour them both.

"Exceptionally." She hesitated, then said, "Give me your sword."

"Get behind me," he said. "I'll handle it."

The creature lunged at them with a lightning-fast swipe of its front paws.

Fenton shoved Crocus back as he dodged, then lunged.

He did not wound the monster, but the attack drove the creature back a few feet.

Behind him, Crocus did something that felt like magic to him, but he could not see it, and it seemed to have no effect upon the manticore. The air grew colder.

It gave a hopping little lunge at him, a feint, from which it suddenly drove in from a different angle.

But Fenton had not honed his skills against Theo's considerable talent and Fair training for nothing.

He lunged, every bit as fast as the manticore, and drove his sword through the monster's eye. Later, he would let the horror of the moment sink in and probably vomit at the memory of the gore, but in the moment, he was entirely focused on preventing it from moving. He dodged a weak swipe of its razor-tipped paws.

The creature twitched, and he yanked his rapier out of its head.

With a convulsive last effort, its tail flipped overhead and the stinger stabbed Fenton near the top of his right shoulder in the thick muscle just above the shoulder blade.

He gave a short, strangled cry of pain before clamping his lips together in resolute silence.

The manticore was dead, and the stinger had fallen away by the time Fenton turned to see if Crocus was injured.

The Fair woman stared at him in horror.

"It didn't hurt you, did it?" Fenton's voice shook, and he cleared his throat. He stepped away from the gory beast toward her.

"I'm not injured." Crocus said. Her beautiful eyes flicked over him. "How do you feel?"

The poison burned, and it was all Fenton could do not to throw himself on the forest floor and writhe in agony. The pain spread from the wound in tongues of fire that seemed to wrap around his chest and up his throat, making his face hot and his hands tremble.

He swallowed and closed his eyes against the blinding light of the sun streaming through the leaves. Then he blinked and focused on her face again, for without that reference point everything seemed to swim around him, and the ground wobbled as if it meant to shake him off into the darkness that lurked at the back of his brain. The burning spread down his back and through his legs, and he felt his knees shaking.

Words seemed terribly complicated. Finally he said, "Quite ill." Then he clamped his lips shut again, for he did not want to weep and scream in helpless agony like some mindless animal.

Crocus muttered something savage under her breath, then did some sort of complicated magic thing that he would likely not have entirely understood even if he'd been able to pay attention to it. His magical gifts were not particularly remarkable, even by human terms, and here in the Fair Lands, the Fair Folk could do more significant magic than humans had ever witnessed.

After some indeterminate period of time, Crocus took both his hands and led him directly into the trunk of a tree which did not seem wide enough, even to Fenton's tormented senses, to serve as a doorway, much less a tunnel.

A chill passed over him, perhaps from the cold wind that cut through his soaked jacket, or perhaps from the poison that flooded his veins. He sucked in a breath as they passed into the tree, and Crocus must have taken it as a question, for she said, "I know of only two cures for manticore venom, and neither are fast. I'm taking you to the dance floor of His Majesty Silverthorn's palace. Dance with me there for your life. Don't say a word."

This made no sense to Fenton at all, but at this point very little made any sense, and much of the Fair Lands had never made sense to him at all anyway.

He stumbled after her, dizzy and sick and resolutely silent in the face of the agony that stole his breath and made his heart race. From the darkness of the strange passage, they emerged suddenly into the middle of the dance floor.

CHAPTER TWELVE
The Search Continues

Theo made a circuit of the entire Overton estate again, looking in all the sheltered copses and thickets in case Crocus had sought refuge from the rain among the vegetation. He rode along the creek, now rushing and swollen, for several miles in each direction. Every minute or so, he called her name, until his throat rasped.

Around nine o'clock, he returned to the manor again, for a lantern and a bracing bowl of hot, rich stew, which he ate so quickly he burned his mouth.

"Lord Selby hasn't returned yet?"

"Not in hours, sir. It couldn't have been past three o'clock last I saw him. No word from his estate, either."

"Blast." Theo hurriedly changed his soaked clothing for dry and his soggy boots for an old, dry pair. He would soon be soaked through again, but for a few minutes, it was a blessed relief.

When he came back downstairs, Anselm told him that Milo, the horse Fenton had been riding, had returned riderless. Theo inspected the horse and its tack, but found no clue about what had happened to Lord Selby.

He set off again, calling all the while. He circled Lord Selby's estate, then crossed the hills to the west of them both.

Near midnight the rain petered out, so slowly that Theo barely noticed until it was only a slight, frigid drizzle. He had long since been soaked through and half frozen, but when he noticed the weather had changed, he realized how long he had been out and turned back toward home.

Sodden and shivering, he stepped into the relative warmth of the hall, where Lily, Anselm, and his mother met him. He dripped icy water into the kitchen and stood by the fire while Anselm heated another bowl of soup and some hot tea for him.

"Nothing, sir. I haven't seen Lord Selby either. Go change into dry clothes."

Theo's troubled frown deepened. "I will. When did my father go to bed?"

"He's out looking as well, sir. He's been out for hours. You just missed him."

Theo blinked. "I suppose I should have expected that. When you see him next, please tell him I'm grateful for his help."

"Of course. I'm sure he knows that, though." Anselm put a reassuring hand on Theo's shoulder. "I could wake Sophie and go out myself." Sophie was his wife, and she often helped in the kitchen with Beth, the cook, though she officially had no such duties.

Theo hesitated, then shook his head. "No. The cold bothers your knee too much to ask it of you. But if there's still no sign of them in the morning, I might be so bold."

Anselm's brows lowered. "I'm not an invalid, sir, and I'll thank you not to imply that I can't be of assistance."

"I'm not. It's miserable out there, Anselm, and this whole situation is my fault." Theo rubbed shaking hands across his face. "Anyway, a bit of hot food is a godsend. You're helping brilliantly, Anselm."

"I can't see any possible way that either you or Lord Selby were at fault," Anselm said.

A soft sound caught Theo's ear, and he turned to see Juniper in the doorway. He stared at Theo with stricken eyes. "It's my fault, isn't it?" he whispered.

"Of course it isn't," Theo said, with fierce conviction. "Come here."

The young fairy sidled in, eyes on the floor. Theo put both hands on Juniper's thin shoulders and bent a little to meet his young friend's gaze. "It will be all right."

"I can go search for them too," Juniper said earnestly.

Theo said, with equal sincerity, "You're both brave and capable, my friend, but if Larch is searching for anyone, it's probably you. I would never forgive myself if something happened to you while you were out there alone. Please stay inside."

Juniper caught his breath on a suppressed sob, but nodded. "Yes, sir."

With a quiet word, Anselm brought Theo's attention to the food now waiting for him.

The young man shivered as he wolfed down the soup. "I am going to try the veil next. Maybe I will be able to feel them in there; sometimes I can, you know. If not, I will go on to the Fair Lands and take a poke around the royal grounds. If I don't find anything, I will be back in a few hours."

Anselm's frown grew more worried. "Be careful."

"As always." Theo swallowed the last of the tea and took a deep breath. "I'm off."

Lily followed him upstairs. He changed, still shivering, and when he had pulled on dry trousers but had not yet pulled on a new shirt, she wrapped her warm arms around him. His skin was so cold she almost flinched away.

"You're nearly frozen," she murmured.

"I'm all right." His voice was tight with worry. "Something has happened to them, I'm sure of it. Fenton has roamed these hills in the dark a thousand times. He can't possibly be lost. Either he's injured or dead somewhere in the human world, or Larch captured them, or something else terrible has happened." His voice shook as he shivered.

Lily tightened her embrace, then let her arms fall away as he pulled on a dry shirt and a thick vest over it, then a wool jacket, heavy and practical. He retrieved a sword from the wall and kissed her thoroughly with his cold lips as he buckled it on. He started toward the door, then went back for a second sword, the smallest upon the wall.

Then he jogged downstairs and back to the kitchen.

"Juniper, I've just realized there is something you can do to help," he said to the young fairy.

Juniper looked at him with wide eyes. "I'll do anything, sir."

"You know better than to say those words," Theo said seriously. "Here." He presented the sword to the fairy. "It's a lot to ask, I know, but I'd appreciate it if you could help keep the ladies safe. Anselm is well-trained, so you won't be alone, but it would help put my mind at ease if I knew you were armed too."

The Fair youth swallowed and nodded seriously. "I'll do my best, sir."

"Thank you, Juniper."

With one last kiss for Lily, he turned his attention back to the search. He stepped into the sodden world outside, opened a door into the veil at the edge of the garden, and stepped into the darkness.

The veil was unsettled, and Theo paused just inside the door. He let it close softly behind him and put a hand to the wall, feeling the magic writhing beneath the slimy dampness. He gently pushed a little of his magic into the wall itself, feeling for the veil's response. The magic flinched away, skittish and irritable, before it calmed.

Theo extended his weak magical senses and felt for any Fair or human presence in the veil, but found nothing. Undeterred, he began walking.

For an hour, he walked toward the Fair Lands, taking a meandering, circuitous route. All the while, he resolutely ignored the tickle of strange unseen things upon his neck and at his ankles at times.

The rough stone beneath his feet grew slippery with damp and a thin, slimy coating of mildew. He slowed his brisk pace a little; last time he had encountered this slippery sort of footing, the veil had jerked beneath his feet, apparently trying to make him fall. He had fallen, though he had not hit his head upon the stone, and the veil had reacted with a shiver of glee. When he'd made it to his feet again, damp, bruised, and slightly annoyed, he'd crept forward more cautiously, knees bent, and thus had avoided being thrown to the ground when the veil twitched again.

After some time, his steps began to squish upon water-soaked moss, and he lengthened his strides again.

Yet he still felt no presence of human or Fair Folk. At last he turned back and took a longer route back home, stopping at intervals to focus on his senses.

Still, nothing.

Even Theo's optimistic heart feared the worst. He shoved the terror down in his heart and took a trembling breath.

Then he crisscrossed the veil back toward the Fair Lands, letting his left hand trail along the wall of the passage. Every few minutes, he pressed his magic into the wall, asking, pleading, for the veil to give him some hint of where Fenton and Crocus might be.

The veil's unsettled irritability had faded as the hours passed, and now it seemed eager to assist, if it could. It gave him an easy, relatively safe route back to the Fair Lands, and no tentacled monster lurked at any of the turnings in the corridor.

Yet still he had not found them.

Theo was forced to conclude that either they were dead somewhere in the veil, or they were not in it at all.

When he reached the Fair Lands, he stepped out into a frigid Fair morning. The sky was a deep turquoise streaked with magenta, promising a beautiful clear cerulean as the sun rose. Pink and white streaks of clouds glowed softly as the sun lit them from below. The bush to Theo's left glittered with frost edging every magenta leaf, and the pale yellow and green blades of grass beneath his feet crunched with every step.

Theo circled the grounds with his head held high, gaze flicking around for any sign of Fenton or Crocus. With his weak magic, he tried to sense the presence of anyone else on the grounds. He paused at a strange sense of a great many Fair Folk somewhere in the palace. For an instant, he almost thought he sensed a human presence, but the movement of the others was so constant and complex, that he could not find it again among the sea of Fair Folk. He stepped closer with a vague sense of unease and tried again to find the human.

For long minutes he stood near a rear door of the palace with his eyes closed, but try as he might, he could not sense that human presence again. He had nearly made up his mind to enter the palace and search for the human when the door opened without warning and he found himself face to face with a fairy.

The Fair lord's lips lifted in a slow, cruel smile. "Overton. Why are you creeping about here, as if you have the right to step your disgusting human feet upon Fair royal ground?"

Theo bowed mockingly. "Good morning. I don't believe we've met."

"Oleander Larch, Duke of Feverfew Valley and Special Assistant to His Majesty Silverthorn in matters involving traitors to the crown."

Larch was even taller than Theo, probably of a height with Silverthorn himself. His skin was a fresh, pale green, like that of a new leaf; his aquiline features looked as though they had been sculpted to best advantage him in looking down his nose at inferiors. His hair was a deep chestnut brown that glinted auburn as the light hit it, and his eyes were a bright amber.

"Theo Overton. I'm actually looking for some friends of mine, but I don't want to trouble you." He gave the fairy a sparkling smile and bowed again.

"It's no trouble at all," Larch sneered. "For whom are you looking, and why would you look here?"

"A human and a fairy, my lord, and I'm looking here because I've exhausted all the other possibilities. Unfortunately, unless you have seen them, I shall have to retrace my steps yet again."

"A human and a fairy?" Larch's orange eyes gleamed. "Together? To my knowledge, you are the only human who regularly consorts with fairies. Who might this human be?"

"I am really not sure I ought to say, my lord." Theo smiled apologetically. "However, might I ask if you have been lurking around my estate and the nearby properties? Or perhaps you have sent your servants to investigate there? I have heard of several instances where intruders were detected and then disappeared, as if by magic, or as if hidden by a Fair glamour."

"You may ask, but I will not answer." Larch smiled coldly. "It baffles me that His Majesty Silverthorn allowed you to live at all."

Theo's eyes gleamed with interest. "Do you not intend to abide by His Majesty's edict, then? Shall I assume you also wish ill upon all my allies and have been seeking to do them harm in secret?"

"You may assume whatever you like, Overton." Larch's hand rested upon the hilt of his sword. "You have brought dishonor upon all Fair Folk, and I will correct this error. Where are your Fair allies now, Overton?"

Theo blinked innocently. "I should hope they're all safe well away from you, apparently. If the king has promised that they will face no repercussions for their support of my efforts, what right do you have to take vengeance upon them?"

"The right of a Fair lord to kill any human for any reason at all." Larch stepped forward with a cold smile. "You are small and weak, and yet you dare aspire to the Fair throne's power? As if you are our equals or even our benefactors?"

Theo took a careful step backward. "What Fair allies do I have, then?"

Larch snorted. "Not as many as you think. Mosswing, little Morel, and another two or three I've nearly pinned down."

With no other warning, Larch grabbed Theo by the throat with one hand, and with the other he began to draw his sword.

Despite his wariness and his own remarkably quick reflexes, Theo could not match Larch's lightning-fast attack. The fairy's fingers dug hard into his throat, cutting off the blood as well as any breath.

Theo clawed helplessly at Larch's wrist with both hands as spots danced in his eyes. The rasp of the fairy's sword was barely audible over the roar of his slowing pulse in his ears.

Iron.

He fumbled in his pocket and drew forth the iron horseshoe nail he kept there for emergencies. With it across his palm, he slapped his hand upon Larch's wrist.

The fairy screamed at the touch of iron and lost his grip on Theo's throat.

The young man stumbled backward, gasping, and the fairy shook his hand furiously. "I'll kill you," he hissed.

Theo drew his own sword, the tip wavering as he tried to blink the spots from his vision. "You may certainly try, but I'm rather busy at the moment."

Larch lunged, but Theo had regained enough strength to rip a door in the world and step into the veil. It snapped shut in Larch's furious face.

Theo sank to sit against the wall of the veil. His breath rasped painfully in his throat, and he felt dizzy and sick with the sudden rush of his blood in his ears. For a few minutes, he merely sat, letting the veil settle around him and his pulse slow its panicked pace.

Then he swallowed with a wince and shoved himself to his feet. He still did not know where Fenton and Crocus were, but it was long past dawn. Perhaps they had somehow made it safely back.

He clung to that hope while he walked through the shadows.

Lily and Lady Overton had taken shifts staying awake in the study the previous night. Lady Overton had insisted that Lily sleep first, and, unable to argue further with her mother-in-law, Lily had felt obligated to at least try to sleep. She undressed and slid beneath her covers, then tossed and turned for four hours. She did fall asleep once, but though she slept deeply, she did not sleep long; her fear for Theo brought her to wakefulness far too soon. A little after four in the morning, she had given up on sleep entirely. She pulled on a warm, modest dress and wrapped a shawl around her shoulders, as if she were wearing a blanket, and crept downstairs.

Juniper sat in the chair nearest the door, his feet curled up under a blanket and the sword resting across his knees. He ducked his head to her when she entered, but said nothing.

Lady Overton looked up from where she sat by the fire. The lamp near her was turned up high, but otherwise the room was dark.

"Go back to bed, Lily," she said gently.

"I can't sleep." Lily crossed to her and knelt down so she could look up earnestly into Lady Overton's face. "I might as well be awake down here as up there. One of us ought to rest, and it's your turn."

Lady Overton sighed softly, then said, "All right. I will take a little rest. Sir Theodore just left a few minutes ago. He made Anselm go to bed. If they're not all back safely by eight o'clock, Anselm will ask all the neighboring lords for their assistance."

Lily nodded. "Thank you," she whispered, grateful to be informed of these plans.

"Juniper has just now sat down," Lady Overton said. "The poor boy has been pacing for hours. He blames himself."

"It is not his fault," said Lily. "I do not know if there is fault to be assigned at all, but it can hardly be laid at his feet."

Lady Overton nodded. "If I had my way, that child would never go back to the Fair Lands. He will be happier here, and we are glad to have him." She said this softly, but clearly, as if she hoped Juniper would overhear.

The young fairy glanced at them, then away, as if ashamed.

"Go to bed for a little while," Lily said again. "I can make tea when they return next."

"Thank you." Lady Overton stood gracefully and walked out of the room, pausing only to set a gentle hand on Juniper's shoulder for a moment.

For nearly an hour Lily sat there in silence with Juniper. The young fairy seemed to want to disappear, or at least be ignored, and he remained entirely still, except for once, when Lily heard him take a tremulous breath. Perhaps he was trying not to weep, for he wiped at his eyes surreptitiously.

Lily waited some time after this, for she did not want him to be self-conscious. The sky was beginning to turn gray when she said softly, "Juniper?"

He twitched in surprise and turned to look at her, his turquoise eyes gleaming in the firelight.

"Yes, ma'am?"

"Will you tell me a little of your life in the Fair Lands? It seemed so beautiful when I visited with Theo. How did you come to help him rescue the children?"

The young fairy's lips trembled, and he looked down for a moment. "I am an orphan," he said quietly. "I was very young when my parents died, and I had no one to look after me."

He glanced up at her through his deep purple lashes, and, seeing that she was still waiting with sweet concern in her eyes, he ventured, "I petitioned His Majesty Alder Silverthorn, the previous king, for a job. He would have denied me, for I was only seven years old, and I believe he thought me worthless, but Lord Mosswing's father was there, and he made an off-hand remark about how a king's generosity was more important than a king's pride." He swallowed. "He pricked the king's pride, deliberately I believe, and in doing so, he persuaded the king to offer me a position in the palace. I served there for seven years, until I fled to your world."

Lily sat with this in silence. She knew that in the human world, children were left orphaned and uncared for, but she had not realized that such things happened in the Fair world too.

After a moment, she asked, "How did you come to serve the Wraith?"

Juniper's white teeth glinted briefly as he smiled, though the expression faded in a moment. "After the first few children were spirited away, the entire Fair court was in an uproar. They imagined him a ghost, like your name for him, Wraith, but they called him the Rose, for he left that symbol for the Fair guards. I happened to be serving in a banquet not long after that first rescue, and Lord Mosswing found me alone in a hallway. He asked me what I thought of the Rose's actions. I did not know Lord Mosswing well, but I did know him to be honorable and much kinder than many other Fair lords, and he looks much like his father did, whom I remembered as a benefactor. So I was bold; I told him that no child deserved to be stolen from loving parents, and that even orphan children should be cared for, not used as slaves to dance until death claimed them." Juniper's voice had grown fervent as he spoke, and this last was said with quiet passion.

When he heard himself, though, he caught his breath and said, "I am sorry, Mrs. Overton. I've been too forward."

"Of course you haven't!" she said. "Speak freely, please; we are friends, or we should be."

Juniper hesitated, then said, "Thank you, Mrs. Overton. Lord Mosswing told me how I might help the Rose, and I did so. I passed notes to Lord Mosswing whenever I knew anything of the palace's changing architecture, or the schedules of Lord Willowvale and other noblemen. Only later did I meet Mr. Overton personally.

"I wanted for those children what I did not have myself: someone who cared for them, someone to notice if they were not fed or if they became ill. Mr. Overton was that and more, for he righted the injustices against those children that had so grieved my heart."

"What about you, though? Did you hope nothing for yourself?" Lily said gently.

He blinked at her. "Of course not. Why would the Rose help me? I am one of the Fair Folk, the very people who stole the human children he so valued."

Lily said softly, "Oh, you poor child!"

He laughed softly, embarrassed. "I was, of course, honored to meet your husband several times in the course of his later rescues. A few minutes with a hero! Of course I was honored. I barely spoke a word. He must have thought me almost dumb.

"Lord Mosswing heard that His Majesty had discovered my assistance to Mr. Overton somehow and helped me flee into the veil.

But the passage was confused, and I thought I would die alone in the dark. I almost did.

"Mr. Overton came to rescue me." His voice cracked, and he paused a moment, gathering himself. Tears glistened in his eyes. "Though he barely knew me, he came into the veil for me, and dragged me from the very stone itself.

"Mrs. Overton, I owe your husband my life, and I still don't understand why. Even among fairies, gratitude for help such as I offered does not extend this far. I have nothing to offer to repay him for months of hospitality and protection. Is this what love is? A passion so deep it passes all logic and all hope of recompense? For I don't think that any sort of recompense would ever fully satisfy what I feel I owe him, and I don't know whether it is a weighty burden upon me, or an unbearable lightness that lifts my heart even when I ought to be grief-stricken. For I cannot imagine that I will ever be able to return safely to the Fair Lands, and I have lost everything I ever knew, and yet this world fills me with joy I don't understand, because I love this family and this house and…" His voice cracked again, and he looked away, trembling.

Lily, emboldened perhaps by lack of sleep and nervous tension, walked to him and knelt in front of his chair so she was face to face with the young fairy.

"Juniper, you don't need to repay him," she said gently. "He is delighted to be your friend; surely you can see that."

He nodded tremulously. "I do see it. But I don't understand why." He brushed one pale hand at his eyes, leaving a damp sheen of tears across his cheeks.

"If I may be so bold as to speak for my husband, I would venture to say there are several reasons. One, Theo is delighted whenever he can make a friend."

Juniper nodded again, with a faint, reluctant smile.

"Second, you have proven yourself brave, clever, and selfless, with a generosity of spirit that is uncommon among both men and Fair Folk. Surely you can understand why Theo would love that in anyone."

Juniper pressed his lips together and looked down. "I think you give me too much credit," he whispered.

"I will ask you to trust me on that, then. Third, your binding magic, which you gave so generously, helped him stop the Fair Folk from stealing children while also helping him save the Fair Lands he loves so much."

Juniper gave a soft, wry chuckle. "I didn't do much. His part of it took all the courage."

Lily said gently, "Is it so hard to be loved?"

The young fairy sucked in a sharp breath, and then said, "It is, Mrs. Overton. I shouldn't argue with you. Please forgive me."

Lily's tender heart twisted at this, and she said, "You don't have anything to apologize for, Juniper. I am sorry your life has been so lonely, and so hard, that you find it difficult to be loved, because I don't find it difficult to love you at all."

He stared at her, then looked down. "Thank you, Mrs. Overton," he whispered.

He looked so pale and so overwhelmed that she reached out and put her hand on his for a moment. He twitched in surprise, then grasped her hand between both of his and bowed over it, as if she were a queen.

Then he said, "I will keep watch, Mrs. Overton, if you would like to sleep a little."

Understanding this as the only sort of request he would make for a little time to think, Lily retreated to the sofa nearer the fire.

Anselm entered the room around seven thirty that morning, looking a little haggard but fully alert.

"They haven't returned?" he asked.

Lily shook her head without a word.

The older man sighed. "I'll bring you some breakfast before I set out." Half an hour later, he brought her and Juniper plates, which they ate in front of the fire.

CHAPTER THIRTEEN
Fading Hope

It was nearly noon when Theo reached the human world again. As soon as he stepped out of the veil, Lily ran to him.

She flung her arms around him, shuddering. "You've been gone so long," she gasped into his chest. "I thought…"

"I'm fine," he said. "Are they back?"

Lily looked up at him, her gray-blue eyes stricken. "No."

His knees nearly buckled, and Lily tightened her arms around him. "Come rest, my love," she said quietly. "Your father just came back. He and Oliver and my father and Anselm and all the stable hands have been combing the hills all morning. Your father sent word to neighboring lords, and they're looking, too."

Theo ran a trembling hand over his face and nodded.

Lily kept her arm around him as they walked to the house.

Sir Theodore met them at the door.

"Thank God you're back," he breathed, and crushed Theo in a tight, hard embrace. "Are you hurt? You've been in the veil all this time?" He stepped back and looked Theo over with a frown of concern. "Come, rest."

Theo followed his father down the hall to the study that had been designated as the center of planning as the search continued. Anselm had relinquished his duties to his wife Sophie, who had just brought a fresh pot of hot tea to the room, and he was now out searching with the others. Sir Theodore had been updating Lady Overton and Lily, who were tracking the routes everyone had covered on a map laid out upon a low table. Juniper shot to his feet when he saw Theo, but the joy in his eyes faded when he saw Theo's grim expression.

Theo sank into the nearest chair, fatigued beyond words for a moment, but too full of nervous energy, frustration, and looming grief to actually relax.

His voice rasped when he said, "I've crisscrossed the veil and they're not in there as far as I can tell. I'm sure the veil has killed Fair Folk before and I've never been able to sense the presence of their bodies, so I wouldn't know if they were dead somewhere in there, but if they're alive at all, they're elsewhere.

"I went to the Fair palace and walked the grounds for about an hour around dawn. For a moment, I almost thought I sensed a human, but I think I must have been mistaken. There were hundreds of Fair Folk in there. Perhaps it was a ball; I think they were dancing."

Lily, standing at his side, let her hand rest on his shoulder, and her fingers tickled the soft auburn curls at his neck. He leaned back into her touch, and she shifted her hand.

Her finger brushed the side of his throat, and he flinched.

"What's wrong?" she asked. "Are you hurt?"

"I'm sorry." He swallowed and winced; his throat was terribly sore, and talking hurt quite a bit more than he had expected. "Just an unpleasant little encounter with Larch. He is definitely our lurker, or at least one of them, and I think the others are working for him."

Sir Theodore knelt in front of him. "Theo, you're not telling me everything." His hazel eyes were too perceptive. He reached out and with one freckled finger carefully moved Theo's collar. "You're bruised here and here. It's just beginning to show, but I see it. Your eyes are blood red, and not just from staying up all night."

Theo sighed, then winced when that hurt too. "Larch tried to strangle me. Never fear, I had the nail. I'm all right, just a bit bruised and tired."

Lily's hand trembled on his shoulder.

Lady Overton said gently, "You're probably more shaken than you realize, dear Theo."

"If you haven't found them here, and they're not in the veil, then I should go check the Fair Lands again. I doubt Miss Firethorn can navigate well in the veil, so they might not be near the palace at all. There's no reason for them to be there, really." Theo's voice shook, and he gripped his knees to still his hands, for they were shaking too. "I should call on Cedar; he may know where Miss Firethorn served before. If he does, I'll look there first, because she might have gone there, even if only because it's a little familiar."

Lily entwined her fingers gently with his. "Dear heart, rest a while. You're exhausted, and you're trembling, and you must be famished. You'll be better able to help your friends when you have a little food in you and a little rest."

Theo shuddered and pulled away only to bury his face in both hands. He curled forward in the chair, wracked with dry, silent sobs.

Lily slipped forward, edging Sir Theodore out of the way, and wrapped her arms around Theo's shoulders. She murmured reassurances into his ear, but perhaps they were more wishful thinking than true optimism. For she, too, feared the worst.

Only a few minutes later, Anselm returned from his route, followed in short order by Oliver, Sir Jacob, and two of the stable hands. None of them had found Fenton or Crocus, nor any definitive sign of them.

Theo stood to greet them then wavered, suddenly dizzy, and clutched at the table with shaking hands.

"Sit down, Theo," Lily said. "You don't have to be the host. Just eat and rest, please."

Theo took a shuddering breath and nodded. He nodded to Lily's family, and Sir Jacob started in surprise when he saw Theo's eyes. Theo sat at the table with his head in his hands.

He stared at the rich butternut squash soup that Sophie had put in front of him. A pat of butter melted into the rich bread beside the bowl of soup. A little bowl of small tomatoes and another of strawberries and whipped cream offered hothouse luxuries.

Where would he look next?

"Are you in too much pain to eat?" Lily whispered in concern.

"I'm fine."

"You don't have to be fine, Theo." She cupped his cheek in one gentle hand, and with infinite tenderness, she traced the bruises under his eyes with her thumb. "I'm so sorry," she whispered. "I wish I could…"

He closed his eyes. Tears slid silently down his cheeks, and his breath came unevenly and too fast. But there was no time for weeping, for he would not give up hope.

With a breath like a sob, he straightened. "I'm all right," he said again, as if it were true. He entwined his fingers with hers while he ate with his other hand. The acid of the tomatoes burned his bruised throat, and the milk and honey in the tea did not soothe it as much as he had hoped.

He heard his father relaying what Theo had told him to Sir Jacob, Oliver, and Anselm, but he could not face them. Not yet.

"I need to go look for them, Lily," Theo whispered hoarsely.

Lily stood with him; perhaps she realized only nervous tension had kept him from collapsing thus far. For when he stood, the world heaved like an ocean wave, and the black spots in his vision returned with a vengeance. He sat down suddenly, gasping, and put his head between his knees.

"Just rest a little, Theo," Lily murmured. "I'll help you over to the sofa. Even a few minutes will help."

Anselm helped him to the sofa, and with the servant's strong arm to assist, it didn't matter as much that the headache that had been lurking at the back of his awareness finally could not be pushed aside any longer and came upon him in a rush. His eyes hurt, his throat burned, and his chest felt as though he'd been kicked by a horse. With barely a word of thanks, he curled up on the sofa and let the darkness take him for a little while.

Theo woke with a gasp less than two hours later, much to Lily's dismay. He struggled up to a sitting position. The whites of his eyes were blood red, and the bruises beneath his eyes had deepened as he rested. His voice rasped when he whispered, "They haven't come back?"

Lily shook her head.

Theo gathered himself for a moment, then stood, still a little shaky but steadier than he had been. He looked around the room to see his mother sitting by the fire. "Where has everyone gone?"

Lily and Lady Overton showed him on the map. "Anselm just left to follow the river south. Sir Jacob has gone to Ardmond to ask at the palace if they know anything." The others had gone farther afield, crisscrossing the neighboring estates and making enquiries with everyone as they went.

Theo nodded. "I will go by Cedar's house first. If he can tell me anything, I will follow that lead. If not, I will return to the Fair palace, for I fear I might have missed something."

No one dared speculate aloud that Fenton and Crocus had died in the veil itself.

At his mother's and Lily's plea, he ate a savory meat-filled pastry and a plate of raspberries, grapes, melons, and cheese, with another two cups of tea to wash it down.

Then he said, "Dearest Lily, I will return when I can." He kissed her fingertips one by one, as if he feared he might not have the opportunity again soon, then pressed a kiss to her forehead, another to her lips, and then murmured in her ear, "Thank you. I've run out of courage, but you've given me enough to carry on."

"I love you, Theo." Her sweet, solemn smile brought tears to his eyes again.

"I love you, Lily, with all my heart."

She felt him trembling in her arms, and she feared for him. But she did not call him back when he strode out into the fading afternoon light.

CHAPTER FOURTEEN
A Desperate Dance

A thousand Fair Folk, or so it seemed to Fenton's feverish eyes, danced a thousand confusing dances to the lilting music of unfamiliar instruments.

Crocus kept her eyes focused on his face. Her pink rosebud lips were pressed together tightly.

Fenton thought muzzily that it was strange to be dancing when he felt as though the poison were eating him from the inside out, turning his blood to liquid flame. The music was unfamiliar, and so were the steps, but he stumbled resolutely on, ignoring the rhythm in favor of staying mostly upright.

The burning spread, and he shivered, feverish and chilled, though his shoulder felt like fire. Once he looked away, hoping to see the edge of the dance floor, and Crocus cupped his cheek in one cool hand and gently turned his face back to her. Her bright, ice-blue eyes held his with strange intensity.

The music wore on, and he thought wildly that he ought to beg her to stop. What use was dancing when he was dying? What use was dancing to curry the king's favor if he fell into a screaming jumble of limbs and fracturing sanity in the middle of the crowd of brilliant, beautiful Fair Folk?

The music became even quicker and livelier, and Fenton stumbled, then stumbled again, nearly falling on his face before Crocus pulled him upright. She wrapped her left arm around his waist and pulled him forward, so that his body was pressed against hers. He tried to pull away, vaguely embarrassed and afraid she would be offended, but he had no strength left, and he fell helplessly against her. His cheek rested against her narrow, white shoulder.

She hauled him through the dance, her feet moving in the rhythm. Time had long since lost all meaning to Fenton, but he thought that they had been dancing quite a while, for her cool white skin had a sticky film of sweat upon it now.

He drifted in and out of consciousness, his mind burning and his body shaking with fever and pain. He made no sound, for even in this delirious state, he did not want to be unseemly.

By the time Theo made it to Cedar's house, it was nearly dusk. He pressed a hand to his chest at intervals; his chest hurt, as if his lungs ached in protest of Larch's attack. He had, carefully, in the darkness of the veil, explored the bruises upon his neck and face, but could not ascertain how bad he looked without a mirror. His lips felt oddly swollen, and the skin below his eyes felt bruised and tender. His neck was painfully bruised, and his throat still burned with every breath. But he was alive, and he had no intention of stopping the search until he knew with certainty what had happened to his best friend and his Fair guest.

He knocked upon Cedar's door for the first time in half a year. During the Wraith's activities on behalf of the human children, they had only rarely met at Cedar's house, for it was often safer and quicker for Cedar to meet him nearer their destination.

The Fair lord opened the door himself only moments later. "Theo!" he said in disbelief. "Come in."

Theo ducked his head and followed Cedar down the hall.

"Phlox and Basil got married last week, so I gave them the month off. You'll have to make do with my best effort at tea."

"It's not a social call, unfortunately."

When they entered the parlor, Cedar turned to a little table, where a pot of steaming tea already sat. He poured a cup of tea for Theo and one for himself. "You're always welcome here, but sounds as though something has happened."

Theo managed a grim smile. "Lord Larch is our intruder. But I'm here for another reason. Fenton and Miss Firethorn are missing."

"Miss Firethorn?"

Theo took the seat Cedar offered with a rush of gratitude, for his head was throbbing, his throat burned, his neck ached, his chest hurt, and overall, he felt that sitting down was probably a wise decision.

"You remember she appeared at Fenton's door a few weeks ago, seeking Juniper. She claimed to be his cousin and wished him well. Fenton wanted to trust her, and he offered her hospitality while she searched. He wanted Juniper's permission before letting her know he was staying with me."

Cedar held up his hand at this point. "What is wrong with your voice? And your eyes?"

"Larch tried to strangle me a few hours ago. Anyway, we—"

Theo's eyes widened at the rush of healing magic, and he lost his place in the sentence for a moment. For the first time in hours, he could breathe without pain.

"We…" He blinked. The thread of magic Cedar had slipped into him was not nearly as strong as what he had used after Theo had confronted Lord Willowvale and His Majesty Silverthorn, but it was still more than strong enough to scramble his thoughts. The golden sparkles that danced over his vision were comfortingly familiar, for Cedar had filled him with a tremendous amount of healing magic several times after that bloody triumph. The gold entirely overwhelmed the haze that had been creeping in from the edges of his vision.

He swallowed, still blinking, and said, "Thank you. If you will permit me to skip ahead, we had them over for lunch. When Juniper entered the room, he told her he was safe. She was furious, for we had lied to her, or near enough for her to take it as a lie, numerous times, telling her we did not know where he was, before Juniper was ready to reveal himself."

Theo rubbed shaking hands over his face. "Miss Firethorn fled into an autumn squall. Fenton waited nearly an hour before going after her. It was a cold snap, and windy, and we searched for hours in the cold rain on horseback. Fenton had borrowed one of my horses, and it returned alone late last night. My father and I searched all night, and this morning Anselm, Lily's father and Oliver, and the stablehands joined the search.

"No one has found any sign of them. I've searched the veil backwards and forwards. I did one search of the Fair palace grounds, and that's where I encountered Larch." Theo had to stop and catch his breath, for he felt dizzy with the combination of fatigue and magic and emotion. He looked up to meet Cedar's beautiful turquoise eyes. "I don't think he did anything to them; he didn't seem to know anything about them at all. But he has been the one lurking about the estate, and Fenton's estate, and I believe he may have his lackeys sneaking around too. I assume they're looking primarily for Juniper, although they might be happy to find Miss Firethorn as well.

"So I came to see if you knew anything of her and where she might have gone. For I cannot—I *cannot*—accept that they are dead somewhere in the veil." On this last sentence, his voice cracked.

Cedar said gently, "I don't know her, or anything of her. I've heard the name Firethorn, but I know nothing about the family."

Theo put his head in his hands and closed his eyes. "Miss Crocus Firethorn? You've never heard of her?"

The Fair lord shook his head. "There was a Sorrel Firethorn, a minor lord, I believe, but he died years ago."

"Perhaps he was her father. She wasn't living at his property, though; she said as much when I first met her." The magic threaded his veins, and despite the failure of this lead, Theo felt a faint hint of hope still remaining. "If you were me, where would you look next?"

Cedar's eyes widened a little, and he let out a soft breath. "I cannot guess," he said. "If you're feeling both bold and desperate, and you think Larch might have something to do with their disappearance, I suppose you could petition His Majesty to question him."

Theo frowned. "I think I will."

Cedar rose. "Shall I come with you?"

Theo hesitated, then shook his head. "I think not. I think I'd rather you be here, ready to check for messages."

He stood, buoyed by the faint tingle of magic, and said, "Thank you, Cedar."

"Godspeed." Cedar stood with him.

Theo opened the door to the veil right there in Cedar's study, and stepped in.

As the door closed behind him, he put a hand against the wall and felt for them again, hoping against hope.

With a gasp of shock and joy, he felt a human presence and a Fair presence a long distance away.

He began to run.

CHAPTER FIFTEEN
A Terrible Price

When the music shifted again, Crocus stumbled, whether from weariness or his weight or merely the transition to a new rhythm.

"Please—" Fenton gasped into her neck.

She tried to clap a hand over his mouth, but the angle was too awkward, since her hands had been occupied holding him upright.

He slid downward and fell to his knees on the floor; he would have fallen sideways too, but she caught him and held him, kneeling at his side with her arm wrapped around him.

"Denied," a deep, smooth voice said from above them.

Crocus cried, "Your Majesty, he is human! Surely the law does not hold humans to the same code as we Fair Folk!"

"I did not devise this law, Crocus Firethorn. It is my generosity that allowed you to make this attempt to save his life. Do not blame me for his failure."

"How shall we save him then, Your Majesty?" Her voice shook.

"That is not my concern." The king turned away.

Crocus straightened. "I believe there is something you can do."

He turned and stared at her, his violet eyes steady and cold. He stared at Fenton.

The young nobleman's skin was pale and clammy and burning with fever. His glassy eyes drifted closed.

The Fair king gave a faint twitch of one shoulder, then said, "You're willing to pay the price?"

"Let us say it aloud, so that everyone can witness our understanding." Crocus trembled, and her breath came fast.

"I, Oak Silverthorn, king over all the Fair Lands, will exert the full power of my magic to remove the manticore venom from this human, and in return you, Crocus Firethorn, of clan Firethorn, will owe me your life and magic until I release you or you die."

Fenton made an inarticulate sound at this. His eyes were closed, and he shuddered at intervals, his breath coming fast and shallow.

Crocus said clearly, "I accept, Your Majesty."

The king blinked, as if he were actually surprised by her acceptance of this bargain. Then he said, "Lay him down with the wound upward."

His Majesty Silverthorn watched with a sort of impersonal interest as Crocus gently laid Fenton on his back upon the wooden floor. She laid his trembling hands at his sides, and he shook with fever. He opened his eyes for a moment, but he did not seem to perceive anything. She rolled him carefully to his stomach and pointed at the hole in the fabric. Very little blood had seeped through the layers of fabric, and the hole was not large, though it was clearly visible against the fine cloth.

The king pulled a knife out of his jacket and cut Fenton's jacket from his collar down to the waist, then similarly cut his vest and shirt. He pulled the cloth away from Fenton's back and curled his lip at the wound.

Fenton's smooth, olive skin had a deep puncture wound in the thick muscle above his right shoulder blade. The skin around it was streaked with half dried blood and ichor, and the flesh was swollen and hot. His skin prickled with chill, and he shivered again, his face scraping against the floor.

The king frowned faintly at the wound.

Fenton's breaths had grown shallower and quicker, and the king asked, "How long has it been?"

"Twenty-three and a half hours. It happened only a few minutes before we began dancing. I brought him as quickly as I could."

The king pressed the flat of his right hand to the wound and closed his eyes. He took a deep breath and his face contorted for a moment before he let out his breath slowly.

For long minutes, there was silence aside from the sound of Fenton's quick, labored breaths. The other dancers had retreated some distance away, and their dancing and music seemed to have faded into a vague sort of disquiet.

Crocus watched in an agony of tension. Fenton's brow was still covered in clammy sweat, and his sun-kissed olive skin was pale and sallow.

The king suddenly jerked his hand away from Fenton with a sharp cry and, breathing heavily, said, "It is done."

Fenton groaned and moved a little. He opened his eyes and closed them again, wincing, then struggled up to his hands and knees. His head hung down between his shoulders as he gathered himself.

In this position it quickly became apparent that his jacket, vest, and shirt were in pieces, which began to slide down his arms toward the floor. He sat back, still breathing heavily, and looked around.

"What happened?" he gasped.

Still on her knees beside him, Crocus studied his face a moment before saying quietly, "His Majesty Silverthorn burned the manticore venom from you." She looked toward the king and bowed so deeply that her forehead nearly touched the floor. "Thank you, Your Majesty."

Something in the king's face looked strange to her, and she watched with trepidation as the king opened his mouth, then closed it again. His chest heaved with effort, and his robin's egg blue skin looked pale.

At last he swallowed and nodded once. He shoved himself to his feet and staggered a step, then straightened with his chin high.

Fenton looked after him, still glassy-eyed and dazed. He swallowed and looked back at Crocus.

The music began again, quiet and understated, and the Fair nobility resumed their dancing, avoiding Crocus and Fenton by a wide margin.

Crocus looked down, avoiding Fenton's gaze. She offered him a hand and said, "Can you stand?"

The young nobleman swayed on his knees, and his eyes fluttered closed. He slumped to the side and might have fallen, but for Crocus's wiry strength. He mumbled something she did not understand and tried to steady himself.

"Just sit for a minute," she said quietly. "I don't expect he used much healing magic on you, if he has any to use at all."

Fenton sat on his heels, head drooping, eyes closed, and for some time he was only aware of the strange, unsteady rush of his pulse in his ears and the lingering hollow feeling of pain receded but not quite vanished.

Crocus had slipped her arm through his and held him upright, and he was so dazed that he did not realize this for several minutes. When he did, he gave a halfhearted groan and mumbled an apology.

"Can you stand?" she asked again. The king would return soon, and she wanted Fenton safely out of the Fair Lands before His Majesty returned to claim her. She didn't know what the king would require of her, but she was certain the young Valestrian nobleman would not stand for it. It would make little sense to bargain with the king for his life only to have him throw it away immediately to extricate her from the mess.

"I can try," he whispered, with hopeless, dogged courage that made her blink sudden tears from her eyes.

He shoved himself upward and staggered, steadied only by her arm.

"Do you remember what happened?" she asked gently, partly to see if he was still aware enough to both remember and answer, and partly to give him more time to come to terms with being on his feet.

"A monster," he said. "With a stinger. Magic in my blood. I can't…"

She steadied him. "Come on. Let's get you home," she said.

Crocus pushed her magic into the air and begged the veil to open. It took all her strength and skill to open a sliver of a doorway barely wide enough for her, much less Fenton's broad shoulders. "In here," she coaxed. "Just turn a little to the side and slip in." She wrapped her arm around his waist and guided him, stumbling, into the clammy darkness.

"The veil hates me," he managed.

Crocus wanted to groan, but kept her dismay to herself. She was barely able to navigate the veil at the best of times, and she was not at her best at this moment. Her head ached with fatigue and her heart ached with grief for both herself and the young Valestrian nobleman who depended upon her. She pushed the gibbering fear of the king and the veil to the back of her mind.

"We'll manage somehow," she said reassuringly, and started off.

Fenton leaned on her, but he kept his feet moving and they made good time for almost an hour. She put her hand on the wall at intervals, feeling the magic writhe beneath the stone and brick and moss.

Then, when she thought they ought to be getting close, she put her hand on the wall and felt an unpleasant scaly sort of texture, as if a serpent of unimaginable size lay coiled there. She bit back a shriek and said, "We've made a wrong turn, or the path has changed. We need to go back."

Fenton stumbled and nearly fell as they turned.

Crocus hurried them back the way they had come, trailing her fingers along the left wall. Where was the turn?

There!

She took it. Three steps later, the ground vanished from beneath their feet, and they went sliding down a long, pebble-covered slope, faster and faster, until she couldn't help letting out a cry of pain as the rocks scraped the skin from her hands.

Suddenly they splashed into the edge of an icy pool and slid to a stop as the angle of the slope lessened.

For nearly a minute, neither of them said anything. The only sound was that of their ragged breathing in the darkness.

"Are you hurt, Miss Firethorn?" Fenton whispered shakily.

"I am alive, Lord Selby," Crocus managed.

The tiniest sound caught their ears, and for a moment neither of them understood. Then another little swish in the water, closer.

"Get out of the water," Fenton said. His hand found her shoulder in the darkness and shoved her uphill.

He clambered after her, the pebbles slipping and sliding beneath him.

A louder splash came from quite close, and he said, "Move, Miss Firethorn, uphill, as fast as you can."

Then a voice came out of the darkness. "Lord Selby, I do believe you have the most abominable luck in the veil," Theo said cheerfully as he grasped Fenton's hand and hauled him bodily up the slope only a moment before something slapped the pebbles at the water's edge. "Are you hurt?" Theo was a little out of breath, but he seemed absolutely delighted to have found them.

Fenton's knees scraped on the stones as he tried to get a little farther from the unseen creature in the water.

"Where's Miss Firethorn?" he asked.

"I'm here." Her voice sounded shaky and breathless. "What is that thing?"

Theo flicked light to his fingertips for a moment, then let it subside. "I haven't seen that one before. It has tentacles, though. We'd better move quickly. Here." He opened a door to the veil, and through it a strange sunset glow lit the pebble-strewn slope on which they stood.

"Where is that?" Crocus asked.

"Anywhere but here," Theo muttered. He ducked under Fenton's arm and stood, half carrying his friend toward the exit. "Miss Firethorn, if you would step out, please." He followed her out and let the door to the veil shut behind them.

CHAPTER SIXTEEN
A Dangerous Game

The golden glow from the setting sun lit the magenta leaves and treetops above them, but the bushes around them were already shadowed.

"Where are we?" said Crocus with misgiving. She looked around, her hand going to where her sword would be, if she hadn't left it at Lord Selby's house two days ago. Her breath fogged in the air.

"I don't know yet." Theo's voice was warm and reassuring. "Sit here, Lord Selby." He helped his friend sink to the moss-covered forest floor.

Fenton huffed a weary laugh. "Thank you for your care for my dignity, but I don't mind if Miss Firethorn hears my first name at this point."

Theo chuckled under his breath. "As you wish. What happened?"

He listened as Crocus told most of the story.

"And what bargain did you make with His Majesty for my friend's life?" he murmured at the end.

Crocus looked at Fenton, whose expression was lost in shadow, even to her sharp Fair eyes. She swallowed, then said, "It need not trouble either of you. What's done is done."

Fenton, exhausted nearly beyond coherent thought, managed to say, "I don't agree."

"Neither do I," said Theo. "There are ways, and there are ways of working within the confines of Fair bargains. It would do you no harm to let us know the details, and it might help us devise a way to help you."

The Fair maiden said, with a hint of anger in her voice, "The whole reason this happened is because you lied to me about Juniper. Now you expect me to trust you?"

Theo blinked, then said gently, "I am sorry, Miss Firethorn, but I was honor-bound to protect Juniper, and it was his right to decide whether he trusted you, not mine. I hope you can forgive me."

She gave a frustrated growl deep in her throat and turned away. "It is none of your business what happens to me, anyway. I made the bargain of my own free will. I didn't want to watch him die in front of me."

Fenton would have said something at this, something warm and appreciative and dignified, but words were much too difficult to manage now. Instead, he slumped sideways.

Theo helped him lie on the moss. "Let me figure out where we are, Fen, and I'll go fetch Cedar," he said quietly. "Are you in pain?"

"No," Fenton mumbled. The frigid chill of the moss seeped through his trousers and pressed an icy line against his skin where his clothes had been cut apart on his back. He could not muster the energy to shiver, though.

Theo looked up at Crocus. Her delicate features were silhouetted against the candy pink streaks across the night sky.

"Will you be all right if I leave you for a few hours? I think we're quite far from my friend's estate, even through the veil."

Without warning, fairy light flared above their heads with sudden brilliance.

"No, stay," said a cool voice. A Fair lord, for he was unmistakably a lord, strolled out of the shadows beneath the trees flanked by six enormous wolves. "I do not often have the opportunity to meet uninvited guests."

The cool fairy light danced over his lavender hair. His skin was a pale gray that almost matched the smoky gray of his wolves. His green eyes were bright and cold, and he smiled with teeth that seemed a little more pointed than they ought to be.

Theo rose and bowed deeply. "My lord. I beg your forgiveness. We fled in haste, and did not mean to intrude upon your lands." He smiled as he straightened.

"Fascinating," the Fair lord breathed. He waved a hand and the wolves spread out around them with silent steps. The fairy stepped closer, his gaze taking in Theo, Crocus, and then Fenton, who lay pale and motionless on the moss beneath their feet. "You shall have to play a game with me, of course."

Crocus stiffened. "My lord, we will be delighted to leave your…"

"I insist." The demand was sharp as glass.

Theo said brightly, "What sort of game?" He shot Crocus a quick glance, imploring her to remain silent.

The Fair lord studied him again. "A game of bargains, I think."

"You shall have to teach me how to play, my lord, for I am not familiar with those sorts of games," Theo said, in sparkling good humor.

The fairy's smile took on a dangerous edge. "Then I shall be especially delighted to teach you," he purred. "Let us play like this: You ask me for what you want, and I will tell you the price. If you think my demand too dear, you may suggest something else. When we have come to an agreement, we shall make a bargain."

Theo gazed at him with wide, innocent eyes. "How is that a game, my lord? It sounds merely like an opportunity to get myself in trouble."

"We will play several rounds. Let us say we shall make three bargains. Whoever gets the better end of two of the three rounds is clearly the winner, don't you think?"

"How will we know who got the better end of the deal?"

The Fair lord gave him a toothy smile. "I think it will be apparent."

"What does the winner get as their prize?" Theo asked.

The fairy's eyes raked over the little group. "What do you want?" he asked.

Theo laughed. "I didn't realize we were beginning already! If I win, I should like to be able to call you a friend. If you win, I should like for you to call me a friend."

The Fair lord hesitated, his eyes narrowed. "That was not the first round. If I win, I shall do whatever I want with you. If you win, I will call you a friend, and you may call me whatever you wish."

Theo laughed lightly. "That doesn't sound appealing at all, my lord. Why should I agree to that?"

The lord's lips lifted in another menacing smile much like the silent snarl of his wolves. "Shall I make it more appealing? If you win, you and your friends live. If you lose, I will enlighten you as to the legal rights I have against intruders upon my ancestral lands."

Theo tilted his head and studied him. "I would prefer lesser terms," he said. "If I lose, perhaps we might pay some small penalty. I can offer you some very nice human tea, if you are partial to it."

Astonished, the fairy stared at him for a split second before he laughed. "The alternative is that you all die now," he said, sharp teeth glinting. "My wolves are hungry, and I grow bored."

"Well, you have me at a disadvantage. We are agreed on the prize, then. If you will be satisfied with nothing less, I will play for our lives," Theo said.

As the Fair lord had spoken, several of the wolves moved closer on silent paws, their yellow eyes bright and hungry upon Theo's face.

"Mr.—" Crocus began to say to Theo, when he interrupted.

"I do believe that should be my first request, my lord. Your name. In return, I shall give you mine." He smiled, all warmth and friendliness.

"Done." The fairy grinned. "I am Lord Laurel Bayberry, Marquess of the Eastern Reaches."

This name had been mentioned several times by Cedar as one of the more dangerous and clever Fair lords. As a marquess, he ranked quite high in the Fair Court, but he preferred hunting with his wolves to dances in the capital. Cedar had met him more than once but did not know him well.

Theo bowed gracefully. "I am Theodore Overton the Fourth."

"What is your title?"

Theo held up a finger. "Is that your starting demand for the next round?"

Lord Bayberry blinked. "We haven't finished the first round."

"Oh!" Theo laughed lightly. "I thought we had. I gave you all the title I have."

The fairy shifted and studied Theo with narrowed eyes. "You told me no title. Am I to understand that you have none?"

Theo gave a graceful shrug. "Indeed, my lord. Can we say that I have gained more than you have in that round, for your name is certainly more noble than mine?"

Lord Bayberry's eyes narrowed, and his mouth twisted for a moment in anger before he said, "Indeed. You have startled me, Overton. The round is yours. What is your starting position for the second round?"

"I should like your hospitality for the night for my friends and myself." Theo gestured toward Fenton, who had not yet moved, and Crocus, who had been standing frozen in an agony of fear and indecision for most of this conversation.

The fairy gave a laugh of sparkling disbelief. "Fascinating," he said again. "You have not heard of me, then."

Theo smiled modestly. "Only a very few rumors, and it would be silly to believe the worst of someone on rumors alone. What price would you ask for this, my lord?"

Moonlight glinted on the Fair lord's pale lavender hair as he shifted.

Theo knelt at Fenton's side and felt his pulse at his throat. To Theo's great relief, it was strong and steady. Fenton was unusually pale and drawn, and he seemed so deeply asleep that he could not be woken by anything short of some unimaginable fiery cataclysm, but he did not seem feverish or otherwise ill.

Crocus's ice blue eyes met Theo's for a moment, and he smiled reassuringly at her. Then he looked up at the Fair lord, who had taken a half step closer as he watched this interaction.

Lord Bayberry said thoughtfully, "Do you have any magic?"

"Only a little of my own, my lord, but I like to think I've used it effectively."

"I should like a demonstration of your magic as payment for my hospitality." The Fair lord smiled with a predatory glint in his eyes.

"It may take some time, my lord, and I will require both my friends."

"I accept those conditions."

Theo lifted Fenton enough to slide one arm behind his friend's back, then hefted Fenton up with him as he stood. Fenton groaned softly but did not wake.

"You're all right," Theo murmured. He glanced at Crocus and said, "Walk with me, please." Then he used his free hand to open a door into the veil.

Lord Bayberry gasped.

Theo stepped into the veil with Crocus on his heels. The Fair lord stared at them in shock, and Theo said cheerfully, "I shall return as quickly as possible, my lord."

Then he let the door snap closed.

"You lied to him!" Crocus sounded shaken.

"Only a little. I didn't entirely know what he meant by a game of bargains, and I'm quite sure that sort of game is not the sort one ought to play when fuzzy on the rules."

"Oh. I meant…" She caught her breath, as if on a sob, though it was much too dark for Theo to read her expression. "I had forgotten that. I meant when you said you would return."

Theo said gently, "Miss Firethorn, that was entirely truthful, and I do intend to return to finish our game once I have taken you and Lord Selby to safety. Hold my jacket, please; I've found that it's best if we maintain physical contact in the veil."

He set off through the darkness, setting as brisk a pace as he could maintain while hauling Fenton beside him.

After several minutes, Fenton groaned again, and a little movement let Theo know he was drifting toward awareness.

"We're just on a little jaunt through the veil," Theo said to him. "I'm taking you and Miss Firethorn to my house. We can get word to Cedar more quickly from there, and I'll ask Anselm to let your mother know you're safe."

Fenton leaned hard on Theo but began supporting more of his own weight. "Anything after us?" he mumbled.

"Not yet." Theo stopped to shift Fenton's arm about his shoulders. "How do you feel?"

"Could be worse. A little embarrassed."

Miss Firethorn said, "You've acquitted yourself with admirable courage, Lord Selby. I can't think of anything for you to be embarrassed about."

Fenton let out a soft breath and tried more emphatically to get his feet under him, with little success. They continued through the darkness, Theo's indefatigable energy carrying them onward at a brisk pace.

"Oh, let's turn around," Theo said abruptly, and he led them hurriedly into a side corridor neither Fenton nor Crocus had noticed.

"Was there something there?" Crocus asked.

"I believe so, and I think I've met it before," Theo said with an unusually grim tone. "It has far too many teeth for my liking."

The next half hour seemed interminable to all of them, as they expected to be grabbed from behind at any moment.

At last, Theo said, his own relief almost entirely hidden behind his encouraging cheer, "Here we are." He opened the door and let Crocus out first, then supported Fenton as they stepped out into his garden. The moon was nearly hidden behind clouds, leaving the garden suffused in a soft silver light bright enough to show the bulk of rhododendrons and roses but too dim for the humans to see any detail.

Theo strode across the lawn and opened the door. Not immediately seeing anyone, he began walking toward a guest suite on the ground floor.

"I can walk," Fenton said in a low voice, but he stumbled on his next step, still leaning on Theo.

Theo blew out a dismissive *pfft* and muttered, "When I said that, everyone laughed at me. It's your turn to be supported, for once."

He said, over his shoulder, "Miss Firethorn, I'm sure you won't begrudge me getting Fenton settled. I'll show you to a guest suite momentarily."

The fairy blinked, and said, "Of course." Her hands trembled a little and she clenched them in her skirt. She stopped at the door of the guest suite.

Theo turned to her and said, "I beg your pardon. I'll be out in just a moment." Then he shut the door.

He rang the bell for Anselm, then helped Fenton to sit on the edge of the bed and helped him undress, which was a quick task given the state of his jacket, vest, and shirt. Theo winced in sympathy at the blood and ichor stains on Fenton's shirt. He pulled a new, clean shirt from the chest of drawers over Fenton's head and helped him get into bed.

Fenton mumbled something that might have been thanks, for it had the tone of gratitude, and fell into sleep before Theo had moved his boots to the end of the bed.

Anselm came quickly, frowning in confusion at being called to a guest suite. His eyes were shadowed with fatigue, and he had apparently been about to leave again to continue the search. Theo met him at the door.

"Lord Selby is here. He was stung by a manticore and then danced nearly to death. The poison is burned out, but he's wrung out like a rag and needs a great deal of sleep and several good meals, I imagine. I would very much like it if you would send for Lord Mosswing to help his healing, please."

Anselm nodded, his tired eyes wide with concern. "Shall I get him something to eat now?"

"First thing in the morning. For now, just let him sleep until Lord Mosswing arrives." Theo turned to Crocus. "Miss Firethorn, this is Anselm, a good friend and my manservant. I trust him with my life. Walk with me, please." He strode just a little way down the corridor to another guest suite on the same side of the hallway. "You may stay here. If there is anything you need, please do not hesitate to ask." He smiled warmly at her, then turned to Anselm. "Would you please bring her some warm water to wash and perhaps a midnight snack?" With another glance at her, he added, "You must be famished."

Crocus nodded wordlessly. The fatigue of the previous days had risen until it seemed endless, and it had been nearly a day and a half since she or Fenton had eaten at all. She felt near tears from fatigue alone, not to mention worry for him.

"Yes, please bring her dinner," Theo said more decidedly. "Thank you, Anselm. I'm going to speak to Mrs. Overton briefly, and then I must be off again. Lord Bayberry expects me back promptly."

Anselm said, "I'll fix you a plate before you leave. It's been hours since you left."

Theo blinked. "It has, hasn't it? Thank you. I could use a bite to eat." He bowed to Crocus. "Rest well, Miss Firethorn."

When she closed the door, he turned to Anselm, who had waited a moment longer. "Is everyone still in the parlor?"

"Lady Overton slept this afternoon and is in the parlor now. She insisted that your wife go to bed; she was exhausted. Your father took a short nap and went back out hours ago; he ought to be back soon. I don't think Juniper has slept at all; the poor child is beyond exhaustion, but he will not consent even to a nap. He says you told him to guard the ladies, so the only time he closed his eyes was when Sir Theodore and I were planning what areas we would search next."

Theo sighed. "And you? You look exhausted too."

Anselm gave him a severe look. "I could hardly rest while you were injured and still looking for Lord Selby and Miss Firethorn. Surely you think better of me than that."

"Of course," Theo said, chastened. "Still, I hope you can get a little sleep soon. I'll go speak to my mother, and then Lily, and then meet you in the kitchen, if you can hold out that much longer."

Anselm scowled. "Don't insult me. I assume you saw Lord Mosswing?" At Theo's nod, he said in a low, rough voice, "You looked half dead, Theo. We've all been terrified for you."

Theo put a reassuring hand on his shoulder and said, "I am sorry to have worried you, and I certainly did not mean to insult you. Please forgive me."

The servant gave a choked little laugh. "Don't be ridiculous, Theo. I've never been truly angry with you in my life; I'm hardly going to start holding grudges now. Go reassure your mother."

Theo said, "Thank you." He held the older man's gaze a moment longer and smiled with all the warmth and gratitude that filled his heart.

Juniper shot to his feet when he saw Theo coming down the hall. He bowed and then stepped aside so Theo could greet his mother first.

In the parlor, he embraced his mother and reassured her that he was entirely healed. His eyes sparkled with his customary humor and wit, though they were still shadowed with fatigue, and the gold had faded, leaving his true warm hazel. His voice carried no hint of the painful rasp that had so worried his mother before when he gave the barest outline of how he had found Fenton and Crocus in the veil and brought them safely back to the manor.

Theo turned to Juniper next and said sincerely, "I cannot thank you enough."

The young fairy bowed again, and smiled shyly.

He told them both, "I must return to the Fair Lands tonight, for I have one thing left to do. I expect it will take all night, and much of tomorrow as well, so do not worry."

"Must you go? Tonight?" his mother whispered.

"I have unfinished business with a Fair lord, and I promised to return as soon as I could." He hesitated and then said, "It might take even longer than anticipated, for I shall have to be careful, and it will not do to rush it. If I'm not back by midnight tomorrow night, perhaps you might ask Cedar to call on Lord Bayberry." He frowned. "No, give me another day, I think. The veil has been particularly recalcitrant lately. I shall return as quickly as I can, but don't worry until the day after tomorrow."

His mother trembled and raised her chin. "Be careful, Theo. *Please.*"

"Of course, Mother. Always." He grinned and kissed her on the cheek.

Juniper had stiffened at the mention of Lord Bayberry, but he said nothing until Theo turned to him.

"Bayberry, sir?"

"Don't worry, Juniper. In fact, what I want most for you to do is get a little rest. You've been very brave, and I appreciate it more than I can say." He smiled kindly at the young fairy, who stood at rigid attention before him. Juniper's eyes, too, were shadowed with weariness, but his eyes gleamed in the lamplight.

"Someone must stand guard," Juniper said earnestly.

Theo could not deny this, so he said, "I will ask you to stand guard a little longer. I cannot ask my father or Anselm to do it, since they've been riding out in the cold all day. But after a few hours, I'm sure one of them will relieve you. In the meantime, perhaps you can be the one to tell everyone that Lord Selby and Miss Firethorn have been found safely. Mother, you ought to go to bed as well."

Juniper nodded.

Theo put a hand on Juniper's shoulder and said, "Thank you, my friend."

Juniper let out a breath like a muffled sob, and said, "You're welcome, sir."

After another reassuring smile for his mother, Theo strode away to the stairs and up to the suite he shared with Lily. He slipped in, closing the door behind himself, and walked quietly through the sitting rooms to the bedroom they now shared. It had been his alone, with Lily spending her nights in the opposite suite for those few tense weeks after the wedding, but since their reconciliation, she had slept in his room every night.

She had not woken at his entrance. He knelt beside the bed and kissed her cheek, then murmured, "My love, I would speak with you before I go again. Will you wake up a little?" He brushed her cheek with the back of his fingers, smiling at her in the darkness as she answered sleepily.

"Theo?"

"I must go back, for I've promised to finish a game with a Fair lord."

She sucked in a startled breath and sat up. "What? I don't understand."

His voice was warm and remorseful. "I didn't mean to wake you so thoroughly. Fenton and Miss Firethorn are safely in guest suites downstairs, though Fenton will feel better once Lord Mosswing arrives. I've given my word to Lord Bayberry to return to finish a game of bargains. I will return to you as quickly as I can."

In the shadows of the room, her face was only a pale oval above him as he knelt at the bedside, and he could make out little of her expression. "Don't worry, my love. I only wanted to kiss you before I left, and I thought…" He hesitated, then said even more softly, "I hoped you might want to kiss me too."

Lily cupped his face in her warm hands and leaned closer. With a sigh of deep satisfaction, he leaned in to her embrace. He put his arms around her waist, and her fingertips tickled the nape of his neck, and he nearly groaned with joy.

"Oh, Lily," he murmured into her ear. "I hate to leave, even for a little while."

Her soft cheek brushed his, and she said, "I hate you leaving too." She took a tremulous breath and tightened her arms around him. "Your voice sounds better. Do you feel better?"

With exquisite care, she touched the tender skin behind his ear, then trailed her fingertip down the side of his neck. He flinched almost imperceptibly, for the memory of the pain was still fresh, even if the pain was gone.

She pulled away with tears in her eyes. "I'm sorry," she whispered.

"I saw Cedar, and I feel absolutely fine. It is just reflex, my love." He took her hand and leaned into it, her palm flat upon his neck. Her hand was warm and soft, and her touch was so gentle, that the last, lingering hold of Larch's violence upon his memory faded. He turned to kiss her palm, then her wrist, then smiled at her.

"It's dangerous, isn't it?"

He chuckled so low she might not have heard it, if she had not been so close, breathing the sweet salt scent of his skin. "I do not want to lie to you, my love, so I will not say that it is safe. But do not worry too much for me. Sometimes I can be a little bit clever, and I think I might be able to use this."

Lily's arms tightened on him.

"Also—" He leaned closer and pressed a line of kisses from her cheek to her ear. "I've never been more motivated to come back home. I shall not do anything unnecessarily foolish."

She gave a half laugh, half sob into his neck, and said, "I believe you, and yet I'm not entirely reassured. I love you, Theo. Please be safe."

With more kisses, reassurances, and heartfelt declarations of love, they made their farewells.

Theo closed the door to the room and leaned against the wall for a moment, for he found to his surprise that he was trembling from head to toe, and his eyes were damp with tears.

Though every part of him longed to stay with his beloved wife, it was not entirely that desire which made his heart thunder within him and his chest feel tight with unexpected sobs for which he did not have time. Instead, it was the desperately, achingly deep relief and joy that she loved him enough to weep at his departure.

To be sure, she had given every sign of adoring him, albeit in a quieter way than he showed his own adoration. She had comforted him when he was distraught, hurting, and exhausted.

But for all that Theo showed the world a carefree, delighted version of himself, he had felt the pain of their distance after the wedding deeply. Her sweet tears of fear for him, so tenderly offered, were balm that soothed any last memories of that pain.

With one last, shuddering breath, he focused on the task at hand and set off to the kitchen.

Anselm met him there with a plate, having already made and delivered a tray to Crocus in her room. "I've sent a message to Lord Mosswing already."

Theo thanked him and ate hurriedly. "I'm off. Don't worry too much."

"I can't help it," Anselm muttered.

"Well, don't wait up for me, anyway. It will be hours until I'm back. Certainly no earlier than tomorrow morning, and likely not until the following evening. Get some sleep. I asked Juniper to stand guard a little longer, until you or Father or someone else could relieve him. He's tired, but he's warm and fed, and he'll last a little longer. You and Father have been out in the cold all day." Theo almost added, *I see your hands shaking*, but held his tongue. Instead, when he finished the pork pie and glass of rich milk, he steered Anselm out into the hallway and said again, "Go get some sleep, my friend."

Anselm said, "Be careful."

"As always." Theo grinned.

A minute later, Theo set off back to the Fair Lands.

CHAPTER SEVENTEEN
Fair Hospitality

The veil seemed particularly agitated as Theo traversed it back toward Lord Bayberry's estate. The young man spent nearly three hours avoiding a series of yawning holes in the tunnel floor which opened suddenly the moment before he would have stepped into them. He backtracked and tried another route, and then was forced to backtrack again.

At last, a little frustrated and trying not to be alarmed, he pressed both hands to the wall and let a wisp of magic seep into the squishy moss. His magic met one of the tendrils of the magic underlying the veil itself and caressed it, soothing the magic as one would calm a frightened horse. For almost an hour, he felt it wrestling and thrashing, slowing its protests little by little.

When it lay docile and compliant, he asked the veil to let him get to Lord Bayberry's estate. With a little wriggle of mingled dismay and delight, the veil cooperated. Theo had the feeling that the dismay was a warning, for it came with a sense of danger and an unpleasant scent of blood, though there was nothing in the veil with him from which such a scent could come.

He murmured his thanks and pressed his gratitude into the magic, though he doubted it could understand anything that specific.

A short time later, he opened a door into the moonlight clearing where he had left Lord Bayberry. The sky was strewn with a million twinkling stars, and the pink and cerulean streaks across the expanse seemed especially vibrant.

Two wolves lay in the clearing, and they stood at his appearance. They growled. The silvery moonlight glinted on their fur but did little to illuminate the surrounding forest.

"I've come to finish my game with Lord Bayberry," Theo said courteously. "Will you take me to him?"

One of the wolves turned away, as if it expected him to follow. Theo let the door to the veil close behind him and stepped forward. The other wolf, with a low growl, followed him.

The wolves escorted Theo through the wood on silent feet. Theo would have had trouble following them if they had stayed in the shadows, but they kept to the open spaces of the forest.

After nearly an hour of walking, he came upon an enormous manor nestled in the hillside as though it had grown there. The walls were dark wood and stone, and in the shadows Theo could not pick out the limits of the house with any certainty. The door he faced was easily twelve feet tall, and it was flanked by windows of green and blue glass that gleamed darkly in the moonlight.

The wolf in front of him approached the door, which opened without a sound, and Theo followed the wolf inside. Behind him came the second wolf, and then the door closed.

The entrance hall was lit by a chandelier high above, which cast warm yellow light across the floor and upon the walls in odd patterns. Theo looked up to see that the chandelier was apparently made of hundreds of deer antlers, which gave it a wild, vaguely threatening air.

He followed the first wolf through the hall and to a door, where the wolf growled as it entered an enormous room carpeted in deep green moss.

Theo knocked upon the doorframe.

"My lord, I apologize for the wait, but I do hope the demonstration sufficed." Theo swept a low bow toward Lord Bayberry, who had stood in surprise. The dying embers of a fire glowed softly in a fireplace to his left.

The fairy's lips curled in irritation. He said, "You have returned alone."

"Yes, my lord. Thus I believe I ought to concede that you have bested me in this round." Theo frowned in gentle amusement.

"Is that so?" Lord Bayberry flicked a few fingers in the general direction of the wolves, and they sat at attention, their ears pricked toward Theo.

"It appears so, for your part of the bargain was to provide hospitality for three people for the night, yet the night is nearly gone and I am the only one here to partake of your hospitality. I fulfilled my side of it completely. I do hope you intend to honor your promise, my lord, for I am quite fatigued." Theo gave him a sparkling smile.

The fairy's emerald green eyes flickered, then he said in a low voice, "I cannot argue with that. You shall have the best of my hospitality for the night, in safety."

Theo bowed courteously. "Thank you, my lord. Let us please discuss the final bargain tomorrow, after I have had a little sleep."

One of the wolves growled low in his throat. The fairy's eyes glittered, but he said only, "As you say. Follow me."

He opened the door and led the way down a hall that was open to the sky. The crisp, cold sky was clear and bright with stars, and Theo breathed in the scent of moonlight, snow, and Fair spruce and pine. Lord Bayberry and his wolves escorted Theo down the long hallway and down a large, graceful stair to another corridor. This one was floored in white marble and patches of moss. The walls were polished wood stained a deep blood red, and the ceiling above them was indistinct, lit by mist that emanated its own warm yellow light.

"You may stay here." Lord Bayberry opened a wooden door inlaid with gold. The design was that of a forest upon a mountain hillside, and a hundred wolves with golden eyes peeked from behind the intricately carved trees.

"I commend you on your excellent taste," said Theo, with genuine admiration in his voice. "Even your door is lovely, though it is undoubtedly different than what is currently fashionable in the human world. This is beautiful work."

Lord Bayberry's golden eyes flickered in what Theo took to be surprise, though with the Fair Folk it was rarely safe to assume anything. "Thank you," he said cautiously. He gestured gracefully for Theo to enter, and the young man did so with a smile.

To the left side of the room was a fireplace with a large flagstone hearth. Wood was laid in it, though it was not yet lit, and a neat stack of wood beside it offered plenty of fuel.

"I shall fetch you for breakfast. Would you like me to start the fire for you?"

"Yes, please, unless it will cost me."

The Fair lord stepped into the room and flicked his fingers at the fireplace, which blazed into cheerful flames.

"Thank you, my lord," Theo said.

Lord Bayberry looked the young man over with fascinated eyes but said nothing else before he turned away.

"Good night!" said Theo cheerfully. He closed the door and began to explore the room.

The room was entirely carpeted in soft, dark moss, which had little patches of tiny pink flowers near the walls. A wooden table stood near an enormous window which looked out upon a valley with a little stream burbling through it, all silvered by the moonlight that peeked through the clouds at intervals. The table had a pitcher of cold, clear water upon it, an empty basin, and a little bar of soap that smelled like the winter forest outside.

Theo did not at first see the bed, until he noticed the indentations cut into the stone wall. The steps, for so they were, led up to a little stone landing which gave access to a spacious platform hanging from the stone roof. Fairy lights lined the edges of the platform and danced along the edges of the ceiling and under the platform, lending a constantly shifting warm light to the room. When Theo climbed up to investigate the platform, he found a soft mattress of down topped with fine linen sheets and the enormous pelt of a white bear as a blanket. It swung gently on thick ropes.

The bed would have been warm enough even without a fire, but Theo felt that enjoying that little bit of hospitality would honor his host, so he stripped down to his underclothes and used only the sheet. For five minutes, he reviewed his plan for the following day, and then he drifted easily to sleep, enjoying the unfamiliar sensation of the bed swaying slightly with his every movement.

Theo slept deeply and well, secure in the knowledge that his friends were safe. Despite Cedar's healing magic, which had soothed the pain of Larch's attack and given him strength that carried through the hours afterward, he was still bone tired, and so he did not wake until the knock sounded upon the door the following morning.

He blinked at the ceiling, momentarily disoriented. Brilliant white light poured through the window, but it was below the hanging bed, putting Theo in shadow. The ceiling above him was now revealed to be made of a translucent rose quartz, or the Fair equivalent, which nearly glowed in the morning sun.

A profusion of vines crept up a wall opposite his bed, blooming in scarlet, crimson, fuchsia, and a purple so deep it seemed black.

The knock sounded again, and Theo started up.

He clambered down the steps in the wall. "Just a moment!" he called as he pulled on his clothes again. He straightened his vest and jacket before opening the door with a delighted smile.

"Good morning!" He beamed at Lord Bayberry. "I hope you slept as well as I did."

The Fair lord eyed him suspiciously. "Very well, thank you." Then, with a hint of amusement, he added, "I thought we might have breakfast before beginning the third bargain."

Theo said brightly, "What a delightful offer, my lord, but I fear I must decline. I am human, you see. But please don't abstain on my account."

Lord Bayberry said nothing. He led Theo through a wide hall with a wooden floor inlaid in intricate knotted patterns. They stepped out onto a wide stone patio that looked over the valley Theo had seen from the window the previous night. In the cold morning light, a faint dusting of snow was visible on the flagstones and on the tops of the distant trees visible over the low stone wall edging the patio.

Lord Bayberry strode directly to a table which was already set with two plates. "That plate is human food," he said, the reassurance clear and unequivocal, if not warm or friendly. "I am not so mean a host as to deny a guest breakfast he can eat, though I confess my means of obtaining a variety of foods is limited."

The Fair lord's plate held a slab of very rare meat, a mound of something that looked like vibrant, sky-blue mashed potatoes, and a variety of roasted vegetables, most of which Theo had seen before at Cedar's house, when they had shared a meal. Theo had, of course, not eaten any of them, having been provided a meal of human food instead, but he could imagine what they might taste like from the scent.

His plate, by contrast, held an enormous slab of steaming, crusty bread thickly spread with some sort of fruit spread, and a generous slice of cheese.

Theo blinked and said, in genuine gratitude, "Thank you, my lord. All of that is human food?"

"Yes. Water is safe for you, I believe. I have had it heated, but I have no tea or other safe beverage for you." Lord Bayberry's voice was tight, and Theo imagined he was both embarrassed and irritated by this lack.

"This is perfectly satisfactory, my lord, and I pray you think no more of it, for I did not expect any breakfast at all." Theo gave him a sparkling smile.

With stiff courtesy, Lord Bayberry indicated that Theo should sit first.

If it had been up to the Fair lord, they would have eaten in a tense silence. The golden-eyed wolves sat nearby, and their steady attention might have unnerved someone with more fragile nerves than Theo.

But Theo was not so easily daunted, and he kept up a steady flow of questions, most of which could not be easily answered in one word alone.

"How do you obtain human food, my lord?"

"I was given it by the ambassador to Ruloth some years ago, and I have kept it fresh in case of need."

"Do you often have need of human food?"

"Never before." The Fair lord's eyes gleamed with cold amusement. "I've never needed to keep a human alive for long. How long do humans live without food?"

"Oh, it varies for many reasons, but skipping a meal won't kill most of us. Nonetheless, we do like to eat at regular intervals." Theo grinned. "Your wolves are marvelously intelligent, I think. They knew exactly who I was and where to take me, and they seemed to understand my words. How do you manage that?"

Lord Bayberry's lips lifted in a wolfish smile. "Magic," he said succinctly. "Do you always talk so much, Overton?"

"Perhaps I'm nervous, my lord," Theo said serenely, giving no sign that this was actually the case. "I have heard you are rather terrifying, but this does not align with my own observations, for to me, you seem sophisticated and hospitable. I should very much like to discuss literature with you over tea someday."

The Fair lord's golden eyes gleamed. "Do you always trust your own limited observations over those of more well-informed persons?" he asked.

"Only when it serves my desire to believe the best of someone." Theo smiled warmly, as if inviting Lord Bayberry into his confidence. "For I do dearly love to find the good in someone when it has been deeply buried."

The fairy laughed, the sound bright and hard as ice cracking under the weight of one's boots. "Have you had much experience with Fair Folk, Overton?"

Theo tilted his head. "Not as much as you have, my lord," he allowed, "but more than most humans. Certainly there is much I have yet to learn."

"Indeed." Lord Bayberry gave another toothy smile, and yet, despite the warning in his every movement, Theo imagined that he might, if he wanted, be almost as friendly as Lord Willowvale.

"Have you heard of me?" Theo asked.

"No," Lord Bayberry said. "Should I have?"

"Oh, no, I am not so arrogant as to think anyone should have heard of me. I was merely curious." But the knowledge that Lord Bayberry did not know of his actions as the Wraith, or had not connected those stories with Theo himself, seemed useful.

Theo drank the steaming water Lord Bayberry had provided in lieu of tea, and it was surprisingly satisfying. The patio was quite cold, and his fingers were already chilled. The fairy seemed unaffected by the temperature and icy breeze.

At last, when Lord Bayberry had finished his meal and dabbed politely at his mouth with the napkin, he said, "Let us begin. What is your starting position for the final bargain?"

"In two weeks, I would like for you to come witness an event at the palace."

Lord Bayberry blinked, an extraordinary display of surprise during negotiations. "What event?" he said cautiously.

"I am sorry, my lord, but that's just the thing; I can't explain it, or it won't have its proper effect. I've thought about your dilemma a great deal, and I think you'll find it quite satisfying." Theo sparkled at him.

"What dilemma do you think I have?" The Fair lord's voice was hard.

"I hope I haven't overstepped," Theo said, with warmth and kindness. "I thought this whole game was because you were bored, for surely if you were truly, deeply offended by the intrusion upon your lands, you would have merely killed my friends and me without giving me this chance to entertain you and thus save our lives."

Lord Bayberry's cold expression grew colder. "I am bored, and yet I hate the politics of court. Why should I go to court on your behalf?"

Theo poured another cup of steaming water and wrapped his hands around it. The icy wind cut through his jacket with surprising ease.

"Well, I expect the event you will witness will be entertaining, one way or the other. In exchange for your witness, I offer you an afternoon's diversion."

The Fair lord stood, graceful and distant, and strode away to look across the distant hills. His fur cloak billowed in his wake.

"You overstep your rights here as a guest, Overton," he said quietly. "You are not a friend to be given entree into my private thoughts and frustrations here at the edge of the Fair Lands."

"Of course not, my lord," Theo said, his voice soft and compassionate. "I would not dare presume anything of the sort. I thought merely to offer you something that seemed to my own tastes and preferences to be desirable, if I were in your place. For it seems to me that you are entirely too discerning and sophisticated to turn down the opportunity to witness something I believe will be unique in the Fair Court. Perhaps it might even be talked about for some time, and if so, wouldn't it be desirable to have been present for it?"

"What do you expect me to do in this unprecedented event of yours?" Lord Bayberry turned and, with arms folded across his chest, regarded Theo from the other side of the patio. His yellow eyes gleamed, and the fur cloak that hung from his shoulders shifted in the wind.

"Nothing. I desire merely your presence."

"You offer only entertainment?" The Fair lord's lips lifted in thin amusement. "It must be unusual indeed to justify letting you live."

"I am so confident in the unusual nature of what will transpire, my lord, that if you are not surprised or entertained by anything that happens, I will concede the round and thus the entire challenge to you, and you may kill me right there in the presence of the king and all others present."

The wolves shifted, and one of them growled low in his throat, as if contemplating this intriguing possibility.

"When does the challenge end, then, if I accept?"

"At midnight Monday, two weeks from tomorrow. I do believe it will happen in the throne room of the Fair palace."

"What are you planning?" Lord Bayberry's eyes had sharpened with interest.

Theo said gently, "My lord, if I tell you, it will hardly be surprising, will it?"

The fairy chuckled and said, "It was worth a try. Why should I believe you will be there at all, since you risk so much?"

"I came back last night, didn't I?" Theo laughed lightly. "I will not say I have never lied, my lord, and I know Fair Folk hold that as a deep flaw of the human species, but in this, I will do everything within my power to be there, for it serves another purpose of mine as well."

"If you do not entertain or startle me, I will kill you in front of everyone," the Fair lord said, with precision and a sense of enjoyment. "If—"

Theo held up a hand. "My lord, I cannot promise that *I* will entertain or startle you, although certainly I may. I promise only that you will be entertained or surprised by the events that take place."

"Very well. If I am not entertained or surprised, I will kill you in front of everyone. If I am, then I have lost the round and the game, and I shall have to acknowledge you as friend." This last was said with sharp dismay.

"As much as that prospect displeases you, my lord, I shall account it an honor to reciprocate," Theo said with warmth.

"Why?" Lord Bayberry snapped.

"Shall I tell you all my secrets?" Theo laughed. "Perhaps I merely like making friends, or perhaps it is the sense of victory over a tough challenge, or perhaps it will merely be the triumph of living another day. Does it matter?"

The Fair lord glared at him. "Do you delight in being infuriating?"

Theo fairly sparkled with delight. "I will admit I sometimes find it entertaining, but my lord, please understand that it is a personal failing on my part, not a personal affront to you."

One of the wolves growled. Lord Bayberry snapped a finger at it.

The icy wind whipped past Theo's face, cutting through his thick jacket with ease. He suppressed a shiver.

Lord Bayberry said at last, "Our agreement is settled, and I grow tired of your ridiculous cheer, as if both I and our game are some joke. You have one hour to leave my lands."

Theo bowed deeply. "I understand, my lord. Please believe me when I say I fully understand the grave nature of our game. Thank you for your hospitality last night and this morning."

The Fair lord's eyes flickered in cold amusement. "Until Monday two weeks hence." He gave a faint bow, just shallow enough to edge upon rude.

Theo gave him a sweet, warm smile, as if they were already the best of friends, and said, "Farewell, Lord Bayberry." Then he opened a door to the veil and stepped in.

CHAPTER EIGHTEEN
Gratitude

The first thing that brought Fenton back to wakefulness was a warm, golden sort of comfort that spread from his right shoulder, the one which had been stung by the manticore, through his torso and down throughout his body. His mind felt bubbly and bright, like a glass of the finest sparkling wine, alight with exuberant hope.

It was a thoroughly unfamiliar feeling. Lord Fenton Selby, for all his many admirable qualities, was more inclined to quiet, deliberate joy than effervescent delight, and even joy was not entirely familiar. He was certainly not unhappy, as a general rule, but joyful was a bit of a stretch, seeing as how he had no beloved wife with which to share his life.

Golden light filtered through his eyelids, and he realized it must be daylight already. He blinked, then squeezed his eyes shut, for the sun was high and the room was even brighter than he'd imagined. There was a tall figure nearly silhouetted beside the bed, just removing his hand from Fenton's shoulder.

"Lord Mosswing?" he murmured. "Oh." That explained the golden warmth, which must be Cedar's healing magic.

"I came as soon as I heard." The dark-skinned Fair lord pulled a chair from near the wall and sat a few feet away.

Fenton blinked at him, taking in his casual attire. Lord Cedar Mosswing must have come in haste indeed, for he was dressed more simply than Fenton had ever seen him. A cream shirt of a fabric somewhere between silk and the finest gauzy linen lay open halfway down his dark chest. He wore a fine golden chain with a teardrop shaped gem the color of his turquoise eyes that glittered against his skin. Fenton blinked, momentarily stunned by the realization that Lord Mosswing was not married, and there was no logical reason for this. If anyone could understand his longing for a wife, it would be this Fair lord, who had been similarly fortunate in so many ways and yet remained alone.

But for his friends.

"Where is Theo?" Fenton sat up, checking to see that he was modest and that the world didn't spin before he slid out of the bed and stood.

Anselm, who stood just inside the door, said, "He went back to the Fair Lands just before midnight. Do you need help dressing, sir? I sent to your estate earlier and had some clothes brought." He gestured to the chest at the end of the bed, where a stack of neatly folded clothes waited.

The young nobleman looked down at himself and smiled ruefully. His shirt was one of Sir Theodore's old ones, apparently left in the drawer in case of emergencies. Theo was slighter of build than Fenton, and one of his shirts would not have fit in the shoulders or chest. His trousers were a little worse for wear, with a few spots of blood and dirt upon the cuffs, but could perhaps be salvaged with a good cleaning.

"I'm all right. Thank you, Lord Mosswing."

"Cedar, please." The Fair lord looked at him thoughtfully, then stood. "I commend you. A manticore is no mean opponent." He bowed and stepped toward the door. "I will stay for lunch, I think, in case you need a little more magic."

"Thank you," Fenton said again.

"Lunch will be on the patio, sir," said Anselm.

Fenton murmured thanks yet again, feeling a warm rush of gratitude.

Cedar and Anselm stepped out and closed the door behind them.

Fenton dressed easily, feeling no trace of pain in his shoulder. His stomach growled, and when he straightened from pulling up the clean trousers, the room spun for a moment. He was ravenous, but it would not do to be rude about it. Lunch could not be too far away.

Despite the brief moment of dizziness, his overall feeling was something approaching bliss; other than his concern for Miss Firethorn and Theo, everything seemed suffused with a deep, abiding peace.

He smoothed the front of his new trousers, pulled on clean socks and low boots, and splashed water on his face. He ran a comb through his hair and examined a few tiny pieces of moss that fell to the vanity. He would like a bath at some point, but for now, he felt delightfully refreshed and ready for both lunch and news.

As he strode through the hall toward the patio, he marveled at the beauty of the Overton manor. It was as familiar to him as his own, and yet he appreciated it anew.

The warmth of the autumn sun felt like a benediction when he stepped onto the patio, and the crisp, cool air formed a delightful contrast.

Cedar and Crocus stood to greet him, and he bowed courteously.

"I trust you're well," he said to Crocus.

"Yes." She smiled at him, and her eyes seemed not only friendlier, but warmer than they ever had been before. "I am glad to see you well, Lord Selby."

"I believe that is thanks to your courage, Miss Firethorn. I…"

A fuzzy, disjointed memory of leaning upon her, of his face nearly in her hair, brought heat to his face. He said, with a little gasp of mortification, "I am so sorry."

She blinked at him, her expression showing only gentle confusion. "What could you be sorry for?"

He covered his mouth with one trembling hand, then put his hands back at his sides, facing the embarrassment squarely. "I have a muddled memory, or perhaps it was a dream, of leaning upon you, without any respect for your dignity at all, and I am horrified, Miss Firethorn, to think that you might think me the sort of person who would willingly violate a lady's person." He caught his breath, feeling that he ought to continue apologizing, while simultaneously wishing that the stones of the patio would open and swallow him.

Crocus stared at him in what appeared to be utter confusion, then turned to Cedar. "Are you sure you didn't give him too much?" she asked.

"Reasonably sure." Cedar stood and took his arm solicitously. "Are you dizzy?"

"Only a little." Fenton let himself be led toward the table. "Miss Firethorn, can you ever forgive me?"

The Fair lady's ice blue eyes held his. "Lord Selby, I think Lord Mosswing's magic has affected you more than you realize. If you don't recall, you saved me from a manticore, and in so doing, you were stung. I took you to His Majesty Silverthorn's dance floor. There is a tradition that if two people dance together on the royal dance floor for twenty-four hours without stopping or speaking, they may together ask one boon of the king. We nearly made it, but… you were so very ill, my lord." She stopped, as if her throat had closed with emotion.

That could not be right. She had been furious with him for lying about Juniper.

He swallowed. He did remember the manticore, with its strange fury and the oddly segmented legs beneath a human head. The memory of the burning agony of his shoulder brought an echoing surge of nausea.

"Sit down, Lord Selby," Cedar said gently.

At this moment, Anselm came out with a tray bearing several plates. As he set them down in front of Fenton, the door opened and Sir Theodore, Lady Overton, and Lily emerged, followed by Lady Selby.

Fenton stood to greet them, feeling a swell of affection and appreciation. The Overtons had been so kind to him over the years, and Lily made Theo ridiculously happy, which was what any good friend would want. His mother, of course, had come just after Anselm had sent to the Selby estate for a change of clothes.

Lady Selby quickly crossed to him and wrapped her arms around him. He returned the embrace. He felt a little dizzy and strange, but not ill.

"How do you feel, Fenton?" Sir Theodore asked kindly. "Sit down and rest while you eat."

Fenton sank back down into the chair and his mother took the seat just to his left, resting her hand on his shoulder a moment as if to reassure herself that he was whole. He was about to begin eating when he realized he was the only one with food in front of him. He looked up questioningly.

Sir Theodore said, "Go on. The rest of us had breakfast and can wait for lunch."

The young nobleman's cheeks heated, but he nodded.

"How are you feeling?" Sir Theodore asked again.

Fenton swallowed his bite and said quietly, "Fine, sir." He felt Lily's eyes on him and added, "Did Theo say when he would be back?"

"As soon as he can be," Lily answered. "Today or tomorrow."

"And Juniper's all right?" Fenton glanced at Crocus, but looked down again, feeling unaccountably shy.

Sir Theodore said, "Indeed. We've been searching for you and Miss Firethorn for since you left, and Juniper stood watch for any sign of Lord Larch while we did so. We ate breakfast together and he's taking a nap now. Theo asked for a little binding magic before he left, so Juniper was quite tired. He asked me to give you his regards."

Lily said, with a hint of worry in her voice, "Binding magic? Again?"

Sir Theodore said quietly, "He assured me it was only in case of emergencies, and he didn't foresee any emergencies."

Fenton closed his eyes in relief.

Sir Theodore said, "Anselm, you ought to go back to bed after lunch. I got a few good hours of sleep this morning, and I've had enough tea to keep me going a while longer. I told Juniper he should sleep until he got hungry, and he had a good breakfast, so I doubt we'll see him before supper. You and I will take shifts again tonight, so I'd like you well-rested, if you please. We'll manage dinner, so sleep as long as you want."

Anselm nodded. "Yes, sir."

The rest of the conversation flowed easily around Fenton; eating took a little more concentration than usual, and he felt quietly satisfied with the world in general, though a twinge of concern for Theo would not let him entirely reach the blissful state that Cedar's magic seemed to justify. The birds sang in the nearby trees, and the leaves rustled with a cheerful sort of expectancy.

Autumn was well on its way, and soon there would be pumpkin tarts and spiced teas, half a hundred varieties of squash soup, spice cakes, apple crumbles, spiced cider, apple tarts, and a thousand other warm, comforting foods and scents, a thousand things to make one happy to be at home by the fire.

Anselm quietly removed the dishes when Fenton was finished and replaced them with more, until the young man looked up in tired amazement and said, "Anselm, I do believe you're trying to stuff me like a goose. I'm quite finished, thank you."

Anselm, who never would have broken propriety with any other nobleman outside the Overton household, put his hand on Fenton's shoulder for a moment. "Good. What else can I do for you, sir?"

Fenton found his gaze drawn inexorably back to Crocus, who had listened to the conversation without saying much. "Nothing. Thank you." Then, remembering Sir Theodore's words, he added, "Don't stay awake on my account."

Lady Selby and Lady Overton shared a look which Fenton, in his slightly fuzzy state, did not understand, and Lady Selby spoke for nearly the first time. "Lady Overton, Mrs. Overton, would you mind walking with me for a few minutes? I'd like to admire the burning bushes over there." She gestured gracefully to a bank of graceful bushes that were halfway between their summer green and the exuberant autumn scarlet some distance away.

Lady Overton leaned over and murmured in her husband's ear for a moment, then rose. "Of course, we would be delighted to!" She smiled warmly at her friend and Lily, then turned to Fenton with a conspiratorial smile.

Sir Theodore stood. "Lord Mosswing, would you care to accompany me to the stable? Mrs. Overton's brother has a horse here that I'm not sure you've seen. Theo picked him out."

Fenton had the strange feeling that everyone had conspired to leave him with Crocus in a semblance of privacy, albeit within the confines of propriety, as the ladies were not far away.

This impression was confirmed when Crocus, too, began to rise, and Lady Overton said, "Stay, Miss Firethorn. I'd rather not leave Lord Selby entirely alone yet, injured as he was. Surely you don't mind, do you?"

Crocus shook her head wordlessly, then watched Lady Overton walk away with a strange glint in her eye.

"They seem to have agreed that we must talk," she said, with a chagrinned smile.

"It seems so." Fenton found himself smiling back at her. She really was quite lovely, with her ice blue eyes and her delicate features. "I wish you'd take off your glamour," he said, and then put his head in his hands. "I am so sorry," he gasped. "My tongue has betrayed me. I do not mean to be so ill-mannered. Please forgive me."

Crocus gave a soft huff of laughter. "It is done, Lord Selby. There's no offense in that to forgive." She tilted her head inquisitively as she smiled at him. Her blue hair cascaded over her shoulders, just as it had when it appeared brown, but to his eyes it seemed even more beautiful than before.

The affection in her eyes seemed perhaps a little unjustified, for he did not think he had done anything particularly admirable, but he let it warm his heart anyway.

Fenton considered his words carefully for any hint of impropriety, then said, "Miss Firethorn, I am in awe of your courage and kindness in saving my life. Thank you." He stood and bowed. "Yet I confess a lingering discomfort, for I have a vague and slightly addled memory of you saying something about a bargain for my life."

Crocus licked her rosebud lips and said quietly, "You need not worry about that, my lord. I made a bargain of my own free will, and I will deal with the consequences without endangering anyone else."

Fenton, still standing said, "No, Miss Firethorn, I cannot accept that."

"What do you think you can do about it?"

"I do not know yet, but I am not in the habit of letting beautiful maidens sacrifice themselves for me."

Crocus could not help her soft peal of laughter.

Fenton's gentle brown eyes darkened, and he said, stiffly, "I am sorry you think so little of me. Nevertheless, I do intend to help you, if I can."

The Fair lady smiled up at him and said, "Please sit down, my lord. You misunderstand me."

He sank back into the chair, feeling grateful and tired and slightly dizzy. The bright sunshine warming his shoulders also caught Crocus's hair and the smooth, pale curve of her cheek, and he could not speak for the beauty that suddenly overwhelmed him.

"I do not mean it as an insult," she said gently. "But you have already suffered more than enough for my sake. Let us speak of something else."

Fenton's tender heart twisted at this, for he did not intend to let her face this bargain, whatever it was, alone. Yet he smiled and said, "What topic of conversation would please you, Miss Firethorn?"

She leaned forward. "I would like to know why your friends have conspired to leave us alone together. What do they know that I do not?"

His cheeks flushed, and he looked down at the white tablecloth. "I do not know," he murmured.

"Really?" she asked. "You have no idea?" There was a hint of laughter in her voice.

Fenton blushed more deeply. "I did not say that I had no idea, Miss Firethorn," he said almost inaudibly. "I can make a guess."

"Please do." She gave him a sparkling smile, and the beauty of it stole his breath.

He swallowed and looked down again. He studied the pattern of the lace at the edge of the tablecloth and the play of the light refracted through the water in his tumbler.

Miss Firethorn was one of the Fair Folk. Magic ran in her veins. She fairly glowed in the sunlight, with her sweet smile and her shining eyes and her tumbling blue locks.

It was foolish indeed to set one's heart upon a Fair lady. There were songs about the heartbreak that awaited any man who dared dream of earning the love of a Fair maiden. There was even a song of a human maiden who had lost her heart to one of the male Fair Folk; she pined away for his strange, alien beauty for half a century, never settling for a human husband. Fenton had never imagined that he would see his future in that sad story.

Yet here he was.

"Lord Selby," she prompted gently.

"They meant to be kind, of course." He gave a faint, melancholy smile, and added, "Miss Firethorn, if I might prevail upon you, I find myself rather fatigued after all. Might I ask for you to tell me a little more of yourself? I would find it easier to listen than to be amusing."

She studied his face, and he wondered, with a little trepidation, whether she realized he was already grieving the loss of her presence in his life. Soon she would return to the Fair Lands.

Aside from that pesky matter of the bargain she had made, which he would need to discuss with Theo, he was unlikely to see her much more in the future.

How dull the world would be without her. Theo's sparkling friendship and Lily's quiet kindness would distract him of course, but they would not be able to entirely fill the hole.

Crocus said hesitantly, "Well, my lord, if you must know, I was a servant in the house of Lord and Lady Kauri, but I was not born a servant. I was bargained into servitude in childhood. My mother died during a conflict among the Fair Folk of the hills, though for unrelated causes, and my father died in the war with Aricht. I realized that my father's bargain had died with him and I ought to be free, but it took me some time to muster the courage to take the freedom that was mine by right."

Fenton inclined his head toward her. "I have seen your courage," he murmured.

The Fair lady gave a shy little laugh, and if she had been anyone else, Fenton would have wondered whether it had been designed to seem vulnerable and appealing. But Crocus had never, as far as he knew, indicated that sort of interest in him, nor had she found entertainment in getting his, or any other man's, attention. Nor, for that matter, had she shown any tendency toward calculation in her displays of emotion, other than hiding any sign of vulnerability.

"What you saw was desperation," she admitted quietly. "And…" She stopped, her voice a little choked.

It would have been terribly rude to press her to continue. He wanted to say something kind and reassuring.

"Well, I do thank you," he said, and it sounded thin and inadequate against the immensity of his emotion. But his mind felt fuzzy and warm, and he could no longer keep his eyes open in the bright golden sunlight.

"You are tired, Lord Selby. I shouldn't wonder. I've never heard of anyone living after being stung by a manticore." She caught her breath in what sounded like a sob.

"I owe you my life, Miss Firethorn." With great effort, he managed to open his eyes and smile at her, and then, in a moment of boldness, said, "You are as beautiful as you are courageous."

Crocus blinked, then smiled gently. "I think Lord Mosswing's magic has affected your tongue, my lord."

Fenton closed his eyes again, replaying the words in case they had been offensive. With his eyes still closed, he murmured, "I am sorry if I've said it badly."

"It is not the words but the sentiment, my lord. I don't believe you're thinking quite clearly. I will ask our hosts to take you up to bed."

"No, I'm fine." He couldn't seem to open his eyes, but he managed to say, "You were beautiful before the magic made me fuzzy."

She gave a sparkling laugh and said, "Be that as it may, my lord, I think you are tired."

He didn't hear her.

It was a dream, of course, but it was a pleasant one which Fenton did not want to let go. Crocus, her ice blue eyes warm on his face, danced with him through the garden. There was a white rose in her hair, signifying virtue, purity, and innocence; the creamy white petals set off her blue hair perfectly.

"Shall I give him a little more magic?"

Fenton felt he ought to have an opinion on this topic, but he was far too tired and muzzy to come to any kind of decision about an answer before a gentle, golden comfort seeped into him. He sighed and mumbled, "Thank you."

"You're welcome." Cedar stood over him, smiling. "I'm leaving for the Fair Lands. Please give my regards to Theo when you see him."

Fenton blinked blearily at the Fair lord. "Farewell, then. Thank you." He'd already said it, but it seemed like something that ought to be said again, given how much better he felt.

Cedar grinned, white teeth flashing, and gave him a fond pat on the shoulder. Then he strode off across the lawn. He opened a door to the veil as if he were walking into a large rhododendron and disappeared.

CHAPTER NINETEEN
Ambushed

As soon as Cedar stepped out of the veil onto his own front patio, he knew something was wrong. The transcendent joy that had filled him only moments before, after a certain delightful conversation with a Fair lady, receded behind wariness.

He opened his front door cautiously.

There was no one in the entrance hall, but the sense of wrongness, of an intrusion, remained. He stepped quietly toward the front parlor and peeked inside, then stepped in so he could see the far corner. When he extended his senses to try to pinpoint the Fair Folk, he could sense only that there were at least four of them, but not where they were.

From behind him, a cold voice said, "You are a traitor to the Fair Lands."

Cedar turned and stepped inside the parlor, avoiding the quick, almost silent attack by instinct.

Lord Oleander Larch stood in the doorway, his eyes blazing with righteous anger.

"That is not true," Cedar said. His voice was smooth and calm, as if a mild voice would calm Larch's fury. "I have never betrayed the Fair Lands."

"You supported the Rose." Lord Larch's sword flashed, and Cedar backed away. He was not armed; his swords were upstairs, for he rarely carried a weapon in the veil, and he certainly had not expected to need a weapon at the Overton manor.

Lord Larch waved the point of his sword far too close to Cedar's broad chest for comfort.

Cedar edged sideways, and the point of the sword flicked upward just as he got his hand upon the heavy candlestick upon the nearest table.

Larch stabbed at him, and Cedar stepped back, almost avoiding injury until Larch lunged again, faster than thought. The sword sank deep into Cedar's chest, and the Fair lord gave a strangled cry of pain.

With a snarl, Larch straightened and pulled the sword out, preparing to strike again. Cedar twisted and lunged himself, bringing the candlestick up to strike his startled opponent on the side of the head.

Larch stumbled to the side, stunned, and Cedar grabbed for the sword, but retreated when Larch whipped the blade up between them.

Larch took an unsteady step forward, and Cedar retreated again, edging around the sofa. Two other fairies stepped in the room behind Larch, both carrying swords.

The wound screamed for attention, but Cedar pushed the pain aside long enough to open a door into the veil and step into the darkness. Larch's scream of rage cut off abruptly as Cedar let the door close.

He pressed his healing magic into the wound, and in the safety and privacy of the veil, he let out a soft groan of pain. Then he set off back toward the house of his beloved.

Cedar stepped out of the veil at the edge of the lawn of the Overton estate. The cool night of the human world was fresh and alive with scents and sounds subtly different than those of the Fair Lands. Even after nearly one hundred visits, the world of humans seemed exotic and wonderful to him.

The Overton lawn was shadowed by maples and looming rhododendrons, and he strode confidently through the shadows toward the door. The Fair lady trailed behind him, her hand in his.

He knocked loudly upon the door, wincing as he did so.

"How badly does it hurt?" the Fair lady behind him asked.

"Not worth mentioning." Actually the wound was still rather painful, but it was hardly debilitating. He kept his voice steady to hide the pain, but he couldn't quite hide the catch in his breath when he raised his arm to knock again.

Anselm opened the door just as he began to knock.

"Lord Mosswing!" The servant blinked at him, then at the Fair lady. "Come in, my lord. What's wrong?"

"Is Theo here?"

"He hasn't returned from the Fair Lands yet." Anselm's voice betrayed his worry.

Cedar rocked back on his heels. "That's not good." Suddenly lightheaded, he put a hand against the wall and said, "Would you please ask Sir Theodore if he might speak with me? I would ask his hospitality for the night."

"Of course." Anselm's quick, perceptive gaze took in Cedar's posture. He added, "Please come sit down, my lord and lady." He led them to the nearest little sitting room, an intimate room painted a deep, soothing blue and decorated with numerous pen and ink drawings of various plant species.

Cedar gestured for the Fair lady with him to sit on a white velvet settee, and she did so, primly crossing her ankles and folding her hands in her lap atop the brilliant blue silk of her dress. Cedar stood beside her, leaning his left shoulder against the wall.

Several minutes later, Anselm returned with Sir Theodore and Lady Overton.

"Lord Mosswing? What brings you here at this time?" Sir Theodore smiled and bowed to the Fair lady, who stood to greet them.

"Sir Theodore, Lady Overton, this is Lady Poppy Miscanthus. Lady Miscanthus, Sir Theodore Overton and Lady Helena Overton, father and mother of my long-time friend Theo."

The Fair lady blinked and looked up at him. Her hair was a dense cloud of black corkscrew curls that stood out from her head. Her skin was even darker than Cedar's walnut tones, and her eyes were like shining black gems. She gave the Overtons a graceful bow, sweeping one arm forward, for Fair ladies did not curtsey as in the human custom. Then she looked back at Cedar.

Cedar continued, "This afternoon I was attacked in my home by Lord Larch and several of his men. I agree with you; I believe that he intends to take some sort of vengeance upon all those who aided the Rose. I have long loved Lady Miscanthus, but I kept my hope hidden, for I did not wish to have any suspicion fall upon her if my support for the Rose were discovered. After Theo's triumph, my part in supporting him became public."

He sagged against the wall, and Sir Theodore's sharp eyes saw the movement. "Sit down, Cedar," he said gently.

Cedar might have protested, but the sting of the wound was irksome, and it had been a very long day already. So he sat, careful not to lean back against the cushions of the settee, because he did not want to get blood upon the furniture.

"I thought, when His Majesty Silverthorn conceded to Theo, that the danger was past, and I made my hope known to Lady Miscanthus. She was gracious enough to honor me with the promise of her hand in marriage." He took her hand in his again and looked down, studying the rich cool black of her skin against his warmer brown tone. "While Lord Larch is still free and pursuing whatever vengeance he seeks, I could not leave her unprotected." He drew in a breath, a little unsteady now with the pain that seemed to be rising, and would have continued, but Sir Theodore spoke first.

"Of course she is welcome here, and we will protect her as well as we can. What of you, Cedar?" Sir Theodore could not see through the glamour, but he had obviously perceived something was amiss.

"I'm all right. Just a little bloodied and annoyed." Cedar frowned ruefully.

"Let me see it, if you please. None of us have your healing magic, but we can still bandage you up if necessary."

Cedar debated for a moment internally, then reluctantly let his glamour drop.

Poppy sucked in a quick breath, and he winced, wishing she did not have to see the blood.

"It's not that bad," he said, but Sir Theodore and Anselm had already stepped forward.

"Take off your jacket, please." Sir Theodore was all business, and he paused only to say, "Lady Overton, if you would be so kind as to show Lady Miscanthus to a guest suite, please. I'd like Anselm here with me."

Lady Overton looked toward Poppy with a kind smile. The Fair lady hesitated, then said, "I would rather stay, if I might."

Cedar frowned more deeply. "I'd rather you not have to see it."

She said, with the slightest edge in her soft voice, "Lord Mosswing, I do appreciate your care of my sensibilities and your consideration of my safety these last months, but if I am to be your wife, I should like you to trust me enough to let me see the cost of your heroism as well as the triumph. It would set my mind at ease to know exactly how serious the injury is, so that I do not have to imagine the worst."

Sir Theodore took a blanket from a chair in the corner and draped it over the back of the settee, then nodded that Cedar should sit back against it.

The young Fair nobleman did so, a little muzzy with fatigue and pain. "I'd rather you not see me grumble," he murmured, trying to keep his voice steady. "It's really not that bad, and the magic is already working." He fumbled with the buttons on his emerald green jacket, then his vest, and finally his cream silk shirt, which was damp with pale blue blood from his right shoulder nearly to his waist.

He gingerly pulled his arm through the sleeve and sat back, studying Sir Theodore's face in an attempt to avoid Poppy's eyes.

She slipped her hand into his without saying anything.

Sir Theodore sent Anselm off for hot water and a clean cloth to wash the wound, then said, "You're right. It could be a lot worse. It looks like it's nearly stopped bleeding. When did it happen?"

Fair blood was a pale, translucent blue, and on Cedar's dark skin the color was barely noticeable. He felt that it was wildly inappropriate for Poppy to see him half disrobed, but a small, secret part of him hoped she liked what she saw. Other than the deep, ugly gash, of course.

"Three hours ago, more or less, just as I arrived home from here. I went straight to Lady Miscanthus's house to fetch her and then into the veil." He pressed his lips together when Sir Theodore gently cleaned the wound, then continued, "The veil was unusually cooperative for me, but the walk was long this time. I wish I understood it the way Theo does."

Sir Theodore glanced up at his face. "I don't think anyone understands it. Theo works on instinct, more or less. You did excellently."

When Anselm returned, he and Sir Theodore carefully cleaned the wound, which seemed to hurt less already. Certainly the magic had been working, and by the end of the following day the wound would be entirely healed. The magic seemed to work more slowly on him than it had on Theo, but the wound was trivial in comparison to the one Theo had suffered in the Fair Lands. The tender care of these humans, whom Cedar thought of as family, was balm to his troubled heart.

He ignored the pain as much as he could and said, "Thank you, Sir Theodore."

The words were inadequate, but Theo's family knew more than most how restrained Fair Folk were, and perhaps they understood the depth of love in his words.

"You are most welcome." Sir Theodore met Cedar's turquoise gaze with an encouraging smile. "You're always welcome here, Cedar."

Cedar ducked his head a little, feeling his cheeks flush with pleasure and gratitude.

Sir Theodore helped him put on a new, clean shirt, a human one, for the buttons and collar were different and the cloth had a different texture. Theo had worn Fair clothes often in his exploits as the

Rose, but Cedar had never before worn human clothing. It was similar, but the differences seemed to accentuate the strangeness of this evening.

"You'll feel a great deal better after a good night's sleep, I imagine," said Sir Theodore. "Would you like a little brandy to help you get to sleep?"

Cedar hesitated, then shook his head. "No, thank you. I'd rather be alert in case… well, just in case."

Sir Theodore put a steadying hand on Cedar's elbow as he helped the Fair nobleman stand, and then steered him toward the door. "Should we put you and Lady Miscanthus in the suites nearest us, then? Anselm and I will take shifts on watch."

"I hate to ask it of you," Cedar replied, keeping his voice admirably steady, given how wobbly he felt. Nevertheless, his tone betrayed his concern. "I'm really not sure to what lengths Lord Larch would go. I don't believe he would target Lady Miscanthus—he has no reason to except her connection with me—but I could not risk it. Is Juniper still with you? Larch will definitely target him."

"Juniper is here and has not been seen at our estate, but he did see Larch some weeks ago around Lord Selby's estate, so it is not inconceivable Larch would extend his search to this area."

"I trust Lord Selby is well?"

"Much better, yes."

"Did either of you get any sleep today?" Cedar asked belatedly.

Sir Theodore frowned and said, "I'm off to bed as soon as you're settled. Anselm took a seven hour nap, and he'll be on watch until he gets sleepy."

Anselm added, "I'm quite wide awake, and my only objection is that my employer made me rest before he did himself."

Cedar laughed softly, as Anselm had intended.

Sir Theodore led them up the broad staircase and down the hall before he stopped at a door. "Let me give you this suite, and Lady Miscanthus can have the next one. Someone will stand watch at the top of the stairs all night."

Cedar bowed to his intended with all the grace and elegance of the Fair lord he was. "Goodnight, Lady Miscanthus."

"Goodnight, Lord Mosswing." She bowed to him with a small, admiring smile that made his pulse rush in his ears and the pain recede until he barely remembered it at all.

CHAPTER TWENTY
An Unexpected Invitation

The Fair evening was even colder than that of the human world, but no snow lay upon the ground. The brilliant green grass of summer had turned a crisp yellow-green, and each blade was edged by silvery frost that glinted in the last glow of sunset.

Theo strode up the steps and directly to the front door of Lord Willowvale's mansion. He knocked loudly.

A moment later, a servant opened the door. His golden eyes widened, and he said, "You!" in a soft, surprised voice.

"Good evening!" Theo beamed at him. "Would you please inquire with Lord Willowvale if he will see me?"

"Why?" The servant looked at him in open confusion.

"Because I'd like to visit him." Theo smiled as though wanting to visit Lord Willowvale were the most logical thing in the world. "You're Hemlock, aren't you? I trust you're fully recovered from that unpleasantness in the veil?"

"I am." The fairy hesitated, then added quietly, "sir."

"I am delighted to hear it," Theo said, all warmth and kindness. "I will wait here, if you think Lord Willowvale will not want me inside."

Hemlock hesitated, then nodded. "I will ask him if he will see you," he said.

Theo stood upon the broad patio while he waited. His breath fogged in the chilly air, and he resisted the urge to shiver. Instead, he took a deep, bracing breath, and thought of warm things. The warmth of Lily's embrace. The sweetness of her gray-blue eyes. The fire in his heart when he thought of how much he loved her.

He smiled to himself at the thought of Lord Bayberry's consternation at the conclusion of their game. Was it wrong to delight so sincerely in confounding arrogant Fair Folk? Or arrogant humans, for that matter.

Theo turned and smiled at Hemlock when the door opened.

"He will see you." The fairy looked a little surprised by this, but said nothing else.

Theo followed the fairy through the spacious, marble-floored entrance hall, through a corridor whose walls appeared to be made of green silk banners alternating with patches of flowering lichen, and into a study. The floor of this room was soft green moss, and the desk near the window appeared to have been grown from the floor of a pale wood, sending exuberant shoots from the corners up toward the ceiling.

Theo's eyes followed the wooden shafts upwards to see the ceiling gleaming with fairy light reflected from a mosaic of a hundred thousand tiny bits of mirror. The windows were dark, but Theo knew they looked over the rear of the garden toward the distant mountains.

"Thank you, Hemlock," Theo said, when he spotted Lord Willowvale.

The servant bowed infinitesimally and withdrew.

Lord Ash Willowvale was dressed as casually as the last time Theo had seen him. It was late, and of course the fairy had not been expecting a visitor, much less Theo. His shirt was a pale shell pink, open halfway down his breast bone, and his trousers were a soft fawn velvet, with a hint of a pearlescent sheen upon the folds. He sat upon a green settee with his legs stretched out before the dying embers of a fire in a great stone hearth.

"Overton," he murmured. His pale silvery gaze followed Theo as the young man made his way across the room.

"Your house is lovely, Lord Willowvale," Theo said sincerely. "Does the moss not mind being trod upon?"

"It thrives; there's enough magic running through the floor that it wouldn't dare die." Willowvale gestured toward another sofa. "Since you're here, you might as well explain why you came."

Theo sat and studied the fairy. "I wanted to reassure myself that you had fully recovered."

"Why?" Lord Willowvale's pale eyes flicked over Theo's face, as if he were baffled.

"Is it so unbelievable that I actually care whether you're alive or dead?" Theo huffed softly in laughter.

"It is difficult to fathom," the fairy said coldly. He flicked his hand, and one of the servants appeared in the door. "Bring tea."

The servant bowed without a word.

"I am recovered," Lord Willowvale said after a long silence. "Physically."

"Something else troubles you?" Theo asked.

The fairy wove his fingers in a complicated pattern, then flicked them at the fire. The flames danced merrily in bright blue and green, then violet and red, and finally subsided into the usual yellows and oranges.

Behind them, the servant opened the door and stepped in bearing a tray with a steaming pot of water, two porcelain teacups on saucers, two little tea strainers atop the teacups, and a tin of tea. He set the tray upon the table between the two sofas.

"Thank you. You're Poplar, aren't you?" Theo looked up at the servant with a sparkling smile.

The servant nodded, then shot a glance at Lord Willowvale, bowed, and retreated.

Lord Willowvale straightened with that disconcerting grace of the Fair Folk and spooned tea into the tea strainers, then poured hot water over the tea to steep.

"Do the Fair Lands produce tea?" Theo asked.

"It's from the human world." Willowvale glanced up to meet Theo's gaze. "I don't want you trapped here any more than you want to be trapped here. Probably less, in fact."

Theo laughed. "Thank you, my lord."

"It wasn't a compliment," Willowvale snapped.

"I meant for the assurance that you wouldn't try to trap me here."

Willowvale blew out a dismissive huff. "Even I am not so ignoble as to mistreat a guest, but I did not expect you to know that."

A smile danced over Theo's lips, but he didn't say anything else.

Willowvale tapped his fingers meditatively upon the arm of the settee as he studied Theo. His cold, pale eyes flicked over Theo's hair, a little mussed from his recent trip through the veil, and over Theo's expression of friendly amusement.

"Surely you did not come to the Fair Lands only to see me," Willowvale said. He lifted the tea strainer out of each teacup and put them on a small plate apparently provided for this purpose. Then he indicated that Theo should select a cup.

Theo did so and waited until Willowvale took a sip before drinking.

"Thank you," Theo said sincerely. "This is excellent, and I did need a little refreshment. I confess I did come to the Fair Lands for another reason. I found myself in a game of bargains with Lord Bayberry, and I had to finish it. Do you know him?"

At Lord Bayberry's name, Willowvale's eyes widened slightly. "What did you promise him?" he asked.

Theo's eyes glinted with mirth. "You presume I lost the game."

Lord Willowvale's gaze flickered, just a little, in a way that Theo took as bitter amusement. "You won?"

"If I had lost, I doubt I would be alive to trouble you this evening."

The fairy's lips curled a tiny, genuine smile. "You're probably right. What possessed you to enter into such a perilous game?"

Theo leaned back in the settee with a gentle sigh of satisfaction. "May I compliment you again upon your house before I answer? Even your furniture here is delightful."

"It's a settee, Overton. It's not magic." Willowvale's icy gaze was steady, but less rancorous than usual.

"It's a lovely settee, and I was quite cold and fatigued before I arrived here, and I rather expected you to leave me out on the patio, so I'm both pleased and grateful to have the opportunity to enjoy your hospitality." Theo closed his eyes as he took a warm sip of tea. The spiced scent wafted in his face, warming his cheeks as the fire warmed his cold toes.

He continued, "As for your question, Lord Bayberry insisted upon the game when some friends and I inadvertently intruded upon his lands. We made our apologies and would have departed with no trouble, but he insisted."

Willowvale said, "I don't seem to recall a fairy's insistence on your continued presence being of much effect before." He took a sip of tea, his silvery gaze steady upon Theo's face.

"The situation was a little different. I should hate to throw ice water on this little shred of civility we have managed to build, but I am not entirely sure I want to reveal what induced me to stay, for I should hate for you to later use it against me." Theo softened these words with a gentle smile, as if he thought himself silly to fear such a ridiculous thing. "I do apologize, my lord; I am probably being overly cautious."

Lord Willowvale gave a short, surprised huff of laughter. "I can guess, for you are entirely predictable. Your friends were in danger, or so you thought. For some reason you judged it safer for them to stay and match wits with Bayberry than to flee into the veil. I presume they were incapacitated in some way, and you didn't think you could get them into the veil quickly enough without further injury."

Theo held his gaze.

The fairy said quietly, "I have no argument with your friends, nor any remaining reason to apprehend you. I shall not use your secret, such as it is, against you." He took a sip of tea and looked at the fire. "Though what Bayberry will do is beyond us both. You've picked a dangerous enemy, Overton."

"I'm sure you're right," Theo said with a smile. "Nevertheless, I am not unduly concerned."

"Are you ever?" Willowvale finished his tea and set the cup and saucer back on the tray with a precise sort of finality.

Theo's smile widened to a grin. "Not often." He finished his tea and put the cup and saucer gently back upon the tray. "Might I ask what you will do now that there is no need to catch the Rose?"

Willowvale gave a slight, elegant shrug. "Whatever the king decrees."

"What did you do before seeking the Rose?" Theo asked with interest.

The fairy's silvery eyes rested upon him, and there was a meditative weight to his gaze that would have made most men squirm. Finally, he said, "I fought humans for a time, though I never saw action against the Valestrian forces."

Theo inclined his head, acknowledging the gravity of this tiny confidence, and looked toward the fire. He waited, patient and silent, while the Fair lord decided whether to reveal anything else.

The silence grew weighty, and Theo looked up at last to see Willowvale's gaze upon the flames and his mouth in a bitter twist.

"How is it," he growled, "that when I wished you to be silent, you would not stop talking, like a little yapping dog, with your barbed compliments and sideways insults, and when I wish you to fill up the yawning silence with your stupid chatter, you are wordless and patient and kind?"

Theo inclined his head in apology, but said nothing.

"You would probably like to believe that my time in war made me as I am." Willowvale sneered at the fire, not meeting Theo's gaze. "But the truth is, I saw only little combat, for I was employed by His Majesty Alder Silverthorn, the current king's father, in rooting out traitors in the Fair ranks."

The young man remained quiet, his warm hazel eyes upon Willowvale's pale, hard features.

"Perhaps it is to be expected that having been trained from birth to think the worst of everyone around me, I do so with exceptional skill." Willowvale finally looked up to meet Theo's gentle gaze. "It seems there is no need for a weapon like me if the Silverthorn dynasty is to be held and maintained by the love of a human."

Theo let out a soft, grieved sigh. "Lord Willowvale, surely you cannot believe yourself entirely without purpose or value in the world."

"Can I not?" Willowvale's voice was nearly inaudible.

"You *should* not," Theo said gently. "No one is without value, my lord. If those little street children, dirty and hungry and orphaned, have intrinsic value, then so do you."

Willowvale gave a bitter little laugh, but said nothing else.

For a moment there was silence. Lord Willowvale glanced at Theo, then stared morosely at the fire.

"I am honored by your confidence," Theo said in a low voice, "and I am genuinely grieved that you are so unhappy. Nevertheless, I am sure that you, being so gifted in so many ways, can find some new purpose in life."

"I wonder if it is pleasant to be so full of stupid, baseless optimism," the fairy said, half under his breath. "You have more reason than most to hate me, Overton. Why should you offer me any reassurance? What do you hope to gain from your pretty words?"

Theo hid a smile, for he heard these insults as a panicked last defense of Willowvale's wounded pride. "Why should I not seek to make you a friend, my lord?" he said gently.

"Why should you want to?" Willowvale snarled.

"Why should I not? It seems to me that you might benefit from a friend."

"You cannot benefit from my friendship, I wager."

"Any benefit I derive is not my purpose." Theo looked down at the floor, then up to meet the Fair lord's icy gaze. "I shall leave you, my lord. It is late, and I should not prevail upon your hospitality any longer. I thank you for your kindness to me."

Lord Willowvale's pale face seemed, for a moment, to have a strangely bereft expression before he smoothed it into his customary cold condescension.

Theo stood and bowed. "Will you be entirely insulted if I invite you for tea next Tuesday? I would like to return the hospitality you have offered me here."

Lord Willowvale blinked, then said, "You would invite me for tea?"

"Yes." Theo inclined his head, hiding his smile at the fairy's confusion.

The Fair lord's lips opened, then closed and pressed together. He swallowed. "I accept."

Theo gave him a sunny smile. "I am honored, my lord. I shall be delighted to receive you at four o'clock on Tuesday. Shall I come fetch you? I don't want you to have any difficulties with the veil on the way there."

Willowvale let out a short, sharp breath, and muttered, "I will manage, Overton."

"Then I will bid you goodnight." Theo bowed again.

CHAPTER TWENTY-ONE
Introductions

Fenton woke early, entirely refreshed, with a feeling of vibrant strength and energy that had replaced the muzzy lethargy of the previous day. He dressed in the gray dawn and wandered happily into the hallway. Everyone would surely be asleep at this early hour, so he decided to take a leisurely walk through the garden and eventually make his way to the stables. He would spend a pleasant hour or so in the crisp morning air and the warm, steady presence of the horses before coming in to meet Theo for breakfast.

Fenton had begun to make his way outside when a soft voice hailed him from the top of the stairs.

"Lord Selby."

He looked up and was startled to see Anselm sitting on the top stair with a sword across his knees and a cup of tea beside him.

"What are you doing?" Fenton asked in consternation.

Anselm made his way down the stairs to speak to him quietly. "Lord Mosswing and his betrothed, Lady Poppy Miscanthus, arrived late last night. Lord Larch and several of his men attacked Lord Mosswing in his home, injuring him. Lord Mosswing was concerned that Larch might target Lady Miscanthus next, so he brought her here for a time. They're in the guest suites upstairs. Sir Theodore stayed up yesterday afternoon and made me rest, so I took the night watch. I was just beginning to get a little drowsy, so I thought I might wake him soon."

Fenton frowned in concern. "How badly was Lord Mosswing injured?"

"Nasty sword puncture right about here. Pretty deep." Anselm indicated the location high on his own chest, on the right a few inches below the collarbone. "But his magic is working; he estimated it would be completely healed in a day or two. We put him to bed; Sir Theodore estimated the better he could sleep, the faster he'll heal, and anyway he won't mind it so much while he's resting."

Fenton nodded, still frowning. "Did he mention having injured Larch in return?"

"He did not, sir."

"It is only that I wonder whether he might have bought us a little time to take Larch's actions to His Majesty Silverthorn." Fenton's frown deepened. "Where is Theo?"

"He went back to the Fair Lands after he brought you and Miss Firethorn here. Do you remember?"

Fenton sifted through the jumbled memories. "No." His frown deepened. "He has sent no word back?"

"No, sir." Anselm shook his head. "I cannot think of any good reason why he would be gone so long, but he did say it might take quite some time."

"Nor can I, but I will try to let that reassure me." Fenton forced a smile. "While we await his triumphant return from whatever he's doing, I believe I shall borrow one of his swords and see if I can find anything suspicious around the estate. If I find nothing, might I prevail upon you to let me take your place so you can bring me some breakfast or tell me where I might find it myself? I'm famished." Indeed, the deprivation of the last few days had caught up with him even as he'd stood there, and he felt ravenous.

"If you'll take my place, I'll make you something now. I don't want to leave them unguarded." Anselm handed him the sword.

"Thank you, Anselm. I appreciate it more than I can say." While he waited for Anselm to return, Fenton amused himself by reviewing some of his favorite parries and lunges, careful to keep his quick footwork light and quiet.

After a quick breakfast alone in a sunny little nook hidden between larger, statelier rooms, Fenton walked up to Theo's study and selected a sword.

The rain of the previous days had departed, leaving the air chill and damp. Every leaf and blade of grass was crusted with frost.

In the garden, he did a quick sweep of the areas nearest the manor, then expanded the search to every corner of the extensive garden. He kept his footsteps quiet in hopes of surprising anyone lurking in the bushes.

Despite his efforts, he found no lurking malefactors, nor evidence that anyone other than the Overtons had been in the garden. In fact, the most interesting thing he found was an enormous spiderweb. Each silken strand was laden with dewdrops that sparkled like diamonds in the early morning light. After admiring it, Fenton went around it, leaving it intact, rather than swishing it out of the way with a stick.

By the time he finished the second, more thorough exploration of the grounds, Fenton was beginning to feel a little hungry again. The cold, crisp air was thoroughly invigorating, and he'd spent over two hours tramping briskly around the Overton estate.

He stopped by the stable and patted each of the horses on the nose, smiling and apologizing for the fact that he hadn't brought them any apples. When he returned to the manor, he found Anselm still at the top of the stairs.

"Theo's not back yet?" Fenton asked.

"No, sir." Anselm frowned worriedly. "Would you like some tea?"

"If you don't mind." Fenton took Anselm's place sitting at the top of the stairs and stared meditatively across the spacious entrance hall from this elevated vantage point. What should, or could, he do to free Miss Firethorn from her bargain with Silverthorn? How would one convince a Fair king to free a sworn captive?

A few minutes later, a door opened behind him, and he turned.

A Fair lady emerged, so breathtakingly beautiful that for a moment Fenton could only stare.

Then he stood hurriedly and bowed. "I apologize for the lack of a proper introduction. I'm Lord Fenton Selby, Marquess of Ambervale."

She extended one arm as she bowed gracefully. "Lady Poppy Miscanthus, Baroness of Evenfall." Her voice was soft. Her skin was a deep, cool black darker than any Fenton had ever seen. The morning light through the windows caught the elegant planes of her cheekbones and the curve of her full lips.

"I was not aware until this morning that Lord Mosswing was betrothed," Fenton said, feeling rather helpless in the face of such Fair grace and elegance. "I shall congratulate him when I see him. I hope he is not too seriously injured."

Poppy smiled, revealing straight white teeth that contrasted starkly with her ebony skin. "You are friends, aren't you?"

"Yes. We have known each other for years, though we have not seen each other as often as I would like."

Poppy's smile remained, and her eyes gleamed with interest. "The betrothal is quite new. He asked me yesterday, just after he returned from your world. I was delighted to accept his promise of marriage. When he returned home soon afterward, he was attacked by Lord Oleander Larch and several of his men. After he fought them off, he returned to me, and we set off through the veil. I have never before been through the veil, nor met a human."

At this moment Crocus appeared at the bottom of the stairs, having woken in her room in Theo's wing of the manor and not found anyone on the hall.

She looked up the stairs at Lord Selby and Poppy and her eyes widened. She bowed gracefully.

"Lady Miscanthus. Lord Selby." Her voice was nearly inaudible.

Fenton bowed again. Her ice-blue eyes made him feel warm and fizzy inside, as if he'd drunk a little too much sparkling wine. "Good morning, Miss Firethorn." The fact that she knew Lady Miscanthus intrigued him, but he did not ask about it yet.

Crocus strode gracefully up the steps, eyeing them with interest and caution.

Fenton felt a little out of his depth, having the impression that the two ladies knew each other, or at least knew of each other. "May I introduce you, or do you know each other?"

"I would appreciate an introduction, Lord Selby," Poppy said serenely.

"Lady Poppy Miscanthus, this is Miss Crocus Firethorn. Miss Firethorn, Lady Miscanthus, Baroness of Evenfall."

Crocus said, "I did not think to see you here, Lady Miscanthus. Do you often come to the human world?"

Poppy's dark eyes gleamed with humor. "I have never been here before, but Lord Mosswing spent the entirety of our walk through the veil extolling the virtues and character of his friends here." Her warm gaze rested upon Fenton for a moment, then shifted back to Crocus. "I did not, however, hear your name, Miss Firethorn."

Crocus swallowed and lowered her eyes for a moment. "I have only recently come in search of my cousin, Juniper Morel. I shall not be here much longer, either."

Fenton frowned. "Is that because of the bargain?" His memories of that bargain, and even of the conversation the previous day about the bargain, were shrouded in misty confusion, and he still was not entirely sure what had been promised. Nor why she had done it for him, other than a sense of guilt.

Crocus's smile seemed a little strained. "Don't let the bargain trouble you, please. It is my affair." All the same, she clasped her hands together to still their trembling.

Fenton's tender heart twisted at this, for she seemed so lonely and brave. He would have pressed her for more information, with utmost kindness, of course, but from the bottom of the stairs, he heard Anselm.

"I have prepared a breakfast for you in the rose room, if you are hungry." The servant looked up the stairs. "Mrs. Overton and Lady Overton will meet you there."

He strode up the stairs and took his position again at the top of the stairs. "Lord Selby, I will remain here. Would you be so kind as to keep your sword at hand?"

"Of course."

Lady Overton and Lily were waiting for them and Fenton made the last remaining introduction of Mrs. Overton to Lady Miscanthus.

"I am delighted to meet you both." Lady Overton greeted them with gracious hospitality. "You are welcome here. My husband, Sir Theodore, was quite fatigued from the events of the last few days, so he is still sleeping now, but he will be delighted to take lunch with us."

Over breakfast, Fenton listened as the ladies exchanged careful, polite inquiries about each other.

"How did you meet Lord Mosswing?" Lady Overton asked Lady Miscanthus.

The Fair lady smiled softly. "I have known of him for years, but my family has long abhorred the politics of the Fair Court. Last year, my father and mother were on a romantic retreat in the far mountains, and they never returned. We believe they were somehow taken by the fading of the land; perhaps their carriage fell into one of the mists, or the ground disappeared from beneath them. I was alone."

Her dark eyes shone with tears, and she raised her chin. "Lord Mosswing was unfailingly kind in his sympathy. When others wanted my estate in marriage or my support for their political faction, Lord Mosswing supported my neutrality. My father had shielded me as much as he could, so I did not know the truth of the factions. I did not want to lend my name to something with which I did not agree."

"Will you tell us of your betrothal?" Lily asked. Her eyes were alight with friendly warmth.

She smiled, her lips quivering. "To tell the truth, I had hoped for many months that Lord Mosswing would ask for my hand in marriage, and I wondered why he did not. I felt no coldness in his words or actions, yet he gave no indication that he was interested in anything more than a friendly acquaintance in public. In our few relatively intimate meetings at dinner parties and smaller affairs, he was attentive and warm.

"Yesterday, he found me at my family's estate and proclaimed his adoration in the loveliest words. When I expressed my acceptance, he breathed a sigh of relief, as if he had been afraid I might reject him." Her full lips curved in a sweet smile. "Perhaps I had not made my delight in his presence clear enough. Then he brought me here, and he spent the entire walk explaining his support for the Rose, and his enduring friendship with your family, and his deep trust and respect for you."

She raised one elegant hand and brushed a slight dampness from her eyes. "He did not let me know he had been injured until we were nearly here. I saw that he wore a glamour, of course, but, having been assured through his voice and actions that it was truly him, I did not at first imagine he had been wounded."

Fenton felt obliged to say at this point, "Anselm has assured me that Lord Mosswing will heal quickly and well. I've seen myself how strong his healing magic is."

Lady Miscanthus nodded gratefully. "I'm sure you're right. All the same, it is difficult to see someone you love in pain. Also, I wish he had not felt as though he had to hide it." She looked down and brushed at her eyes again.

Through all of this, Crocus had listened silently.

"Do you then support the Rose, Lady Miscanthus?" she asked quietly.

The lady's dark eyes widened. "Of course! Not only did he risk his life again and again for the sake of helpless children, he saved the Fair Lands themselves! Have you not heard?"

Crocus licked her lips. "What I have heard is difficult to believe, and I was no longer in the Fair Lands when he met the king. What I heard of that meeting sounded more than a little garbled."

Lady Miscanthus said, "Perhaps later you can speak with Lord Mosswing to hear the truth of it. He was there."

At this moment, Anselm knocked upon the doorframe and said, "Lord Cedar Mosswing." Cedar stepped into the room behind him, and Anselm added, "Let me go get you some breakfast, sir."

"Thank you," Cedar said. Everyone stood to greet him, and he bowed to each in turn.

Cedar was wearing the same clothes as he had the previous night, and there was the faint edge of glamour about them. Fenton imagined he was concealing the tear in the fabric.

"How do you feel?" Fenton asked him.

"Much better, though perhaps a little tired." Cedar's dark skin looked a little pale, and he moved a little more gingerly than usual, but he did indeed look remarkably well, considering the wound Anselm had described.

Fenton noticed, with amusement and warmth, that when Cedar looked at Lady Miscanthus across the table, a faint flush came across his dark cheeks. That was probably what he himself looked like when he looked at Miss Firethorn, though she did not return his affection as Lady Miscanthus returned Cedar's.

Fenton looked down at his clasped hands. "Lady Overton, Mrs. Overton, if you don't object, I think I will check the garden again."

He bowed and exited the room. He didn't really expect anyone to be lurking in the garden; in fact, he was more alarmed about the fact that Theo had not yet returned. He found Anselm in the hallway and asked, "Has there been no word from Theo?"

"No, sir." Anselm's frown was nearly as worried as Fenton's.

"I believe I shall take a walk in the garden, Anselm. If you receive anything, please let me know."

"Yes, sir."

CHAPTER TWENTY-TWO
Waiting for the Rose

At lunch, when everyone was gathered in the dining room, Lady Overton shared what Theo had said about perhaps sending Cedar to Lord Bayberry's estate if Theo were not back by midnight that evening.

"Bayberry!" Cedar stared at her. "Surely he hasn't gone there! Why would he do that?"

So Crocus recounted the events while the others listened in growing concern. The story was new to Fenton too, for he had remembered little of the evening, and nothing of Lord Bayberry, for he had been unconscious before Bayberry had arrived.

Juniper shuddered at the mention of Bayberry's name.

"What do you know of Bayberry?" said Sir Theodore.

"Not much. I saw him once in court, when I was quite young. He did not often come to court; I think he hated it. He and his wolves stalked through the court as if they owned it, and I heard a rumor that the wolves ate some poor child just outside the palace, but I never knew if it was true." Juniper raised his chin. "But Theo is terribly clever, and I am sure he will get the best of Bayberry."

The words sounded exactly like what they were: a child's attempt to reassure himself.

Crocus met Fenton's eyes across the table, and she sighed softly.

Sir Theodore tapped his fingers upon the table meditatively. "Did he say anything about what he was doing?" Sir Theodore asked.

"He said he gave his word to Lord Bayberry to return to finish a game of bargains," said Lily.

Anselm said, "He did say he expected it to take all yesterday morning, and he did not expect to be back until evening."

With a carefully steady voice, Lady Overton said, "He said to give him today as well."

With a frown of concern, Sir Theodore stared at the table and pressed his lips together. Finally, he said, "I do not think I want to wait until midnight to inform Bayberry of the error of his ways."

"I do not intend to wait that long," Fenton agreed. "When shall we leave?"

Crocus glanced between them. "Did you not hear how dangerous Bayberry is? At least come up with a plan before you storm the mountain lord's stronghold."

Cedar said, "I will be honored to accompany you. But as much as I fear Theo has gotten into trouble, I have seen him in action, and I think we ought to give him a little more time. He is really quite clever."

"I am well aware of how brilliant my son is," said Sir Theodore, with terribly polite precision. "I am also more acquainted than most with how cruel certain Fair lords can be."

Lady Overton put a gentle hand on her husband's, and he said, "Forgive me, Cedar."

Cedar inclined his head. "I am entirely in agreement, Sir Theodore, and there is no offense to forgive."

The silence grew heavy, until finally Fenton said quietly, "If we must wait, perhaps we might come up with a plan."

So while the ladies listened in growing tension, Sir Theodore, Fenton, and Cedar tried to imagine how they might convince a Fair lord to release a captive, how they might reach his mountain stronghold, and how they might oppose his wolves and whatever other magic he had.

Juniper listened in silence for hours. In the late afternoon, he finally said to Sir Theodore, "I should come too, sir."

"What?" Crocus looked at him in horror. "Absolutely not."

He blinked in surprise. "I do not mean to be impertinent, Miss Firethorn, and I know you have risked much for me. But I owe Mr. Overton my life, not to mention my friendship, and I cannot simply stay here while I might be able to help him."

Sir Theodore shook his head. "Juniper, Theo would never forgive himself if somehow you were hurt in trying to save him."

The young fairy's lips trembled, but he said, "Then he ought to respect my choice to risk myself for my friend, as he does. For what use is setting such a valiant example and then getting upset when someone follows it?"

Fenton gave a soft, choked laugh, and put a hand on Juniper's shoulder. "You've already set a valiant example for us all, Juniper. Please, let us not argue about this; I don't think any of us would ever forgive ourselves if we knowingly took you into danger now."

Juniper's purple eyebrows lowered in frustration, and he said, "I will not consent to be left here as a child."

They spent the afternoon resting in turns and the conversation took much the same turn over an early dinner, though they had not come to any sort of concrete plan.

After dinner, they moved to the spacious sitting room that had been so much used in previous days.

The fire died to embers, but the room was warm enough that no one felt inclined to build it up again. It was just after ten o'clock by now, and the world outside was inky black, for shadows blanketed the moon and blocked all hint of its silvery light upon the lawn.

"Something must be wrong." Fenton paced back and forth across the study.

Lily had been pale and silent for hours. In her heart, she purposed to follow the men into the veil, for she would not be left behind while her husband was in danger, whether she could actually be of use or not.

Cedar frowned at Fenton and Sir Theodore. "The veil hates you both. It might be better if you both stay and I go alone."

"With all due respect, Cedar, I could not live with myself if I didn't go. You needn't coddle me in the veil, either; I won't slow you down." Fenton squared his shoulders and met Cedar's turquoise gaze.

"He's my son." Sir Theodore's voice brooked no argument. "I'd prefer you stay, Fenton, for I don't want you injured in the veil, but I'll not impugn your honor by saying it twice."

Poppy's dark eyes gleamed with emotion, but she said nothing.

Lily said, "I will come too."

"But…"

"He's my husband!" Lily's voice cracked.

At this moment, a slight sound caught their ear.

Anselm was at the door, so he was first into the hallway. "Thank God!" The relief in his voice told everyone that Theo was back.

"Good evening!" Theo said cheerfully, and he followed Anselm back into the study where everyone had gathered. He crossed first to Lily and, heedless of the onlookers, kissed her full on the lips. "I missed you," he said, his voice soft and sweet, the words for her alone.

Then he looked up and around with a smile. "You all look so serious." He kept one arm around Lily, pulling her close.

"We were planning to storm the Fair Lands and rescue you," said Sir Theodore.

"They were about to argue with me about whether I ought to be allowed to come or not," said Lily.

Theo's eyes sparkled. "You know she threatened Lord Mosswing with one of my old swords?" he said proudly.

Poppy's eyes flicked to Lily in surprise. "Really?" she murmured.

"I didn't know how to use it, but I didn't yet realize he was a friend." Lily flushed pink with embarrassment. "I am most sincerely sorry, Lord Mosswing."

Cedar gave a low chuckle, and he said quietly, "Mrs. Overton, I cannot say I have ever before been so delighted by the wrong end of a sword. It gave me great pleasure to know you would use a blade on someone for your husband's sake."

"I don't know if I really could have used it."

"I'm grateful you didn't," he said warmly.

Theo bowed to Poppy, and Cedar realized, with a twinge of embarrassment, that he had not yet introduced them, so he did so. Theo bowed over her hand, then straightened, his eyes glowing with friendship and warmth.

Then he said quietly to Anselm, "I hate to bother you so late, but I'm famished. Would you mind seeing if there's anything left over from dinner?"

"Of course not." Anselm glanced at him more critically. "You look exhausted. Why don't you tell them about it while I make you a plate?"

Theo nodded and sank into the chair nearest the fire.

"Well, I spent the first night at Lord Bayberry's, as promised, which gave him the victory on that bargain, for he gained the better end of the deal. The third bargain is still in progress, you might say, but I am confident of the resolution. The negotiating was conducted outdoors, in the cold, hence why I'm a bit out of sorts." He didn't look remotely out of sorts, in the normal sense of the word; if anything, he looked pleased with himself and the world, and his good humor had at first distracted everyone from the fatigue in his posture.

"I was on my way back here at last, and the veil was being particularly disagreeable. I found myself passing close to Lord Willowvale's estate, and I thought I ought to drop in upon him and see if he had recovered from that little issue with the binding magic.

"He has, and we spent a surprisingly pleasant hour or so having tea together. It was most welcome, for by this time I was quite frozen and tired. In return, I invited him here for tea next Tuesday at four o'clock."

Cedar stared at him in disbelief. "You invited Lord Willowvale for tea?"

"I did." Theo's eyes gleamed. "What's more, he accepted the invitation."

"Why would you do that?" Crocus breathed. "Are you utterly mad? Do you know how dangerous he is?"

Theo's smile widened. "I do, actually." At Crocus's look of disbelief, he added gently, "I understand that you will not want to see him. I issued the invitation, and I will receive him, but no one else is obligated to attend."

Lady Overton murmured, "You're conducting an all out assault, aren't you? He won't know himself by the end of next week."

Theo beamed at her, then turned as Anselm stepped back into the room with a tray generously laden with roast pheasant, baked pears, roast squash, and an enormous, well-buttered roll. "Oh, thank you, Anselm." He nearly groaned in relief.

"When did you eat last?" Lily asked. She stood beside his chair and twined her fingers into his coppery curls. He leaned into her touch with a grateful sigh.

"Lord Bayberry had breakfast for me yesterday morning, much to my surprise, and of course there was tea with Willowvale last night. But that was a long time ago, and I must have walked thirty miles in the veil since then."

Crocus blinked and said, "Where did you sleep last night?"

"I don't trust the veil enough to sleep in it, especially as obstreperous as it has been lately, so I found a sheltered little nook in the Fair Lands and took a nap this morning. Then I had a brief run-in with a troll, which sounds more exciting than it was, and the rest of the time I was walking back here." He closed his eyes in bliss as he took a sip of steaming tea. Then he added, "I found a little colony of those rope-bear creatures that seem to dislike you so much, Lord Selby. They are every bit as unpleasant as we have suspected."

Fenton blinked. "You're not injured?"

Theo shook his head.

"Anselm and I will take shifts at the top of the stairs again," Sir Theodore said firmly. "You, Theo, will sleep late tomorrow."

Theo frowned. "What's this about taking shifts? I thought we were done with that now that Lord Selby and Miss Firethorn are safe."

The attack on Cedar, and Cedar's concern for Poppy's safety, was explained while Theo ate, and by the time he finished, he agreed that it would be wise for someone to keep watch.

"I can take a shift," he offered.

"You are going to bed," his father reiterated firmly.

"Yes, Father." His eyes sparkled merrily, but he didn't argue.

A few minutes later, everyone had departed for their respective suites, and Sir Theodore had taken the first watch near the top of the stairs in the entrance hall.

CHAPTER TWENTY-THREE
Gracious Hospitality

The next few days were full of quiet hospitality in the sudden chill of autumn. The first morning after Theo's return, Lily woke to the early light streaming across the bed and Theo smiling drowsily at her.

"Good morning, my love," he murmured.

"Good morning, dearest." She smiled when he closed his eyes again. "Go back to sleep."

He gave a soft hm and reached for her hand, which he kissed and then held to his cheek. "I love you."

When they woke again, the light was richer and warmer. Theo dressed in a cream shirt, a vest with an elegant, understated pattern of green and gold, and a slim-fitting green jacket and trousers that set off his lean figure to perfection.

Lily eyed him with consternation. "You look so fashionable. How am I to look the part of your wife if you dress like this every day at home?"

Theo laughed. "I'm only dressed up because Fenton and Cedar have guests; I should hate to be discourteous by being too casual this early in our friendship."

She bit her lower lip, and he said gently, "Are you nervous? You look lovely in everything, dearest Lily. It is only us men who must use additional decoration to be presentable."

She couldn't help a chuckle, and he added, in a lower voice, "Nothing you wear does you justice anyway. I wish we could dispense with it altogether."

Lily's cheeks heated, and she felt a surge of pleasure when he said it that way, with his voice just a little husky.

With a sparkling, teasing smile, he took both her hands in his and kissed them one by one, his eyes warm and sweet as he held her gaze. "But if you must choose something, let me assure you that my only desire is for you to feel as beautiful as you are. You delight me in *every* way, Lily."

She leaned in to his embrace, and his kisses assured her that he was not at all concerned with which dress she chose.

When Theo and Lily finally made their way downstairs, flushed and smiling, they found breakfast long over, and Sir Theodore, Lady Overton, and their guests reading poetry to each other in the library. Anselm was stationed in the corridor in a comfortable chair with a sword across his knees and a cup of tea on a diminutive table beside him. Through the open door of the room, he was able to listen to the poetry. This was attributable more to the Overton tendency to treat him as one of the family whenever possible than to Anselm's enjoyment of poetry; indeed he generally found it rather silly. Nevertheless, he appreciated the gesture, and he did enjoy the warmth and sweet friendships developing among the Overton guests.

Crocus had drawn Juniper to one corner, where the younger fairy had been explaining the last few years of his life, especially the last year in which he had been recruited by Cedar to aid the Rose, his services to the Rose, and his flight to the human world for refuge when his actions had been discovered by His Majesty Silverthorn. Crocus listened in rapt attention, glancing at Fenton, Cedar, and the others at intervals, and she asked quiet questions now and then.

Theo and Lily stopped to greet Anselm and thank him for his vigilance, then stepped into the room.

"How are you this morning, Theo?" Fenton asked. The young nobleman had slept deeply the previous night, relieved to his soul by Theo's safe return.

"I am delighted to see nearly all of my favorite people in one room!" Theo sparkled at them with effervescent delight. "I believe we're lacking only your family, Lily, and Anselm, who is so faithfully protecting us."

Out in the corridor, Anselm smiled to himself. Another young nobleman might have said the same words with mockery or condescension; Theo said them in genuine friendship and gratitude and a determination that Anselm's service not be overlooked.

Theo conferred quietly with his father for a moment, then stepped out into the hallway to take Anselm's place while Anselm went to fetch Theo and Lily a light, late breakfast, since lunch was still a few hours away.

After a moment, Fenton joined him in the corridor. "Why are you standing watch, Theo? Shouldn't you be in there, enjoying it all?"

Theo glanced at his friend. "Shouldn't you?"

Fenton looked down but didn't say anything.

"You look troubled." Theo's voice was soft and compassionate. "Is it because of Miss Firethorn's bargain with the king?"

Fenton nodded once.

"We'll figure something out." Theo met Fenton's dark gaze with an encouraging smile. "He hasn't called her to service yet. Don't you think you ought to be in there, letting her know how charming you are?"

Fenton chuckled, low and sad. "I don't think she finds me charming, Theo. I think she hated me, then she pitied me, and now she ought to resent me, but she's too kind to show it openly."

Theo's mouth dropped open. "Have you suddenly gone blind and stupid, my friend? I was in the room barely five minutes, and I saw how her eyes soften when she looks at you. I don't think that's resentment."

Fenton's dark eyebrows rose. "I think your optimism has gotten the better of you."

"I think not." Theo's voice was gentle. "I am sorry for my part in the dishonesty that so angered her, but I think she is wise enough to recognize your character if given half a chance."

Fenton smiled faintly. "Thank you, Theo."

Theo put a hand on his shoulder and murmured, "Just wait. We'll free her somehow. I am working on a plan already."

When Anselm returned, Theo ate with Lily, admiring her all the while with those lovely warm eyes that made her feel delightfully cherished, as indeed she was. After they had finished eating, Lily joined the poetry reading, and Theo drew Cedar off to one side, with a nod for Fenton and Juniper to join them.

"Miss Firethorn, would you join us please?" Theo asked a moment later.

The Fair woman diffidently joined their little cluster at the table by the window, which Anselm had just cleared of Theo and Lily's breakfast dishes.

"Would you please tell us the exact wording of your bargain with His Majesty Silverthorn?" Theo's hazel eyes focused with startling intensity on Crocus, and she twined her trembling hands together in her lap.

"It isn't any of your concern, Mr. Overton," she said quietly. "I made the bargain of my own free will."

"I understand that, and it was most courageously and selflessly done." Theo inclined his head to her in something like a seated bow. "All the same, it does not impugn your honor to give us the full details of His Majesty's hold over you."

Her pink rose-bud lips quivered, and she looked down. She took a tremulous breath. "I have no wish for Lord Selby to feel any guilt over it," she whispered.

Theo said, in a voice so kind and gentle that tears came to her eyes, "Then please let us help you, if we can. At least let us try! My friend is already wracked with guilt, and even a thread of hope would be a gift to him."

Her ice blue eyes flicked to Lord Selby's face, and for a moment their gazes held, pale, cold blue and deep, warm brown.

Crocus swallowed and said, "Lord Selby was insensible, I think; at least he did not seem aware of anything. We had not quite danced long enough to ask a boon of the king. I begged him for mercy, since Lord Selby is human, but the king stood upon the law.

"I said that there was one thing His Majesty could do, and he asked if I was willing to pay the price. We made the bargain aloud, so everyone in the court heard. He was to exert the full power of his magic to remove the manticore venom from Lord Selby, and in return, I owe him my life and my magic until he releases me or I die."

Her voice throughout this had been quiet but clear, and she had fixed her gaze steadily upon the center of the table. Now, for a brief instant, she looked up to Fenton's face, and their eyes met again.

He sighed, soft and grieved, and said, "I wish you hadn't. It cost too much."

Theo said, with tightly controlled anger, "Lord Fenton Selby, I will thank you not to value your life so little. Miss Firethorn accounted it worth saving at great cost, and I agree with her. The only question is what to do next."

Fenton covered his face in his hands and turned away.

Theo put a hand on his shoulder and spoke into his ear. "Fen, you cannot blame yourself. It is entirely unjust, and I will not stand for it in this house. You know it is not your fault."

Fenton rubbed both hands over his face and took several deep, shuddering breaths, regaining something of his usual composure before he turned around. He nodded once to Theo, acknowledging the words, if not entirely accepting them.

"Lord Mosswing, what can you tell me about His Majesty's motives? Does he often put lovely Fair maidens in his power this way, and if so, for what purpose? Is it only maidens, or only commoners, or has he put others in his power this way?"

Cedar frowned thoughtfully and glanced at Poppy. "I have never heard of him targeting maidens in particular, and I do not know his purpose. I have heard of a few others who have bargained their lives and magic to him, but I do not know what induced them to do so, nor what demands he has made upon them in service." His bright, gemlike eyes rested upon his betrothed, as if in question.

Poppy inclined her head gracefully, and Cedar continued, "In recent days, His Majesty has spoken of the hold that Mr. Overton has over the Fair Land with awe and wonder, and I fear he may be trying to take back, or replicate, that power for himself."

Theo's copper eyebrows drew downward. "I don't wonder that he should try to take back power, but I do wonder what he means to do with such power. He held it before and it did not serve his ends."

"What is his end, then?" Poppy asked quietly.

Fenton asked, "Is there a way to find out what he has demanded of the other captives?"

Theo said, "I shall ask Lord Willowvale when he comes for tea. Perhaps he will be able to shed light on the king's purposes."

At the urging of all the Overtons, Fenton and Lady Selby stayed the rest of the day and overnight. The following evening, Fenton and his mother returned to the Selby estate, for it seemed a little silly to both of them to prevail upon the Overtons longer.

Before he left, Fenton took a walk with Crocus in the garden. They were not unaware of the risk, but Fenton steered them through the paths closest to the patio, always within sight of the others on the patio, who were both chaperones and additional eyes alert to any sign of Lord Larch or any of his lackeys. Fenton wore one of Theo's swords, just in case.

They walked in silence for some time. "Miss Firethorn," said Fenton at last, "I know the circumstances have not been ideal, but I have enjoyed this time with you."

Crocus frowned up at him. "I would have thought you would regret offering me your hospitality, for that generous impulse seems to have resulted in a great deal of pain and trouble for you and your friends."

Fenton met her blue eyes and smiled, with a sweet sort of melancholy that touched Crocus's heart. "I do regret the trouble it has caused them," he allowed. "But I would gladly suffer any number of other troubles myself if it would improve your situation in any way."

The Fair maiden swallowed and looked away. "You are too kind, Lord Selby. It is dangerous to be so generous, and I wish you would not put yourself to any trouble for me."

The young nobleman sighed, and said, almost inaudibly, "I cannot please you in this, Miss Firethorn, though I always wish to please you."

"Why?" Her eyes widened. "Why should you wish to please me?"

Fenton laughed, soft and despairing, and said, "Is it not entirely obvious that I adore you far more than is remotely proper? Our acquaintance is too short to justify my presumption, especially since your impression of me is, of course, shadowed by my lies on Juniper's behalf, however well-intentioned they were. I would not dare presume that you feel the same way. Nor should you."

Fenton had not dared look at Crocus while he said this, so he did not at first realize that there were tears in her eyes.

"I am sorry," she whispered. "I cannot return your affection."

The words struck the young gentleman like a blow, and for a moment he could not breathe. He had not truly expected her to say anything openly encouraging his pursuit. He had not phrased it in a way that anticipated encouragement, because he had wanted her to feel entirely free to reject him, if she so chose.

Still, the finality in her words twisted in his guts like a knife.

"I understand," he said at last.

She gave a soft, pained inhale, as if she meant to weep, like he wanted to, but she said nothing else. So they walked in silence, the fallen leaves crunching beneath their feet.

The Overton garden had been exquisitely designed for beauty in every season, and though the rhododendrons and roses and many other flowers were no longer blooming, the maples were scarlet and gold, the birches showed their silvery skin, and the chrysanthemums flaunted their rich orange and purple hues. The peace of the garden, and the golden sun that warmed the cool air, seemed to mock Fenton's despair.

What was there to say now?

Finally, he managed, "I do hope that if I come visit again, as Theo is sure to insist, that my presence will not trouble you."

"Of course it will not," she said.

He heard the sharp edge in her voice as irritation and said nothing else.

An hour later, Fenton and his mother bid the Overtons and their guests farewell. "Farewell, Miss Firethorn," he murmured. "Good night."

"Good night, Lord Selby," she replied.

The following day, Fenton ate breakfast with his mother.

"You like her, don't you?" Lady Selby said quietly. "Did you tell her?"

"Yes." Fenton kept his gaze focused on his toast.

"What did she say?" Lady Selby sounded baffled.

Fenton swallowed. "She said 'I cannot return your affection.'"

Lady Selby blinked, then blinked again. "I thought fairies could not lie," she said to herself. "Ah, but she has been careful with her words."

The young man laughed under his breath, low and hopeless. "Mother, I do appreciate your endless faith in me, but it seems Miss Firethorn finds me less charming than you do. It is not actually impossible that a lovely maiden might refuse me."

She frowned at him, then put a hand on his wrist. "Dear boy, that young lady is quite enamored with you, if not deeply in love."

"Mother." Fenton stared at her in frustration. "I love you, but you are wrong. She was quite excruciatingly clear. I think I would have noticed if she had intended me to take encouragement from her words."

"I'm sure you would have. She meant to discourage you, indeed. But I do not believe it was from lack of interest or affection." Lady Selby patted his wrist. "I believe she intended to protect you from… well, whatever horrible thing she believes will result from her bargain."

Fenton's gentle eyes darkened. "I must humbly disagree. Nevertheless, I will talk to Theo about it. Perhaps between us we can come up with a plan."

Fenton spent that afternoon riding alone, pondering what he had heard and what little he remembered of the interminable dancing in the Fair Court.

At the top of the ridge between his estate and and the Overton lands, he sat atop his horse for a while looking at the Overton garden. From this vantage point, he could see Lady Miscanthus, Miss Firethorn, and Mrs. Overton on the large patio. Miss Firethorn was not wearing her glamour, for her pale blue hair shone in the bright afternoon sunlight. They were sitting at the table where the family so often enjoyed meals outside, as well as card games and strategy games. At the other end of the patio, Cedar, Juniper, and Theo appeared to be deep in conversation. Theo had his hands shoved in his jacket pockets and seemed to be listening intently to Juniper.

Theo looked up and waved, and Fenton waved back.

Fenton turned his horse away before Theo could turn the wave into an invitation.

They were happy and peaceful, and Fenton was not ready to face that yet. Instead, he rode a leisurely route all across the hills, up to the ridge from which the changing colors of the trees would be most spectacular, down through the apple orchard, and across the river to the edge of the forest.

By the time Fenton made his way home that evening, a note from Theo had already arrived.

Dear Fen,

I am not the only one disappointed that you did not join us this afternoon. Will you honor me with your company tomorrow? Come for lunch and stay for supper, if you can. Your mother is welcome too, of course.

Theo

For the following five days, the routine was much the same. Fenton drove his mother to the Overton manor every morning, and they enjoyed lunch with the Overtons and their guests. Afterwards Lady Selby and Lady Overton enjoyed poetry and tea and read silently at opposite ends of a sofa by a fire.

Sometimes Lady Miscanthus, Miss Firethorn, and Mrs. Overton joined them for tea and poetry, but the two older ladies spent much of the time in quiet companionship. They had been friends far too long to need to entertain each other, and reached the comfortable stage of friendship where simply being in the same room was enjoyable.

This is not to say they did not speak at all.

"I already thanked Theo for what he did for Fenton, but I cannot convey the depth of my gratitude, Helena. I know it was difficult for you and Sir Theodore as well." Lady Selby spoke into the comfortable silence.

Lady Overton replied, "I cannot say you are welcome, because I had little to do with it, but I will say that I rejoice with you in his safe return." Then, carefully, she added, "What is your opinion of Miss Firethorn?"

Lady Selby focused on her stitches for a moment, then set her embroidery down. "I was cautious at first, but she has won me over. I believe she is quite terrified of the bargain she made for my son's life." She frowned thoughtfully. "Yet not only did she make it impulsively, for love or guilt or altruism, she has rejected every offer he, and your son, have made to help her out of the bargain. She believes it too dangerous for them, and she means to protect them at her own expense." She pressed her lips together, apparently debating with herself, and then said, "I do believe that she loves him, whether she has admitted it to herself or not. She discouraged him, but you've seen how she looks at him."

Lady Overton frowned in sympathy. "Poor boy," she murmured. "He believed her, didn't he?"

"He did." Lady Selby shook her head regretfully. "I do not know enough about the Fair Folk to even imagine what a solution might look like, nor whether it is even possible for one of them to marry a human. Still, it speaks well of her character that she is trying to protect him."

In another room, Lily was getting a little more comfortable in her role as hostess, though she still felt a little like a guest herself in the Overton manor. Crocus could not read Valestrian, but Poppy could, and she and Lily took turns reading poetry and novels to the others. Poppy was quite accomplished in many aristocratic arts, and she recited Fair poetry to them. Lily was enthralled with her voice, for it was like a musical instrument, able to carry pathos and exaltation, grief and love, and when she spoke, every line of every poem seemed more beautiful than it had when merely read upon the page.

Crocus watched in quiet admiration as Poppy recited a particular love poem with passion and eloquence.

"That was exquisite, Lady Miscanthus," she said.

The Fair lady smiled kindly. "I am sure you could do the same, Miss Firethorn, once you learned the words. The trick is to feel the emotion, and anyone with a tender heart can do that."

Crocus looked down. "Thank you." She clasped her hands tightly in her lap, so that the skin across her knuckles grew even whiter.

CHAPTER TWENTY-FOUR
The Day of the Tea

The Tuesday on which Lord Willowvale was to come for tea dawned bright, clear, and cold. A thick coating of frost silvered the lawn. From their windows, Theo and Lily could survey much of the garden, and Theo spent several minutes looking carefully for any footprint in the frost, or any other sign, of the mysterious intruder.

After breakfast, Fenton rode up, and he, Cedar, Juniper, and Theo selected horses. Anselm drove the ladies in an open carriage, and all together they took a leisurely ride up to the highest hill near the Overton estate, where they dismounted from their horses and stepped down from the carriage. From this vantage point they could see the changing colors of the leaves in all their glory.

The sight was breathtaking. The Overton manor gleamed white against the fading green of the lawn and the brilliant scarlet, orange, and golden leaves of the trees scattered throughout the garden. Crimson and gold dahlias bobbed above heuchera, and nearby burning bushes had turned a dazzling red.

Cedar had visited the human lands in autumn before, and had even stood on this very hill at the peak of the display, but the beauty of it still brought him nearly to tears. The Fair Lands were beguiling to both Fair Folk and humans alike, with their vivid colors and unpredictable threats, with the thrill of danger and splendor at every turn. But the purity of this autumnal display, with its vibrant color and the crisp wind in their faces carrying the faint scent of a distant wood fire, seemed both exotic and charmingly winsome to the Fair lord.

With impulsive boldness brought on by the beauty of the view, Cedar put his hand over that of Poppy, and his joy was complete when she twined her fingers into his. This was no mere practicality, holding hands to maintain contact through the veil. This was mutual enjoyment and appreciation of beauty and of each other.

Theo had already wrapped both his arms around Lily and pressed a kiss to her temple, as if it were the most natural thing in the world to kiss one's wife in full view of one's friends and acquaintances and even a servant. Lily flushed, but she could not resist when he murmured in her ear, "Dearest Lily, I really thought I would like for you to see the beauty around us, but now I find myself entirely, selfishly overcome by your beauty, and I wish very deeply that you would appreciate me instead of the leaves."

She turned her face into his chest to muffle her helpless giggle, and he added, even more softly, his breath tickling her ear, "Why did I think to bring all these lovely friends of ours? I really think you could appreciate me better without an audience."

He was rewarded by another, even deeper flush, and he laughed, low and delighted. Then he took one of her hands in his and began pointing out distant landmarks for the others. When Lily had almost recovered her composure, he bent to kiss her on the lips, with complete disregard for Juniper's wide eyes.

Fenton stood by the carriage studiously ignoring the two happy couples. He said something to Juniper, and then turned to admire the view.

After some minutes, Theo pulled Lily a little distance from the others. "I'm sorry, Lily, I shouldn't have done that."

Lily, emboldened by her delight in his kisses, said, "I hope you don't think my blushing meant I wanted you to stop." This admission made her blush again, but her eyes sparkled.

He gave a soft, agonized groan. "I didn't want to stop either, but I realized we were being cruel to Fenton. I meant to be a better friend than I am." He ran one hand over his face and took a deep breath. "Let me think."

A moment later, he drew her back toward the group with an effervescent smile. Fenton was speaking softly to one of the horses, and Crocus was standing some distance away, looking over the colorful vista with wide eyes.

"Miss Firethorn," Theo said with a radiant smile. "Isn't the view lovely?"

"It is," she replied quietly.

"I do think the view is best enjoyed in pleasant company. Shall I drag Lord Selby over here to you? He's quite charming, and I am sure he would make himself delightful."

Lily said in shock, "Theo!"

Crocus glanced between them, then across to Fenton, who had moved to the other horse in front of the carriage. He had apparently heard none of this.

"I can't imagine he wants to entertain me, sir," said Crocus quietly. "He's already unhappy enough; please don't force him to put on a happy face for my sake."

Theo said more gently, "You seem to think he would feel speaking with you as a burden. I believe it is the other way around; he does not want to burden you with his presence. He believes you resent him for your captivity."

Crocus's fine features tightened. "Do you always pry into things that don't concern you?" she muttered. "I cannot deny that I resent the bond, but I can hardly blame him for it. If I'd been cleverer, perhaps I would have come to some other solution, but I could hardly watch him die there in front of me."

Theo said, with warmth and sincerity, "He is the very best and bravest of men, and a wonderful friend, besides. I am most thankful to you, Miss Firethorn."

"I have seen his courage." Crocus crossed her arms and looked away.

Theo said more softly, "He is also tender-hearted. If you are troubled, he would be honored if you would allow him to comfort you."

She shot him a sharp glance. "Why are you extolling the virtues of your friend, as if I have not noticed them already?" Her voice had the slightest bite. "I am not blind to his charms, Mr. Overton, as I am not, actually, entirely stupid! Even if I were, I doubt his qualities would go unnoticed.

"I do not want to think of him grieving over me, as if I deserved it, when the entire situation was my fault!" At this she snapped her mouth shut and turned away, her arms crossed protectively in front of her.

"Forgive me, Miss Firethorn," Theo said gently. He would have said something else about how her situation was not hopeless, but at the shimmer of tears in her eyes, he thought better of it and merely bowed solemnly.

He withdrew without another word and made his way over to Fenton.

"I believe Miss Firethorn is in need of a little encouragement and charming conversation," Theo murmured to his friend.

Fenton blinked at him. "I don't think she wants to talk to me."

"I think she would appreciate your presence very much, whether she will admit it or not," Theo said with confidence.

With some doubt, Fenton strode over to her and said, "Miss Firethorn? I trust you're enjoying the view?"

She swallowed and raised her chin. "It is beautiful," she allowed.

Fenton bit his lip, wondering what to say, and ventured, "From that hilltop north and west to the river is my land. This side is the Overton estate. Across the river there belongs to Lord Radclyffe."

Crocus's pale blue eyes followed his pointing finger, and she glanced up at him. She seemed receptive, so he continued quietly, "Lord Radclyffe's son Sir Michael was also part of the Rose's league. They both have binding magic, so they were more help than I was in the end."

The Fair woman said quietly, "I'm sure your support was very much appreciated."

"More than it deserved." Fenton glanced at her. "I am sorry, Miss Firethorn, but I assure you, if anyone can free you, it is Theo."

"You have a lot of faith in him." She sighed. "I doubt the king can be induced to release me, and I have no urgent desire to die, so I must come to terms with my captivity."

Fenton said quietly, "I doubt I can convince you that there is hope, but whatever comes, I am sure you will face it with courage and grace."

Crocus looked up at him more thoughtfully, her icy blue eyes taking in the strong, straight line of his jaw and the warmth of his eyes. When he met her gaze, her cheeks pinked slightly and she turned away.

"Your estate is beautiful," she whispered. "I think some lady will very much enjoy the colors, when you marry."

Fenton tried to smile. "I am glad you find it so."

Some distance away, Theo stood behind Lily, with his arms wrapped around her and his chin resting upon her hair. He murmured something, and she twisted to smile sweetly up at him, as if he delighted her.

Farther away, Cedar and Poppy stood side by side, her hand in his with their fingers entwined in a manner that would have been entirely too intimate, if they were not betrothed. They seemed to be in such awe of the colors of the foliage that they did not need words; they merely enjoyed the sight together.

Anselm and Juniper had retreated some distance away, giving the various couples a semblance of privacy.

Fenton said quietly, "Thank you for coming, Miss Firethorn. I know the circumstances are not ideal, but the view is more beautiful because you are here."

"Why must you be so kind, Lord Selby?" She sighed. "It would be easy to resent you if you were loathsome."

The young lord covered his shock with an elegant cough, and replied, "I am sorry to disappoint you. I am only being honest."

Her lips tightened, and she said, "I wish you had been so from the beginning."

"I wish I could have been."

At three fifty-seven that afternoon, Lord Willowvale came trotting up the long, curving drive to the Overton manor on a bay horse. One of the stable hands met him, and he handed the reins to the young man with a cold nod.

Willowvale strode up the steps and knocked. He was dressed in the Valestrian style, wearing an elegant black jacket, a richly embroidered claret vest, a white shirt and cravat, and dark gray trousers. Compared to the Fair fashion, the outfit was muted and boring, but in Valestria, Willowvale had hit exactly the right style to indicate a serious, thoughtful mind in a man—or fairy—of means.

Anselm opened the door almost immediately, and welcomed the Fair lord in with a polite bow. "Come in," he said.

Although he hadn't exactly told Theo or the elder Overtons, Anselm had kept a sharp dagger in his jacket for months. He had long feared that someday, some fairy would either follow Theo through the veil, or find the house through some other means, and attempt to take some vengeance upon the family.

Of all the Fair Folk he had feared, Willowvale was the name most often heard and the face most imagined, and his was the mission that had most threatened Theo. Now, when Anselm saw him face to face, it was all he could do not to slip his hand inside his jacket to take hold of his knife.

Just in case.

After lunch, Theo had asked Lily and all his guests to move to his parents' wing of the house, and they had been comfortably installed in the library and a sitting room for an hour already. Theo had been there for a while, ensconced happily on a settee with one arm around Lily. This physicality had quietly scandalized all the Fair Folk, though if pressed Cedar would have admitted he was very much looking forward to a similar intimacy with Poppy, once they were married. Fenton studiously ignored the impropriety, for he understood Theo was not only delighted in his lovely wife, but also intentionally bringing the

Fair Folk into this quiet, comfortable, familial atmosphere. They took turns reading to each other and played games.

Shortly before Willowvale was to arrive, Anselm brought the group tea and pastries, and he and Theo returned to the other side of the manor.

Theo stirred the fire while Anselm waited by the door for Willowvale's arrival.

When the Fair lord arrived, Anselm brought him to the elegant little sitting room Theo had selected.

"Lord Willowvale!" Theo greeted the fairy with a radiant smile and a bow.

"Overton." Willowvale gave a faint, stiff bow and stalked into the room. His silver blue gaze flicked over the room and all its furnishings, taking in the understated elegance and comfort.

"Anselm has gone to fetch us tea. Sit down." Theo indicated one of the deep leather chairs in front of the fire and stood in front of the other, waiting courteously for Willowvale to sit first.

The Fair lord sat. Though the Fair Folk were nearly always graceful, Willowvale was often so tense and irritated it made his movements stiff, and this time was no exception, though perhaps it was not irritation this afternoon but some other uncomfortable emotion.

"Did you have any trouble getting here?" Theo asked.

"No. I couldn't get myself any closer than Ardmond, so I hired a horse there and rode the last three miles."

This news did not entirely displease Theo, for he was not delighted with the thought of Willowvale knowing how to access the estate directly from the veil. Nevertheless, he put on a sympathetic expression and said, "You must be chilled. Autumn has come suddenly this year, and it's cold and windy this afternoon."

Willowvale said, in a passable attempt at small talk, "The Fair Lands also grow cold."

Theo smiled and leaned forward to stir the fire a little more. "Move the chair forward if you'd like. I asked the cook to make something warm for tea."

The fairy did not move the chair, merely stretched his feet a little closer to the flames and eyed Theo with a furrowed brow.

"What do you hope to gain by befriending me, Overton?" he said at last. His voice was not exactly warm, but it was not as biting as it might have been, either.

"A friend." Theo's smile sparkled with sincerity and warmth.

Willowvale's lips tightened.

When Anselm entered the room, Willowvale tensed almost imperceptibly. The servant carried a heavy tray laden with two small china plates bearing cinnamon scones, two ramekins filled with steaming baked spiced apples, a little bowl of clotted cream and an accompanying tiny spreader, a pot of hot tea, and two teacups on saucers.

"Here you are, sirs." Anselm put the tray upon the table between Theo's and Willowvale's chairs and retreated. He stationed himself in the hallway, out of sight but able to hear and intervene if Willowvale offered violence.

The fairy studied Theo surreptitiously as the young man poured tea into both cups.

"There's cream and sugar, if you'd like."

"That's unnecessary."

Theo offered Willowvale the clotted cream first, and he looked at it with a faint sneer.

"What is it?"

"Clotted cream. It's delicious on the scone. I like to put the baked apples over the top and eat the whole thing with a fork, but you can eat them separately too. If the scone isn't all sticky, you can pick it up. Or even if it is, I suppose."

Willowvale shot a sharp glance at the young man, but Theo's sparkling humor was not malicious. With a doubtful look, the fairy followed Theo's example.

They ate in silence.

The fairy's cold eyes flicked to Theo at intervals, as if he questioned what the young man would say next.

Finally Theo said, "Do you like it?"

"Yes." Willowvale looked slightly displeased by the admission, but added, with visible effort, "You humans have a talent with food, considering your pathetically weak magic."

Theo laughed in unreserved delight. "It burns you to say something pleasant about humans, doesn't it?"

Willowvale snarled, "Do not mock me, Overton!"

"Why should I stop now? I don't mean it unkindly, you know." Theo refreshed Willowvale's tea, apparently blithely unconcerned by the fairy's trembling rage. Then he looked up with a warm smile. "It must be difficult to be pleasant to me, when you hate me so much. I appreciate your effort."

Willowvale's face contorted for a moment in silent fury, but he said nothing else. He sat back in his chair and crossed his arms. If he had been less dangerous, it might have looked like the pose of a petulant child.

"Lord Willowvale, when I visited you in the Fair Lands, you offered me some excellent human tea. How do you obtain human tea, if travel between our worlds is so often difficult?"

"I bought a generous supply in Ardmond and brought it back in those trunks. Also, Ambassador Brookbower sends some to the palace occasionally. His Majesty bestows it upon his favored courtiers and officers as gifts at times."

Theo brightened. "I would be happy to send some back with you, if you'd like. I have a lavender black tea that is delicious in spring with lemon pastries."

Willowvale stared at him. "Do you seek to put me in your debt?" he asked.

"Of course not!" Theo said. "I don't have the memory to keep up with debts with fairies. There is no reciprocation expected. It is a gift in the human tradition, not the Fair tradition."

Willowvale's troubled expression deepened. "This is not a fair trade, for it does not repay what you owe me," he said in a low voice. "Surely you can't have forgotten."

Theo blinked. "I confess I have. What do you think I owe you, my lord?"

"Quite a few deep punctures." Willowvale's gaze did not flicker. "You're only an idiot when you want to be, so you cannot convince me you have actually forgotten that."

Theo looked down, then leaned forward to stir the fire again. He sighed softly. "No, my lord Willowvale, I have not forgotten, but I have forgiven you. Can you not put it behind you as well?"

The fairy looked at the fire. "It is not guilt that assails me, Overton." The bitter grief in his voice belied this, but Theo didn't argue. "It is a deep sense of the utter pointlessness of all my efforts on behalf of the Fair crown, and thus of my entire existence." He gave a faint, disgusted growl deep in his throat, then muttered, "I dare say you have always been pampered and cherished, so I do not expect you to understand this. I should not have said it at all."

Theo refreshed the Willowvale's tea again, and the fairy took the cup and gulped it down, as if hoping the liquid would soothe his heart as well as his throat.

The young man settled back into the seat with a thoughtful glance at Willowvale, but he said nothing else.

The Fair lord stared at the fire, his face set in a grim scowl. When the silence had grown long, he muttered, "If a friend of yours were so hopeless and devoid of purpose, what advice would you give him?"

Theo, wisely, let the silence after this grow until Willowvale could stand it no longer and shifted his shoulders irritably against the back of the chair.

"I would advise such a friend gently, with consideration for his very real grief over what he has lost," Theo said at last. "Perhaps I would advise him to find something to fill his time, something that would give him a sense of purpose and value, however small, while he reordered his world to fit this new understanding of his place in it.

"I might, were I so invited into this friend's private anguish, even dare ask him for help with some difficulty of my own. Not at first, of course, but if I thought he might be receptive. In this way I might benefit from his considerable knowledge and skill while also helping him see that he does have value, and talent used for one purpose can certainly be turned to another, kinder purpose."

Willowvale's eyes glittered when he glanced at Theo. "If only you were so confident in this friend's changed heart," he muttered. "But no, this enemy is far too clever and dangerous to be trusted so quickly, and you will not ask him anything."

Theo shrugged. "It is a pity, for I do have a difficult puzzle to solve, and I have the feeling time is running out. I don't know enough about Fair bargains."

The Fair lord's silver-blue gaze rested upon him in sudden, sharp interest. "Is that so?" There was a faint burr in his voice, like the purr of a pleased cat.

"Indeed. Shall I pose the question to you, just as an exercise for your wit?" Theo's steady gaze rested upon the fairy's face.

After a moment, Willowvale nodded once. "I presume this about Lord Bayberry."

"No, my lord." Theo gave him a sparkling smile. "That bargain is entirely to my satisfaction. This problem is a bit thornier. His Majesty Silverthorn made a bargain with a fairy, saying, 'you will owe me your life and magic until I release you or you die.' The fairy accepted. I want to free this fairy."

Willowvale gave a faint, disbelieving snort. "I think that will challenge even you, Overton," he murmured.

"Indeed. That is why I would venture to ask your opinion of the matter."

The fairy narrowed his eyes in thought, and as he did so, the harsh unfriendliness of his mouth softened a little. "What prompted the fairy to make such a bargain?" he said at last. "He must have been desperate."

"Indeed, it was desperation." Theo did not clarify that the fairy in question was female.

Willowvale steepled his long, narrow fingers and tapped them lightly together. "I am not aware of any loophole in a bargain phrased so clearly. The king must have wanted him. Do you know any reason why?"

"I do not."

Willowvale sighed and relaxed a little into the chair as he stared at the fire. "I wonder what would induce the king to release the fairy."

Theo glanced up at a motion in the doorway and nodded that Anselm could come in. "A little more tea, please, if you don't mind. Thank you."

The fairy stared meditatively at the flames. "Is the fairy important to the Fair Lands in any way?"

"Not to my knowledge."

Willowvale's brows lowered slightly. "Perhaps His Majesty is merely gathering power, and the fairy's identity is immaterial. He was quite piqued by your hold over the Fair Lands."

"In that case, would he not seek to make similar bargains with others?"

Anselm entered with a new pot of tea and took the empty one away without a word.

"Indeed." Willowvale watched Theo pour steaming tea into his cup. "That is different."

"Butterscotch and vanilla. Do you like it?"

"Yes." Willowvale's lack of a sneer when he said this was nearly an expression of enthusiasm, and Theo beamed at him.

"I'll send some back with you, then."

The fairy hesitated, then said, as if it pained him, "Thank you." Then he grumbled something to himself and turned back to the fire.

Theo's smile widened, but he said only, "If you were me, and you hoped to free this fairy from the king's power, what would you do?"

"*I* wouldn't do such a thing," said the Fair lord, with a curl of his lip. "But if I were advising you, I would suggest that it might be possible to pay for a life with a life."

Theo frowned faintly. "I had considered that, yes, but that leaves me no closer to my goal. I will die for this captive if I must, but I do think that between us we ought to be able to come up with something a little more clever."

Willowvale gave a dismissive *pfft* and said, "I wasn't suggesting you sacrifice yourself, nitwit. I was suggesting that you find someone else willing to die."

"That's even more horrifying, my lord. I can't ask someone to do that."

"What if someone volunteered?" The Fair lord shot a sideways glance at Theo, his pale eyes glittering in the fire light. "Someone who saw nothing else worthwhile and thought it might be interesting to do one unselfish thing, just to see what it was like."

Theo let out a soft breath. "My lord Willowvale, let us not explore such desperate plans yet."

Willowvale half shrugged one shoulder and took a sip of tea, then murmured, "It is an option."

"The generosity of the impulse does you great credit. Nevertheless, I will not consider it." Theo's voice was full of warm conviction.

Willowvale raised his pale eyebrows but said nothing else.

The silence that followed seemed somehow more comfortable. Theo and Willowvale sipped their tea in silence.

"What do you know of Lord Oleander Larch?" said Theo at last.

Willowvale gave a faint, snide smile. "Cruel, arrogant, entirely devoted to the Fair throne, though not particularly devoted to Silverthorn himself." He studied Theo with his pale, hard eyes. "Do you think to use him to free your captive?"

"I have no idea how, but I did wonder if it might be possible."

"I will think on it." Willowvale glanced out the window. "Silverthorn does not know I am gone, and I have no doubt overstayed my welcome."

Theo sighed regretfully. "I am sorry you cannot stay longer."

The fairy laughed, soft and bitter, as if he did not expect Theo to hear it at all. "That cannot be true. You humans lie so easily. It is disconcerting for my kind."

"It is true, my lord." Theo met his eyes. "I hope you will come for tea again, too, though I wonder if it is more trouble than it is worth to you, since you must traverse the veil to get here."

Willowvale pressed his pale lips together and his eyes flicked to the side, as if he could not meet Theo's sparkling hazel eyes. "You cannot wish that," he muttered. "You've repaid my hospitality, such as it was."

Theo shrugged. "I do wish it. Reciprocate the offer, if you feel you must. My offer stands. Tea, next Tuesday at four o'clock?"

Willowvale hesitated then nodded sharply. "I will come." Then, with an awkward, irritated movement unlike his usual grace, he bowed and said, "Thank you."

"You are welcome, Lord Willowvale. It has been a pleasure." Theo returned the bow.

Willowvale began to stride toward the door, but Theo called ahead, "Anselm, do you have the tea I mentioned for Lord Willowvale?"

"Yes, sir." Anselm presented a little package wrapped in brown paper and tied with a green velvet ribbon in a bow.

Theo took it and handed it to the fairy with a smile. "I do hope you enjoy it. I like it best with cream and sugar."

Willowvale was apparently unable to muster another word of thanks, for he merely bowed again sharply and followed Anselm down the corridor to the front door. A few minutes later, he was trotting briskly down the drive toward the road to Ardmond.

CHAPTER TWENTY-FIVE
The Plan Takes Shape

For the following three days, Theo took himself to his private library from before dawn to well after everyone else had departed to their rooms for sleep at night, emerging only once or twice to ensure that his guests were well entertained. Fenton spent much of the time with him, though he didn't exactly know what Theo was looking for.

Theo read every account of every bargain between a fairy and a human or between fairies recorded in every book he owned, then emerged, smiling, to watch Fenton and Cedar teaching Juniper how to play chess.

The Fair Folk played a game similar to chess in concept, but made more dynamic by the illusions cast upon the pieces and the propensity for certain spelled pieces to move out of turn to devour the pieces of the opposing side. The human game, by contrast, employed different strategies, for one's pieces could not be relied upon to act with their own initiative when given the chance, or to hide their nature before attacking by ambush. Fenton was a skilled chess player, and Cedar, while not as experienced, was not new to the game either.

Poppy looked on with affection and murmured to Crocus, "It is good to know your young cousin has been so well cared for."

Crocus nodded sharply. "It is." Her voice was a little rough, and Poppy glanced at her.

Theo said, "May I speak with you privately, Juniper?"

Crocus watched with open interest as Theo drew Juniper out into the hall. They were gone for only a few minutes, but when they returned, Juniper looked paler and more tired, and his purple eyebrows were drawn down in a worried frown.

Later, when Crocus was able to speak with Juniper for a moment alone, she asked what Theo had said to him.

Juniper's clear turquoise eyes held hers. "Miss Firethorn, I appreciate your care for me, but Mr. Overton spoke with me in confidence, and I will not betray that, even to you."

Crocus almost flinched, for she felt the words as a rebuke. Nevertheless, she pressed, "Did he insist that you not repeat what he said?"

"It was a private conversation." He set his narrow jaw. "Miss Firethorn, you have friends here, if you will but accept their friendship. These are the kindest and most generous of humans, and I am more than half inclined to stay here, though Lord Mosswing says he believes His Majesty Silverthorn will grant my plea for clemency. I am happier here than I have ever been." He did not say it, but the unspoken addendum to this was that he could not be cajoled into revealing even the smallest confidence.

"You look tired," she said softly. "Are you well?"

"Very." He smiled, the expression full of sweetness and innocence.

Nevertheless, Crocus did not miss that Theo ensured that Juniper had a rich, satisfying lunch, and then, with unexpected solicitousness, shooed him to his suite for a nap.

The Rose was planning something, and she feared it.

For three more days, everyone enjoyed the gracious Overton hospitality. Theo had apparently completed his research, for he enjoyed every meal with his guests and played chess and parlor games with carefree enjoyment.

Every evening, he met privately with Juniper. The young fairy grew more pale and tired, and he frowned worriedly when he thought no one was watching.

At last, Crocus could not stand it anymore, and she cornered him after dinner. "What does Mr. Overton do to you to make you so pale and shaky? It's not right!" she hissed.

He blinked at her. "He doesn't do anything to me," he said.

"Then why have you grown so white and weak? Your hands are shaking, and you're about to meet with him again, and it will only be worse."

He twisted his hands together and said, "Miss Firethorn, I appreciate your concern. But whatever is happening, I do it of my own free will, for the friendship and love of these humans, who have been more family to me than I have had in many years."

She did flinch at this, and said, with tears in her eyes, "Forgive me, Juniper. I should have come for you earlier."

He blinked. "I did not mean that as an accusation," he said earnestly. "I never would have expected you to come for me at all! That you have is generous and kind, and I am grateful, Miss Firethorn. I mean only to say that they have not manipulated or taken advantage of me."

"You're thirteen years old, Juniper! How would you know if you'd been manipulated?" Her voice cracked. "That man could charm anyone into doing whatever he wanted, and you wouldn't even know until far too late to do anything about it."

Juniper laughed softly and looked down. "I do not doubt it. Nevertheless, do not fear for me, for I am in no danger. Rather, I have been given a small opportunity to help a dear friend do something selfless. I am honored to accept it."

For a moment, Crocus could not breathe for the injustice of it! She had finally, belatedly, been able to come to her young cousin's aid, and he absolutely refused to recognize that he needed her help.

Finally, Juniper's earnest expression convinced her that even if he were wrong, she had little chance of convincing him of it.

"I fear for you," she said at last.

Juniper gave her a slight, respectful bow. "I thank you for your concern, Miss Firethorn," he said.

Theo had finished bidding Lily a temporary farewell, for the ladies were retreating to a smaller parlor for dessert and poetry, while the men were debating between chess and a game of illusions in another room. He looked toward Juniper, and the young fairy immediately inclined his head and stepped out into the hallway. "Will you play tonight, Juniper?"

Juniper nodded, smiling, and then they strode off together toward the room where the men would spend the next hour or two before bed.

Crocus watched with misgiving and growing frustration.

The following morning, she arrived in the breakfast room just as Juniper did; Cedar and Poppy were already there, as were Theo and his pretty young wife. Sir Theodore and Lady Overton were eating privately this morning. Everyone stood to greet Crocus and Juniper.

Crocus's gaze, so sharp and perceptive, did not miss Juniper's pallor. The young fairy smiled sweetly at everyone in turn and sank into a chair with a faint sigh, as if he were very tired, but he did not seem uncomfortable or in pain.

Nevertheless, Crocus's worry and frustration boiled over into anger. When Theo offered her a seat beside him, she remained standing and said in a shaking voice, "Why are you preying upon my cousin? Poor Juniper is exhausted!"

Theo blinked at her and glanced at Juniper, who stood again, his pale lips pressed together in dismay.

"I'm all right!" Juniper said hurriedly. "Please, Miss Firethorn, do not worry."

"He's not!" She glanced at him, then fixed her eyes on Theo again. "He's a child, Mr. Overton. I beg you stop, or I will make you stop!"

There was such pure and magnificent anger in these words that Theo could not help the wondering smile that played across his lips.

"Do not mock me with your smiles and your pretty words!" Crocus cried.

"I do not mock you," Theo said, with a respectful half bow. "I am entirely in agreement with you in my admiration for Juniper's courage, and in my grief over the weight of what I have asked of him."

"Then why do you keep asking?" she snapped. She put her hand on her hip, where she had kept her sword, before it had been left at Lord Selby's house, then clenched her fists.

Theo licked his lips, apparently considering his words carefully, then said, "Forgive me, for I cannot help but fear that if I tell you, it will not work, or not as I have planned it. I can only assure you that I do not ask it for myself, and if I could bear the cost for him, I would do so."

Crocus stood in silent, trembling fury for several seconds, looking between Theo and his gentle warmth that would charm even her, if she let him, and Juniper, whose wide-eyed innocence rent her heart. "How can you do it?" she finally whispered. "How can you be so cruel?"

Theo bowed a little and said into the brittle silence, "Miss Firethorn, I am sorry you think the worst of me. I would ask, however, that you respect Juniper enough to let him act upon his courage."

He did not otherwise defend himself, though Lily wanted him to, and he did not make any apology or explanation for his action. He only waited, holding her chair out with exquisite courtesy, letting her decide whether she would sit at the breakfast table or whether she would storm from the room.

Cedar said gently, "Miss Firethorn, perhaps I might speak with you after breakfast about what happened in the Fair Lands between the Rose and His Majesty Silverthorn."

She pressed her lips together and gave a sharp nod, though it was anyone's guess as to whether she would allow even the Fair lord's words to change her opinion.

Breakfast was a tense, mostly silent affair. Theo kept a sharp eye on Juniper and ensured that he was offered seconds of everything, and that he drank a second glass of rich milk, which the young fairy had decided he liked quite a lot after his initial skepticism.

When they had finished, Cedar escorted Poppy and Crocus to a little gazebo in the garden on the south side of the manor, which was sheltered from the chilly wind. All three of the fairies wore cloaks borrowed from the Overtons, though the cold bothered Fair Folk less than it did the humans. Crocus held her anger against Theo as close as she held the cloak to her chest.

He had brought her and Lord Selby safely away from Lord Bayberry, which was to his credit, but she had difficulty reconciling this with Juniper's clear exhaustion. What could possibly justify his demands of the poor child?

"Miss Firethorn, will you listen to what I know of Theo Overton? It may help soothe your worry for Juniper." Lord Mosswing spoke quietly. He really had quite a nice voice, deep and smooth; on him, the Fair noble accent she had always told herself she despised sounded charming and elegant rather than snobbish. Perhaps it was the unmistakable compassion and kindness in it.

Of course, his voice was hardly as attractive as that of Lord Selby.

She blinked at the thought and scowled. "I will listen, but I doubt your words can change my mind," she said sharply.

While Cedar gave a measured, thoughtful account of the work of the Rose, his own contributions to that work, and the Rose's meeting with the Fair king, Theo sat deeply in thought in the library for some time while Lily sat with Juniper at a little table with a children's book. The young fairy could not read Valestrian and had already finished Theo's meager collection of books in the Fair tongue. The previous day, Lily had offered to teach him to read Valestrian, and he had accepted this offer with wide-eyed delight.

After half an hour, Theo stood and said quietly, "I believe it is time I go speak with His Majesty Silverthorn again."

Lily looked up in alarm. "What? Why?"

Theo glanced at the door, reassuring himself that no one else was present, then said, "I have the beginning of a plan to free Miss Firethorn from the Fair king's service. Pray do not reveal even that hint to anyone, though. If anyone asks where I am, please say that I've gone on private business."

Lily grew a little paler. "Will it be dangerous?" she asked.

Theo drew closer and took both her hands in his. "This part of the plan is not likely to be especially perilous," he said reassuringly. "I imagine the latter part will be rather unpleasant." He smiled warmly and added, "but, my love, sometimes I can be rather clever, and I've almost worked it out. I pray you set your mind at ease, for I would much rather think of you enjoying the fire and the pleasant company than beset with worry."

"How can I not worry about you?" Lily said with a tremor in her voice. "I love you."

Heedless of Juniper's blushing, Theo leaned in to kiss her on the lips, then wrapped his arms around her. "I love you more," he murmured. "I cannot say that I do not appreciate your worry, my love; it warms my very soul to know you care about my safety. But do not worry overmuch about this meeting. I should be back before dinner."

He turned to the young fairy and said, "Are you quite well, Juniper? I think you ought to rest today."

"Fine, sir," Juniper managed. He was torn between intense embarrassment at the open display of affection between Theo and Lily, and his delight at being included in this moment, as if he were part of their family.

Theo studied his face, then nodded. "All right. Have a pleasant, quiet day of rest. Stay inside, if you please."

"Yes, sir." Juniper ducked his head, hiding a smile. Theo's care for him always felt like an unexpected gift. The young fairy had felt his wounded, lonely soul coming alive again in the gracious hospitality of the Overton manor, filled as it was with love and kindness for family and friend alike.

Theo kissed Lily again and murmured, "My dearest, I adore you."

Then, stopping only to pack a simple lunch, don a heavy coat, and retrieve a sword, he turned his face toward the veil.

The passage through the veil was unusually free of dangers, and Theo felt almost suspicious of it until he stepped safely into the garden just east of the Fair palace facing the main entrance. It was not yet noon, and this late in the year, the frost edged each scarlet and indigo leaf, each bare twig, and an enormous, perfect spiderweb between two bushes a short distance away.

Theo stopped to admire the spiderweb, on which the tiny ice crystals gleamed. Then he approached the palace. His steps crunched on the ice-covered grass. Birds sang cheerily in another part of the garden, but nearer him, the garden was silent and almost forbidding, despite its brilliant beauty.

The young man walked up the broad steps and knocked.

When the door opened to reveal a fairy servant, Theo smiled radiantly and said, "I would like to request an audience with His Majesty, please."

The fairy blinked. "Overton?" he said uncertainly. His skin was an unusual, slightly unsettling shade of lemon yellow, and his eyes were a deep red, a color which would have been lovely in a wine glass but looked more than a little unnerving to human sensibilities as an eye color. His hair was a brighter scarlet, and it was intricately braided back from his face and fell to his shoulders.

"Yes. I don't believe we've met," Theo said warmly. "Theodore Overton the Fourth, but you may call me Theo."

The fairy swallowed and stepped back. "I'm a servant," he said, rather unnecessarily.

"You still have a name," Theo prompted. "Although I suppose you may think it beneath you to introduce yourself to a human."

The fairy blinked again. "Corydalis," he said, as if surprised by his own answer. "Follow me."

"I take it you've heard of me?" Theo said brightly as he followed the servant down a gorgeous hallway floored in dark gray flagstones edged in vibrant yellow moss. The walls were covered in an exuberant display of paintings and tapestries which competed with each other in color and design and movement, for some of them changed their design when one wasn't looking right at them. Between these works of Fair art were flowering vines clinging to the walls beneath, which were entirely hidden behind the leaves, and might have been plaster or stone or something else altogether. The ceiling above them was mirrored, and when Theo glanced up, he had an unsettling moment of vertigo. He shook his head and focused on the servant in front of him.

"*Everyone* has heard of you by now," the fairy said, with a hint of hidden laughter beneath his cool words. "Wait here." He opened the door to an elegant sitting room floored in brilliant white marble.

Theo strode to the window while he waited. The window looked out upon a valley which he was quite sure was not nearby at all, and he was not sure whether that meant the window merely displayed something distant, or whether there was a strange connection between the two places through the mirror, or whether he had passed to this far place without knowing it. Upon examination, he found that if the window opened, it was not by physical means, which led him to suspect it merely displayed the distant valley without providing a means to reach it.

The door behind him opened, and he ceased his fascinated study of the window to turn and greet Corydalis.

"His Majesty will see you." The fairy looked Theo over again, his strange eyes filled with fascination. "Did you really stop the fading of our lands?" he asked. "And defy His Majesty while you did it?"

"Yes," said Theo simply. "I did."

The fairy stared at him a moment longer, then said, "Thank you." He turned and strode away, and Theo followed.

The throne room had not changed significantly since Theo's visit with Lily not quite two weeks earlier, but he had the impression that some of the mosaics and windows had rearranged themselves. Vines now covered the wall behind the throne itself, blooming in a profusion of shades ranging from deep burgundy through magenta to pale pink, though with no discernible arrangement of colors. Many of the Fair Folk had considerable facility with plant magic, so Theo was reasonably sure that the riotous display was what the designer had intended.

"Your Majesty." Theo bowed both as he entered the room and once he reached the dais, where the king sat upon the magnificent throne. Previously it had been made of gold inlaid with silver, but now it seemed to be carved of dark wood with sparkling silver inlaid in a floral pattern that spread outward from the place where the king's head would rest.

"Overton." The king smiled, and if there was no warmth in it, there was also no hint of simmering anger or hostility. His violet eyes gleamed with fascination. "Why have you come?"

"I have come on behalf of a friend," Theo said with another bow. "She has found herself in a difficult situation, and I thought I might ask for clemency for her."

"Do tell." Silverthorn's smile widened. "Who is this friend?"

"Miss Crocus Firethorn."

The king's gaze did not flicker. "You want her freedom."

"I do, Your Majesty."

"Why?"

"I believe all people ought to be free." Theo hesitated, then added softly, "Moreover, her freedom is important to my closest friend, and I would do him any kindness within my power."

The Fair king straightened almost imperceptibly upon his throne. "What will you give me for her freedom?" he asked.

"What do you want?" Theo spread his open hands.

Silverthorn sighed softly and looked over the room, his gaze resting on the few fairies in the back of the room before he looked back at Theo. His pale blue lips twisted in anguish. "I want to not require a human to keep the land from falling into mist."

Theo inclined his head in a respectful bow. "How shall I help you toward that goal, Your Majesty?" he said, without a trace of condescension or snideness in his voice.

"If we lace the binding magic through a fairy, will it hold the land firm?"

"I do not know, Your Majesty," Theo said honestly. "I imagine, if the fairy loved the land and the Fair Folk with his whole heart, it might work, just as it is holding the land firm through the strength of my love. But I do not believe your father's love, which upheld the land for decades, relied upon binding magic; I used it only because I had access to it, not because it was the best magic for the task."

"What do you know of Fair magic?" the king asked.

"Not much," said Theo modestly. "I've read quite a bit, but my own magic is quite insignificant, as you know."

Silverthorn was startled enough by this to smile, and the expression transformed his face from alien beauty nearly into transcendence. "Magic to traverse the veil is hardly insignificant. You exaggerate your shortcomings, Overton."

Theo shrugged and smiled. "It is always better to exaggerate one's flaws than one's strengths, I think, for then one can allow others to be pleasantly surprised rather than bitterly disappointed."

The king narrowed his eyes. "How shall you pleasantly surprise me, then?"

"If I pleasantly surprise you, will Miss Firethorn go free?"

Silverthorn chuckled low under his breath. "No, Overton. For her freedom, I require more than that."

Theo sighed and studied the king. "How will you learn to care for your land, Your Majesty?"

The king blinked, then blinked again, as if the question were unexpectedly unsettling. Finally, he said, with a catch in his voice, "I don't know." He stood at last, and between his great height and his elevated position atop the dais, he towered over Theo. He crossed his arms tightly across his chest and stared down at the young man, who maintained a warm, friendly smile.

Silverthorn paced to the rear of the dais and back, then away again. When he reached the throne a third time, he looked at Theo with cobalt eyebrows drawn sharply downward.

"I don't know what I want," he said, with an uncomfortable twitch of his shoulders. "I don't think I want to let her go at all."

"Why should you want to keep her captive?" asked Theo, his expression all warmth and innocence.

The king's lips twisted again in dismay. "Shall I not have power over my own people?" he asked. "Is it not my right and duty to rule them, as my father before me did?"

Theo blinked. "But the hold you have over her is not that of king and subject, but of master and slave, is it not?"

Silverthorn rolled his shoulders, as if the question weighed upon him. "Is it really that different?" he asked. "As king, I have the right to command her, and as master I have the same right. What difference does it make? The degree of control is greater. That is all."

Theo frowned at him and considered his words. "Your Majesty," he said gently. "Might I suggest that you know this is wrong? Why should you want such a great hold upon a maiden, when you already hold such power? You have not called for her to attend you yet, have you?"

The king shrugged one shoulder carelessly. "No, I have no need of her service." He turned to pace again. After a moment, he cleared his throat and said, as if irritated by his own words, "I care not that she is a beautiful Fair maiden. I want her because she was free, and now she is mine. You took the Fair Lands. Can you not understand that I want them back?"

Theo said softly, "Your Majesty, I entreat you not to pursue this path. The Fair Lands will not thrive under a yoke of bondage."

Silverthorn laughed bitterly. "Will they thrive under a human, absent and ignorant of our ways? What choice do I have?"

The king paced away again, his silvery-white cloak billowing with the speed of his agitated steps.

Without a word, Theo waited while the Fair king paced back and forth, his pale lips pressed tightly together in dismay.

When Silverthorn reached the front of the dais a fourth time, Theo bowed and said, "Your Majesty, if I show you the quality of a human, and the strength of human friendship, will you let her go?"

The Fair king stopped dead in his tracks and stared at the young man. "How do you propose to do that, and what good will it do?"

"If you recall Miss Firethorn to the Fair Lands for service on Monday, you will find that she is not without human friends."

"What difference does that make to the Fair Lands?"

"If nothing else, it will reassure you that while you learn to love, the Fair Lands are in no danger from us." Theo inclined his head.

"I am not afraid your love will fail." Silverthorn laughed, low and cold. "I am galled that your love is necessary at all."

Theo frowned at him. "You think that if you have such a hold over enough of the Fair Folk, the land will no longer need love, and will instead be sustained by duty and obligation?"

"Something like that." Silverthorn's smile was more a baring of teeth than any expression of warmth or kindness. "If the land can be bound by love, it can be bound by promises and bargains just as well."

"What a sad view of life!" Theo exclaimed. "Shouldn't you be eager to learn how to love rather than seeking alternatives? My life is made rich and full by love, and what pain occasionally results from those connections is nothing compared to the joy of loving generously and well."

Silverthorn laughed, the sound sharp and cutting, and the Fair Folk gave a belated, echoing titter. "All right, Overton. You shall have a bargain for her. Show me love that is neither yours, nor benefits you in any way. Show me love that brings you pain, and yet you judge it worthwhile. Show me your victory in defeat. Then you shall have her."

"Whose love shall I show you but mine, Your Majesty? I have no right to command anyone else."

"That is your problem, not mine."

Theo studied Silverthorn as the Fair king shifted his shoulders beneath his cloak irritably. "Will Lord Larch be present on Monday?" he asked.

"Yes." The king's pale blue lips lifted in a cool smile. "I believe he considers your power over the Fair Lands a personal affront."

"I wonder," said Theo meditatively, "how Lord Larch will react when you free Miss Firethorn."

Silverthorn let out a soft, awed breath. "You really are mad," he muttered. "You truly think to win her, do you?" His violet gaze swept up and down Theo's trim form. He rested his hand on the jeweled hilt of his long, narrow sword. "I imagine he will be furious," he said almost gently, as if he had, for a moment, been assailed with moral qualms about what would come of the challenge.

"I'm sure you're right." Theo smiled radiantly at the Fair king, as if entirely unconcerned, even delighted, by the prospect of Lord Larch's wrath. "What sort of magic does he have?"

The king chuckled quietly. "He is particularly strong and possesses an unusual magic, rare in both our kind and the Unseelie. I don't know whether humans can see it at all, but to Fair eyes, it looks like flame, and I am told it feels like a fiery torment beneath one's skin."

Theo's smile wavered a little, and he said, with a faint, thoughtful frown, "Does it actually cause permanent damage?"

Silverthorn laughed again under his breath. "He spent but little time in the conflict with Aricht, but I was told he killed a few humans there by magic. They were left charred husks, burned up from the inside out. I execute my own traitors, so I cannot say with certainty it would be lethal to one of the Fair Folk, but I have been assured by one who crossed him that even his minor flare of temper was quite agonizing."

"Poor souls," Theo murmured.

The Fair monarch gave him another cold smile, with a cruel glint in his violet eyes. "Do you want to disavow the bargain?"

Theo pressed his lips together and looked down with unwonted seriousness. Then he looked up, his warm eyes a little sad. "No, Your Majesty. If you will recall Miss Firethorn on Monday, I will uphold my part of the bargain."

Silverthorn's eyes glittered, and he sketched the barest hint of a bow. "As you say, Overton."

Theo bowed deeply and replied, "Until Monday, Your Majesty."

When he left the palace, Theo turned toward Lord Willowvale's manor house. A path of magenta moss took him nearly halfway across the garden before curving away to the south around a sheltered grove of cyan willows. Ten more minutes' walk brought him to Lord Willowvale's front door. He knocked.

"Overton." Alyssum's gaze swept up and down Theo. "Why are you here?"

"I would like to speak with Lord Willowvale, if he will see me."

Alyssum nodded. "Come in." He left Theo in a sitting room for only a few minutes before returning to say, "Follow me."

Lord Willowvale was in a private study, and he stood to greet Theo. "Overton," he said, with the faintest hint of warmth.

Theo bowed and looked around with unbridled admiration. "What a lovely room!" he exclaimed softly.

Willowvale blinked. "Thank you."

Vines adorned with golden, bell-shaped flowers cascaded down one wall and crept across the floor. Willowvale had apparently been sitting in an overstuffed leather chair, with a steaming mug of some Fair beverage on the windowsill. Soft blue-green moss carpeted the floor in uneven patches, broken by little mounds of flowers and sections of bare hardwood inlaid in intricate patterns of contrasting wood. The brilliant Fair sunlight flooded the room with gold, highlighting every elegant line of the bookshelves behind the chair and every intricate detail of the floral tapestry upon the near wall.

Theo tore his attention from the beauty of the room and said, "Forgive me for the interruption. I will be brief. I came to invite you to my conversation with His Majesty next Monday. I believe it will be quite exciting, if not enjoyable."

"Next Monday." Willowvale's pale eyes flicked over Theo's figure.

"Yes." Theo gave him a sparkling smile. "I would very much appreciate your presence, my lord."

Willowvale blinked. "Why?"

"You shall see the conclusion of my effort to free a friend from His Majesty." Theo's smile was warm, if a little sad.

The Fair lord straightened almost infinitesimally. "You found a solution."

"Of a sort." Theo inclined his head. "Until then, my lord."

With a bow in farewell, Theo left Lord Willowvale staring after him, the Fair lord's eyebrows drawn downward.

The veil smelled of iron and ash, and Theo wondered whether it was now so aware of him that the scent reflected his mood, or whether that was merely a coincidence. He pressed a hand to the cool stone at his feet and tried to convey the question with a gentle tendril of magic. The veil did not seem to have enough of a consciousness to answer, and the only result of this effort was that Theo was alerted to the presence of a monstrous creature closing in on him unheard.

He ran, hurdling yawning chasms and slithering stony protrusions, and had nearly reached a place from which he could open a door to the Overton estate when something clipped his right foot and sent him sprawling with his heart in his throat.

He flicked a bit of light to his fingertips as he drew his sword.

The golden light danced across the scaly face of a beast so alien he could liken it only to the mythical dragon, if the dragon had white eyes like a blind cave creature, a beak like a turtle, and feet with far too many claws.

It flicked its forked orange tongue at him. Theo clambered to his feet. His knees were bruised, and the palms of his hands were bleeding, but he was not seriously injured. With a bit of light and sword in hand, he prepared to defend himself.

Then he realized where he was, and he opened a door and stepped out into the human world. The door snapped closed just before the monster reached him.

Theo looked around in delight. He was near the top of one of the hills to the east of the Radclyffe estate, an area nearly as familiar to him as Lord Selby's land. This particular hill was only about seven miles from the Overton manor. At this height, the wind was icy, but the intense, late afternoon sun promised that in the shelter of the Overton gardens, it would be warm enough for a game of croquet or tennis, if one wore a coat. He sheathed his sword and set off down the long slope.

After half an hour, he found his right ankle becoming more painful, and his pace slowing as he climbed another hill. He entered the veil again to see if there was a shorter path and found, with some relief, that there was. So it was that he exited the veil only fifteen minutes later to find his father and Lady Miscanthus playing tennis against his mother and Cedar, while Lily, Crocus, and Juniper watched.

Lily saw him first and ran to him with a smile that made his heart beat faster. "Theo!"

When she threw her arms around him, he picked her up and spun her around with a delighted chuckle.

"My love." He kissed her on the lips in full view of everyone, then drew her closer, so that her head was against his chest. He rested his cheek on her hair for a moment, drinking in the comfort of her presence.

"What happened to your hands?" she asked, for his palms were scraped bloody and rough.

"I fell in the veil." His sparkling smile reassured her, as it was intended to. Then he looked up. "Where is Lord Selby?"

"He did not come today." His father met his gaze.

Theo frowned, thinking.

"Did your meeting with the king go well?" asked Lily quietly.

He smiled again, warm and sweet and bright. "It did. I believe I shall go visit Lord Selby this evening." He glanced up again to meet Crocus's eyes. "His absence is undoubtedly lamented."

Crocus looked down and swallowed. "It is better for him to stay away, I think," she said quietly.

Theo's tender heart understood this for what it was—a wish for Fenton to be free of any heartache when she must return to the Fair Lands, for him to be free of any entangling emotions.

"Nevertheless, I shall entreat him to visit us tomorrow and the following days, for his presence is required both for practical reasons and for reasons of enjoyment." Theo smiled radiantly at her, as if he hoped, by his own delight, to make her delighted too.

Crocus pressed her pale lips together and looked away.

As the sun sank below the distant hills and the chill wind gusted, Theo bid his friends and family farewell, mounted his horse Milo, and trotted off to the Selby estate. Dressed as he was in thick, warm clothes, and looking forward to the familiar hospitality of his friend, he didn't mind the frigid wind in his face.

"Come in!" said Richard, Anselm's counterpart in the Selby household. "I'll let Lord Selby know you're here."

A few moments later, Theo was ushered into the little dining room where Fenton was finishing dinner with his mother.

"Good evening, Lady Selby," Theo said with a bow. "It is lovely to see you again."

"Theo." The lady smiled at him. "Of course you'll dine with us."

Theo laughed and bowed again. "Thank you, I will, if it's no trouble. I am honored, as always."

They made small talk for several minutes as they waited for Richard to bring Theo a plate. Once Theo had started in on a delicious piece of roast pheasant, Lady Selby said, "Theo, may I assume you have come up with some clever plan to extricate Miss Firethorn from her service to the Fair king?"

Theo blinked at her, momentarily rendered speechless with his fork halfway to his mouth. "I actually came to invite you both to tea and parlor games tomorrow, and apple crumble and whipped cream afterward," he managed.

Lady Selby chuckled under her breath. "Oh, you dear boy," she said gently. "As if I didn't know you to be the Wraith. Of course you have a clever plan."

Theo flushed and ducked his head. "I should have known you'd realize it. You were always perceptive."

Smiling, the lady stood and said, "I'll let you two conspire in privacy, then. Do please let me know if I can help in any way." She patted them both on the shoulders and swept from the room.

Both young men bowed as she departed, then looked at each other.

"There will be apple crumble tomorrow," Theo said.

Fenton laughed and looked down. "I'm sure."

"Fen, I would be most honored and delighted if you would come. Please." Theo smiled gently. "I know it is painful, for you think there is no hope. But I do, in fact, have a plan. It is not, perhaps, a good or pleasant plan, but it *is* a plan, and I am fairly confident it will succeed."

Fenton's eyes widened. "To free Miss Firethorn?" he breathed. "What must I do?"

Theo sighed almost inaudibly. "Oh, Fen, if all men were as kind and honorable as you are, there would hardly be need of kings or laws at all." At his friend's steady look, he said, "We shall accompany Miss Firethorn to the Fair Lands when His Majesty calls her to service."

"What must I do, Theo?" Fenton's gentle, dark eyes held Theo's gaze.

"I am still thinking about it," Theo admitted, though he had the shape of the plan already in his mind. "When I have it more clearly, I'll tell you your part. I think, though, that it would be both pleasant and beneficial if you spent time with Miss Firethorn in the coming days."

Fenton let out a soft, grieved breath. "I cannot imagine she wants to spend time with me, Theo, and I have no wish to make myself the cause of her distress."

"She will be grieved either way," Theo said, swallowing hard. "You might as well give her the comfort of knowing the generosity of your heart and the pleasure of your company."

Fenton blinked, then blinked again, studying Theo's face. "Am I to die for her, then?" he said, without a tremor in his voice. "If so, I should like to know now, for I ought to at least give my mother a little warning, and there are legal arrangements to be made."

"You will *not* die!" Theo said fiercely. "It is out of the question."

"Do you know when she will be called to service? If it is not death I will face, then is it captivity? Am I to bargain myself for her freedom?" Fenton's dark eyes met Theo's bright hazel ones. "I will do what I must, only I would like to know what I face so I can make any necessary arrangements for my absence."

Theo licked his lips, then shook his head. "I am sorry, Fen," he murmured. "I will tell you when I have it more clearly in mind."

Fenton nodded once, then smiled faintly. "Thank you, Theo."

"Come tomorrow morning," Theo said, his voice warm and kind. "Please."

"All right. I will."

With a few words of affectionate farewell, Theo departed for home.

CHAPTER TWENTY-SIX
Grief and Encouragement

When Lily awoke the next morning, Theo was already gone. He had stirred the coals in the fireplace and added more wood, so the room was pleasantly warm when she rose and dressed. She stepped out into his private sitting room to see him sitting with tea cup in hand, staring at the fireplace.

"You look troubled, my love." She came and sat by him, nestled close as he wrapped his arm around her.

He sighed softly. "I am going to have to do something I do not want to do." His voice had an unusual rasp in it, and she twisted to look up at him more closely. He gave her a melancholy smile.

"I'm sure there is a good reason." She bit her lip, taking in the faint redness of his eyes, as if he had not slept well, or perhaps had wept while she had been sleeping.

"The alternative is even worse." He swallowed. "Anyway, he'll forgive me for it, which is both reassuring and crushing me with guilt."

Lily blinked. "Who will?"

"Fenton. Fenton Selby, the kindest man I've ever known." Theo made a soft, strangled sound and covered his mouth with one hand, as if to keep his grief neatly contained.

Lily twisted to wrap her arms around him, and he closed his eyes and rested his head against hers.

For some time they made no sound, for Lily knew that words would not help now. Theo shuddered once, as if holding back a sob, but otherwise he merely sat in silence, twined against her, his cheek against hers.

"He's coming soon, I think," he said at last, his voice steady.

"What shall I do?" she asked. "How can I help?"

His hazel eyes were sad. "Don't tell him anything. I will tell him what I can, but not yet."

She swallowed. "As you wish," she said softly.

Theo kissed her, sweetly and tenderly, and they descended the stairs to breakfast hand in hand.

They entered the dining room to see no one else there yet. Juniper entered a few moments later.

"Good morning, Juniper." Theo greeted his young friend with a smile. "How are you feeling today?"

"Better, sir." Juniper smiled and ducked his head.

"I am delighted to hear it," Theo said, then added, "Although I believe I've asked you not to *sir* me, my friend."

"I'm sorry, sir. I can't help it."

Lily laughed at the young fairy's cheeky grin.

Soon after this, Cedar joined them, then Poppy, and then Crocus. Juniper's customary shy courtesy prevented him from saying anything else, after polite greetings to his elders, for much of the meal.

Then Poppy said kindly to the young fairy, "Lord Mosswing informed me of your courageous service to the Wraith and his friends, and of how you were forced to flee the Fair Lands. I see that you are happy here, but if ever you do wish to return, and it is safe for you to do so, you will always be welcome with us."

Juniper blinked, and his pale cheeks flushed. "Lord Mosswing speaks too highly of what I did," he murmured. "I did only what I believed right."

"That is commendable and rarer than it ought to be." Poppy's white teeth contrasted sharply with her coal black skin as she smiled. "I think you are too modest, my friend, for so I should like to count you, if I may."

Juniper's blush deepened. "As you wish, my lady. I am honored." He ducked his head. "Thank you."

"Juniper, I wonder if you might like to meet some of the children you helped rescue." Theo smiled at him across the table. "I visited them last week, and it was immensely encouraging. I think you might find it so too."

The young fairy's eyes widened. He hesitated, then said quietly, "I would like it very much, sir, but I imagine they would fear me, and I would not like to distress them."

Theo said kindly, "It is likely they will fear you at first. Yet I think it might be good for them to see that not all fairies are cruel. I would be glad to take you this afternoon, if you would like to go."

Juniper bit his lip and looked down at the table. Then he nodded and said, "Yes, sir, if you think it will benefit them."

Though she was slightly apprehensive, Crocus did not protest this plan. However, she did interject, "May I come too?"

"Of course." Theo smiled warmly, then looked at Cedar and Poppy. "I don't believe it would be an imposition if you would like to come as well, though it might take a little while for the children to be entirely comfortable. I believe His Majesty Alberdale would be glad to meet you, too."

Juniper tensed and seemed to shrink into his seat a little. He swallowed. "I'm sure he has more important things to do."

Theo's smile softened, and he said gently, "Juniper, he and my parents have been friends for many years, and I might be so bold as to call him a friend myself. There is no need to be apprehensive."

The young fairy nodded, but his eyes were still wide.

"I'll send a message to let them know we're coming. We will depart right after lunch."

The reply from the palace came an hour later, noting that His Majesty Alberdale would be ready to receive Theo and his friends for a short introduction before they visited the children.

There had been so much social time that it seemed pleasant to everyone to spend a little time quietly that morning. Lily continued teaching Juniper how to read Valestrian. Juniper retrieved the books in the Fair tongue which he had borrowed from Theo, and these were offered to Crocus, Cedar, and Poppy. Cedar and Poppy read quietly on a sofa near the fire, sneaking admiring glances at each other when they thought no one would notice.

Crocus also accepted a book, which she intended to read, but she found herself watching the others more than she actually focused on the words. Lily's attention to Juniper tugged at her heart; the human's smiling encouragement to Juniper seemed entirely genuine. The youth seemed increasingly comfortable with the Overtons, and while she could not deny that their hospitality was both generous and pleasant, she also could not entirely forget that they had lied to her about Juniper's whereabouts.

Still, it seemed that Juniper was less tired this morning; whatever Theo had been doing to him, he seemed to have stopped, at least for now. Crocus tried to let that reassure her. Fenton arrived with his mother during this quiet time. Lady Selby and Lady Overton retired to a quiet corner to enjoy needlework together, and Fenton joined Theo in a game of whist, for which they enlisted Sir Theodore and Anselm, for Cedar was quite happy reading beside Poppy.

"I don't remember all the rules," protested Anselm good-naturedly.

"Then you ought to be on Theo's team," said Fenton. "He always has the best luck."

Theo grinned but did not argue with this, for he did win far more often than seemed reasonable, and that without any cheating at all.

Crocus was intrigued to see the Overtons and Fenton treating Anselm as if he were part of the family. The man obviously understood his position in domestic service, yet here, in this quiet, intimate environment, he was comfortable, respectful, and yet fully respected. It endeared the Overtons and Fenton to her in a way she did not want to fully acknowledge, for their lies to her still rankled. Nevertheless, she could not deny that there was some logic in their decision to lie, and Juniper did seem to be happy. Also, her heart turned toward Fenton, with his courage and his courtesy and his quiet kindness.

After lunch, they departed for the palace. Anselm drove a carriage in which Lily, Juniper, Cedar, Poppy, and Crocus rode, and Theo and Fenton rode alongside. The ride was delightfully sunny, though the breeze was frigid, and even Fenton's troubled heart felt lighter in the brilliant sun. At the palace, they were admitted with smiles from the guards.

When they emerged from the carriage, all the Fair Folk wore human glamours. Cedar said quietly, "Theo, I thought it best that we not advertise our true faces to everyone in the palace, yet shall I assume your king will want to see us?"

"Indeed," Theo replied.

When the ladies were all comfortably installed on their preferred gentleman's arm, Anselm bowed to Theo and departed for the servants' kitchen, where he knew many of the palace staff and knew there would be hot tea and cream-filled pastries waiting. "Give them my regards," said Theo.

"Of course, sir."

Juniper looked after Anselm as if he wished to follow him. Theo put a reassuring hand on the young fairy's shoulder for a moment, but didn't say anything.

With Theo and Lily in the lead, the entire group headed to the king's private study, where he had said he would receive them. The fairies looked about with wide, wondering eyes, fascinated by the beauty of the Valestrian palace. The floor was marble, which was familiar, but the walls had no trailing vines or intricate, moving mosaics, nor was the ceiling of any hallway mirrored. None of the tapestries lunged at them, nor did the windows show places far distant. Yet the stonework was detailed and precise, and the tapestries were elegantly designed and richly woven, and the symmetry of the rooms told of a long, peaceful history.

Crocus's hand tightened upon Fenton's arm when they reached the antechamber to the king's study and the guards stared at them with narrow eyes.

"Good afternoon, Marcus," Theo said brightly. "His Majesty is expecting me, and he approved my guests already."

"Are you really Theo Overton?" Marcus said.

"Yes, I am Theo Overton," Theo said with a gleam in his eye. "I like your caution, too."

Marcus's shoulders relaxed a little, and he opened the door for them. "Security has been increased," he said, without apology.

"Of course."

Theo led the group into the study, where the king sat behind a great wooden desk with several stacks of paper in front of him. "Your Majesty." Theo bowed deeply, and the others followed his lead. Poppy and Crocus bowed in the Fair fashion, while Lily alone curtsied.

His Majesty Lance Alberdale's eyes glinted with curiosity, but he greeted Fenton and Theo first with an affectionate smile. "Good afternoon, Lord Selby, Mr. Overton, Mrs. Overton." His sharp gaze took in Theo's easy, erect posture, and he said, "I take it there has been no repeat of that little incident." There was the faintest question in his voice.

"No, Your Majesty." Theo's sparkling smile assuaged the last of the king's concern. "May I introduce my friends?" At the king's nod, he continued, "Lord Cedar Mosswing, Duke of Flamefall, my long-time friend and a great ally in the Fair Lands. He assisted with nearly every rescue, and I cannot tell you how grateful I am for his healing magic."

Cedar dropped his glamour and bowed again gracefully, though with a faint hint of tension in his shoulders.

The king said warmly, "Lord Mosswing, I have heard much of your courage, and I am more grateful than I can say that you were with Theo when he faced your king. I am glad to know there are Fair Folk of courage and compassion. You do your people proud."

Cedar blinked in shock, then said, "Thank you, Your Majesty."

"Lady Poppy Miscanthus, Lord Mosswing's betrothed," Theo said.

Poppy dropped her glamour, and the king almost flinched at her beauty. Her skin was so dark that in the relatively dim room, it was more difficult to read her expression than that of anyone else in their group, until she smiled, and her white teeth stood out sharply against the rich black of her skin. She bowed again, the motion as graceful and elegant as that of any queen. Cedar could not help a slight, proud smile to see his beloved's beauty recognized by the human monarch.

"Miss Crocus Firethorn," Theo said.

Crocus watched the king's eyes widen as she let the glamour fade. He looked at her blue hair curiously, but said nothing about the color. She bowed to the king, extending one hand properly.

"And this is Juniper Morel, a young ally at first, now a dear friend as well," said Theo. "You remember Lord Mosswing recruited him right out of the Fair king's staff, and he aided our cause out of sheer moral courage and compassion for the children. When His Majesty Silverthorn discovered him, Lord Mosswing helped him escape, and he has been with us ever since." Theo had, of course, informed the king of the young fairy's presence at his estate months earlier, but he wanted the opportunity to commend Juniper to the king in the young fairy's presence.

Juniper bowed deeply, his hands clenched to keep from trembling, and dropped his glamour.

His Majesty Alberdale said, "I am deeply grateful to you, Juniper. Such courage and compassion, especially in one so young, are truly exemplary."

The young fairy's eyes widened, and he blinked in surprise. "Thank you, Your Majesty," he murmured.

With a warm smile, the king said, "Thank you for coming today. It is always an honor to become acquainted with those of courage and good character. I understand you are to meet the children." His expression grew more sober. "As requested, I did let Mr. and Mrs. Porter know you were coming. The children are a little apprehensive, but I am sure you will be kind." This last was said in the gentlest tone of warning possible.

After they had agreed and the king had bidden Theo a fond farewell, they left the king's study. Theo led them cheerfully through the palace to the manor in which the children were still housed.

The Fair Folk, no longer wearing their glamours, looked about the palace and the courtyard with open admiration. Lily thought this was both endearing and slightly amusing, for to her eyes, the Fair palace was more extravagant and riotously beautiful than anything in the human world.

Theo led them through the little gate in the white fence surrounding the garden around the guest manor and up the flagstone path toward the door. None of the plants were blooming this late in the year, but the maples near the corners of the house were a lovely scarlet, and the heuchera in the flower beds boasted every shade from deep burgundy to bright yellow, and deep purple loropetalum offered leaves in a shade any flower would be proud to bear.

Theo knocked on the door.

John Porter opened the door. "Good afternoon, Mr. Overton." His gaze flicked over the Fair Folk, and he bowed slightly.

Theo said warmly, "Is Mrs. Porter here? I had hoped the children would be playing. I believe my friends would find it quite encouraging to see them enjoying themselves, just as I did."

"Yes, sir." John led them through the house and out into the sheltered garden in the back, where the children were indeed playing.

When the children caught sight of the group, the revelry came to a sudden halt. Some of the children seemed frozen, and others edged closer to John or to their nearest friend.

"Children, you remember Lord Selby and Mr. and Mrs. Overton," said John reassuringly. "These are some of their friends. Mr. Overton?"

Theo introduced them one by one, just as he had to the king. Then he addressed one of the older boys. "When I visited a few weeks ago, I enjoyed the games with you very much. I'm not sure if Juniper was ever able to play in the Fair Lands at all, so I thought we might teach him a few of the games Lord Selby and I so enjoyed. Perhaps you would be willing to show him how to play Follow the Leader?"

The boy's eyes flicked cautiously at Juniper, then he fixed his eyes on Theo again. "Do you want me to?" His hands clenched at his sides, and then he shoved them in his pockets.

"It would be kind." Theo smiled gently. "Would it help if I played with you?"

The boy gave a jerky nod.

"All right. I do think you'll be the best leader, though. Perhaps some of the others can go next, and then Juniper, and then Lord Selby and me?"

The boy nodded again.

In her soft, elegant voice, Poppy said, "Lord Mosswing, Miss Firethorn, I believe the children are a little frightened. Might we go sit there on the patio, so the children can see us from a distance, and perhaps grow a little more comfortable?"

Cedar graciously assented, inwardly delighted by the thoughtfulness of his beloved, and Crocus followed them to the wrought iron chairs on the brick patio. Fenton would have accompanied them, for he thought it much preferable to sit by the Fair maiden he so admired than make himself look ridiculous in Follow the Leader.

Then one of the little girls looked up at him and said, "Will you push me on the swing?" No gentleman could possibly refuse such a charming request from such a sweet, hopeful child, and he followed her to the wooden swing hanging from one of the branches of a large oak tree to one side of the lawn.

After several minutes swinging, the little girl said she was ready to play something else, and, with increasing confidence, grabbed Fenton's hand and tugged him toward the group that was jumping rope.

Fenton took a spot at one of the ends of the two ropes, while Theo was convinced to take a turn in the middle, which he did with great skill, to the delight of the onlooking children.

"I didn't know gentlemen knew how to jump rope!" said one girl in surprise.

With two more jumps, Theo was free, and he said seriously, "Well, it isn't commonly known, but even gentlemen were children once."

The older children laughed, while one of the youngest looked a little confused by this.

"Would you like a try, Juniper?" Fenton asked.

Juniper, more confident now, nodded, and in a moment he had leaped between the swinging ropes. Like all fairies, he was quick, and he had good rhythm, for nearly all fairies had at least this much musical talent. Moreover, he was in high spirits, or what passed for high spirits given his shy temperament. To the cheering of the children, he jumped, knees high, and duplicated nearly every one of Theo's tricks successfully on his first try, until, with one little misjudgment, the rope tangled in his feet.

The children clapped and cried out in admiration. Cheeks flushed, the young fairy grinned and ducked his head as he stepped out of the ropes to give one of the human children a turn.

"Well done!" said one of the boys approvingly, and Juniper's blush deepened.

"Thank you," he said.

One of the girls said to him, "You can play stick and hoop with me if you like."

"I don't know how. Will you teach me?"

The child gave him a horrified look. "You don't know how to play stick and hoop? What did you play in the Fair Lands, then?"

Juniper shook his head. "I don't remember playing more than once or twice, when I was quite small. Mostly I worked and tried to stay out of trouble."

One of the older boys, who had earlier introduced himself as Walter, said, "You didn't have an easy time of it there?"

Juniper shook his head again and bit his lip. "No." Then with a shy smile, he said, "I would like to learn your games. I am glad you are happy here. I did hope that for you, that even if I was discovered and executed, at least you would be safe back in the human world."

Walter blinked. "I didn't realize." He swallowed. "Well, I'm glad you're safe too," he offered after a moment.

Juniper said, "I have Mr. Overton to thank for that, just as you do." He took a bracing breath, then said in a rush, "Would you like to see a little magic?"

The boy studied him, then cautiously said, "It won't hurt anyone, will it?"

"I would never," said Juniper. "It's only a little glamour. You can put a glamour on things, you know, and even in the air, if you're good at it." He knelt and formed the magic into the image of a teapot and two steaming cups of tea sitting on a low table. "I've learned to enjoy tea since I've been here in the human world. I had never tasted it before; it was only given to His Majesty Silverthorn's favorites, and the ambassadors and envoys to the human world were able to purchase it." He glanced up to see the children looking at him, fascinated.

"Can you make a kitten?" asked one of the little girls.

Juniper obligingly formed the image of a little black and white kitten which he cupped in his narrow hands. "I don't know the animals of your world well, but there were some kittens in Mr. Overton's barn a few months ago."

"Did you get to pet them?"

Juniper grinned. "I did!"

The little girl reached out to pet the image of the kitten, and her hand went right through it to Juniper's hand. She jerked back, as if he'd burned her, then stared at him. "You feel like a person." There was a hint of accusation in her voice.

"I am a person," he said gravely. "I'm a fairy, but I'm still a person." He let the kitten image fade and held out his empty hands, palms upward.

The girl reached out tentatively to touch his hand again, the touch light and careful.

One of the boys said, "Why do fairies have strange colored hair?"

Juniper flinched reflexively when one of the other girls touched his deep purple curls, but her touch was timid and careful, not like the harsh grip one of the older fairy servants had so often used. "It isn't strange for us," he said, keeping his voice steady.

From the patio some distance away, Crocus watched with fascination as Juniper sat cross-legged on the grass and let the children examine his hair and slightly pointed ears. Fenton came to stand nearby, his arms crossed and his lips curved in a faint smile.

Theo stood nearer the children, his eyes sparkling.

Juniper asked if anyone would be frightened, then, receiving reassurances that everyone would be brave, he used his glamour to make the image of a tiny peryton, which was both fierce and entirely lacking any power to frighten, since it was so small. The illusory peryton consented to pose with great dignity to be examined by the children, and then disappeared in a puff of pink and purple sparkles for the amusement of the children.

After an hour and a half, some of the children had begun a game of hopscotch at one end of the yard, while another group was engaged in an energetic game of tag. Juniper looked a little overwhelmed, though he seemed happy. Theo approached his fairy charge. "Are you ready to go home?"

Juniper smiled up at him. "Yes, sir." He took a deep breath and looked across the yard again. "You were right, sir. This was encouraging. Thank you."

Theo put a hand on the young fairy's shoulder affectionately. "Good. You can just call me Theo, you know."

Juniper laughed under his breath. "I do, sometimes. In the veil, I did, because I wasn't sure it was you and I wanted to be sure. But I think my respect has grown since then, and it seems harder now."

"I am still the same person, and we are closer friends now, I should like to think." Theo smiled radiantly at him.

The fairy flushed and looked down. "Yes, Theo, sir." He laughed again, almost inaudibly, at Theo's theatrical sigh. "Thank you."

The sincerity that filled his voice twisted in Theo's heart, and the young man said gently, "You're welcome, Juniper."

When they met Anselm in the courtyard to return home, Juniper said impulsively, "Might I ride up front with you, sir?"

Anselm looked to Theo and said, "I would be delighted, if you think it's safe."

Theo frowned. "If you wear a human glamour, and keep your hood over your face, I suppose we might risk it. Lord Selby and I will stay close, of course. Anselm, you're armed?"

"Yes, sir."

"All right."

Juniper climbed up to sit beside Anselm in the narrow driver's seat and pulled his hood forward to obscure his face from any onlookers.

The drive back to the Overton estate was quiet. Cedar and Poppy made polite conversation about the beauty of the human world and the kindness of the Overtons in hosting them. Poppy asked Crocus if she had enjoyed the afternoon, and she said, with some surprise, that she had.

"It seems that Mr. Overton and Lord Selby are quite popular with the children," Poppy said with a smile.

"Yes." Crocus could not help but agree. She had felt a such a sense of protectiveness over Juniper, though she had not known him, that seeing him smile while playing with the children had soothed some of her worry.

The following morning Theo drew Juniper into one of the smaller rooms on the first floor, away from the others. Theo questioned Juniper in great depth about binding magic, and they experimented together for hours.

Finally, Juniper said, "I really don't think it's possible."

"All right." Theo sighed. "Well, it was worth a try. We have a plan, nevertheless."

Juniper's eyes widened. "You're really going to do it?"

"Absolutely."

Juniper nodded, his eyes wide. "I'll give you everything I can."

"Thank you, Juniper."

The young fairy bit his lip. "Are you not terrified?"

Theo let out a soft, grieved breath. "Fear is the least of what troubles me." He swallowed and said, "You might as well rest until tomorrow night, if you can give me the magic then. Miss Firethorn will be recalled Monday."

Juniper nodded gravely.

CHAPTER TWENTY-SEVEN
Heartache and Solace

Monday morning, Theo rose even earlier than usual. Lily found him in his dressing gown staring out the window of their sitting room, with his hands shoved in his pockets.

"Good morning, my love," she said as she wrapped her arms around his lean waist.

"Morning." He managed a melancholy smile. "Miss Firethorn will be recalled to the Fair Lands today. Fenton, Cedar and I will accompany her when she returns."

Lily nodded, feeling the heaviness in these words. "How can I help?" she asked gently. She looked up at his dear face, at the hazel eyes which always danced with wit and joy, and it grieved her to see him so troubled. She raised a hand to cup his cheek.

He leaned in to her touch and closed his eyes for a moment. Then he met her gaze and said, "I know you are brave, my love, but I will ask you to stay here with Lady Miscanthus, Juniper, and my parents."

She blinked. "I would rather help you." Her voice shook, and she straightened a little, wanting him to see her determination. "Surely I can help you more there, even in some small way, than by playing hostess here. Besides, your parents are more than capable."

He sighed, and there was such a weight of grief in his eyes that she could not bring herself to continue the argument. "Dearest Lily, please. I beg you to stay here in safety, for I fear I will not be able to do what I must do if… if you are watching, and if I do not know you to be safely away from… from what we face."

A chill terror swept over her. "What will you face?"

He looked down, unwilling to meet her eyes, but he drew her closer. He wrapped his arms more tightly around her, as if he meant for her to perceive his faint shudder. He swallowed. "I would rather not say, my love," he whispered, then pressed a kiss to her hair.

"Is there nothing I can do to help?" Desperation made her voice shake, and she twisted in his arms to look up at him.

He kissed her again and said, "Pray for us, my love, and be of good courage." He kissed her cheek, her ear, where he whispered of his love and gratitude, and then her neck, before bowing low over her hands and kissing them each in turn. "Thank you, my love."

She wanted to argue, to plead with him to let her do something more, and perhaps, if she had had skill with a blade, or more significant magic, she would have. But the depth of his relief at her agreement to stay in the human world lent weight to his plea, for he should face this challenge, whatever it was, without the added worry for her safety.

"I will stay," she said reluctantly, "if, and only if, you promise to return to me whole."

"I will do my best, dearest Lily."

When they descended to the dining room to meet their guests, Theo put on his bright smile as if by magic. But Lily knew him better now than she had just a few months ago at that party where he had been so troubled just before he had rescued her brother and Araminta from Lord Willowvale. Now she could perceive that his smile was not entirely carefree, and his eyes had the faintest shadow of concern hidden behind the sparkling friendliness. Still, the facade was nearly convincing, even to her, and she breathed a sigh of relief, if not joy, that he had been so honest with her in private.

If she could not help him in the physical confrontation, at least she might offer some rest and comfort for his troubled heart.

CHAPTER TWENTY-EIGHT
Miss Firethorn Is Called To Service

After breakfast, Fenton arrived, as handsome and quietly charming as ever. Crocus resolutely ignored the way her heart leapt within her when she saw him enter the parlor where everyone had gathered for tea and games.

"Good morning." He greeted them and bowed politely to everyone in turn, smiling. Was it her imagination, or was he perhaps a little graver than usual? He was never frivolous, not like Theo, full of effervescent delight and witty remarks and sparkling humor.

Still, he seemed a little more pensive than usual. For a moment, when she forgot herself and what she knew she ought to do, she met his gaze and smiled. His eyes were so warm and so kind that she couldn't help the smile that came to her lips.

Then she remembered, and she wiped the smile from her face and looked away. She felt his inaudible sigh as if it were her own, a soft, despairing grief that had no outlet.

Theo pulled Fenton out into the hallway to speak with him privately.

"His Majesty Silverthorn will call Miss Firethorn to service today," Theo said. "I do not know how he will make his call known, but somehow he will. When she answers his call, you and I and Cedar must go with her. I've already told Cedar."

Fenton blinked. "What will we do?"

Theo's eyes grew unwontedly serious, and he said, "You'll see." There was a strange, tight tone to his voice.

"I have a feeling you're planning something terribly clever and horribly dangerous, and I wish you wouldn't, Theo." Fenton held his friend's gaze.

Theo smiled reassuringly. "Don't worry about me. You just be yourself to His Majesty, and he'll understand."

"Won't you tell me what you're planning?" Fenton said in a choked voice.

"I don't think it would help matters, and it might make your part more difficult. Can you please trust me, Fen?"

Fenton sighed and dropped his head. "You know I do," he murmured. "I fear for you, Theo. This isn't your fight."

"You're my dearest friend. I can't walk away and let you face His Majesty alone. Please don't ask it of me."

Fenton swallowed and said with quiet resignation, "All right. What do you want me to do?"

"Take this." Theo held out his hand, which appeared empty.

When Fenton clasped it, the binding magic snapped between them like fire, and Fenton let out a gasp of pain. As quickly as it had come, the magic settled into his heart, leaving only the memory of its fiery path up his arm.

"Are you all right? It doesn't still hurt, does it?" Theo said.

"It's all right. Feels warm, I think." Fenton rubbed his chest, then said, "No, I can't even feel it."

"Draw on it when you need a little extra strength." Theo's hazel eyes were grave. They were so often dancing with mirth that for a moment, Fenton's fear rose.

"What have you done, Theo?" he asked quietly.

"Just given you a little reinforcement. Pull on it as hard as you want. It won't break."

Fenton almost questioned him further, but he knew Theo would not tell him any more.

Theo smiled, as warm and reassuring as ever, and ushered him back into the parlor.

It was decided that Juniper and Lord Selby would oppose Theo in chess, which Theo would play with his chair turned away from the board. Juniper would test the new strategies he had learned against Theo's mental image of the board, and Fenton would lend assistance and advice as necessary. Meanwhile, Theo could observe his lovely wife reading poetry to Crocus, Poppy, and his mother. Cedar, Sir Theodore, and Fenton were engaged in a game of Yacht, a dice game of chance and strategy. The humans had suggested Liar's Dice, but then realized Cedar would be at a distinct disadvantage in this.

Crocus split her attention between Lily's reading of a poem, apparently famous, about a hero's journey across the world to rejoin his beloved, and surreptitiously observing Fenton. Crocus did not know how the hero in the poem had become separated from his beloved, for the poem was quite long and Lady Overton had suggested that she begin in the middle, with the hero's passionate declaration of love for his betrothed. If Lily had read the beginning, Crocus would have missed it anyway, for she found that her eyes were continually drawn back to Fenton.

The young nobleman smiled encouragingly when Juniper made a particular move in chess, then turned back to the dice game. After his move, and after congratulating Sir Theodore on a lucky roll, he studied the chess board again.

Juniper put his hand on his remaining bishop but did not move it. Fenton pointed to a rook on the other side of the board, and Juniper withdrew his hand.

The young fairy chewed his lip. "You really are terrifyingly good at this, sir," he said to Theo.

Theo laughed. "You are improving rapidly. I am sure you will beat me soon."

Fenton said, "Don't hold your breath, Juniper. He has encouraged me like that for a decade, and I've only beaten him twice, and I think he let me win." Crocus was more intrigued by the warmth in his eyes than by the words, for it seemed that the affection between the friends was stronger than any resentment that might have arisen.

When Theo had triumphed yet again, to Juniper's consternation and Crocus's incredulity, Fenton said, "Ah, well, better luck next time, Juniper. Not victory, mind you, but better luck."

Theo turned around to survey the board with a little flicker of satisfaction in his eyes. "You played very well, Juniper." Then, to Fenton, he said, "Perhaps you might like to take a walk in the garden with Miss Firethorn."

Fenton hesitated and glanced at her, then down at the board. "I shouldn't trouble her," he murmured.

Guilt pressed upon Crocus so heavily that for a moment she could not breathe. It was not fair at all that Lord Selby should feel guilty about troubling her, for had she not brought trouble to his very door? She had repaid his hospitality to herself, and his protection of her cousin, with anger and peril and coldness.

Watching his guidance of Juniper in this human game, and the vulnerability in his eyes before he looked away, she felt regret and remorse roll over her like ocean waves.

She stood. "I would like that, Lord Selby," she said softly, before she could change her mind.

He blinked, and for an instant there was, if not hope in his eyes, a flicker of gratitude. "I would be delighted to escort you, Miss Firethorn."

Theo and Cedar rose too, for even now Theo and his father insisted that no one ought to be alone in the gardens or anywhere outdoors while Lord Larch remained a threat.

Fenton offered Crocus his arm, and she put her hand upon it in the human style. Although it was quite proper, it still seemed a strangely intimate gesture to her Fair sensibilities, especially since she had rarely been treated with such respect in the Fair Lands. Theo and Cedar followed at a distance, offering escort for both propriety and safety.

The air was frigid, but there was no wind, and the sun was bright and strong, warming their shoulders through their cloaks. Fenton led Crocus to a sheltered little nook in the garden from which they could look up at the distant hills covered in the spectacular colors of the trees. He took off his cloak and spread it upon the bench. If she had realized what he was doing, she would have protested, but the gesture was so alien to her that she merely looked at him in confusion when he indicated that she should sit upon it.

She did so, feeling the guilt nearly choke her, and she said nothing.

The day was so clear and bright that the hills receded before them in an exuberant display of the beauty of the human world. Scarlet-leaved maples, dogwoods, and oaks nestled between yellow poplars, beeches, birches, and sycamores. The treetops danced in the breezes that caressed the hillsides.

"Your world is beautiful," Crocus said at last.

Fenton nodded. "It is." There was a faint catch in his voice, as if there were something else he wanted to say.

They sat in silence for several minutes until Fenton asked, "What was your home like in the Fair Lands?"

Crocus hesitated. "I do not want to cause you pain," she said at last.

Beside her, separated by a proper space of twelve inches, that might have been twelve miles, Fenton chuckled, soft and despairing. "Miss Firethorn, I will suffer any pain for you, if it could help at all. Please do not let fear of that make you withhold even this small confidence."

She pressed her lips together and looked down at her hands clasped in her lap. Her knuckles were white.

Fenton shifted beside her. "Forgive me."

"There is nothing to forgive." Crocus swallowed. Using her glamour, she sketched a landscape in the air in front of them, overlaid on the human world and temporarily hiding it, at least from their vantage point upon the bench.

Crocus cleared her throat. "When I left the Fair Lands to search for Juniper, the hills were fading. The mountain tops were disintegrating into mist, and some of the outlying villages had entirely disappeared."

The crisp, clean lines of the snow-covered mountaintops against the pink-streaked sky grew hazy, and the sky itself seemed to fade in that direction.

"The fading was visible from the house in which I was bound to service, but I did not know anyone who was taken by the mist." Nevertheless, she felt her throat tighten with emotion. "When we were in the Fair Lands and you fought the manticore, I caught a glimpse of the mountains again, for we were in the same part of the Fair Lands as that house, though miles away. The mountains were solid and bright in the sunlight."

The glamour shifted to show this, and Fenton nearly gasped at the beauty, for the mountains seemed even more real than before. The snowy peaks gleamed in the slanting golden light of the Fair sun. Trees of a thousand colors clustered like vibrant flowers upon the distance slopes, cerulean and indigo and scarlet vying for prominence with gold and green.

"He did that, didn't he?" Crocus gestured at the mountains. "He kept them from falling into mist."

"I almost wish I'd seen it, but I'm glad—" Fenton's throat closed with emotion so deep it shook him, and he swallowed. "I'm glad I didn't. I don't think I'm strong enough to watch someone I love suffer like that and hold my peace."

Crocus glanced at him. "You've been friends a long time."

"Since we were boys. But I've known most of the noblemen my age just as long." Unspoken in this, but clearly conveyed, was that none of them were quite like Theo.

"Were you never jealous of him? It is hard sometimes, I think, to be the quiet one, when someone shines so brightly beside you."

Fenton smiled and looked down at the grass. He plucked a stalk and rubbed it between his fingers, forming the words and then discarding them as inadequate.

Finally he said, "Once, for a moment or two, jealousy called, and I thought about answering. But then I thought of how much colder and darker my life would be, if I saw him as competition rather than a friend." He looked up to meet her eyes, full of grace and wonder. "Why should I turn something bright and generous into something small and mean, and hurt us both in doing so?"

Crocus sighed softly. "What a lovely heart you have."

Fenton laughed under his breath and glanced at her, then at the distant hills. "I am glad you think so, Miss Firethorn."

She let the glamour fade, and they sat in silence before the bright beauty of autumn in the human world.

"Thank you, Miss Firethorn," Fenton said at last.

"Thank you, Lord Selby," she murmured, for she felt the guilt that pressed upon her fade for a moment in the peace in his presence.

A sound like a hunting horn rang in her head, and she stood without thinking. "The king calls me to service," she said. She looked at Fenton, squashing her terror resolutely down, so that he saw only a little flicker of fear in her eyes, for she could not entirely hide that. "Farewell, Lord Selby. I thank you for everything."

"Theo!" Fenton cried over his shoulder. "Wait, Miss Firethorn!"

She opened the door into the veil and wondered at the ease with which she did so. His Majesty Silverthorn's call must have given her some extra measure of magic, at least for the purpose of fulfilling his command, for never before had she managed it without a great deal of effort.

Then Theo was at her side, and he caught her hand to keep her from stepping into the veil. "Wait for Lord Mosswing," he said. Then over his shoulder, he said, "Hurry!"

But the call of the king's magic in Crocus's mind seemed to govern her feet, and she stepped into the veil without conscious thought. The two young men stayed at her side, and Theo held the door open for a moment, his hand in hers.

Then the veil snapped closed in his face, leaving them in the echoing pitch dark. Theo shoved his magic into it, but it did not open again.

"He will follow us." He kept his voice steady and reassuring. "Draw your sword, if you please, Lord Selby, and I will do the same. We'll keep Miss Firethorn between us."

With that, he led them through the veil toward the Fair Lands.

In the dark of the tunnel, with the dank scent of damp stone and half rotted moss in her nostrils, Crocus found herself entirely speechless for several minutes.

Theo's hand was warm and strong, his narrow fingers slightly calloused from years of practice at swordplay. She had expected his hands to be softer; apparently not all human noblemen were as pampered as she had assumed. Fenton's hand was similarly calloused, but wider, with a reassuring solidity to his grip. His hand was cooler, for his hands had been loose in his lap while they had talked on the bench in the chilly air, while Theo must have had his hands in his pockets. Between them, she felt an unexpected surge of gratitude, for they did not intend to let her pass through the veil unprotected.

Then her fear rose. "You shouldn't have come!" she snapped, for terror made her voice sharp. "The Fair Court isn't safe for humans."

"Forgive me, Miss Firethorn, but neither Lord Selby nor I could countenance leaving you in servitude to His Majesty Silverthorn." Theo's answer came out of the darkness ahead of her.

"What are you going to do about it?" Her voice shook. "What can you possibly do about it?"

Fenton said mildly, "Theo, I do think it is time you explain your plan to me, so that I might play my part better."

"Just be yourself," Theo murmured, and if there was the slightest catch in his voice, no one mentioned it.

CHAPTER TWENTY-NINE
A Convergence of Bargains

Five minutes later, Theo stopped.

"Miss Firethorn, I entreat you to stay by Lord Selby's side as well as you can." Theo's voice was steady. "And forgive me, if you can ever bring yourself to do so."

"What?" Her question was lost in dismay as Theo opened the door to the Fair Lands.

Crocus was astonished to find that Theo had brought them directly to the rear of His Majesty Silverthorn's throne room. Perhaps this was a display of his skill or power, or perhaps it was merely for convenience, but in either case, it impressed the Fair king.

His Majesty Silverthorn stood in shock from where he had been sitting upon his throne.

The Fair throne room was full of onlookers, who had been standing in small groups along both sides of the central space. The fluted columns that lined the room shone in the bright light that flooded the space from the tall windows. The floor was now cobalt glass tiles in an intricate trellis pattern, edged in brilliant green moss. Blue flowers of a thousand varieties cascaded down the sides of the steps up to the dais upon which the king stood.

Lord Willowvale stood near the front of the room, taut and lean. He was dressed in a silver jacket trimmed in white, with narrow, well-cut trousers of a darker silver. The attire would have been outrageous in Valestria, or anywhere in the human world, but in comparison to the other Fair Folk in the throne room, it was muted and severe. Lord Willowvale's pale skin, icy blue eyes, and white hair, combined with this attire, gave an impression of single-minded focus and relentless purpose.

On the other side of the room, Lord Bayberry's eyes locked onto Theo with terrifying intensity. There was a space around him, as if even the other Fair Folk feared him. His wolves, which had been seated at his side, stood, their ears pricked.

Theo stepped out of the veil in front of Crocus and Fenton and bowed deeply to the king. Then, in a clear, carrying voice, he said, "Your Majesty, I offer myself in place of Miss Firethorn. My magic is small, and my life is short compared to that of the Fair Folk, but I believe you hold some grievance against me, so perhaps my death might suffice to buy her freedom."

Fenton's horrified gasp was the first sound to break the silence. "No, Theo!"

"Why would you do that?" Crocus breathed.

But Theo looked only at the king.

"Your Majesty." Lord Willowvale stepped forward with a graceful bow. "Might I have a word with you privately?"

The Fair king glanced at him, then back at Theo. "Yes," he said at last.

Lord Willowvale strode confidently up to His Majesty Silverthorn and leaned close to speak into the king's ear.

A moment later he stepped back, his gaze not leaving the king's face.

"You would do this of your own free will?" the king asked.

"Yes, Your Majesty." Lord Willowvale gave another, deeper bow to emphasize his words.

His Majesty Silverthorn stared at him, then swallowed. "What has come over you?" he murmured, as if to himself. "No, I cannot allow it."

Theo said, "Your Majesty, I will also note that your agent Lord Larch seems to desire some revenge against the Rose and all who aided him. I should be grieved indeed if any of that vengeance fell upon my friends rather than me. Perhaps, if you see fit, Lord Larch might execute your judgment against me, and thus end his campaign against my friends as well as purchase Miss Firethorn's freedom."

Theo bowed again more deeply.

The Fair king opened his mouth, but before he could say anything, Fenton cried, "No, I beg you, Your Majesty, let it be me! Do not forget that he holds your lands with his love! If he dies, your lands are in more danger, but while he lives, your Fair Lands are safe. Let it be me who dies for her. I will buy her freedom gladly."

The Fair king stared at him, his pale lips twitching. "What magic have you wrought, Overton?" he breathed. "Who is this?"

Fenton stepped forward and put himself in front of Theo. "My name is Fenton Selby, Marquess of Ambervale, Your Majesty. Theo is my oldest and dearest friend." He bowed deeply and flicked a hand at Theo as he did so, as if to shoo Theo away from danger.

"Theo, take her and go," he said over his shoulder.

Theo would have wept at his friend's courage, if there had been time.

"Overton, I concede that…" His Majesty began.

Lord Larch cried, "Your Majesty!"

Silverthorn's violet eyes blazed at the interruption, but he turned to the Fair lord with icy control. "Yes, Larch?" he said, omitting the lord's title in rebuke.

"If you will not kill him, I will," Larch snapped.

For a split second, the Fair king glanced at Theo.

The young man, pale and resolute, pressed his lips together and said nothing.

"Proceed," said Silverthorn.

Fiery magic ripped from Larch's hands and tore into Fenton.

The high, keening scream that came from the young nobleman brought Theo to his knees.

"No!" cried Crocus, and she flung herself toward the king.

On her knees before the Fair king, she begged for Fenton's life. "Your Majesty, please! I will serve you to the end of my days. Kill me instead! Why would you let Lord Larch kill him for the Rose's crimes! And the Rose served the Fair Lands, so why should his deeds be considered crimes at all? *Please*, Your Majesty, please stop!"

Fenton's wordless, horrifying wail went on for far too long until he gasped for breath and began again.

Crocus wept, her face buried in her hands.

The air crackled with magic. Human pain echoed in the vast room, layer upon layer of anguish, pure and unsullied by conscious thought or desire.

Lord Willowvale twitched, his hand on his sword hilt, and finally said, "Your Majesty."

"That's enough!" snapped the king in a voice like a crack of thunder.

The flood of magic that illuminated Fenton's bones in fiery agony abruptly vanished.

He fell to his knees, gasping.

His skin was cold, and his heart burned within him.

For a moment, his mind felt like a tattered rag, emptied and shredded by the passage of too much magic for a human to endure.

The thread of magic in his heart steadied him, and he pulled on it as if he were climbing a rope up from an abyss, hand over hand, thought layered upon thought, until he remembered who he was.

Slowly, trembling, Fenton struggled to his feet.

"Your Majesty, thank you." The world wavered, and Fenton licked his dry lips. "Set her free, as you promised." His throat rasped, as if he had been screaming. Perhaps he had. He couldn't remember.

Lord Larch said, "Why is he not dead?"

Lord Willowvale said, "Your Majesty, if I might speak to you privately a moment, please?"

He stepped closer and spoke directly into the king's ear. His Majesty Silverthorn kept his eyes upon Fenton, who stood with his feet braced in the middle of the room. The young nobleman blinked rapidly, trying to get the strange, red-tinged darkness to fade from his vision.

After a moment, the king nodded once.

"Miss Crocus Firethorn, you are released from your service to me from this moment." His Majesty Silverthorn said in a clear, ringing voice. "Lord Larch, you are relieved from your position."

"What?" The Fair lord stared at the king in horror. "Why?"

"I have no further need for your services. Your influence upon the crown is at an end. You will keep your ancestral lands and title."

The fairy straightened, his eyes blazing with fury. "Is this because you esteem the stubbornness of a human over my undisputed talent and distinguished service? Are you so easily swayed by human wiles?"

"Silence, Larch," the king said, with a razor edge in his voice. "I owe you no answer."

Fenton finally managed to make out Crocus through the haze over his vision, but he could not seem to make his feet move yet. Nevertheless, he felt a slow, steady trickle of strength that flowed from whatever magic he had been clinging to through the maelstrom of Larch's destructive power. He closed his eyes and imagined himself resting his forehead against the rope, somewhere on the cliff as he climbed from a bottomless abyss of agony toward something like sanity again. His hands cramped, and his breath rasped, but the rope held firm between his fingers, and he continued without looking back.

"How can a human withstand Larch's power?" Crocus stood in front of him. "I don't think that's possible."

She wrapped one arm around Fenton, steadying his trembling, and looked back toward the king.

"By your leave, Your Majesty, I will return with the humans to their world."

"I have released all claims to you. Go in peace."

Finally, Fenton's fractured mind began to put the pieces together.

What was the slow, steady trickle of strength but the fiery magic that had threaded his veins earlier? It had the same fierce love in it, the blazing heat which he had not at first recognized as love.

Theo.

Lord Willowvale stepped forward, and Fenton turned unsteadily to look back to where his friend had been standing.

Theo lay crumpled face down on the cobalt tile floor.

Fenton stumbled forward and fell to his knees beside Theo. With trembling fingers, he felt for a pulse in Theo's throat, but his own heart-beat was so unsteady, and his fingers were shaking so badly, that he could not tell if Theo were alive at all. Was his chest moving?

Too exhausted to sob, he could not think of what to do.

"Move," Lord Willowvale muttered. "Let me turn him over."

The Fair lord knelt beside Fenton. He grasped Theo's shoulders with his pale hands and turned the young man over with unexpected care. He pressed his fingertips to Theo's throat, then his wrist, then hissed in frustration.

"He can't be dead." Fenton could not look away from Theo's face.

He was so deathly pale. His copper eyelashes gleamed against his skin; they were damp, as if his eyes had filled with tears before he'd collapsed. His mouth was open, and there was a little blood on his lips, but only a little.

Willowvale leaned in closer, putting his ear to Theo's lips.

"He breathes," the Fair lord said. "I can't say how long that will last." He looked up at the king. "Your Majesty, I request that you call for Lord Mosswing."

From his position at the top of the dais, the Fair king gave a curt nod. "Do so."

There was some commotion in the back of the room, which Fenton could not parse into words, much less comprehend.

Theo moaned softly before his eyelids fluttered open for a brief moment.

Lord Larch's voice rang out across the room, clear and cold and powerful. "I challenge you, Theo Overton, to a duel to the death. Now."

Theo breathed, "I cannot answer it, my lord." His voice was nearly inaudible.

"Why?" Crocus whispered in horror. "You lost your challenge, Lord Larch." She stood before the dais, trembling, and then stepped closer to Fenton and Theo.

"Only due to his interference!" Lord Larch stalked forward, flicking his narrow blade in short, sharp movements at his side. "In consideration of your deplorable lack of magic and of His Majesty's ruling, I shall limit myself to a blade. Put your sword in your hand and get your feet under you, for I mean to run you through."

Theo sighed. "I cannot."

Fenton stood, swaying. "I will answer it for him."

Larch hissed in outrage. "I'll kill you first, then him. My claim against him remains. How dare you interfere, Overton?" His voice cracked.

Theo managed to open his eyes for a moment. "He's my friend." This seemed so utterly exhausting that for a moment he could say nothing else. "Help me up," he breathed.

"Idiot," Willowvale muttered. He put a restraining hand on Theo's chest and shoved him back down, then stepped forward. "I will stand for Overton."

He drew his sword and stood in the center of the throne room, straight and tall and utterly confident.

"Why would you stand for him?" Larch said in disbelief.

Willowvale's eyes danced with a deep, terrible humor. "He is my friend," he said.

Lord Bayberry, who had stood silent all this time, so that Fenton and Theo had entirely forgotten he was there at all, stepped forward as well. He put his hand on the hilt of his sword, but did not draw it. "He is also my friend." His voice was as cold and hard as the marble beneath their feet.

Willowvale glanced at him. "How?"

"I owe you no explanation, Willowvale." Bayberry's lips curled in muted irritation. "Larch, select a second, if you so choose, for I will not relent once we begin."

Larch hesitated. "My lords, I have no wish to duel you."

"Nevertheless, you will, unless you withdraw your challenge for now and forever against Theo Overton." Bayberry gave a wolf-like smile.

Theo struggled to a kneeling position, but could not manage to gain his feet. "And my friends and family, and all humans," he gasped. Fenton had stepped back to stand at his side, and he gripped the shoulder of Theo's jacket, steadying them both.

"I did not say I would not fight. Only that I have no wish to," Larch said at last, his mouth working with fury. "Who shall it be first?"

"I claim first right," Willowvale said, just as Bayberry said, "Me."

Willowvale laughed, low and cold, and said, "My lord Bayberry, I know not whose claim ought to take precedence, but I ask your leave to kill him first."

Bayberry's wolves growled, but the Fair lord said, "As you wish, my lord." He gave a slight, elegant bow to Willowvale and took a step backward.

Fenton swayed and braced his feet farther apart, unwilling to lean on Theo's shoulder.

His fingers cramped, locked as they were in the collar of Theo's jacket. Theo sagged until he leaned against Fenton's leg, eyes closed again.

Still, Theo managed, "Fen? You're all right?"

"Yes." Fenton did not know if it was a lie, for he could barely see the duel which was about to begin through the darkening haze over his vision. "I think I'm going to faint."

Crocus grabbed his arm. "Sit down," she said. "You're both more dead than alive. What did you do, Mr. Overton?"

Fenton laughed under his breath, eyes closed. The sound of steel rang out, and Larch screamed something insulting, but Fenton could not be bothered to care. "Something terribly clever and horribly dangerous. I was right, Theo."

Theo murmured, "It worked, didn't it? He poured enough magic in you to kill a dozen griffins, and yet you're alive."

"Are you?"

There was a long, disconcerting silence, in which Fenton waited with growing horror, until he felt the power of the binding magic wrapped around his heart, strong and steady.

Theo mumbled, "I'll be all right."

One of the fairies wounded the other, but neither Fenton nor Theo was able to muster the energy to open their eyes and observe who it was.

Bayberry's wolves suddenly burst into snarling fury, and there was another cry, this time of outrage and terror.

Fenton nearly fell over when Theo slumped into him. Fenton could not help him up, for he felt as weak as a newborn kitten, and he merely held Theo for a moment until Crocus could help him. The Fair woman eased Theo to the floor, where he lay limp and silent.

Steel rang upon steel, until the whole world seemed to be nothing but the ringing of blade against blade.

At last, there was silence.

CHAPTER THIRTY
The Cost and the Crown

The very silence seemed ominous.

Footsteps approached, slow and steady, and Fenton looked up through the red haze to see Lord Willowvale standing above them. Pale blue blood stained the right side of his silver jacket, apparently from a wound in his side. Nevertheless, he stood straight and proud.

"Overton," he said in a low voice. "Are you still alive?"

Theo gave no sign that he had heard Willowvale's voice. The Fair lord knelt beside him and pressed his white fingers against Theo's throat.

He stood again. "Where is Mosswing?" he said in bitter frustration.

A shadow fell across them, and Fenton and Crocus looked up to see Silverthorn at Willowvale's shoulder.

"What did he do?" the king asked quietly. "Why should Larch's magic have affected him?"

Fenton's grief and despair rose like ocean waves in a storm, and he bowed his head to his knees. His eyes filled with tears, for Theo's reassurance that he would be all right seemed born more of optimism than of any reasonable hope.

Fenton found the taut thread of binding magic in his heart, red as blood, and he clung to it with all the strength of their lifelong friendship.

Willowvale murmured something Fenton could not decipher through the crush of fatigue and desperate, fading hope. The fairy knelt beside him and pressed his white fingers, streaked with pale blue blood, against Theo's throat again.

He said sharply, "Mosswing!"

Then Cedar was there, his hand upon Theo's chest. For one minute, two, perhaps three, there was no apparent change in him.

"Fix it, Mosswing," said Willowvale hoarsely.

Cedar's hand trembled, and he did not respond.

Theo's faint, steady breaths stuttered, then grew stronger, and he groaned weakly. He curled onto his side and gasped, "Fen?"

"I'm here." Fenton put a hand on Theo's shoulder.

Cedar lifted his hand and said quietly, "Theo, you're so full of healing magic I doubt you can answer me, but if you can tell me what you did, I can direct the magic a little better."

For a moment, Theo could only breathe. The air felt golden and sparkling inside his lungs, as bright and painful and beautiful as life itself. It took considerable effort to parse out this question, and he couldn't think of the words to answer it at the end anyway. So he mumbled, "Fenton."

Cedar had already put a hand on Fenton's shoulder, filling him with the same blinding golden magic, and Fenton's mind felt bubbly and light, the yawning agony of Larch's magic drowned in the beauty of Cedar's power.

Willowvale's silver-blue eyes had been focused on Theo. When Cedar turned to Willowvale, he raised his snowy eyebrows in surprise.

"May I offer you a little healing magic, Willowvale?" Cedar said quietly. "You're bleeding."

Willowvale shrugged one shoulder, not quite hiding a wince. "I don't expect you to treat me like a friend, Mosswing."

Cedar's turquoise eyes flickered, and he said, "All the same, I will do so, if you will accept it."

Willowvale hesitated, then gave a faint, reluctant nod.

When Cedar put his hand on Willowvale's shoulder, the pale fairy inhaled sharply. "You're very strong," he said in a low voice.

Theo mumbled, "Willowvale?"

Willowvale gave a faint huff of amusement and said, "I'm here. I doubt you're ready to brave the veil yet. Lord Mosswing and I will take you to my manor to recuperate. Larch is dead."

Theo took a deep, shuddering breath and tried to push himself up to hands and knees.

"Sit down, Overton," Willowvale said in a low voice. He put a hand under Theo's arm and steadied him from one side while Cedar took his other arm. Together, they helped him into a sitting position.

Silverthorn had been observing this from several steps away, apparently fascinated by this display. Now he stepped forward.

He sank to one knee in front of Theo, who stared back at him with dazed eyes. The king's dark blue hair set off the crown of silver thorns upon his head. His violet eyes glittered with interest and some strange emotion that neither Theo nor any of the others could identify.

He extended a hand to Theo. "Walk with me," he said in a low voice.

Willowvale said, "Your Majesty, I'm not sure he's competent to understand the words, much less obey. Lord Mosswing's healing magic is quite overpowering."

The Fair king studied Theo's ashen face. The young man's eyes gleamed with gold, but his skin was deathly pale, and his eyelids drifted closed again.

"Perhaps Lord Selby can explain what you did and why he is yet alive. I was under the impression that Lord Larch's magic was unmatched, and yet you two humans, with barely half a scrap of magic between you, withstood him." The king's deep, smooth voice somehow seemed both intimate and carrying, as if he meant the crowded onlookers to hear every word.

Fenton brushed at his eyes. "I don't know. Something with binding magic."

The king's violet eyes rested on Theo again. "Well?" he prompted, almost gently, if a Fair king were capable of gentleness.

Theo's white lips gave a faint quirk, and he managed to open his eyes. "I have a friend who is especially gifted with binding magic," he breathed. "But you can't fight war magic with binding magic. Not really."

Cedar reached out to put his hand upon Theo's shoulder again. Theo's eyes gleamed almost entirely golden, the hazel lost in magic.

"So I didn't fight it. I bound Lord Selby's life to mine, and I wouldn't let him die." Theo closed his eyes and sagged against Cedar's steadying hand. "I bound my life to the land, because Lord Larch's power came from the magic of the Fair Lands, and even he is not strong enough to rip the world apart."

Fenton whispered, "You felt everything?"

Theo half shrugged and smiled, the gold in his eyes glittering. "I don't know. All I knew is that I couldn't let you face Larch alone, and all I had was binding magic."

Silverthorn let out a soft, awed breath. "That is incredible."

"It shouldn't be."

The king proffered his hand again.

Theo sagged, then managed to lift his hand to put it into the king's. The king hauled him to his feet, where he stood, swaying. Cedar shoved past Willowvale to steady Theo when the young man's knees buckled. The king dropped Theo's hand but said again, "Walk with me."

Fenton, dazed and slightly dizzy, followed. Willowvale stalked beside him, lean and terrifying, for he had not sheathed his blade and did not, apparently, intend to. Crocus slipped her arm around Fenton, and he would have enjoyed her touch significantly more if he were not entirely in despair at Theo's imminent death. For what else could the king possibly mean but to kill him?

Theo's steps steadied slightly as they followed the king the length of the throne room.

At last, they stood at the foot of the dais.

Silverthorn stepped up one step and turned to face Theo. He looked across the room, ensuring that every eye was upon him, then focused on Theo again.

Willowvale said quietly, "Your Majesty?"

"Fair lords and ladies, and all subjects of the Fair crown: hear me now.

"The Fair lands require love to hold together. For generations, we kings have forgotten how to love, and the land has faded, moment by moment. I have tried to learn how to love to hold the land together as is my right, my duty, and my privilege.

"I have come to realize that I will never love the Fair Lands enough to sacrifice myself for them.

"Therefore, I hereby abdicate all rights and duties as rightful king of the Fair Lands, and in my place, I present to you Theodore Overton the Fourth, who loves this land and will keep it together.

"Swear your allegiance now."

With no more fanfare than this, Silverthorn removed the crown from his head and put it firmly on Theo's head. One of the points dug into Theo's skin before the king straightened it, and a drop of crimson blood trickled down his forehead.

Theo, half blind with magic and entirely dazed, said, "Your Majesty, I—"

Silverthorn stepped down to the floor, then deliberately knelt. He drew his sword and held it by the blade, hilt upward, before Theo.

"I, Oak Silverthorn, do swear—"

"Stop!" Theo cried, breathless and desperate. "Please stop, Your Majesty."

Silverthorn paused, his violet eyes fixed upon Theo's face. "What would you ask of me?" he said quietly.

"You have learned to love after all," Theo said. "For you are putting the good of your land above your own preferences and comfort, above your own prestige and public honor." He blinked, blinded by the golden sparkles and dizzy with the rush of magic in his veins.

Silverthorn, on his knees, stared at him. "I cannot love as you do, and the Fair Lands need more than weak affection."

Theo lifted the crown from his head with trembling fingers and carefully, gently, put it back on Silverthorn's dark blue hair. "You love enough to sacrifice your crown to a human. That does not sound like weak affection to me."

The Fair king held his gaze. "I doubt it is enough."

"It is a good start, Your Majesty." Theo's eyes glittered golden, and he extended a hand to the king.

Silverthorn stood, graceful and terrible, and he said, "Go in peace, then, Overton, and know that you will always be welcome in the Fair Court. You, and your friends."

Theo bowed, then staggered as he rose, dizzy and nauseated and almost entirely lost in the golden swirl of magic that kept his blood pumping when by all rights, he ought to have been a burned out husk upon the cobalt floor. Only Cedar's quick hand under his arm saved him from hitting the floor.

"Come, Theo," the Fair lord said. "I will take you home."

Theo sagged against him and murmured, "I can't walk that far."

Willowvale took his other arm and said to Cedar, "My house is not far." Then over his shoulder he added, "Lord Selby, can you walk?"

"Yes."

They didn't even make it out of the hall before Fenton pitched forward and would have fallen but for Crocus; she caught him with one arm, and Cedar nodded to Willowvale that he should take Theo, while he stepped back to help Fenton.

By the time they were halfway across the garden, both Theo and Fenton had steadied; Cedar's magic was coursing through their blood, and his ferocious strength kept them moving. Fenton said nothing as he walked, but he stood straighter and looked about with wide eyes, the rich brown shot through with gold. He smiled at Crocus, sweet and shy and happy.

Theo bubbled over with words, magic-drunk and delirious with remembered pain and stupefying fatigue. "Lord Willowvale, you were magnificent! I am delighted that you will honor me with your friendship. Lord Mosswing, I hope you were not in distress when he called for you. I must commend you again for your strength and skill. Your magic is quite overpowering." He stopped suddenly and bent over with his hands on his knees, breathing heavily.

"What is wrong?" Cedar asked. He kept one hand under Theo's shoulder, for the young man was now trembling violently in a way Cedar had not seen before.

"I think I might be sick," Theo said thickly. He closed his eyes and swallowed, for the sparkles were blindingly bright, but closing his eyes did nothing to soften the brilliance.

After several long moments, he straightened and staggered onward.

Willowvale said, "Around this copse to the left, then straight up the path."

"Lord Mosswing, you really do not get enough credit, for your magic is astonishing. I cannot express to you how much I appreciate it." Theo squeezed his eyes shut again, but it made no difference. "Lord Selby, I cannot see you at all. Please tell me you're well." There was an edge of desperation in this plea, even through the blissful haze of magic.

"I am quite well," Fenton said, and pressed his lips together, for he did not wish to babble. Theo sounded ebullient and vivacious, as sunny and sparkling as ever, though perhaps a bit more free with his words than usual. He was witty and bright, as brilliant as the magic that blinded him. Fenton feared that in contrast he would sound dim-witted and dull, and for this moment, with Crocus supporting him already, he could not bear the thought of appearing even stupider than he already must seem.

Willowvale opened the door and barked orders at someone. "Do you want a bed or a couch?" he said to Theo.

Theo blinked at him. "Lord Willowvale, is that blood on your jacket? Are you injured?"

"Come on." The fairy gripped Theo's arm more firmly and hauled him only a short distance down the hall to a sitting room. "Lie down here." He nodded to the couch opposite. "Put Selby there."

Within a few minutes, Theo and Fenton were both staring blearily at the fairies. Willowvale stood by the fireplace with his left hand pressed against the wound on his right side, watching with sharp eyes while Alyssum and and Tansy, two of the servants, set out tea platters nearby. They removed the young men's boots and tucked blankets around their feet, then stirred the fire.

"Good afternoon, Alyssum, and… and…" Theo blinked. "I'm sorry, I can't…"

"Tansy, sir," the fairy said.

"Tansy," Theo repeated. "Did you know those are toxic?" He was trembling as if in a fever, and his voice shook too.

"I was named for the beauty of the flower, sir, not the poison." The fairy shot a glance at Willowvale, as if he expected to be reprimanded. The Fair lord merely raised his gaze to the ceiling.

"Lord Selby? Are you well?" Theo asked again, with his eyes closed.

"Fine," Fenton mumbled. He would not have expected, under any circumstances, to have been comfortable sleeping in Lord Willowvale's house. Nevertheless, Cedar's magic in his veins and the sudden relief of being horizontal produced such a rush of comfort and relaxation that he sighed and fell asleep.

"Cedar," Theo said.

"I'm here. Go to sleep." Cedar glanced at Willowvale, who nodded, and then pulled up the nearest chair to sit between Theo and Fenton. Willowvale leaned against the mantel of the fireplace, lean and graceful, still holding his wound.

"Lord Willowvale was bleeding. Can you help him?" Theo's voice was fading. "I feel odd, Cedar."

"I already gave Willowvale some magic. You're dead drunk on it, Theo. I don't wonder you feel strange." Cedar frowned at him. "Now stop talking and go to sleep."

"I like talking," Theo muttered. "When I'm talking, sometimes I surprise myself, and no one asks me questions. I feel fizzy."

"Go to sleep, Overton," Willowvale said at last. "Mosswing, can you send a message to his wife? She'll want to know when he'll be back."

"Yes, of course."

"Thank you," Theo mumbled. There was a faint, wet hitch in his words.

Cedar leaned forward to hear him better. "Theo, what was that you said?"

The young man didn't answer, having already fallen into the welcoming darkness. But the Fair lord leaned closer and listened to his breathing with a frown, then put his hand on Theo's shoulder and slipped a little more magic into his friend.

"What is wrong with him?" Willowvale asked quietly.

The dark Fair lord shook his head and said, "Larch's magic is especially cruel, but I have learned a little about human bodies, and I have directed my magic accordingly." Cedar's turquoise gaze rested upon Willowvale with a strange sort of satisfaction. "I did not think to see you by his side."

Willowvale's pale lips lifted in amusement. He left his place at the mantel, strode to a chair some distance away, and sank into it with an almost inaudible catch in his breath.

After a moment, he said quietly, "When you became friends with Overton, did it come naturally, or did he achieve it by sheer force of will?"

Cedar laughed softly. "A little of both, I think."

The silence drew out, until Willowvale murmured, "Tea?"

"Yes, please." Cedar stood. "I will send the message to his wife and be back in a moment." He looked toward Crocus, who had been standing silently near Fenton's motionless form.

Willowvale inclined his head. "You may sit," he said mildly to the Fair woman, indicating another chair near the fire.

She licked her lips, then nodded once. When she was sitting, she said, as if bewildered, "I don't understand what just happened."

Willowvale made a strange, choked sound of laughter under his breath and said, "I think that is to be expected with Overton."

Crocus's pale eyes glinted as she looked at Theo's ashen face, then she turned her attention back to Fenton, whose pallor looked just as unnatural with his olive tones.

Alyssum brought a pot of steaming water and the butterscotch and vanilla tea Theo had given Lord Willowvale the previous week, as well as another tea which Willowvale had procured from the ambassador to Aricht.

"Tea?" Willowvale offered curtly, and Crocus shook her head.

It was too strange to think of drinking tea with Willowvale, as if she and the Fair lord were friends, or allies, or as if the two young human men were not unconscious on the couches near at hand. As if they had not stepped between her and the Fair throne's weight, and between each other and Lord Larch's terrible power.

"How badly are you hurt?" she managed at last, for she felt that, as frightening as Willowvale's name had always been, she owed him that, for he had, after all, stood between the humans and Larch's sword.

His pale lips lifted in a faint, grim smile. "Not as badly as Larch was before I let Bayberry have him. I did not want Bayberry to hold any grievance against me for taking all the fun."

Cedar returned and accepted the butterscotch and vanilla tea with a flicker of appreciation. "From Theo?" he asked.

"Yes."

They spent the day in a strange silence. Willowvale disappeared after an hour or so to change out of his bloodied clothes and reappeared a short while later in an equally severe suit of pale blue, the color of both his blood and his eyes. Just after he returned, one of the servants appeared to ask Lord Willowvale where he would like to eat.

"I will eat in the dining room. Will you join me?" Willowvale asked.

"I will remain here," Cedar said, with a polite smile, and Crocus said the same.

Willowvale nodded to the servants to indicate that they should follow these instructions, then said, "Ask for whatever you need."

Their pale host retreated to eat alone in his dining room and did not reappear for several hours, but Cedar and Crocus did not leave the room in which Fenton and Theo lay insensible. They ate on little tables which the servants brought, and the food was both delicious and plentiful.

Lily read the message from Cedar with tears in her eyes.

Dear Mrs. Overton, Miss Firethorn is entirely free. As for your husband and Lord Selby, all is well, or will be soon, for friendship like theirs cannot be broken by something as small as Larch's magic. It may be several days before we return, for neither of them is fit to travel yet, and I believe His Majesty Silverthorn may wish to speak with Theo again.

Lady Overton was right—Lord Willowvale does not know himself, and he surprised us all. Theo also triumphed in the final bargain with Lord Bayberry, and there is no more to fear from that quarter.

Please convey my deepest respect and regard to Lady Miscanthus.

With all respect and sincerity,

Cedar Mosswing, Duke of Flamefall

Near dusk, Fenton stirred. He blinked at the unfamiliar ceiling, for it sparkled both with crystalline beauty and with the golden healing magic that flowed in his veins. "Where is this?" he croaked.

Then Crocus was at his side, and she said, "I think you ought to lie down a little longer, Lord Selby."

The beauty of her blue eyes, full of gentle concern and admiration, made him momentarily speechless.

Cedar said, "We are in the house of Lord Willowvale, who stood for Theo in the duel and has offered his hospitality while you and Theo recover."

"Where is Theo?" Fenton shoved himself to a sitting position, which left him breathless and dizzy, his head full of sparkles and his mind fuzzy and bright. "How is he?"

"He is here, and he will be fine." Cedar did not mention the wet sound to Theo's breathing that had so worried him, for it was finally almost gone.

Fenton sagged in relief and nearly fell off the couch.

"Eat this, and go back to sleep," Cedar said firmly. He pushed the human back onto the seat and handed him a plate with a pastry on it. "Miss Firethorn will be in a guest suite tonight." As soon as Fenton had finished eating, the Fair lord slipped a little more healing magic into him.

Fenton fell easily back into the golden light, as rich and lovely as summer sunlight, and as he dreamed, he smiled for the beauty of the magic and of a certain pair of ice-blue eyes.

A thick, wet cough made Theo curl up on his side, and he coughed again. His bones were molten fire, and his muscles cramped so that he groaned with every breath.

Cedar's hand on his shoulder brought golden relief, and he fell into sleep again.

When he woke again before dawn the following morning, the sparkles in his vision were nearly gone, no longer overpowering all rational thought.

He sat up, and even that slight movement was enough to set his head spinning. He trembled from head to toe, but he did not feel feverish, merely weak and drained and fatigued beyond description.

The room was shadowed, but the Fair moonlight spilled in through the open drapes of several windows. There was a motionless shape upon the opposite couch, and an equally motionless shape sprawled in a chair in the corner. Theo knew this one to be Cedar, for his boots were in the moonlight.

He stood, swaying and dizzy, and looked around the room again, noting no one else.

When he took a step toward the opposite couch, the room spun sickeningly, and he pitched forward, barely catching himself before he bashed his face into Fenton's forehead. He braced one hand on the couch arm and pushed himself back to sit on his heels.

Theo put one trembling hand upon Fenton's chest to feel his friend's slow, steady breaths. For a moment, relief overwhelmed any other emotion.

Then he doubled over with his head to the floor and let the grief rise.

Wracking sobs shook him.

Fenton woke after some minutes, unable at first to identify the uneven gasping on the floor near him as anguished weeping.

When he understood the sound, he shoved himself up to sit and said, "Theo?"

Theo caught his breath and coughed, hard and wet and painful. "Forgive me, Fen," he rasped.

Fenton cast his mind back over everything he could remember. "For saving the woman I love?" he asked.

Theo choked on a grief-bitter laugh. "For manipulating you."

"What?"

"I knew you would offer yourself in my place." Theo's grief nearly swallowed him whole. "I had to do it." He caught a rough breath. "If your sacrifice were impulsive and sincere, not planned, it would satisfy the terms of my deal with the king. It might not have worked if you'd planned it. I couldn't be sure."

He coughed again, and in the corner, Cedar stirred, but he did not interrupt this moment.

Fenton said, "You didn't manipulate me."

"I did!" Theo's voice cracked. "I *know* you! I relied upon your best impulses and took advantage of them. Can you forgive me, at least a little, since Miss Firethorn is free?" He buried his face in his hands. "I'm so sorry, Fen," he breathed. "I'm so sorry! I would have done it any other way, if I could have. I should have been more clever. I should have…"

"Theo!" Fenton reached out to grip his friend's shoulder. "You were brilliant."

"I'm so sorry." Theo shuddered as if he would come apart.

"You didn't manipulate me at all." Fenton's voice was steadier now, for he felt more awake and aware, and Theo's grief appalled him. "I would do it again, a thousand times if I had to."

Theo clasped his hand over Fenton's on his shoulder, as if to keep himself anchored, for the dizziness was rising, and he did not want to lose his mind entirely.

"You've done nothing that requires forgiveness." Fenton shook Theo gently. "In fact, I owe you my deepest gratitude."

Theo stared up at Fenton's face, just visible in the reflected moonlight.

"For once in my life," Fenton said quietly, "I was able to stand between you and danger, at least a little. Can you not see what a gift that is?"

Theo bowed his head, and his shoulders shook.

"Moreover, do you not see how magnificent it is that I was able to be a part of freeing Miss Firethorn? Perhaps you could have done it alone, and certainly I would be glad she were free, but this way I did not have to stand aside while you were the lone hero."

Theo gave a choked little laugh. "You are too kind. This was no gift."

"It was!" With his hand on Theo's shoulder, Fenton felt his friend's soul-crushing grief shake him again. "You always do the glorious, extravagant, sacrificial thing, with love and honor and compassion, and you do it alone, protecting the rest of us. I am honored that you trusted me this much. You could not manipulate me into this. I did it freely, and I would do it again, without hesitation."

Theo sagged. "Thank you."

"Thank you, Theo." Fenton steadied Theo's shoulder. "Please, my friend, feel no more grief."

Theo coughed, the sound soft and bloody. "You humble me, Fen."

"Cedar!" Fenton said sharply. "Theo, please, rejoice with me, for I feel nothing but gratitude."

Theo gasped at the rush of golden magic that flooded his lungs and his pain-fogged mind with light. The rush and swirl of magic stole words from his tongue, leaving him filled with mingled grief and joy and relief.

He would have thanked Fenton again, if he could have found the words, but the sparkling golden magic carried him into sleep before he could remember how to speak.

CHAPTER THIRTY-ONE
A Different Answer

Lord Willowvale entered the room just ahead of the servants who brought breakfast. Cedar had hauled Theo back to his couch some hours before, and the young man now rested in something closer to healthy sleep. He had turned his back to the sunlit room and buried his face in the velvet couch cushion. The golden light spilling through the windows warmed his shoulders and lit his hair to gleaming copper. Fenton had been drowsing with his head on his fist, and he straightened in surprise when their Fair host stepped in.

"Is everyone still alive?" Willowvale said, with a sharp glance at Theo's motionless figure.

"Yes." Cedar stood to greet their host with a bow, and Fenton did so more slowly, finding himself a little light-headed with the movement. He sank back down to the couch, and Cedar put a hand on his shoulder. The golden magic that slipped into him was too gentle to confuse him, but it still filled him with a sense of bright optimism and gratitude.

"Miss Firethorn will join us for breakfast here." Willowvale looked impeccable in white from head to toe. "Have you been made comfortable, Mosswing?"

"Yes. Thank you."

"Selby?" Willowvale's silvery eyes flicked over Fenton with interest.

Fenton smiled. "Yes, thank you."

Crocus joined them a few minutes later, and she crossed immediately to Fenton, who stood again to greet her.

"Are you well, Lord Selby?" Her ice blue eyes seemed unaccountably warm, and her rosebud lips trembled as she smiled.

"Yes, thank you, Miss Firethorn." He bowed over her hand, full of golden magic and gratitude.

They ate in silence, Willowvale, Cedar, Crocus, and Fenton, and though it was not exactly a comfortable silence, there was a strange peace in it. Willowvale inspected every item on Fenton's plate before letting the servant place it in front of him, and he watched with sharp attention when the servant poured human tea for his human guest. Cedar ensured that Willowvale did not miss anything, for Fenton was entirely pre-occupied with surreptitiously admiring Miss Firethorn and did not even think to check that all the food provided was human food and not Fair.

Just as they finished eating, Theo groaned softly as he drifted toward wakefulness. When he opened his eyes, he was at first too confused to even sit up, for all he could see was the golden sparkles of magic and the emerald velvet of Lord Willowvale's couch.

Fenton said something, and Theo struggled to a sitting position, which took far more effort than it seemed like it ought to require.

Willowvale said, "I will leave you." He stood and bowed sharply, then stepped out of the room and closed the door.

"Fen?" Theo blinked blearily, for the sparkles obscured the room, and he could not remember where he was.

"I am here." Fenton stood, only slightly unsteady, and stepped closer. He sat next to Theo, shoulder to shoulder.

"I'm sorry, Fen." Theo ran shaking hands through his disheveled curls.

Fenton laughed softly and leaned his shoulder against Theo's, for his friend was trembling and nearly blind with magic. "I meant every word of my thanks, Theo. If you persist in doubting that, I must become offended, and I would much rather not have that between us."

Theo rested his aching head in his hands and leaned more heavily against Fenton. "Thank you." He had known Fenton would forgive him, but still it seemed an inconceivable grace.

The silence that drew out was more comfortable, more familiar.

After several minutes, Crocus approached with quiet steps, cautiously, as if she almost feared to interrupt this sacred moment.

"Mr. Overton?" Her voice shook.

He raised his head and looked at her through the fading golden sparkles. "Miss Firethorn."

She knelt in front of him, trembling and awed. "I do not fully understand what you did, but I am grateful."

He closed his eyes and nodded. "You're welcome," he mumbled.

"I am sorry I thought the worst of you," she whispered.

He managed a wan smile.

Willowvale entered the room an hour later, having apparently decided he had given them enough time for whatever reconciliation might be necessary. Theo was half asleep slumped on the couch, his mind full of shimmering golden light and his tongue temporarily stilled by the immensity of the emotions that had rent his heart. Fenton was sitting beside him, relaxed and sleepy but ready to catch his friend if he fainted. Crocus sat across from them, her hands primly clasped on her lap. They had made a little conversation, but it was apparent to her that Fenton was both reluctant to speak of his own heroism and more than a little dazed himself. Cedar hovered protectively, crossing and uncrossing his arms at intervals as he meandered about the room, examining the paintings and other decor without touching anything.

When Willowvale entered, Theo perked up a little, though it was obviously more by force of will than any actual alertness. "Good morning," he managed.

"Overton." Willowvale's pale lips twitched in something that was almost, but not quite, a smile. "You're awake."

Theo laughed to himself, for this seemed like a ludicrous exaggeration of his faculties, and he said, "Thank you, my lord, for your hospitality."

Willowvale nodded once.

Theo blinked and asked, "What day is it?"

"Tuesday." The Fair lord's silvery eyes glinted.

Theo stood, swaying, and said, "I am to host you for tea today."

Lord Willowvale was startled into a genuine chuckle, and the expression transformed him. "I don't think you're in any shape to be hosting anyone."

Theo looked toward Cedar. "I need to see Lily. She'll be worried."

"I sent her a message last night," said Cedar gently. "Sit down, Theo."

"I'm fine." His smile was, if not as sparkling as usual, at least sweet and kind.

Willowvale said, "Sit down, Overton. My hospitality is not so mean as to necessitate you walking home in your current state."

"I never thought it was." Theo blinked, and then put a hand out to steady himself on Fenton's shoulder. The world danced and spun.

In the end, Cedar poured more golden magic into him, and he slept on the couch for another four hours. Willowvale offered books and refreshment to his other guests and retreated to a chair in the corner, as if he did not want to leave but did not want to trouble them with his presence, either. To Fenton, this seemed like an oddly vulnerable action, but he did not say this aloud, for he did not know what Theo had previously said to their Fair host.

Crocus ventured at last, "Are you not as affected by Larch's magic as Mr. Overton?" For Fenton was pale and fatigued, but mostly alert, and he had taken only a brief nap after lunch.

Fenton swallowed and shook his head. "I think… I don't know how he did it, but I think Theo funneled it through me, so that I was the channel through which the pain flowed, and he was a rock on which it caught and swirled before it passed into the ground."

Willowvale interjected from his chair, "I suppose young Morel's binding magic made that possible."

Crocus tensed. "You may suppose whatever you like, Lord Willowvale, but I certainly cannot vouch for that."

The Fair lord chuckled under his breath, as if her fear amused him. "I have no further quarrel with Juniper Morel, Miss Firethorn, nor does the crown, for His Majesty pardoned all who aided the Rose when Overton bargained with him last month."

Crocus's lovely eyes widened, and she stared at him. "Juniper is free to return if he chooses, with no threat from you or the crown?"

"Yes."

Crocus looked back at Fenton, who nodded and said, "Yes, Theo used Juniper's magic."

Hours later, when Theo was awake again and had voiced his intention to return to the human world with more conviction, they made their farewells.

"Thank you, Lord Willowvale, for your courage and your hospitality." Theo bowed deeply to him and straightened with only a little wobble, and his smile sparkled with its customary warmth and friendliness.

Willowvale gave a jerky nod.

"Perhaps you can come to tea on Friday?"

The Fair lord hesitated, then said quietly, "I would think you've seen more than enough of me, Overton. You've triumphed thoroughly already. What else do you want of me?"

Theo blinked. "You promised to come to tea, my lord. I am sorry that I was indisposed today, but I should hope that a little delay would not offend you so deeply as to induce you to retract a promise made to a friend."

Willowvale opened his mouth, then closed it again. He tilted his head.

Theo's tender heart twisted at the Fair lord's expression, and he said gently, "I do hope you will come. Tea with a friend is always a pleasure."

The fairy looked away, then back at Theo. "Shall our friendship endure a little longer then?" he asked. "I thought you would have done with it at the earliest opportunity."

"I have no such intention, my lord. I do not take my friendships so lightly."

"Not even mine?"

"Especially not yours. I spent a great deal of effort to earn it."

Willowvale laughed, low and clear and, to Fenton's astonishment, not at all bitterly. "All right, Overton," he said. "I will come to tea. I've never had a friend before, you know."

Theo bowed again. "Until Friday, my lord."

Then he turned and opened the door into the veil in the very wall of Willowvale's study.

Pale and silent, Crocus stood to the side as Theo led the way into the veil. Cedar followed him, then Fenton.

"Are you not going with them?" Willowvale said to her.

Fenton, Theo, and Cedar stopped and looked back at them.

Crocus said uncertainly, "I had hoped…"

Fenton leaned one hand against the worn wood of the veil wall, as if to hold himself up. "Miss Firethorn, I would, of course, be honored if you would be my guest in the human world, but I would hate for you to feel obligated toward me in any way, especially since you have already made it clear you do not return my affection. I have no expectations."

He bowed gravely to her.

The Fair maiden's pale cheeks pinked. "I believe I said I *could* not return your affection, not that I did not wish to."

Fenton blinked, then blinked again. "Shall I declare my affection again, then, in hope of a different answer?" he murmured. "Would it offend you if I did so, as if yesterday's events should change your mind?"

"I would be grieved if you did not, for I would hate to miss the opportunity to give you my answer now that I am free." Crocus raised her chin and stepped forward, her hands twisted together.

Fenton shoved off the wall of the veil and stepped back out into Willowvale's study. He took Crocus's hands in his and met her gaze.

"Miss Firethorn, my heart has not changed," he said simply. "I admire your courage in seeking Juniper to the human world, and I grieve the hardships you have suffered in your own world. You are beautiful to me in every way. I would be honored and delighted to spend my life pleasing you."

"I cannot entirely understand why you should say such lovely things," Crocus said, her voice shaking, "but I can think of no higher joy or honor than tying my life to yours." She caught her breath on a joyful sob, her eyes still locked on his.

Fenton's sweet smile turned into an expression of awed joy. "You accept my proposal?" he whispered.

"With all my heart."

CHAPTER THIRTY-TWO
Home Again

The veil smelled of blood and ash and crushed rose petals. Theo closed his eyes as he led them through the darkness, for it was no use trying to see in the dark and he was too tired to keep his eyelids up anyway. His heartbeat thudded in his ears, harsh and uneven, and he felt too many emotions to manage his usual encouraging patter of conversation, but Cedar's magic in his veins kept him upright until they reached the human world.

He opened the door with a twist and pull of magic and leaned dizzily against the wall while the others stepped out into the crisp bright autumn.

When he attempted to step out after them, the ground rose and receded like the waves of the sea, and he stumbled and fell headlong on the frost-covered lawn.

Cedar's magic brought him back to consciousness, but he could neither walk nor think clearly, much less give a coherent account of what had happened. However, Sir Theodore, Lady Overton, Lily, Juniper, and

Poppy had been waiting anxiously for their return, and within a few moments Theo and Fenton had more than enough help from strong arms and tender hearts to get them into the house and into their respective beds.

Cedar filled them both so full of healing magic they would sleep through the night.

Crocus recounted for everyone what had happened before Cedar had arrived in the throne room.

"Where were you?" she asked at the end. "I thought you were to follow us immediately?"

"I tried." Cedar nearly groaned. "The veil fought me every inch of the way, and then two of Larch's lackeys barred my way into the throne room. I arrived as soon as I could."

Lily read by Theo's bedside with her hand in his, for he seemed to breathe more easily with her touch, and she did not want to be farther from him than necessary anyway. She ate dinner at his bedside, too, but unlike the previous time, when she had been desperately hoping for forgiveness and reconciliation, no guilt pressed upon her. Theo's face was terribly pale, but no scratches or bruises marred his handsome features, and when she shifted her hand in his, he turned his head toward her with a smile, though he didn't wake.

She slipped into bed with him gently, for she could not imagine what sorts of pain or unseen injuries might be lingering. Even Cedar hadn't been entirely sure; he said both young heroes had soaked up his healing magic like parched earth soaked up water.

Theo woke well before dawn, full of sparkling humor and energy entirely excessive for that early hour. He admired Lily's delicate features in the faint moonlight that filtered through the sheer curtains. Then he slipped closer and pressed a gentle kiss to her cheek.

"Theo?" she mumbled.

"I love you," he whispered.

"How do you feel?" She slipped one arm around him, her warm skin sending thrills through his body.

"Far too awake." He laughed softly at himself and kissed her again. "I'll get up so my thrashing doesn't keep you from sleeping. Have sweet dreams, my darling. All is well."

After assuring her in no uncertain terms that he was truly healed, he rose and dressed in the gray dawn light, stirred the fire in the sitting room so it would be warm when she got up, and then strolled down to the kitchen to fix himself a snack. He had slept through both lunch and dinner the previous day, and the sense of well-being that pervaded him had come with a healthy appetite.

He was surprised to hear a low conversation coming from the kitchen.

"Good morning," he said as he entered.

"Good morning, sir!" Juniper shot to his feet and bowed deeply. His companions were Fenton, who put his plate down and stood to bow to Theo, and Anselm, who was standing nearby and also bowed.

"I imagine you're hungry too," said Anselm with an affectionate smile. "Wait a moment, and I'll fix you a plate."

"How are you feeling, Fen?" Theo asked. He pulled over one of the wooden chairs from where it stood near the wall and sat in it, his eyes searching Fenton's face.

"Magnificent." Fenton grinned at him and took another bite of the enormous ham and cheese sandwich Anselm had fixed him. "I woke up just a little while ago and found myself ravenous. I came down to help myself to your food, and found Anselm and Juniper already here."

"What are you doing up so early?" Theo blinked at them.

Anselm laughed quietly. "My body has entirely forgotten what normal hours are; I'm too old to stay up nights and then switch back to days without a little confusion. So I thought I would start some bread rising and make use of my time. Juniper came in just before Lord Selby did."

Theo turned his attention to the young fairy, who said earnestly, "I woke early because I've been resting so much after giving you all that binding magic. Everyone has taken such good care of me that I truly can't sleep any more, sir!"

Juniper did look remarkably well-rested, his eyes bright and his cheeks slightly flushed with embarrassment and the heat of the nearby oven.

"Juniper, I owe you a very great debt of gratitude for your strength, courage, and generosity with your binding magic," Theo said gravely. "You helped us free Miss Firethorn and keep both Lord Selby and myself alive while we did it. I really cannot imagine how I might repay you."

Juniper blinked suddenly tear-filled eyes. "Thank you, sir. I am glad I was able to help." His voice sounded suddenly young and awed.

Anselm cleared his throat. "Theo, if I might interject…"

They all turned to him.

"I spoke with Sophie, and we are in agreement. Juniper, if you would like a legal place in the human world, Sophie and I would be delighted to formally adopt you."

Juniper's mouth opened, but he said nothing. His chest heaved with a deep, silent sob, and then he buried his face in his hands and sank to his knees on the floor. He bowed forward, his shoulders shaking.

Anselm knelt beside him and wrapped his arms around the young fairy. "You're all right."

Juniper asked something, and Anselm shifted to sit on the floor facing him and pulled the Fair youth closer, so that Juniper buried his tear-streaked face in Anselm's shoulder. He clung to the servant as if he feared being swept away in a storm.

"I'm sorry," he finally managed. He hid his face in his hands. "I'm sorry. I didn't… I didn't expect…"

Anselm let him straighten but did not entirely remove his arm from the young fairy's shoulders. He said, in his quiet, steady, reassuring voice, "I can't offer you what the Fair Lands can, Juniper, but I can promise that Sophie and I will treat you like a son. The Overtons pay me quite well, and you will not have to work, although it is customary in the human world for adults of my station to work. I can teach you what you need to know for service in a noble house when you're older, or I can arrange an apprenticeship if you want to pursue a career as a craftsman. You will be safe and loved as long as either of us lives."

Juniper wiped at his face and leaned in to Anselm's embrace again. "Why would you do this?" he whispered.

"I would be proud to call you a son," Anselm said. He glanced up Theo and Fenton, who had been observing in silence, and smiled faintly. "Also, it seemed likely to me that one of these young noblemen might have thought of the same thing, so I wanted to speak first. I'm not as young or rich or noble or handsome as they are, but Sophie and I have loved each other for many years. I would like to think there is something appealing in that."

Juniper shook with suppressed sobs, and he had no words. Anselm wrapped his arms more comfortably about the young fairy's shoulders as if he expected to be sitting on the cold stone floor for some time.

Theo said softly, "I had thought to talk to Lily about it, but I wanted to wait until Miss Firethorn was free, in case I didn't survive. But I cannot deny that Anselm has made a compelling offer, and I would be a heel if I tried to press my own case now."

Fenton rubbed his hands over his face and said in an aggrieved sort of apology, "I confess my mind has been too occupied to think of such a solution at all, though of course you know you would be welcome at my house at any time."

The young fairy gave a choked laugh. "I am overwhelmed by your generosity. All of you have been so kind." He smiled, tearful and flushed, and rested his head against Anselm's shoulder. "Thank you." He closed his eyes and brushed at his cheeks again.

Perceiving that Juniper would like to be alone, or alone with Anselm, Theo stood quietly and moved away. He finished making the sandwich Anselm had begun for him, then picked up the plate and an apple and moved to the far end of the large kitchen. Fenton followed.

"How are you really feeling, Fen?" Theo asked.

"Fine." Fenton blinked at him. "You're the one I'm worried about. Do you even remember walking back through the veil? You collapsed in front of everyone."

Theo hesitated, then admitted, "My memories are rather thoroughly jumbled. I do remember your lovely proposal to Miss Firethorn. Congratulations." He smiled, his heart warm and full.

Fenton flushed and looked down at the last bit of sandwich in his hand. "Thank you, Theo." He grinned shyly. "Thank you."

"You really have forgiven me, haven't you?" Theo said softly.

"Of course I have," Fenton said in shock. "How could you think otherwise?"

"I'm having a hard time forgiving myself." Theo shoved his plate away and buried his face in his hands. "I would have done it another way, if I could have thought of a way I could be sure would work."

Fenton shook Theo's shoulder until Theo looked up to meet his eyes. "Either you truly meant to die for Miss Firethorn, which is appallingly unjust and heroic, or you trusted me to do what I did, because it was what was necessary. If you could have told me, you would have! I appreciate your judgment of my character, and I am relieved to my soul to know that I haven't disappointed both you and myself by my actions." Fenton said more quietly, "I cannot properly convey how grateful I am for what you did for Miss Firethorn and the pain you bore for me. It would grieve me deeply if you let unnecessary guilt come between us now, after this incredible triumph."

Theo swallowed. "You really are the most generous of men, Fenton," he murmured.

Fenton laughed, the sound warm and rich and all the sweeter for its rarity. "What a thing for you, of all people, to say! Please, feel no more guilt, for I am grateful beyond words." The sincerity of his smile, and the strength of his hand on Theo's shoulder, reassured Theo that everything was right between the two of them.

Theo made them tea in silence, for Anselm and Juniper were still sitting on the floor, talking quietly at intervals. He put a cup in front of Fenton and sat with his own cup without speaking for several minutes.

"The Fair Lands really are beautiful, aren't they?" said Fenton at last, smiling into his tea cup.

"You mean Miss Firethorn."

"Of course I do."

Whatever guilt had lingered was gone by the time they finished their tea, transformed into gratitude and another thread of friendship binding their hearts together.

CHAPTER THIRTY-THREE
A Conversation With a Friend

Riding a hired chestnut gelding, Lord Willowvale trotted up the curving Overton drive at five minutes to four on Friday. He had dressed in the human style, much like on his previous visit, with a dark, well-fitted jacket and a wine-red vest over a crisp white shirt and cravat. Narrow, dark gray trousers set off his trim figure.

Anselm let him in almost immediately. "Good afternoon," he said politely. He did not trust the fairy, not yet, but Theo and Fenton had both explained how he had stood for Theo in the duel with Larch, which story helped Anselm resist the urge to put his hand upon the hilt of his hidden dagger.

Willowvale nodded, which wasn't exactly an extravagant display of courtesy, but was more than he'd graced the servant with on his previous visit. Anselm decided to credit Theo with this development, and led the Fair lord to the sitting room where Theo was waiting to host his guest for tea.

Theo stood to greet the fairy with a bow and a sparkling smile. "Welcome! I hope you didn't have any trouble getting here."

The Fair lord blinked. "Not more than usual." His pale silvery eyes flicked over Theo's lean, elegant form. "You seem well," he said, with a faint question in his voice.

"I'm entirely healed and entirely grateful to Lord Mosswing for his magic. And you, my lord?"

"I am whole." Willowvale's slightly startled look might have been in response to Theo's question or to the lack of condescension in his own answer.

"I am delighted to hear it. Please, make yourself comfortable." Theo gave him another radiant smile and indicated one of the chairs by the fire.

The fairy stalked across the room and took a seat with the uncanny grace of the Fair Folk. He regarded Theo with cautious fascination, barely glancing up when Anselm brought a tray on which two plates each bore a tasteful arrangement of expensive cheeses and cured meats, cream-filled pastries, and hothouse raspberries. Two cups and saucers stood beside a steaming pot of tea.

"Thank you, Anselm," Theo said with a smile.

For several minutes, Theo merely acted as a gracious host, ensuring that Willowvale had cream for his tea and that his seat was close enough to the fire.

Finally the Fair lord said, "I wonder if you will answer a question that has perplexed me."

At Theo's friendly expression, he continued, "How did you induce Bayberry to claim you as friend and stand against Larch?"

Theo grinned. "Did he? I barely remember that, but I assumed he must have, since I lived to the next day."

Willowvale blinked, then blinked again. "How did you manage it?"

The young man took a sip of tea. "Well, I told you I found myself in a game of bargains with him, didn't I?" He explained the game of bargains, and how he had won the first round and conceded the second in order to get Fenton and Crocus safely away.

Willowvale stared at him, his tea forgotten. "You really are mad," he muttered. "What was the third bargain, then? Everything rested upon that."

"I told him I had realized the game was devised to assuage his boredom, and I promised him entertainment if he came to court on Monday. If he were genuinely entertained or surprised by something that day in court, he must concede the round and game to me, and if he were not, I would concede, and he could kill me in front of the king and all the court."

The Fair lord stared at him, his snowy eyebrows drawn down. "You were so confident he would be surprised?"

"Surprised or entertained." Theo looked down at his tea, remembering Fenton's unflinching courage. "I imagined that either my cowardice in letting Lord Selby bear Larch's wrath in my place, or Lord Selby's heroism in doing so, would startle him enough to win that round. Certainly the rest of the day ought to have been entertaining enough to satisfy him."

Willowvale narrowed his eyes slightly, then let out a soft, wondering sigh. "The king was wrong. You're not mad as a March hare; there's no thought in that. You're crazy like a fox."

Theo smiled modestly and took another sip of tea. "Well, I was more focused on getting Miss Firethorn free and keeping Lord Selby alive than on what came afterward. But I do believe I have you to thank for startling Lord Bayberry."

The Fair lord chuckled, low and awed, and then the absurdity of it overcame him, and he laughed, loud and free, the sound as bright and joyous as Theo's smile. He laughed until he wiped tears from his eyes, and he laughed again when he looked back at Theo.

"You brilliant, mad idiot," he muttered. "You probably knew I would do that before I did."

Theo's answering chuckle was warm and genuine. "I really wasn't sure exactly how it would play out, and I certainly would not presume to be sure of what you would do, but I knew I wanted you there." He leaned forward to meet Willowvale's gaze seriously. "I am honored and grateful that you answered the challenge for me, Lord

Willowvale, but I will not consider it a debt I owe you, because I am not in the habit of keeping track of debts with my friends."

The Fair lord blinked, then smiled again, as if he could not help it. "Call it a gift in the human tradition, then."

Theo laughed aloud. "All right, I will."

Willowvale's smile lingered, and he said quietly, "Selby's all right, I assume?"

"He is." Theo's relief was evident in his voice.

The fairy sat back in his chair with a faint sigh. "All is well, then," he said. "You've achieved everything you wanted."

Theo's smile widened, and he said, "I am pleased, indeed, my lord." Then, impulsively, he said, "Thank you for your reassurance on the matter of Juniper Morel's status in the Fair Lands."

Willowvale gave a careless half shrug. "As far as I know, the child has no reason to want to return to the Fair Lands at all, but it wouldn't be right to have him kept away by fear."

Theo blinked and studied the Fair lord more closely, and Willowvale raised one eyebrow as if in a faint challenge.

Rather than commenting on this statement, Theo contented himself with refilling their tea cups.

After a moment, Willowvale straightened and pulled a letter from an inside pocket of his jacket, which he handed to Theo. "From Silverthorn."

This much was apparent, for the wax seal upon the letter had a crown of thorns which glittered with silver dust and a faint gleam of magic.

Oak Silverthorn, King of All Seelie, to Theodore Overton, IV:

In recognition of your service to the Fair Lands, you are hereby offered a position of Special Advisor to the Fair throne, with all rights accompanying. You shall have the right to offer your opinion on any matter without repercussion. You and yours shall henceforth be welcome in the Fair Lands and shall be offered the hospitality and respect of the Fair throne without limit or recompense and shall be provided human food safe for your consumption.

In return, I, Oak Silverthorn, do hereby request that you visit the Fair Lands as often as you will, and speak with me as often as you will, for I greatly desire your counsel and to follow your example.

With respect,

HM Oak Silverthorn

Theo smiled and said, "Would you mind waiting while I write a reply?"

"I had expected I would." Willowvale took a sip of tea and added with quiet contentment, "It is no hardship to enjoy tea with a friend while I wait."

CHAPTER THIRTY-FOUR
Strength Upon Strength

The week after Crocus accepted Fenton's proposal was one of exquisitely joyful relief and quiet companionship. As it was socially questionable for a young lady to stay at her betrothed's house overnight, Crocus spent the week at the Overton manor, and Fenton and his mother drove over every morning. The various couples went on numerous carriage rides together to see the last beauty of the autumn leaves and to see the frost-covered hills glitter beneath the setting sun. They played card games and dice games, games of chance and games of strategy, and they read to each other.

This peaceful interlude was broken only by the arrival of Lord Willowvale, whom Theo hosted for tea alone, for no one else was quite ready to call him a friend. An unexpected ally, perhaps, but not yet a friend. Theo was delighted by the tea, however, and his optimism seemed both entirely fitting and deeply amusing to the others. For who would have thought Willowvale, of all people, would call a human a friend?

The following afternoon, Crocus and Lily had tea together while Theo and Fenton went riding together for the first time since their return from the Fair Lands. Both young heroes had been, if they were honest, a little unusually tired in the days immediately following their triumph in the Fair Lands, and this was the first occasion on which they felt able to fully enjoy a brisk ride along the windy hills.

When they left, Theo had bowed over Lily's hand with utmost courtesy, then swept her into a tight embrace which would have been scandalous before anyone else, but with Fenton and Crocus, it meant he considered them family.

Fenton looked away with a flush on his cheeks and laughter in his heart, and fixed his eyes on Crocus's slightly shocked face. Her wide blue eyes were so very lovely that his internal laughter faded, and instead a shy, wondering joy filled his heart. He bowed over Crocus's hand and, with a feeling of boldness, let his kiss linger just a little longer than it ever had before. Her hand was strong in his, and he liked the strength. Yet her fingers trembled, and when he looked up at her with a smile, she blushed most becomingly.

"I look forward to seeing you again at dinner, Miss Firethorn," he said. Though they were betrothed, it seemed presumptuous to say *Crocus* before Theo, especially since she was a fairy. Would that offend her? He would have to ask Theo if he knew Fair customs during an engagement, for it would not do to offend her now.

"I look forward to seeing you again, too." Her voice trembled a little too, but it seemed a warm, shy sort of tremble, and, smiling, he held her gaze for a moment longer before following Theo out into the cold. The light of love in her eyes was like a fire in his heart, and he barely noticed the wind at all.

In the sitting room, Anselm and Juniper brought tea for Lily and Crocus. The young fairy had asked to accompany Anselm as he fulfilled his duties throughout the day, and though he was not exactly working, he did offer an extra hand whenever he had the opportunity. For several minutes, the young lady and the young Fair maiden merely enjoyed the repast in silence. The sweet, spicy scents of baked apples and cinnamon scones perfectly complemented the subtle vanilla scent of the black tea.

At last Crocus set her teacup down and smiled nervously. "Mrs. Overton, I confess I am very little acquainted with human marriage customs, and I would be grateful for your guidance."

Lily's eyes lit up. "I am honored that you thought of me. You must have a dress, of course. Has Lady Selby made mention of this?"

Crocus nodded. "There is a dressmaker coming next week." She licked her lips, and then said quietly, "Lord Selby," and then she stopped, for the sound of his name on her lips was so sweet, so beloved, that for a moment she just wanted to savor it. "Lord Selby said that he had asked Mr. Overton to accompany us to the palace tomorrow to formally file the petition of marriage with the king. Will you come too?"

"If you would like me to," said Lily, with another sweet smile.

The Fair maiden hesitated, then said quietly, "I haven't really had a friend before, only fellow servants with whom I was required to spend my time, and there was little affinity between us. I would like to count you a friend, if I may. Your husband…" She stopped and looked down, then carefully dabbed at her eyes with her napkin. "What he did for Lord Selby, and what they both did for me, is… I cannot express my gratitude and awe." She took a tremulous breath and looked up. She swallowed, and then said in a rush, "Mr. Overton nearly glows with joy when he speaks of you, or when he looks at you, or you look at him, or even when someone says your name, and I would like very much to make Lord Selby even half that happy."

Lily smiled and reached across to put her hand on Crocus's. The fairy twitched in surprise, and then gripped Lily's smaller hand with something like desperation. Lily said gently, "Lord Selby is more reserved than Mr. Overton, as I am sure you are aware, but he is utterly delighted that you have agreed to marry him. Surely you see that in his eyes."

Crocus nodded. "I do. I just…" She looked down at the tea and huffed a soft, rueful chuckle. "I want to make him happy enough that he counts it worth the cost. Because my freedom was *very* dear, Mrs. Overton, and I cannot forget it." She pulled away and covered her face with her hands.

Without another word, Lily stood and moved around the table. She wrapped her arms around Crocus's shoulders, and, after a moment of stiffness, the Fair maiden shuddered and began to weep softly, hiding her face.

When Crocus's uneven breathing had steadied, and she had wiped tears from her face for the last time, Lily said quietly, "He counted your freedom worth the cost even before you accepted his proposal. You cannot repay him, and he would not want you to try. He wants you to live and be happy. He found his joy in loving so deeply and so selflessly."

The Fair maiden took a deep, steadying breath. "I shall spend my life trying to love him so well."

Lily smiled and shifted away, so that Crocus could see her face. "I think he will be entirely pleased with your efforts." In her warmest, kindest voice, she added, "Our husbands are such good friends, I would like to think we will be as well. Will you call me Lily, please?"

Crocus swallowed and gave her a tremulous smile. "Then you must call me Crocus."

Lord Fenton Selby and Miss Crocus Firethorn formally petitioned His Majesty Alberdale for permission to marry, for not in several hundred years, as far as anyone knew, had a human, much less a nobleman, married a fairy.

Crocus, though she did not show it openly, was secretly terrified of this event, for she had little knowledge of human kings, and Silverthorn had been terrifying.

Yet when Fenton had bowed and stated his desire to marry her, His Majesty Alberdale had smiled kindly and asked them each in turn why they wanted to marry.

"Because I love her, Your Majesty," said Fenton with such sincerity that when the king turned to Crocus, emotion nearly choked her, and she had to clear her throat before she echoed his words.

"Because I love him, Your Majesty." She flushed pink as she said it. She almost expected the human king to mock her, or somehow take advantage of this vulnerability, because in her experience, the powerful often did such things.

Instead, the king's clear eyes held hers for a moment longer, and then he nodded once. "Good," he murmured. He smiled and looked back at Fenton. "Your petition is granted. My congratulations, Lord Selby."

They rode back to the Overton estate with Theo and Lily, lost in a haze of delight.

"Will you walk with me in the garden a while?" Fenton's dark eyes were as warm as his smile. He added, "I have a cloak for you." He proffered one of her new cloaks in an elegant navy blue wool embroidered with silver crocuses at the hem.

"I would be delighted to." Crocus couldn't help the soft smile that came to her lips. She let him wrap the cloak around her shoulders, which he did with utmost respect. She slipped her hand into his arm and walked with him out into the frigid winter brilliance. A light snow had fallen that morning, and the ground was carpeted in several inches of pristine white.

The snow squeaked beneath their boots. Fenton led her in a meandering path, though she suspected he would eventually stop at the little gazebo near the ice-topped pond. The bare branches of the trees and most of the bushes lent a beautiful, desolate air to the garden, but there were evergreen hedges thick with scarlet berries and conical cypress trees that lent a little green to the otherwise dormant garden.

"Thank you for the boots. My feet are quite warm."

"You're welcome." He smiled down at her. "Are they comfortable?"

"Very." In the weeks before the wedding, Fenton seemed determined to shower her with every manner of thoughtful gift. A dressmaker and a cobbler had visited her at the Overtons' estate, and she had been enjoined to tell them all her preferences. Scarcely a week later, a profusion of dresses and boots and several cloaks had arrived, all both lovely and serviceable. She had discarded her old dress with a relieved sense of finality, for it was both unsuited to winter weather and quite threadbare. "Did you know how badly I needed something warm?"

He looked down. "I can't see through Fair glamours," he said. She raised her eyebrows at him questioningly, and he said, as if confiding something embarrassing, "Juniper did mention that your clothes were rather worn."

The warmth in his eyes, the way he said it so gently, caught at her heart, and transformed what might have been embarrassment, or shame, if she thought about it too hard, into something sweeter. "Thank you," she said simply.

He sighed in quiet relief.

When they reached the gazebo, Fenton brushed the snow from one of the benches. They were well within sight of the patio, but no one was there, for since they were formally engaged, no supervision was necessary. To Fenton, this felt simultaneously scandalous and long overdue. Yet in this now-sanctioned privacy, he could not think what to say. He looked down at his hands in his lap.

Crocus took a deep breath and let it out slowly, as if she were every bit as nervous in the awkward silence as he was.

He laughed under his breath, low and quiet, and said, "I care so much for what you think of me that I fear to say anything at all."

Her answering chuckle was as light and bright as the tinkle of bells, but there was an undercurrent of tension in it. "I fear to disappoint you, after you bought me at such a price."

He turned to look at her in genuine surprise. "You shouldn't fear that."

"I'm quite sure I shall someday, if not very soon." She caught her lip between her teeth. "I have given you my whole heart, but I do not think it is enough." She twisted her pale hands together but did not look away from his face. "You deserve so much more. I was no great lady even in the Fair Lands, and here…"

With a gentle hand, he reached forward to cup her cheek for a moment, then took both her hands in his. His warm, olive skin contrasted sharply with her alabaster skin, nearly white now in the cold. He kissed both her hands one after the other, and the audacity of this both surprised and pleased him. "I am sure we will both disappoint each other in time," he said seriously. "But my love is not so weak as to fail or fade when the first blush of infatuation wears away." He smiled, warm and kind and gentle, and said, "I do not fear that yours will either, for what I have seen of your love is fiercely strong. Together, we can build strength upon strength."

With tears in her eyes, she laughed softly and kissed his hands in return, to his deep, shocked delight. "I am the most fortunate of women," she murmured. She held one of his hands to her cheek and closed her eyes. "I would like for you to promise me something," she said, with a sudden flash of inspiration and boldness.

"What?" He smiled at her, shy and sweet.

"If there is anything I can do, ever, to delight you, or please you, or make your life better in any way, I want you to tell me." She almost laughed at his surprise and added, "I don't know your human customs, but I know I love you now, and I want to love you more and better every day."

The joy that filled Fenton's heart stopped his words for a moment, and he could only smile at her with tears in his eyes. At last he said quietly, "I think we're off to a very good start. I look forward to making progress, day by day, in knowing and loving you more deeply."

"I shall enjoy every minute of it, dear Fenton." She smiled, tears filling her eyes, and said, "Fenton," again, because his name seemed so lovely and so beloved.

The sound of his name on her lips made his heart leap in delight. "So shall I, dearest Crocus."

ABOUT THE AUTHOR

Thank you for purchasing this book. If you enjoyed it, please leave a review at your favorite online retailer!

C. J. Brightley lives in Northern Virginia with her husband and young children. She holds degrees from Clemson University and Texas A&M. You can find more of C. J. Brightley's books at www.CJBrightley.com, including the epic fantasy series Erdemen Honor, which begins with *The King's Sword*, and the Christian fantasy series A Long-Forgotten Song, which begins with *Things Unseen*.

PROLOGUE

When Claire was seven, she had a very strange dream. Impossibly tall trees towered above her, the sound of their distant rustling like whispers. The air in the dappled shadows was cool and still, broken only by a murmuring of unseen water. Claire looked down at her bare feet, skin pale against the deep green moss covering the earth. Static made her pink nightgown cling to her slim legs.

Where was she?

A fluttering overhead caught her ear, and she looked up, her eyes searching the shadowed branches. Nothing was visible, but the whispering of the leaves seemed to increase ominously. She began walking carefully toward the sound of water, chewing her lip.

What was this place?

Her feet padded on the moss as if it were thick green carpet, soft and cool against her skin. She made her way through sparse brush, the leaves parting before her invitingly.

Screech!

The sudden cry behind her made her start in fear, and she froze, looking back into the shadows. It was darker, as if the sun had not only disappeared behind a cloud, but descended to the horizon in a matter of moments.

Her heart thudded, and she whimpered a little. Another angry cry gave wings to her feet.

She flew through the brush, tiny twigs and leaves slapping her in the face and across the arms. She glanced behind her once, not sure what she expected to see.

Green eyes glinted in the twilight.

Claire cried out and stumbled when her foot hit a nearly buried rock. She fell headlong, her hands splashing into a pool of water.

"You aren't right. You're not what you're supposed to be!"

Claire looked up to see a boy of about her own age glaring down at her.

"There's a… a…" She pointed helplessly behind her, too terrified to look for the eyes of the creature that had pursued her.

"Yes. A cockatrice." The boy's blue glare intensified. His eyes were rimmed in red, and she had a fleeting thought that perhaps he had been weeping. "You should know better than to wake a sleeping cockatrice." His eyes flicked behind her with a frisson of fear, and he grabbed her shoulder. "Back you go, then." He pushed her into the pool of water, hurrying her deeper while glancing over his shoulder. A final shove sent her flailing, the water closing over her head. Her last glimpse of him was of his silver-white hair plastered down by water, one arm flung up against a beaked maw that struck with cobra-like speed. Claire screamed, water filling her mouth.

She woke, trembling and sweaty, tangled in her blankets.